There's Music in These Walls

There's Music in These Walls

A HISTORY OF
THE ROYAL CONSERVATORY OF MUSIC

EZRA SCHABAS

THE DUNDURN GROUP
TORONTO

Copy-Editor: Jennifer Gallant
Design: Jennifer Scott
Printer: University of Toronto Press

Library and Archives Canada Cataloguing in Publication

Schabas, Ezra, 1924-

There's music in these walls : a history of The Royal Conservatory of Music / Ezra Schabas.

ISBN-10: 1-55002-540-6
ISBN-13: 978-1-55002-540-8

1. Royal Conservatory of Music. I. Title.

MT5.T6R884 2004   780'.71'0713541   C2004-904463-X

Conseil des Arts du Canada   Canada Council for the Arts   Canadä   ONTARIO ARTS COUNCIL CONSEIL DES ARTS DE L'ONTARIO

1   2   3   4   5   09   08   07   06   05

We acknowledge the support of the Canada Council for the Arts and the Ontario Arts Council for our publishing program. We also acknowledge the financial support of the Government of Canada through the Book Publishing Industry Development Program and The Association for the Export of Canadian Books, and the Government of Ontario through the Ontario Book Publishers Tax Credit program, and the Ontario Media Development Corporation's Ontario Book Initiative.

J. Kirk Howard, President

Printed and bound in Canada.
Printed on recycled paper.

www.dundurn.com

Dundurn Press
3 Church Street, Suite 500
Toronto, Ontario, Canada
M5E 1M2

Gazelle Book Services Limited
White Cross Mills
Hightown, Lancaster, England
LA1 4X5

Dundurn Press
2250 Military Road
Tonawanda NY
U.S.A. 14150

There's Music in These Walls

For the teachers of The Royal Conservatory of Music, 1887–2005

Table of Contents

Preface

I first heard of the Royal Conservatory of Music (RCM) during a visit to Toronto in September 1949. I met several musicians who praised it and others who unkindly condemned its teaching policies and examination system. It seemed to be the only music school of any stature in Toronto and held an important place in the city's musical life. I didn't know then that its influence extended across Canada, thanks to its examinations and publications, which served as a benchmark for most Canadian English-speaking teachers, especially those who taught piano; they expected their pupils to perform well before RCM examiners and earn high marks. Nor did I ever imagine how the Conservatory would become part of my life in the years to come.

I put first impressions of the school aside until thirty months later, when my wife and I decided to move to Toronto. Since I had already taught music in two American universities, I looked first into teaching at the University of Toronto. Music instruction there was mainly in the hands of the Conservatory, which, in the spring of 1952, was going through a major reorganization. The degree-granting university courses were not in need of new staff, so, in April, I went to see Dr. Ettore Mazzoleni, principal of the RCM, about joining the school's faculty as a clarinet instructor. He was cordial and cool, which, I would discover, was typical of him. He did not offer me a job, although the wind department at the school did not appear to be all that active and could have benefited from some new blood. I didn't know at the time that Mazzoleni was coping with serious personal and professional problems. Appointing new teachers was, understandably, not on his mind.

We (my wife, our two baby boys, and I) moved to Toronto in August 1952. I couldn't have chosen a better time. The Conservatory's reorganization had been completed, and Edward Johnson, former manager of the Metropolitan Opera Company of New York and chairman of the Conservatory's board of directors, was temporarily in charge until a new head of the school could be found. Johnson had wanted the Conservatory to get a new lease on life since he joined the board in 1945. Now retired from the Met, Johnson, a Canadian, resided in Canada for most of the year. In his seventies, he still seemed full of energy and feisty to boot.

Johnson hired me in September to be director of the Conservatory's publicity and concerts and of its Concert and Placement Bureau, which had been established in the late forties. These positions provided me with a rare opportunity to observe the school's and Toronto's musical life for the next eight years. I was also an active clarinetist and played in orchestras and chamber groups on the CBC and with faculty and graduates. Later on, from 1960 until the present, I taught, administered, and consulted at the Conservatory and the Faculty of Music of the University of Toronto. The Conservatory was and is a microcosm of Canadian musical history, and I have been lucky to be part of it.

This narrative is a personal and independent account of the Conservatory's first 118 years. Being so close to it, including during the period when I was its principal (1978 to 1983), has been, I think, an advantage. However, to forestall criticism, I have not spared myself in the text when I endured rocky times, and I have been frank and, I hope, unprejudiced in judging colleagues, institutions, and the events around them. You may not agree with me. Some of my memories are short, others long. For example, I remember most events of the fifties as if they happened yesterday. However, as a general rule I have trusted my memory only when documentation was not available.

Let me also say that this is not a history of music in Toronto. I have studiously avoided writing about the Toronto Symphony, the Mendelssohn Choir, and other important musical groups and individuals except when they were part of the Conservatory story. Nor is it a history of the Faculty of Music, although the Faculty has played a prominent role in the RCM's story and is addressed accordingly.

I have used the University of Toronto Archives extensively. It has voluminous material on the Conservatory from 1886 to 1975 as well as on the Faculty of Music. The University records at the archives have also been revealing. The RCM has kept nearly all of its board minutes and other valuable documents. The Faculty of Music Library, the Opera Division of the Faculty, the Music Division of the National Library of Canada, the archives of the Canadian Opera Company, and the archives of the Toronto Arts and Letters Club have all been useful, as have interviews and conversations with Toronto musicians and descendants of Toronto musicians. I have drawn heavily from my own files and the files of others. But this history is not exhaustive; there is ample room for more research and evaluation of the Conservatory's work.

PREFACE

I want to thank Dr. Ann Schabas for spending countless hours reading and editing my manuscript. If this text reads easily and well and covers the necessary ground it is due to her painstaking work. Next, I thank Dr. Dorith Cooper for researching much of the material I suggested as well as other material she found independently. A scholar of Canadian music, she shared her views with me, challenged me when she saw fit, and demanded answers. I also thank Robert Creech, who spent two days with Ann Schabas and me in Ireland clarifying the Conservatory's separation from the University of Toronto and copying pertinent correspondence and documents for my use.

A Chalmers Fellowship provided me with the financial assistance to embolden me to pursue this project. I thank the Ontario Arts Council for administering this competition. I also thank Dr. Peter Simon, president of the RCM, for supporting the project. He has had extensive input in chapters 11 and 12. Conservatory Vice-President Colin Graham has provided financial information about the Conservatory and helped me in many other ways. I thank Patricia Wardrop for generously lending me material from her Conservatory board files, Berthe Jorgenson, director of the Canadian Opera Company archives, Barbara Sweete and Kelda Cummings of Rhombus Films, Linda Armichand of the University of Guelph library, Edwina Carson, Joanne Mazzoleni, Clare Piller, Michael Remenyi, G. Campbell Trowsdale, Jonathan Krehm, and William Vaisey.

The Conservatory staff has been of great assistance. I thank Dean Rennie Regehr, Dr. Jack Behrens, Patrick Dagens, Barbara Sutton, Leigh Bowser, Carole Chapman, Kate Sinclair, Akbar Ahmad, and others too numerous to mention. I also thank George Hoskins, the late Dr. Norman Burgess, Eileen Keown, Mark Jamison, Louise Yearwood, Shaun Elder, Paul Caston, Robin Fraser, and Gordon Kushner. Among the teachers I consulted and thank are Angela Elster, Andrew Markow, Joan Barrett, Carol Pack Birtch, and John Graham, as well as former teachers Lois Birkenshaw-Fleming, Donna Wood, Eileen Fawcett, and Joseph Macerollo.

At the Faculty of Music I thank Tina Orton and Michael Albano of the Opera Division, and John Beckwith, John Weinzweig, Kathleen McMorrow, Suzanne Myers, Carl Morey, and John Fodi, among others. I thank Maureen Nevins of the National Library for her assistance, as well as Florence Hayes.

J. Kirk Howard, president of the Dundurn Group, has been very supportive; Jennifer Gallant has been an attentive and conscientious copy editor; and Jennifer Scott, assisted by Andrew Roberts, has done well in executing the book's design. I thank them all.

I thank those whom I interviewed and are not mentioned above: Peter Allen, Mario Bernardi, Dr. George Connell, Robert Dodson, the late Harry Freedman, Dorothy Johnson, Mildred Kenton and the late

Robert Spergel, William Krehm, John Kruspe, Joseph Macerollo, Margaret McBurney, John Milligan, Burke Seitz, Andrew Shaw, Stanley Solomon, George Welsman, and Arthur E. Zimmerman. A list of interviews and dates can be found in the appendices.

And finally, I thank the wonderful people at the University of Toronto Archives: Garron Wells, Harold Averill, Marnee Gamble, Loryl MacDonald, Lagring Ulanday, and Barbara Edwards.

Prologue

THE SETTING

Y ork, as Toronto was first known, was a settlement of sorts as far back as the seventeenth century. It grew rapidly as a trading and commercial centre after the War of 1812. Most of its immigrants were from Great Britain and brought their political outlooks, religions, and music with them. They also brought with them Orange Lodges, religious and ethnic rivalries, entrenched social and sexual discrimination, and open racial and religious bigotry.

From 1840 Torontonians paid handsomely to hear great musicians: John Braham, Ole Bull, the Germanian Orchestra, Jennie Lind, Adelina Patti, Henrietta Sontag, Sigismund Thalberg, Anton Rubinstein, Henri Vieuxtemps, Henri Wienawski, and Hans von Bülow.[1] Touring opera companies also played to large and appreciative audiences, performing works such as Rossini's *Il barbière di Siviglia*, Donizetti's *L'elisir d'amore, Lucia de Lammermoor*, and *La Fille du Régiment*, Bellini's *Norma*, and works by Auber, Meyerbeer, and Verdi.[2] In addition to music, most Torontonians obviously liked drama — although many of its Methodists and Presbyterians frowned upon it.

Nineteenth-century Toronto valued its concert halls and theatres. Among the larger ones were the Pavilion Music Hall at the Horticultural Gardens and St. Lawrence Hall. Smaller ones included St. George's Hall, the Royal Lyceum, the Grand Opera House, the Royal Opera House, the YMCA's Association Hall, Temperance Hall, Shaftesbury Hall, and Convocation Hall at University College. Over a ten-year period, 1874–83, three of these arts venues were destroyed by fire. First was the Royal Lyceum in 1874. The Royal Opera House was erected on the same site seven months later, but it too was wiped out by fire in 1883. The third, the Grand Opera House, burned down in 1879. It was rebuilt within fifty-one days![3]

The city was prosperous. Its affluent and growing middle class, eager to keep up with the times, saw to it that electric street lights supplanted gas lights, horse-drawn streetcars gave way to electrically powered streetcars, and new railways — the Belt Line and the Humber Line — were installed to bring Toronto's outlying districts closer to downtown. In 1892, despite a slump in the economy, the cornerstone was laid for a new city hall on Queen Street at Bay, designed by the brilliant architect E.J. Lennox. This enterprising city, which combined Loyalist gentility and brash Yankeeism, provided a promising market for music teachers and music schools.

Musicians go to where the work is, and there was work indeed in Toronto. Music schools, especially, were on people's minds. Conservatories had been appearing in major cities in Europe since 1794, when the Paris Conservatory was created to provide skilled instrumentalists for the new First Republic's military bands. Other conservatories, notably Leipzig's and the Royal Academy of Music in London, set standards for other European schools in the first half of the nineteenth century, and this paved the way in North America for Boston's New England Conservatory, the Peabody Conservatory in Baltimore, and the Oberlin College Conservatory in Ohio; all three were founded between 1865 and 1868. England also followed suit. The Guildhall School of Music, founded in 1880, was and continues to be supported by the City of London. The Royal College of Music, also in London, was founded in 1882 by the Prince of Wales (later Edward VII).[4]

Toronto's musical leaders envisaged music schools similar to those many had attended in Europe, schools that would offer both amateur and professionally oriented students a wide range of musical subjects under one roof. Furthermore, they wanted these schools to reassure parents that their children were studying music in respectable, bona fide surroundings and with good teachers. There were many music teachers in the city, but they were unlicensed, unlike teachers in public schools; anyone claiming to be a music teacher could place a shingle across his or her front door and give lessons to the unwary. Music was becoming part of popular education and Toronto's citizens increasingly sought competence if not excellence in its instruction.

And so, as Toronto grew, the demand for music schools grew. The city's population of over 100,000 in 1885 reached 140,000 by 1890. Involvement in good music — playing, singing, or listening — was synonymous with good living, and Toronto, with its positive stance towards life, however conservative and puritanical, was a surefire market for music instruction. The census of 1890–91 noted that 91 percent of Torontonians were first- or second-generation British. Their traditions and values clearly prevailed in education and the arts.[5] Immigrants from other lands were quick to adapt to British-

Canadian ways of life, including its music. The U.S.A. may have been known as the land of opportunity, but so was Canada — especially Toronto.

Certainly late Victorian Toronto was no musical backwater. Most of its approximately one hundred churches had choirs, some very good ones. Here is how the population of the pious "city of churches" was divided: 32 percent Anglican, the denomination most responsible for good music at its services; 23 percent Methodist; 19 percent Presbyterian; and 10 percent other Protestant denominations. Of the remaining 16 percent, 15 percent were Roman Catholic and 1 percent Jewish.[6] Singing enriched worship, and none knew this better than the churches. Their organists and choirmasters — the positions almost always went together — were usually from Britain, and they became Toronto's most prominent musicians.

Toronto could also claim several secular choirs that sang eighteenth- and nineteenth-century repertoire — mostly religious in origin. They performed in churches and concert halls, albeit most of the halls would be deemed acoustically unsuitable by present-day standards. The city, fortunately, had many amateur choral singers who experienced the joy of music in the best way, through participation, and this helped to make them likely supporters of music generally. In 1900 Toronto was known as the choral capital of North America, thanks to its many fine choirs. New York, Boston, Chicago, and Cincinnati may have relished their symphony orchestras, but Toronto could take justifiable pride in its choirs.[7]

Two rather inconsequential and short-lived music schools had appeared in Toronto in the 1870s and early 1880s. And then, in 1886, came the Toronto Conservatory of Music. Our story begins.

Chapter One

TORONTO HAS A MUSIC SCHOOL

The founder of the Toronto Conservatory of Music (TCM), Edward Fisher, was born in Jamaica, Vermont, in 1848. The son of a prominent doctor, he had studied piano and organ at the New England Conservatory, America's leading music school at the time. He gave public recitals on both instruments and was organist and choirmaster at several Boston churches. Despite Boston's sophisticated musical environment, Fisher threw up his work there at age twenty-five to study in Berlin, one of Europe's leading musical centres. After a year in the newly created German capital the adventurous and peripatetic Fisher moved to Canada to become director of music at the Ottawa Ladies' College and conductor of the Ottawa Choral Society, Ottawa's leading choral organization.

After successes in Ottawa, Fisher went on to Toronto in 1879. Perhaps the move was motivated by a plan to start a music school, but that was several years away. First he took on the post of music director at St. Andrew's Presbyterian Church on King Street, facing the present-day Roy Thomson Hall. He eventually enlarged the St. Andrew's choir and renamed it for public concerts as the Toronto Choral Society. Over the next twelve years the society performed Handel's *Messiah*, *Samson*, and *Israel in Egypt*, and other major works by Mendelssohn, Gade, and Schumann. Fisher also held the music director's post at the Ontario Ladies College in Whitby, just east of Toronto.[8] Ladies' colleges usually had thriving music departments that were much like mini-conservatories.

Fisher, a handsome man with a commanding presence, was soon circulating amongst Toronto's high society. He lived well, entertained in style, and belonged to the Lambton Golf Club and the Royal Canadian Yacht Club.[9] His wife, Florence, was a member of the distinguished Massachusetts Lowell family, of whom James Russell and Amy were the most notable. In 1898 the Fishers had a large and attractive house built on 166 Crescent Road in Rosedale, at that time an up-and-coming neighbour-hood.[10] Harry Adaskin, violinist and long-time member of the Hart House String Quartet, described Edward Fisher in 1913, the year of his death, as "a charming elderly man with white hair and mus-tache, ramrod straight, and with courtly manners."[11] Most important, Fisher was astute in business matters, which complemented his musical skills and organizing ability. These qualities would be need-ed for a director to succeed in an unsubsidized and income-dependent school.

Left: Edward Fisher.

Right: Florence Lowell Fisher.

By 1886 Fisher was ready to fulfill his mission to create a music school. First, he enlisted the aid of a few of Toronto's leading citizens, most of them rich, with social standing and a desire to serve the community. They helped him to form the school and appoint its board of directors. Foremost among them was George William Allan. From a wealthy family, he had been mayor of Toronto at the age of thirty-three in 1855. Generous to a fault, he donated five acres of land to the Horticultural Society of Toronto in 1857, and then gave an additional gift of land to the same society for the creation of Allan Gardens, Toronto's first civic park. Dedicated to public service, he was one of Canada's first senators, president of the Upper Canada Bible Society and the Ontario Society of Artists, and chancellor of Trinity College. Allan was also a patron of the Canadian artist/explorer Paul Kane.[12]

Fisher and Allan — they made a good team — incorporated the Toronto Conservatory of Music (TCM) on November 20, 1886. A provisional board of directors met with Fisher on December 14, elect-ed Allan president, appointed Fisher music director and secretary pro tem, and struck a committee to draw up bylaws and stock subscriptions. To get the school moving, shares were set at $100 each. Fisher himself bought fifty, which suggests that he was a man of means who believed in his project. Three leading piano manufacturers and piano dealers — Octavius Newcombe, Heintzman & Co., and A. & S. Nordheimer — bought ten shares each, as did four other individuals with no musical connections. An additional twenty-one people bought five shares each.

The list of shareholders reads like a Toronto who's who of the 1880s: Sir John A. Boyd; banker and director of over forty companies George A. Cox; music publisher I. Suckling; past-president of *The Globe* James Maclennan; incumbent president of *The Globe* Robert Jaffary; and head of the Toronto Electric Light Company Henry Pellatt, who was later responsible for building Casa Loma — an eccentric Toronto landmark and tourist attraction. Its turrets still loom over the city. Boyd and Cox were elected first and second vice-presidents, respectively, of the new TCM.[13]

The conscientious board met eight times between January and August 1887. Setting the school's location was paramount and, after considering several alternatives, the board finally decided to rent the two upper floors of a three-storey building at the southeast corner of Yonge Street and Wilton Avenue (later Dundas Street) — today the site of Dundas Square. A music store was on the ground floor. The lease would run from August 1887 until August 1889.[14] These early board meetings

003

were also devoted to approving the bylaws, making faculty appointments, and setting tuition fees. Fisher had the board's confidence, and his recommendations were almost always accepted without contest.

A number of leading Toronto musicians were appointed to the faculty, as were several other musicians who had moved to Toronto to work with Fisher. Francesco D'Auria, voice teacher, conductor, and composer, was one of his first high-profile appointments and one

Wilton Avenue building.

of the few to get a guaranteed annual salary ($1,200). He would remain with the Conservatory for seven years. Born in Italy, D'Auria had conducted the orchestra on Adelina Patti's U.S. tour in 1881–82 and had worked in Cincinnati and New York before coming to Toronto. He even formed a short-lived Toronto symphony orchestra for a few concerts until it went under for lack of funds.[15]

Other prominent teachers engaged for the school's first term included English-born Arthur Fisher (no relation), who taught violin, piano, voice, and theory — one had to have several strings to one's bow in those days. He also founded the St. Cecilia Choral Society, was violist in the Toronto String Quartet, composed more than one hundred works, and wrote for the *Musical Journal*.[16] Arthur Fisher left the TCM in a huff in 1893 because of a salary dispute. Bertha Drechsler Adamson, also English-born, taught violin and conducted the Conservatory String Orchestra, which later served as the nucleus for the first Toronto Conservatory Symphony. She would also be the first violin of the Conservatory's second string quartet, from 1901 to 1904.[17] In order to make ends meet, both Fisher and Drechsler Adamson also taught at the Toronto College of Music on Pembroke Street. This rival school opened a year after the Toronto Conservatory of Music.

TCM teacher contracts dictated that the school keep a prearranged portion of student fees, from 20 to 35 percent, with the balance going to the teacher — a pattern that changed little in the school's next hundred years.[18] This so-called commission was necessary because the Conservatory had no other source of income.

The first short-lived Conservatory String Quartet was formed shortly after the school opened. It gave two concerts at the YMCA's Association Hall in the spring of 1889. The Conservatory, with some foresight, paid for the quartet's expenses and kept the first $100 of paid admissions to cover costs. If the admissions exceeded $100 — there is no record that they did — the quartet would keep the rest.[19]

The TCM calendar offered courses in voice and in all the major instruments: piano, organ, strings, and winds. There was also a wide variety of other courses: orchestral and ensemble playing, music for public schools, church music and oratorio, musical theory and composition, Italian, French, German, Spanish, music history, musical acoustics, elocution, and piano and organ tuning. The calendar listed twelve piano teachers, four for voice, one for sight-singing, three for languages, and several others for orchestral instruments. There were four ten-week terms for classes and private instruction. Courses were divided into elementary and preparatory (intermediate and advanced) levels. If these courses were pursued diligently, the student could then enter the school's collegiate (professional) department, which trained aspiring performers and teachers.

The calendar confidently reassured prospective students and their parents that the school was a guarantee against the all too prevalent evils in piano and other musical instruction, i.e., incompetent teachers and faulty methods. The professional course took three years and led to the Associate of the Toronto Conservatory of Music (ATCM) diploma. This program branched in the third year: some students studied for the Performers' ATCM and others for the Teachers' ATCM, which paralleled the Ontario Normal School music program. Two years after opening, the Conservatory introduced the fellowship diploma (FTCM), to be granted to associates who specialized in two or more subjects, such as piano and theory. Its theory requirements were especially stringent.

Far Right: Francesco D'Auria.

Centre Top: J.W.F. Harrison.

Centre Bottom: Giuseppe Dinelli.

Above: Humphrey Anger.

On first entering the school, would-be students would encounter a charming young woman, Marion Ferguson. Her job was to help assign students to appropriate teachers and courses. She had come to Toronto to study piano and organ, but, after meeting Mrs. Edward Fisher and then Fisher himself, her career took an unexpected turn. Her insight and intelligence led the Fishers to believe that she might have executive ability. Accordingly, Fisher engaged her as the Conservatory's first secretary/registrar at $200 per annum. No wiser Conservatory appointment was ever made. Miss Ferguson served the school for the next fifty years under three music directors, all of whom depended on her in countless ways and freely admitted that no one knew the TCM's workings better than she did. She was equally helpful with students, who turned to her for guidance when needed. Mildred Kenton, who studied at the TCM in the twenties, said that it was always a joy to enter the school's lobby and be greeted with a friendly smile and a few welcoming words from Miss Ferguson.[20]

Marion Ferguson, c. 1910.

Three piano companies made bids to rent pianos to the Conservatory: Mason and Risch, Newcombe, and Nordheimer.[21] Nordheimer won out. It provided as many upright pianos as needed at $40 each per year, a grand piano for concerts, and two square Chickering pianos.

Now, with pianos in place, the stage was set for the school to begin. The grand opening was held on September 5, 1887, a banner day in Toronto's musical history. To mark the occasion, Charlotte Beaumont Jarvis wrote a Victorian ode, the first lines of which read:

> As when to weary watchers of the Night
> Appears the silver star which ushers in
> The dawn of day, ere yet Aurora's robes

Sweep through the portals of the east and leave
A train of saffron glory, so to us,
Weary of waiting, shines the welcome star
Which ushers in the dawn of brighter day
For Music and her votaries ... [22]

The Conservatory advertised widely that Toronto finally had a music school of merit, and the press reported the opening with enthusiasm. As expected, women students far outnumbered their male counterparts, and most of them studied piano. Every stylish Toronto living room had a piano, and every well-brought-up young lady was expected to play it. In the school's first twenty-five years 92 percent of its graduates were women.[23]

No matter, studying the piano at the TCM was a serious matter if one wanted to earn a diploma. Technical studies were mandatory, the repertoire — surprisingly similar to repertoire today — was extensive, sight-reading and transposing demands were rigorous, and accompanying ability was expected. Students of other instruments were also expected to learn the piano so that they could play — and hear — transcriptions of music for orchestra, choir, and smaller ensembles.

Undeniably, piano students at all levels were the school's bread and butter. The TCM's first course calendar said unabashedly, "The piano is an accompaniment to civilization, and it has grown to be an almost indispensable article in every household where there are pretensions to culture and refinement. It is well-nigh an orchestra in itself, and is indeed the people's instrument." Other piano companies — Mason and Risch, Gerhard Heintzman (not to be confused with the Heintzman family company), and the Bell Company of Guelph — looking for goodwill and more business, confidently joined the original piano company shareholders by buying TCM shares as they became available. More generally, the great interest in piano playing had created a boom in Canadian piano manufacturing. The industry employed as many as five thousand workers and turned out thousands of pianos annually from the 1880s until the Great War. It was helped in no small measure by prohibitive protective tariffs that were mainly directed at American manufacturers, who reciprocated in kind with tariffs of their own.[24]

To return to the study program, there were four terms of ten weeks each. Classroom teaching, as in European conservatories, was preferred to individual instruction. The classes lasted one hour and were held twice weekly with a maximum of four students. Fees varied according to the instrument and the level of advancement: first-grade piano cost $6.00 per term, while third-grade piano (only Fisher gave this class) was $15.00. Organ first grade was $12.50, and second grade was $17.50. Voice first grade was $10.00. And so on. Private instruction was more costly: students paid up to $35.00 per term for twenty half-hour lessons. Costs also varied depending on the teacher. You took your choice, according to your pocketbook.[25]

To supplement the formal offerings, there were a number of "free advantages," such as quarterly concerts and fortnightly recitals. A *soireé musicale* — French names were in fashion — was given by faculty members at the University College Convocation Hall on October 20, 1887, and a student concert was held at the much larger Horticultural Gardens Pavilion a month later.[26] There were also open lectures for students on a variety of musical subjects and free instruction in elementary harmony.

An enthusiastic Fisher told the first annual general meeting (AGM) of shareholders on January 18, 1888, that enrolment had grown from an initial 282 students to 360, and that he was engaging more teachers to meet the demand. He stressed the need for "a new building constructed on proper acoustic principles," since the present quarters were already inadequate. To show that he had no small dreams, he told the shareholders, "We should push boldly on and aim at making this institution second to none on the continent, and the peer of the celebrated conservatories of Europe." Fisher, knowing where the student market was, expressed his concern that there was no residence for the fifty out-of-town women students who had to seek lodgings throughout the city.[27]

There were formal examinations at the end of the school's first year. The TCM had engaged the American pianist William Sherwood as its external examiner.[28] Sherwood had studied in Europe with Theodor Kullak and Franz Liszt and concertized widely after returning to the United States, including performing the American premiere of Grieg's Piano Concerto. He taught in Boston at the New England Conservatory until 1889, when he went to the Chicago Conservatory to head its piano department. Eight years later he formed his Sherwood School of Music. Sherwood, who remained a TCM examiner for many years, was known for his tolerance and words of encouragement that helped examination candidates through this trying hurdle in conservatory music study. Edward Fisher was often his fellow examiner.[29]

Louise McDowell, a Fisher student, wrote her mother in June 1890 about being examined by Sherwood and Fisher. McDowell, after playing Chopin's *Fantaisie-Impromptu*, wrote:

Mr. Sherwood never interrupted me, although he did the other girls, and when I was through he said, "That was well played." Then he took up the Spinning Song, but he only took parts here and there, and principally showed me how to play them. Then he said, "Now we'll have some Bach!" Fancy! Those old inventions, and I think I was almost the first to have them. Well, I turned up the first one and started off and actually played it through with only one or two mistakes. When through, he said, "That was very well played" and Mr. Fisher smiled at me and looked so pleased. I had to smile back. Just to think I couldn't play them for him. Well, then Mr. Sherwood turned over to No. 4, and I started off once more, but he stopped me about half-way through, and told me it wanted to be a little more gliding, and added that he knew I could do it all right for he could see I had strong musical feeling.[30]

Obviously, examinations were pleasantly informal, and it was deemed acceptable for examiners to instruct at them. Examinations were especially popular at elementary levels as progress reports to convince doubtful parents that their money was well spent. Examinations prompted teachers to work harder so that their pupils would get good marks. The pros and cons of examinations for children, from beginning to advanced grades, were rarely debated a century ago.

Edward Fisher taught piano, organ, church music, oratorio, and piano ensemble classes, at which his students played transcribed orchestral music. A hard worker, he did all of this in addition to his administrative and examining duties. In 1889 he produced the school's first ATCM graduate, the excellent J.D.A. Tripp.[31] After graduation, Tripp studied in Europe with two greats — Moritz Moszkowski and Theodor Leschetizky — and eventually returned to the TCM to concertize, conduct, teach, and examine. He was its first West Coast examiner.

Organ was not neglected. A reed organ was rented for the school's first three months until Fisher could find a better instrument.[32] He also purchased a Technicon, a mute keyboard used for practice to strengthen fingers and help muscular control. It cost $13.50![33] Later, he bought a $260 Miller pedal piano for organ students to practise pedalling.[34] To save the day, J.W.F. Harrison, a leading English-trained organist, then donated a three-manual organ. What became of it, however, remains a mystery.[35] Soon after, an organ built by Warren & Sons (later Karn-Warren) that cost $4,225 was installed in Association Hall.[36]

Harrison was the conductor of the well-known choir of men and boys at the Church of St. Simon-the-Apostle. He, Fisher, and later A.S. Vogt were the most prominent organ teachers. Vogt, Canadian-born and, like Fisher, Leipzig-trained, also taught piano at the TCM. Prominent in the community, Vogt was music director at the Jarvis Street Baptist Church, secretary of the Canadian College of Organists, president of the Canadian Society of Musicians (1893–95), and the only Canadian organist to play at the 1893 Chicago World's Fair.

Lessons in voice and other instruments were, of course, not as popular as piano lessons at the TCM. Nevertheless, there were a number of excellent vocal students training to be oratorio and opera singers. The vocal courses were formidable by any standard. Singers were required to study standard works in four languages and demonstrate that they could accompany themselves on the piano. They took extensive theory classes, too.

Fisher and his board, letting no grass grow under their feet, realized that an affiliation with a university would help to prepare their students for university music examinations and enhance the prestige of the school generally. Accordingly, in June 1888, he approached Toronto's University of Trinity College.[37] (Trinity did not federate with the University of Toronto until 1904.) Trinity had been giving B.Mus. and D.Mus. degrees since 1853, and had formally created its Faculty of Music in 1881.[38] It spelled out its terms to the Conservatory board, which approved them on November 16, 1888. TCM students who passed the first and second examinations towards the ATCM would be exempt from Trinity's first B.Mus. examination, and TCM students holding the ATCM would be exempt from Trinity's first and second B.Mus. examinations. Although Trinity had a faculty of music, its sole music professor gave no classes or lectures. Thus, one didn't have to attend Trinity to take its examinations; one did pay fees, however, much as at the TCM. Examinations were money earners.

A zealous Trinity advertised in London in 1890 that its examinations were now being held in both Toronto and London, England. This raised the hackles of a number of leading British musicians, who were affronted that Trinity, a Canadian-based university, was granting *in absentia* degrees to students in Britain. They implied, further, that standards in Canada were lower than in England. Perhaps they were, since Trinity did not require its candidates to have arts prerequisites or take literary tests, as did English universities. Persistent British opposition to such colonial intrusion finally forced Trinity to discontinue its London examinations. One TCM and Trinity examiner, the English musician Dr. E.M. Lott, staunchly defended Trinity during this period. As his reward he was appointed Trinity's professor of music in 1891.[39] Trinity stopped giving examinations in 1904, when it surrendered its degree-granting powers to the University of Toronto.

For its second year, 1888–89, the Conservatory rented additional space at nearby 5 Wilton Avenue. Fisher went to England in the summer of 1889 to look for a cello teacher and convinced Giuseppe Dinelli to accept an "exclusive" appointment at the TCM at $1,000 per annum.[40] *Exclusive* was a key word in teachers' contracts to prevent them, not always successfully, from teaching privately or at other music schools. That year, when the TCM started including exclusivity clauses in contracts, seven teachers resigned in protest, including Herbert L. Clarke, a twenty-two-year-old cornet teacher who would become one of the most famous Canadian musicians of his time.[41] He worked instead at the Toronto College of Music, where there was better orchestral instruction, thanks to its founder and music director, Frederick Torrington. Clarke went on to a career in the United States, where he was soloist with, among others, Patrick Gilmore, John Philip Sousa, and Victor Herbert. Also a conductor and composer, he returned to Canada for five years (1918–23) to lead the Anglo-Canadian Leather Company Concert Band, an outstanding group that played at the Canadian National Exhibition (CNE) and did the first band broadcast on CFRB Toronto in 1926.[42]

Other prominent musicians joined the staff in 1889–90 and in the two to three years following. One was the English organist, composer, and conductor Humphrey Anger. Fisher installed him as head of the theory department in 1893; Anger later became a TCM shareholder.[43] Influenced by English theoreticians such as Ebenezer Prout, Frederick Ouseley, John Stainer, and Hubert Parry, he developed the theory department along English lines and used primarily English textbooks. Anger introduced revenue-producing theory instruction by correspondence in 1895. Ever productive, he also wrote books on harmony and form, and a three-volume work entitled *Treatise on Harmony*. His work determined the path theory teaching would take at the Conservatory for more than fifty years.[44]

Knowing well the advantages gained from blowing its own horn, the TCM cited press notices from Toronto magazines and newspapers in its fourth annual calendar, 1890–91. The journal *The Week*, reflecting an all too common Canadian syndrome, admired the Conservatory for organizing and maintaining a school "on much the same grounds and in the same manner as that of Boston." (It was referring to the New England Conservatory.) It applauded the TCM for creating a musical environment and even praised its office as "most beautifully and comfortably fitted up, decorated in graduated tints of pale terra-cotta and furnished with every convenience." Sections of reviews of student concerts were quoted from the *Toronto Globe*, the *Toronto Mail*, and *The Empire*. A quote from *The Empire* read that educational progress was "one of the chief glories" of Canadians, and in musical instruction none showed its "higher aims" better than the TCM.

Despite a discouraging economic depression, Toronto grew steadily in the early 1890s, as did the Conservatory. Massey Music Hall was built in 1894, the city's first *real* concert hall. It initially seated thirty-five hundred and had, many felt, unrivalled acoustics.[45] Unfortunately, Hart Massey, the hall's generous benefactor, failed to buy additional land to the south of the hall that would have allowed for more backstage space, a shortcoming that has limited even the most rudimentary staged events ever since. Its neo-classical facade — one might call it just plain — was attributed to Massey's daughter, Lillian. She was, incidentally, also responsible for the classical Faculty of Household Science building on the southeast corner of Bloor Street and University Avenue. Built by the Masseys in 1912 and named after her, it now houses a trendy clothing store. Massey Hall — the "Music" part of its name was eventually dropped — would be the site of many large-scale Conservatory concerts in the years to come.

Then the University of Toronto senate made a significant move. On March 13, 1896, it approved the University's affiliation with the TCM, but over some objections, including those of President James Loudon.[46] It was the beginning of a long relationship between the two schools. The next year the TCM buoyed its reputation still more by appointing Albert Ham, a distinguished British organist/choirmaster, to the faculty. Ham taught a number of fine singers in the years to come, was music director at St. James Cathedral, and conducted the National Chorus in its annual concerts from its founding in 1903 until 1928. He was also the first president of the Canadian Guild (later College) of Organists.[47]

Now, with a growing enrolment and income to boot, the TCM installed steam heat and electric lighting in its Wilton Avenue buildings. These overdue improvements notwithstanding, Fisher knew that the Conservatory must find better quarters. Fortunately, this was not long in coming. A brick building of considerable size on the southwest corner of College Street and Queen's Avenue (soon to become University Avenue) was singled out at the TCM annual general meeting on January 20, 1897, as a building that, with improvements, "including a music hall, alterations, architect's fees, etc.," would be a suitable school building. There was little mention of its splendid location. The cost broke down to $17,000 to purchase the property and $13,000 for improvements. The board of directors, a group that was as prudent as it was daring, secured a mortgage — a special bylaw had to be approved by the shareholders to do this — and renovations of the three-storey building were completed in less than ten months.

Initially, its main building extended about fifty feet on College Street and sixty feet on Queen's Avenue. To underscore the advantages of the school's new home, the number of classrooms was increased from seventeen to twenty-five, and most were quite spacious. The long-awaited music hall had excellent acoustics and seated 500, although, years later, fire regulations, wider seats, and structural considerations reduced its capacity to 360. One observer remembered its kitsch interior as "finished in buff pressed brick, having a wide wood dado, and an artistically modelled plaster frieze consisting of cherubic figures dancing and performing on musical instruments."[48] An up-to-date electro-pneumatic organ that worked (!) — many an organ didn't in those early days of electrically powered organs — was installed in the hall, thanks to Vogt and Harrison, who supported Fisher in making the change from the traditional wind-supported instrument.[49] There were also several offices and two small halls used for junior recitals.

The new building had a welcoming and attractive lobby that was later enlarged. More studios, a connecting women's residence, a cafeteria, another small recital hall, and two buildings to the west were added over time. There was also space for a small library, but no meeting place for students and faculty.

College Street building, c. 1960.

The official opening was on November 22, 1897, which, fortuitously, was also St. Cecilia's Day (St. Cecilia is the patron saint of music). TCM President Allan, University of Toronto President Loudon, and Trinity College Provost Welch all spoke. Members of the teaching staff gave a program that pleased the capacity audience, with many turned away. Thus launched, the College Street site would be the focal point of Conservatory activities for the next six decades.

Trinity recognized Fisher's fine work by awarding him an honorary doctorate on October 25, 1898.[50] In the same year, the enterprising Fisher set up examination centres in other parts of Ontario, and, shortly after, across Canada. These centres were a continuing source of revenue for the Conservatory and helped to develop its image as a national school. Examinations also embroiled the TCM — and other Canadian schools and musicians — in a year of controversy (1898–99) with the Associated Board (AB), one of Britain's major examining bodies. The dispute was more concerned with sheen than substance, and when it was over many wondered what the fuss was all about.

Its roots went back to 1889, when the Royal Academy of Music and the Royal College of Music in Britain had decided to combine their examinations instead of administering them separately. The result was the Associated Board. Evidently, the scheme turned out well; standards went up and, one can presume, so did profits. (Eighty years later this writer found out first-hand that AB profits from examinations continued to pour in!) In 1893, Percival J. Illsley, organist and choirmaster of St. George's Church in Montreal, wrote to the Associated Board stating that practical examinations given by a recognized English institution were needed in Canada. Frederick Torrington also wrote around the same time to Sir Alexander MacKenzie, principal of the Royal Academy, asking in a general way for the same thing.[51] Obviously they didn't think TCM examinations were good enough!

The AB dragged its feet and waited until 1898 to initiate examinations in Canada. But times had changed. Canadian examinations had improved, and the schools now giving them — Torrington's Toronto College of Music, the TCM, and the Dominion College of Music School in Montreal (founded by Illsley in 1895) — resented the competition and said so. The Associated Board's honorary secretary, Samuel Aitken, didn't help matters by reminding them that they had invited the AB to Canada in the first place, and besides, he added undiplomatically, English examiners would expose inferior Canadian teaching. He implied that the fear of losing money was at the root of Canada's objections. Aitken made it sound as if the colonials were misbehaving, needed a spanking, and should wisely accept guidance from their superiors in the mother country. This was, of course, like waving a red flag in front of a bull.[52]

Canadian musicians closed ranks, and in March 1899 almost one hundred of them affixed their signatures to "An Account of the Canadian Protest Against the Introduction into Canada of Musical Examinations by Outside Musical Examining Bodies." This document was circulated widely. The press, smelling a good story, spun out the AB and the Canadian arguments. The AB, unhappy with these developments, retaliated with "The Case of the Associated Board," a pamphlet prepared and signed by Aitken, on March 29, 1899.

The TCM board of directors had, early on, asked Lord Minto, the Governor General, to use his influence to keep the AB out of Canada. His Excellency did not do so. In fact, he supported the AB, stating that it would raise standards in Canada. To rub salt on the wounds of his colonial subjects, he reminded them that the AB's diplomas were "practically the only ones that carry any value in the eyes of the musical world."[53] The TCM board, repulsed but not vanquished, retaliated by posting a letter in

Theory examinations, 1899.

several newspapers discrediting Aitken. His inflammatory reply was "deemed unworthy of attention," said the board. To top it all, A. Morgan Cosby, who had been an active board member since the school's beginnings until his resignation in 1896, had the effrontery to propose transferring two of his TCM shares to Aitken.[54] The board, undaunted, haughtily exercised its power to forbid such transfers and turned him down. What led Cosby to do this is baffling. Clearly, the AB could not be stopped, but the furor delayed its gaining a foothold in Canada's examination sweepstakes. For ten years it functioned under McGill's aegis, and then, after 1909, independently.[55]

Fisher, as always seeking to improve the Conservatory, appointed Alexander Cringan to the faculty in 1897.[56] A graduate of the London Tonic-Sol-Fa College, Cringan was director of music in the Toronto public schools and would do much to perpetuate the sol-fa system of sight-reading in English Canada. The TCM flourished, thanks to its new building and an improved Canadian economy. As the millennium approached there were more frequent 6 percent dividends to shareholders — the TCM was in a profit mode most years — and Fisher's salary was raised from $2,500 to $3,000 for his administrative work, plus $2,000 for his teaching. (The provident board added a rider — no salary if he gets a "permanent" illness!)

The elocution department, renamed, pretentiously, the Toronto Conservatory School of Literature and Expression, thrived, as did a new program, the Fletcher Music Method. It aimed to introduce ear training, rhythm and time, and sight-reading to young children through the use of toys, rhythmic handclapping, games, and other musical and non-musical devices. The founder, Evelyn Fletcher, born in Woodstock, Ontario, had been trained in Europe. She taught at the TCM and at the Bishop Strachan School from 1894 to 1897 before moving on to the New England Conservatory, where her reputation and method blossomed.[57] A proud Fisher told the shareholders at the 1900 AGM that the New York–based *Musical Courier* now ranked the TCM the third-largest music school on the continent.[58] Size clearly mattered.

In 1901 the Conservatory commissioned J.W.L. Forster to do a portrait of George Allan, its president since the school's founding.[59] Allan died just five months later, to be succeeded by the TCM's vice-president, Sir John A. Boyd. The succession had no visible effect on the school's governance or on its academic programs. Fisher began publication of a bimonthly TCM journal in December 1901, promising that it would be devoted to "educational work" and "home and foreign notes." It was not frivolous, to be sure, and he hoped it would attract new students. Presumably, it did.

For the first issue, A.S. Vogt, proud of his Canadian roots, wrote an article on foreign study, urging students to study at home and go to Europe only towards the end of their training. Canadian and American teachers, he felt, provided the thorough technical groundwork and close personal attention younger students needed.[60] Mostly true, the piece did no harm to school enrolments. Eight years later Fisher echoed Vogt, perhaps for more mercenary reasons, saying that American schools were superior to Europe's and that studying music in Europe was a lottery.[61] It made sense, at least for the great majority of pianists, but less so for singers. However, it didn't apply at all to instrumentalists and composers, areas in which TCM instruction was uninspiring. Nevertheless, both statements clearly showed a growing pride in Canadian instruction, important in counteracting the country's pervasive colonial mentality.

Over the next few years the Conservatory expanded its quarters south to Orde Street and west. It took out mortgages, made calls to shareholders for money, and posted subscriptions for new shares. Fisher guided his board through this expansion as surefootedly as any astute businessman, accountant, or corporate lawyer. He was living proof that a music school director should be able to read a balance sheet as competently as he could read music. His personal rewards were salary raises every few years.

At the board meeting of December 5, 1901, Fisher brought forward a letter from the University of Toronto asking for a meeting with TCM officials; the University was planning to introduce its own music examinations in performance and theory leading to a licentiate diploma. These would be in addition to administering examinations for its B.Mus. and D.Mus. degrees begun several years earlier.[62] The board, after recovering from the shock, met on January 9 and fired off a lengthy letter to the University the next day asking why. It pointed out that the Conservatory was a pioneer in the field, that it received no financial support from government, and that it depended heavily on examination revenue, all familiar and really sound arguments. The letter went on to describe the TCM's proficient examination system and its service to the musical and educational world. It concluded by hoping that the University would reconsider its position before initiating its new examinations in June 1902.

The University, in defending its action, complained that conservatories, while exploiting their affiliations to universities, generally did not prepare their advanced candidates sufficiently to pursue professional degrees.[63] Right or wrong, it was commonly known that the Associated Musicians of Ontario, a relatively independent group of leading musicians, had urged the University to give its own examinations to insure quality and objectivity. The Associated Board fracas may have indirectly provoked this critical storm.

The TCM board hoped that its examiners, who had agreed to examine for the University, would withdraw from the latter commitment. They didn't. The examinations proceeded, and a few examiners worked for both schools. In the following years the University sent examiners to different parts of Canada, enabling many advanced music students to earn Toronto licentiate diplomas.

Putting examination worries aside, the TCM delved earnestly into developing neighbourhood branches in the Greater Toronto Area. This made sense for young children unable to travel independently to College Street. Branches were still another manifestation of TCM expansion and were an important part of the TCM for the next eight decades. Each branch had its own head or principal, teaching staff, studios, and, if large enough, a recital hall. Certainly the branches helped to increase student enrolment.[64] The number of students taking examinations also increased, in spite of the University's encroachment on the school's territory. Fisher tirelessly worked away at organizing more examination centres. In 1907, the TCM examined 1,504 students across Canada, of whom more than half came from outside of Toronto. The numbers continued to grow until the Great Depression.[65]

The Conservatory's travelling examiners were its unsung heroes in the school's early days. In his article "The Conservatory in the North," J.W.F. Harrison wrote that as a TCM examiner in 1909 he travelled six thousand miles in forty days, by train, steamer, horse-drawn carriage, and automobile. He examined in twenty different communities, distributed instructional materials, and promoted the TCM wherever possible. In one town, Harrison recalled, he examined a number of French Canadian students, which was unusual for an English-based examining system.[66]

The TCM, it must be said, paid little attention to orchestral training and even had to engage an orchestra at great expense to dress up its commencement exercises. The only other comparable music school in Toronto, the Toronto College of Music, had a much stronger orchestral instrument program, and Fisher couldn't help comparing it to the TCM's feeble efforts. The College's head, British-born Frederick L. Torrington, had been Toronto's leading musician until Fisher arrived on the scene.[67] An organist and violinist, he migrated to Canada in 1856 at age nineteen. After sojourns as a church choirmaster, bandmaster, and violinist in Montreal and Boston, he returned to Canada as director of Toronto's Metropolitan Methodist (now United) Church. Then he revived the defunct Toronto Philharmonic Society, a large choir and orchestra, in 1872–73. (There is an imposing life-size portrait of him by J.W.L. Forster hanging in the Edward Johnson Building of the University of Toronto.)[68]

Torrington had directed an impressive music festival in 1886 at the Mutual Street Arena (actually a skating rink) involving several thousand children and adults. When he was in Boston, he had worked with Patrick Gilmore, the great organizer of the National Peace Jubilee of 1869, and some of Gilmore's talent must have rubbed off on him. Much good came from Torrington's festival, since it helped influence millionaire Hart Massey to build Massey Music Hall in 1894.[69] Like Fisher, Torrington had been caught up in music schools, and, as already noted, launched the Toronto College of Music one year after the Toronto Conservatory opened its doors. The College affiliated with the University of Toronto in 1890 and, in 1891, started the Toronto Orchestral School.[70] It met one evening a week and gave several public concerts annually. Torrington was convinced that orchestral instrumentalists needed "the necessary routine experience to play in our local orchestras." Budding orchestral players, therefore, preferred his school to the TCM.

To address the TCM's shortcomings in this area, Fisher engaged the talented young Canadian pianist Frank Welsman in the spring of 1906. He had studied for four years in Leipzig and Berlin with Martin Krause and Arnold Mendelssohn and had already concertized in Canada. He would teach piano and also, more urgently, organize a Conservatory symphony orchestra.[71]

Welsman had Fisher's complete confidence. The TCM announced that it would give the orchestra "financial and other support and derive no pecuniary advantage from the concerts given by the orchestra. The proceeds will be devoted entirely to the Orchestra itself and used in promoting the greater efficiency of the organization in the future."[72] The TCM orchestra soon came to pass. It was composed of advanced students, teachers, competent amateurs, and professionals, of whom most worked mainly in Toronto theatres. The TCM paid Welsman five dollars for each rehearsal and performance — not much, but adequate for the times.[73]

Welsman, who also played the violin and viola, was a resourceful organizer, and, although an inexperi-

Frank Welsman, c. 1908.

enced conductor, showed unmistakable talent on the podium. The orchestra of about fifty players rehearsed evenings and gave its first concert at Massey Hall on April 11, 1907. The program was a little spotty: the Beethoven Symphony no. 1 minus the last movement, the first and second movements of the Bruch Violin Concerto in G Minor with Frank Blachford as soloist, and other assorted short works. A far better concert was given on October 11 and drew good notices from the press. *Saturday Night* wrote, "People who have been wont to sneer whenever a local orchestra was mentioned had to admit that under Mr. Welsman's musicianly direction they had accomplished wonders considering that they had only one season's rehearsing."[74]

The next concert, on December 10, featured two complete works, the Beethoven Symphony no. 2 and the Saint-Saëns Second Piano Concerto in G Minor with "Miss Caldwell" as soloist. The highlight at its final concert at Massey Hall on April 9, 1908, was the magnetic — and eccentric — Russian pianist Vladimir de Pachmann. He played the Chopin Piano Concerto, no. 2, with the orchestra and then concluded the concert with a Chopin etude, op. 25, which brought down the house. According to *The Globe*, after six encores de Pachmann "bussed the conductor in full audience view and thoroughly European fashion on both cheeks."[75] Staid Torontonians were aghast at such behaviour. More important, this concert proved that the orchestra was ready to leave the TCM and go out on its own. And so, within two years, Welsman had created the Toronto Symphony Orchestra, a group that lasted until 1918. It was the first but not the last time that the Conservatory spawned a professional musical organization.

The TCM generously let its symphonic offspring keep the music and music stands it had bought for the Conservatory symphony and donated $100 towards its first year as the city's orchestra.[76] Frank Blachford of the TCM staff was concertmaster. In 1909 and 1910, respectively, cellists George Bruce and Leo Smith joined the orchestra and the TCM faculty. Evidently Welsman helped convince the English-born Smith to move to Canada.[77] He had an interesting background, having played under Arthur Nikisch, Hans Richter, and Edward Elgar. Also a composer, Smith would teach theory, history, and composition, as well as cello, at the TCM. A modest and likeable man, Smith called all of his male students "dear boy" and his female students "dear child." He was, in short, very much from an earlier age.[78] Years later, an amusing feud broke out between Smith and Ernest MacMillan. Smith had built a lovely house on Park Road in Rosedale in the twenties. Then, in 1932, MacMillan built a house on the adjoining lot that was taller than his neighbour's and in part blocked out the sun from Smith's house. Smith was unforgiving, and, so the story goes (it could be apocryphal), they never spoke to each other again except at formal occasions.[79]

But back to the TCM. On February 22, 1910, came a bombshell. The Ontario Parliament altered its Assessment Act, to wit, forbidding all educational institutions exempt from land taxation to pay dividends to their shareholders. Instead, they must direct all their profits "to the purposes of the institution."[80] The TCM was in good shape financially. Its real properties were worth $100,483; it had outstanding stock of $61,100, a surplus of $25,024, and owed only $24,800 in mortgages. The TCM's resourceful board therefore came up with what seems, to this day, an ingenious solution "to enable it to comply with the new law without injustice to its shareholders." A new TCM was created, the old TCM Ltd. becoming a private trust with three members of the new TCM board as its trustees. Each shareholder was asked to surrender his shares and in return received bonds and/or other forms of debentures in the same amount as their shares. Since the final valuation came to $193,000, the new conservatory could purchase the old conservatory for this price without hardship.[81] Because setting up a bond issue would take time, the new TCM took out a mortgage to repay the limited company. Just a year later bonds were issued, with one vote in the new company per bond.

To convince the "ex-shareholders" that all was well at the TCM, the new board — its members would be called governors, not directors — produced imposing enrolment and examination figures at the AGM of October 5, 1910. There were 1,800 students at the school, of whom 25 percent were from other provinces, the U.S., and the West Indies; 1,608 examination candidates; and 61 examination centres (46 in Ontario, 7 in Manitoba, 4 in Saskatchewan, 3 in Alberta, and 1 in British Columbia).

A few weeks later Fisher reminded the board that the twenty-fifth anniversary of the Conservatory was approaching, and this led the board to discuss his retirement and pension.[82] Some wondered if their sixty-two-year-old music director would ever retire, given that he loved his work so much. And then came a surprise: two new music schools, the Canadian Academy of Music and the Hambourg Conservatory, opened their doors in Toronto in 1911–12. (The Academy had absorbed the small Metropolitan School of Music, founded in 1893, and made it its Parkdale Branch.) Both schools aimed to fill gaps in Toronto's musical instruction that they thought were not adequately addressed.

The Academy, housed in spacious quarters on Spadina Road north of Bloor Street, was founded and financed by the wealthy philanthropist Colonel Albert Gooderham. (It was known as the Columbian Conservatory of Music in its first year.) Gooderham believed that Canada's gifted young musicians merited the very best instruction and should not have to go abroad for advanced study.[83] This sounded a bit like Fisher and Vogt, although Gooderham put his money where his mouth was. He wanted a school on a par with leading ones in Europe and the United States, and for this he needed great musicians and teachers. Thus the energetic and intrepid Gooderham sought out an international faculty to entice Canadian students to attend his school. One of his first "catches" was Luigi von Kunits, a fine concert violinist and conductor, who turned down the conductorship of the Philadelphia Orchestra to come to Toronto. (Leopold Stokowski was the Orchestra's second choice.) In addition to teaching a number of outstanding violinists in the coming years, von Kunits would, in 1922, become the conductor of the New Toronto Symphony Orchestra, which later became the TSO that is still with us in the twenty-first century.

By contrast, the Hambourg Conservatory, at the corner of Wellesley and Sherbourne — then one of the most fashionable sections of the city — was an intriguing family enterprise. The directors were Michael, a pianist who had studied with Nicholas Rubinstein in Moscow and St. Petersburg, and two of his four sons: Jan, a violinist and pupil of Otakar Sevcik and Eugène Ysaÿe, and Boris, a cellist and pupil of Hugo Becker in Frankfurt. The much younger Clement — he was only ten when he arrived in Canada — was a pianist and, later in his life, a manager of jazz events. Michael's oldest son, Mark, was a gifted pianist who enjoyed a brilliant international concert career. He remained in London, where the family had lived after leaving Russia and before coming to Canada. When visiting Toronto he would give the occasional master class at the Hambourg Conservatory.[84] The Hambourgs, thanks to their international connections, added flavour and dimension to Toronto's musical life. Boris Hambourg joined the Hart House String Quartet when it was formed in 1923 and remained with it until its demise two decades later.

Fisher reassured the board that the TCM was doing well despite this formidable competition, but, significantly, he did increase the TCM's advertising budget.[85] Now the Fisher years were drawing to a close. With little warning, Edward Fisher died of a heart attack on May 31, 1913. Humphrey Anger, a mainstay of the TCM theory department, died just ten days later after a brief illness. Fisher had done admirably in his twenty-six years at the Conservatory. A populist, he firmly believed that Canada needed music instruction at all levels, and he was rewarded for his efforts by the school's growth, its faculty (some of whom were outstanding), and its fine College Street building, the best of its kind in Canada. An optimist, an idealist, he compromised judiciously when necessary but never lost sight of his goals. Fisher had proudly developed a large and prosperous school. Compare the number of staff in 1887 to that of 1912: piano teachers from twelve to sixty-four, organ from two to ten, voice (including sight-singing) from four to twenty-nine, theory from three to four, and other instruments from twelve to twenty-one. Since the school's inception, a total of 655 diplomas had been earned by 589 students.[86] The Conservatory would continue to improve in the next decade. The Fisher years had provided the groundwork and set the stage.

Chapter Two

MUSIC EDUCATION AND MONEY

It was a foregone conclusion that the Conservatory board would choose Augustus S. Vogt as its new music director.[87] Vogt clearly had the musical and administrative qualities required to run the growing school. He also had an excellent reputation as a piano teacher and examiner, and his Mendelssohn Choir had reached great heights, thanks to his organizing ability, meticulous direction, and inspired leadership. Short in stature, he nevertheless had a commanding presence, and he was strict and uncompromising, quite the opposite of the more temperate Fisher. Musicians, amateur and professional alike, admired him. With Fisher gone and Torrington aging, Vogt soon wore the crown as Toronto's leading musician.

Not surprisingly, Vogt viewed the music director's post differently from Fisher. For him it was a total commitment. He believed that in order to devote sufficient time to running the school, he should *not* teach. The TCM board fixed his annual director's salary at $5,500, $500 more than Fisher's, although Fisher had earned another $2,500 teaching piano and organ.[88]

In 1917, four years later, Vogt resolutely resigned as director of his beloved Mendelssohn Choir because of Conservatory duties. He had founded the choir in 1894, broken it up three years later, and re-established it in 1900. It became one of the finest large choirs — many thought the finest — in North America.

First, Vogt dealt with teacher appointments. In England in the spring of 1913, he had, at Fisher's request, looked for a replacement for the ailing Humphrey Anger, and he confidently recommended thirty-three-year-old Healey Willan for the post. Already a prominent organist, choir director, and composer, Willan was, additionally, an authority on plainchant and the Anglo-Catholic liturgy and its music. However, he needed more money than Britain could provide to support his large family — his wife, three sons, his mother, and his sister. The Toronto job offered $3,000 annually, excellent for the times, with the promise of another $1,200 as organist/choirmaster at St. Paul's Anglican Church.[89]

Willan's appointment to the Conservatory was especially significant since he was to be one of English Canada's leading composers for the next fifty years.[90] He composed prolifically, his pieces all stubbornly post-Romantic in style and feeling and redolent of turn-of-the-century English music. It was neither Canadian in spirit nor radical to any degree. Many musicians revered him as a master of his craft, while others less reverently thought he and his work had an inhibiting effect on at least one if not two generations of Canadian composers. As a teacher the jury is still out. He could spend hours with a student on an inspired one-on-one basis — he usually addressed his male students as "old man" — and yet could read lifelessly from a music history book to a class for an hour without comment.[91]

A.S. Vogt.

Personally, Willan exuded much charm. He harboured a storehouse of clever limericks, some of them off-colour. A debonair dresser, he affected an upper-middle-class appearance, used a cane, and wore spats in winter. In his later years, Willan wrote mercilessly about 1913 Toronto. He found Yonge Street, Toronto's main thoroughfare, "about as interesting as an English village street. It seemed like the last place in the world for the development of music."[92] There was no orchestra and few visiting concert artists. "The only annual event of musical interest was the Toronto Mendelssohn Choir Festival — about three days of it at Massey Hall, usually in February. Even with the Mendelssohn Choir, in those days one felt a dearth of music. Sir Robert Falconer, the president of the University of Toronto, told me when I arrived: 'You'll find a great difference here; it's a young country; the errand boy has not yet learned to whistle'." Willan regularly attended the Toronto Arts and Letters Club to socialize with friends. A devoted member, he set its constitution to music and wrote a choral march for its choir and orchestra. The club's setting and membership resembled that of an English men's club and contributed

Healey Willan, c. 1920.

to Willan's illusion that he was forever an Englishman in a Canadian setting. (Women were excluded from the Arts and Letters Club until 1985.)

But back to Vogt. He hired two new piano teachers as his replacement. The first was Danish pianist Viggo Kihl, who had studied with Robert Teichmüller in Leipzig and had given recitals in England, Europe, and South Africa. He would teach at the Conservatory for the next thirty years. A list of his pupils is impressive: Mona Bates, soloist and teacher; Arthur Gold, of the Gold/Fizdale piano team; Weldon Kilburn, piano and voice teacher and Lois Marshall's accompanist and coach for many years; Gwendolyn Williams, who married the violinist Adolph Koldofsky and had a rich career as an accompanist in Los Angeles; and Ida Krehm, who would win three major awards within three weeks in 1937 when she was twenty-five: the Schubert Memorial Award, which included three appearances with the Philadelphia Orchestra under Eugene Ormandy, the U.S. National Federation of Music Clubs cash prize, and the Naumburg Foundation Award, which included a sponsored Town Hall Recital in New York.[93]

Kihl's eccentricities were long remembered by his students. He had the disconcerting habit of playing an invisible piano as he walked the Conservatory's corridors. He usually wore starched high collars, more Victorian than post-Edwardian, but he still appeared unkempt. And — horrors! — he reeked of garlic. Yet he was a fine teacher, analyzed music brilliantly, and provided solutions to technical problems with clarity.[94] Ida Krehm said that in her first weeks of study with Kihl at age twelve he wouldn't let her play the piano. Instead, he had her bring down her arms and hands repeatedly to the keyboard in a relaxed manner, in order to strengthen her hands and develop flexibility in her arms. Krehm attributed her large sound to those first weeks of Kihl's lessons.[95]

The other piano appointment was the American Paul Wells. He had been a pupil of the Australian pianist Ernest Hutcheson in Baltimore and then had studied with Josef Lhevinne and Leopold Godowsky in Europe.[96] Wells also taught a number of outstanding TCM students, including Muriel Kerr, a child prodigy who became a Juilliard teacher and director of her own school in California, and TCM teachers Gordon Hallett and Scott Malcolm. Both Wells and Kihl were active faculty members who gave recitals, played in chamber groups, and wrote about piano study and pedagogy.

Vogt soon came to grips with the Conservatory's associateship (ATCM). An ardent believer in the value of examinations, he was concerned that the variable standards of the groups that administered them — the Associated Board, the University of Toronto, and others — devalued the diploma. He also frowned upon examination bodies that allowed performers to earn advanced diplomas by examination only. However, he took the politic course and concluded that it was best to leave the ATCM as it was, while initiating a new and more demanding licentiate diploma (LTCM). The more prestigious LTCM would require a minimum of one year's resident study at the TCM prior to the examination. It remained the Conservatory's most advanced diploma until 1947.[97] While he was at it, he abandoned the FTCM — the two-subject diploma.

The TCM's new music director diligently kept an eye on profits and losses. In February 1914 he warned new teachers that if their classes were not large enough at the end of their first year, their names would be "taken from the roll of teachers," i.e., they would lose their jobs. He also informed teachers who taught fewer than twenty pupils that they might have to share their studios, since the school's studio space was at a premium. Like any good manager, he wanted his equipment and space used to the maximum to achieve maximum profits.[98] A month later he informed the TCM board that there would be no salary guarantees in the coming year. He didn't seem worried about teachers leaving the school to join the competition.[99]

The Great War had a sobering effect on the TCM as it had on Canadian life generally. Enrolments declined in the first two years, but examination registrations continued to grow. With no lack of modesty Vogt claimed this was due to his reorganizing its administration and graded schedules.[100] He also noted with a hint of delight — probably justified — that Bertha Drechsler Adamson, long-time conductor of the Conservatory Strings, had "laid down the baton for good." It was a hard time for her. The strings had been floundering for a number of years with Adamson, and when Frank Blachford took them over it was a clear turn for the better. Adamson, age sixty-six, had more troubles three years later when her star student, Harry Adaskin, left her to study with Luigi von Kunits. According to Adaskin, neither Adamson nor her violinist daughter Lina forgave him for his "ingratitude."[101] In a way Adamson was no different from other teachers who let emotions affect their thinking; the teacher becomes proprietary and overlooks a pupil's changing needs.

In 1922, Adaskin, constantly looking for solutions to his bow arm problems, spent the summer studying in Chicago with Leon Sametini, an Ysaÿe student.[102] Returning to Toronto, he moved on — as did a number of other von Kunits pupils — to study with the extraordinary and quite mysterious Polish violinist Henri Czaplinski, a new teacher at the Hambourg Conservatory. When he informed von Kunits that he was leaving him, he quoted von Kunits as saying, "I am not surprised. It's well known that, if a Jewish pupil has a choice of a Jewish or a non-Jewish teacher, he will always choose the Jewish teacher." One would not have expected such a comment from von Kunits, but, like Adamson, he hated to lose pupils, and a number of Jewish violin students — convenient scapegoats — were among those who left him. Anti-Semitism was rife in Toronto in those years.

With school profits declining, Vogt cut administrative staff salaries.[103] At the October 1915 annual meeting, he announced that the annual — and expensive — Massey Hall graduation concert had been dropped and would be replaced by several senior student recitals.[104] He added that the school needed a Massey Hall

Bertha Drechsler Adamson.

of its own that could seat about twelve hundred people. With considerable prescience, he predicted that this would be realized only "when the present valuable property on which the present Conservatory buildings stand is converted into funds which may be applied to an equipment appropriate to the institution's very evident national opportunities and responsibilities." The next year, with the war raging, Vogt contradicted himself and bragged, "These three years have been the most successful artistically and financially in the entire history of the institution."[105] So much for Fisher's work. "O fading honors of the dead!"

In 1916 Vogt asked his former pupil, Ernest Seitz, to join the piano faculty. Seitz had studied in Germany with Josef and Rosina Lhevinne from 1910 to 1914. Much like the older Frank Welsman, he was thoroughly taken with German life and culture and spoke German fluently.[106] An October 1914 European tour had been fixed for the twenty-two-year-old virtuoso, but events would have it otherwise. Having spent that fateful summer with his family in Canada, he was unable to return to Europe. As an alternative, he gave a debut recital at Massey Hall in 1915 and evidently stunned Toronto's musical world. Now the TCM piano department, with Seitz, Kihl, Wells, and Welsman, was probably second to none in North America.

Seitz had been a child prodigy; he was alleged to have played "The Blue Bells of Scotland" by ear at age four without any previous lessons. He came from a wealthy family: his father, Joseph Seitz, was the founder of the Underwood Typewriter Company of Canada. Over his performing career, Seitz would be soloist with the Toronto Symphony eighteen times, perform frequently at Toronto Promenade Concerts ("The Proms"), give more than three hundred broadcasts, and tour widely in Canada. Additionally, he gave a successful New York recital in 1922 and played with the New York Philharmonic, the New York Symphony, the Philadelphia Orchestra, and the Boston Symphony.

Ernest Seitz, c. 1916.

Considered by many to be Canada's leading pianist between the wars, Seitz toured Western Canada in 1925, earning splendid reviews. Of interest was Regina's comment: "Part of the audience's enthusiasm was pride that the distinguished artist was a Canadian, and, unlike other Canadians in the musical world, he continues to make his home in his native country and contribute to its cultural development."[107] His students included Muriel Gidley, who was also a fine organist; Reginald Godden and Scott Malcolm, who played together frequently as a two-piano team; Earle Moss, a leading TCM teacher; Charles Peaker, another fine organist and teacher; and Lorne Watson, head of music at Brandon College for many years.

The handsome and personable Seitz is probably most famous for composing the 1918 song "The World Is Waiting for the Sunrise," with lyrics by his boyhood chum and, later, Hollywood actor Gene Lockhart. By 1983, Seitz's royalties had totalled well over a quarter of a million dollars, an amount far more, as Healey Willan had ruefully pointed out, than Willan's total royalties from his enormous creative output. Seitz also wrote several other tunes through the years.[108]

Sir John Boyd, president of the Conservatory for fifteen years and a loyal member of the TCM board since the school's founding, died on November 23, 1916. Searching for a successor, Vogt and the board approached Sir Edmund Walker, a self-made banker who was president of the Canadian Bank of Commerce and chairman of the University of Toronto's board of governors. Walker, a large man with a decided air of authority, was one of the most public-spirited Canadians of his time. He hit it off with Vogt — he is reputed to have said that Vogt would have been just as successful heading a bank as heading the Conservatory — and together, in 1918, they persuaded the University of Toronto to make the Faculty of Music a teaching body.[109] Next, they engineered the merger of the TCM with the University, a merger that would last seventy years. A 1919 provincial Act sealed it. Now the TCM's properties and assets were vested in the University. Two years later, the TCM's operations came under the control of a University-appointed board of trustees.

Sir Edmund Walker.

What lay behind the merger? Why did the Conservatory so willingly lose its independence? One reason was that $184,000 of TCM bonds would soon come due, and the TCM did not have the resources to redeem them. The University, however, did. Another concern was the TCM's hold on the examination market, which was continuing to be tenuous because of the University's formidable competition. A merger would allow the schools to share the market for examinations, examiners, and, ultimately, teaching faculty.

The University of Toronto had also been looking for solutions to *its* examination problems. It had often and unsparingly criticized the Toronto College of Music for giving its own advanced examinations — the College gave associate and licentiate diplomas much like the TCM — despite its affiliation with the University. The Hamilton Conservatory, another affiliate, also provided a further irritant since it was about to initiate examinations. The University — steadfast — believed that it alone should give advanced examinations. Matters came to a head in February 1918, when a University senate committee haughtily attacked those competing affiliates. "More and more the university examinations are becoming one among several of similar character, and there may be further development in outside affiliated bodies which will neutralize even more the purpose which the University had in establishing its examinations." The committee recommended that the University dissolve its affiliation with all three music schools in examination matters, which it did![110]

Then the University of Toronto created its Faculty of Music. Walker and Vogt, both wily schemers, had worked it all out behind the scenes. Walker had good relations with Sir Robert Falconer, the University's president, and had, in fact, chaired the search committee that recommended Falconer's appointment in 1907. As for Falconer, he supported the merger and appointed Vogt dean of this first "legal" faculty of music. ("Faculty of Music" had been improperly used on examination papers as early as 1904.) Now in control over both bodies, the elated Vogt wrote to Walker about the Conservatory's role within the University:

> [The Conservatory] would elevate local musical life and at the same time obviate the necessity of professional students going abroad to complete their musical education. Its reputation and usefulness would be greatly enhanced as a part of the University of Toronto. Such a step would also facilitate the standardization of musical examinations throughout the province. The dignity, permanency, and further development of the Conservatory along the highest artistic lines, would unquestionably be assured.[111]

What an admirable brew of business, education, and art! The triumphant TCM could now claim victory over the competition, the Toronto College of Music and the Hamilton Conservatory.

Healey Willan was appointed to the Faculty of Music but continued to teach at the TCM. Other staff in the new Faculty included conductor, composer, and organist Albert Ham; Ferdinand Albert Mouré, also an organist as well as bursar of the University; and Herbert Austin Fricker, conductor of the Mendelssohn Choir. The only doctors of music on the staff were Vogt and Ham. Ham actually had an earned doctorate from the University of Dublin in addition to an honorary doctorate from the University of Toronto (1906). The University, however, saw to it that all the Faculty's staff would have appropriate credentials by shamelessly awarding honorary doctorates to Willan (1920), Mouré (1922), and Fricker (1923).[112] To make the merger legal, the TCM board members resigned en masse and then were immediately reappointed by the University's governors.[113] There were few changes in its membership, and the move had no effect on the board's standing or operations. For convenience — and to save money — Faculty lectures were given at the TCM's College Street building with its studios and pianos. Everyone seemed happy.

Returning to September 1917, Vogt reported that the war continued to affect TCM enrolments and revenues adversely. Then the question arose about the competing Canadian Academy of Music. Its success had provided still another, if more subtle, reason for the TCM's seeking shelter under the blanket of the University. The Academy had absorbed the Metropolitan School of Music in 1912 and had been strengthened further when the Toronto College of Music joined it in 1917, immediately following F.H. Torrington's death. Then Frank Welsman, whose Toronto Symphony had more or less disbanded by 1918 because of lack of support, left the TCM to join the Academy and took some of his best students with him. At the Academy he became the third of a management trio of Peter Kennedy, Academy head since 1912, and Alfred Bruce, managing director. (In addition to von Kunits, other Academy faculty included Albert Ham and W.O. Forsyth, both of whom joined the school in 1919, and Ernest MacMillan, who joined it a year later.) It was clear that, by Toronto standards, the five-year-old Academy was as much a first-class school as the TCM, and its teachers were earning as good if not better fees. Welsman was appointed music director in 1922, strengthening the Academy still more.

To meet fire with fire, Vogt went to New York in early 1918 to find a piano replacement for Welsman and a violin teacher on a level with the Academy's von Kunits. He returned empty-handed.

Fortunately, TCM examination registrations picked up in 1917–18, thus prompting Vogt, once more and rather tastelessly, to compare his work to Fisher's.[114] "Little progress was made in our examinations in the five years prior to and including 1913; the number of entries for 1918 now shows an advance over 1913 of 2,015 — an increase of about 115 percent — net revenue from $4,949 to $10,353." Then came the world flu epidemic, followed by a smallpox scare, which together nearly caused the closure of the school in 1918–19. Vogt went on a six-month health leave in November 1919, and a committee of teachers, composed of Willan (chairman), Kihl, Wells, and Seitz, took over during his absence.[115] Willan stayed on as Vogt's assistant when the latter returned, receiving a stipend of $175 a month. This appointment prompted Vogt to propose reducing his own salary, but the board would have none of it.[116]

One of Vogt's lasting contributions was initiating the *Conservatory Quarterly Review* in 1918. Leo Smith, an accomplished writer in addition to his talents as a cellist, composer, and theory teacher, took over as editor, a post he held until 1935 when the *Review* folded. The journal more or less paid for itself. Copies cost fifteen cents, and prominent teachers, music publishing companies, music stores, piano manufacturers, and piano dealers regularly advertised in it. The first issue concentrated on teaching. There were articles about piano playing by Seitz, Wells, and Kihl, and a piece by G.D. Atkinson, "On the relation of Psychology to Music." In the voice section, two of the TCM's leading teachers, David Dick Slater and Dalton Baker, wrote about vocal technique, Albert Ham about training the boy's voice, and Healey Willan about how English choir schools function. The *Review* had an organ section and news about concerts, events, and examinations at and outside the Conservatory. Examination results were published in issues following examination periods.

In addition to reporting TCM news events in the *Review*, Vogt wanted Smith to editorialize on a wide range of musical subjects and give "a running commentary on musical life, which would aim to inculcate criteria, and to reflect the attitude of a man of taste."[117] In one issue, Smith wrote a perceptive piece on Debussy, helped in part by his having been in the orchestra when Debussy directed the London premiere of *Pelléas et Mélisande*.[118] He described Debussy as "dark, extremely quiet and reserved, his one idea to let his art speak for itself without the element of personal intrusion." Several of his editorials dealt with "creating standards in a large country of old and new parts and uneven economic development." He wrote perceptively about his experiences as a TCM examiner in a remote prairie town, where, in spite of bad weather, parents left their farms and struggled over poor roads to get their children to the examinations punctually. "The little girls wore their party frocks, and the graceful thank-you after the ordeal is over would melt the heart of a public prosecutor," said Smith. "But the teacher in their district seemed to have thought the Prelude and Fugue was just a double-barrelled name for one item — and the young candidates had prepared only the Prelude."[119]

Sir Edmund Walker used the November 1920 issue of the *Review* to explain the TCM/University of Toronto merger and made this pointed comment: "It is a great satisfaction to those who have laboured to bring this about that the importance of musical training has thus been acknowledged by the State." There was nothing substantive in this acknowledgement, since it would be more than a decade before Ontario would really recognize musical training with material assistance.[120]

The school gradually returned to normal after the Armistice, with more students enrolling and more examination centres in operation. Finally, in 1920, Vogt found two musicians from abroad to join the faculty, violinist Ferdinand Fillion and the Swiss pianist Carlos Buhler. There was a bonus in the Fillion appointment: his wife, Fern Goltré-Fillion, a Belgian soprano, would also teach voice and opera at the TCM.[121] Husband and wife promptly gave a joint debut/recital on October 7. Fillion played the Mendelssohn Concerto, the Bach *Chaconne*, and four short pieces, including Sarasate's *Ziguenerweisen*, to good press, while Goltré-Fillion, a lyric coloratura, sang a number of short English and French songs and the challenging "Bell Song" from Delibes' *Lakmé*. Other than politely reporting her work the press was non-committal. Goltré-Fillion's skills led her to appear in local Gilbert and Sullivan productions and, interestingly, in a series of Jenny Lind recitals with her versatile husband at the

Sketch of Leo Smith.

49

piano. Dressed as Jenny Lind, she patterned her programs in part after those of the "Swedish Nightingale," who had, incidentally, sung at Toronto's St. Lawrence Hall more than a half-century before.

Thanks to Goltré-Fillion, opera came to the Conservatory for the first time in 1923. She formed a company of brave, if not foolhardy, singers who presented Wolf-Ferrari's *The Secret of Suzanne* in the totally unsuitable TCM concert hall. Augustus Bridle of the *Toronto Star* commented on the setting: "… a little stage with a large organ for a background and wings, with the pipes for a border, a piano for an orchestra, screens for doors, no curtain, no proscenium, but the whole thing tastefully laid out to give the suggestion of an elegant room." Goltré-Fillion sang the title role, and performed, according to Bridle, "with a delicacy and light humour … her light, flexible voice an ideal instrument for such a work."[122] The popular Horace Lapp was the pianist.

Ferdinand Fillion played frequently at the Conservatory with Seitz, Kihl, Wells, and Smith. One of Fillion's pupils was Geoffrey Waddington, later head of music at the CBC. Waddington, from Lethbridge, Alberta, received a Sebastian Klotz violin from the Heinl Company in 1922 as a reward for his progress with Fillion.[123] The Fillions moved to Pittsburgh in 1925. Carlos Buhler stayed with the TCM only until 1923.

Undoubtedly the school gained momentum in the post-war years. With studio space at College Street more than ever at a premium, some teachers had to be moved to branches. Conditions improved in 1922, when an expansion of the main building was completed at the considerable cost, for those years, of $69,000.[124] In addition to new studios, the reception hall was extended and sofas and armchairs were added to give it an air of quiet elegance.[125] There was good news, too, from the women's residence, a building that had previously belonged to the T. Eaton family; it was filled to overflowing.[126] Next, a costly central heating plant was installed at the main building, and opera chairs replaced the austere hard-backed wooden chairs in the concert hall. The board approved these projects and also approved changing Vogt's title to principal and Willan's to vice-principal.[127]

Hoping to assure his place in Canadian musical history, Vogt proudly recorded in his September 1921 annual report that the "absorption of the Conservatory by the University is being welcomed throughout the country because it signifies permanency, dignity, and prestige. Examinations are being conducted by the Conservatory and immediately under the direction of a great 'State' University." Was the University of Toronto's reputation and standing as supreme as Vogt intimated? Or maybe it was just good politics and a chance for the self-supporting TCM to show its gratitude to the University for getting it out of a financial hole. In the end, money, as always, fuelled the TCM's engine.

The Chilean pianist Alberto Guerrero joined the Conservatory faculty on March 1, 1923. Guerrero's credentials were exceptional. From a wealthy, cultured, and liberal family, he had broad interests and had played a leading role in Chile's musical life as pianist, teacher, music critic, and contemporary music advocate, before leaving his country at age thirty to make his debut in New York.[128] Two years later he joined the faculty of Toronto's Hambourg Conservatory, where he remained for five years before joining the TCM. A fine musician with a courtly and elegant personal manner, he would teach many outstanding pianists in the next thirty-five years, but especially in the forties and fifties. Here are a few of his pupils: William Aide, Ray Dudley, John Beckwith, Helmut Blume, Paul Helmer, Stuart Hamilton, Malcolm Troup, Ruth Watson Henderson, and Guerrero's second wife, Myrtle Rose Guerrero, whom he married after a twenty-year liaison. His most famous student was Glenn Gould.

At the annual meeting of October 3, 1923, which, incidentally, President Robert Falconer attended (he went to several board meetings in this period), Vogt reported record enrolments of 2,653 students at the main building and an additional 3,515 in TCM branches across the city. There were 1,000 more examination candidates than the preceding year, and the faculty had grown from 193 to 207. The report was all about quantity, not quality. Vogt did, however, stress the need for a new building, although this fell on deaf ears at the University.

About a mile away, the Hambourg Conservatory was also thriving in its own small way, but, unlike the Canadian Academy of Music, it was hardly a threat to TCM supremacy in instruction except in string instruments. Michael Hambourg had died in 1916, leaving the management of his Conservatory to his sons Jan and Boris. The school had a reputation for giving specialized training to young musicians by internationally known teachers. Photos of distinguished artists, with inscriptions of affection to one or another of the Hambourgs, hung on the Hambourg Conservatory walls, which helped the school's ambiance, as did its intimate recitals and parties for the rich and famous. The always hospitable and generous Hambourgs lived on the building's third floor.

Jan Hambourg had left for Paris in 1920 with his wealthy wife, Isabelle McClung, who, incidentally, for many years prior to her marriage had had a lesbian relationship with the American writer Willa Cather.[129] Young Samuel Hersenhoren, who would become a leading Toronto violinist and conductor, followed him there and stayed on for several years to continue his studies. Another of Jan's students, Broadus Farmer, later taught two future concertmasters of the Toronto Symphony, Albert Pratz and Hyman Goodman. After Jan's departure, Boris Hambourg ran the school in spite of his frequent tours with the Hart House String Quartet.

Such was the situation when Vogt made his move to clear Toronto of the TCM's major competitor, the Canadian Academy of Music. Vogt, the empire builder, seemed to have got wind of the Academy's interest in merging with the TCM. (Vogt or Walker might actually have dropped the idea with its president and benefactor, Albert Gooderham.) A cryptic minute of the TCM board meeting of February 12, 1924, hints at what followed: "A very comprehensive discussion then took place regarding the Canadian Academy of Music. Dr. Vogt was asked to report further."

He didn't waste time. At the next board meeting, on April 2, Vogt was given authority to offer up to $100,000 to purchase the Academy. The two schools finally settled on $115,000 on May 23, $15,000 in cash and the remainder in bonds at 5 percent, payable half-yearly.[130] Vogt wrote the same day to Sir Robert Falconer, asking him to approve the purchase. His *raison d'être*, Vogt explained, was that "the combined effort of the Conservatory and Academy would make for an effective control of the teaching situation in Toronto and at the same time exercise a great influence on the Local Examination problem throughout Canada, in which the two schools are now actively competing, to the detriment of their individual interests."[131] The University agreed and guaranteed the bonds.

It was typical Vogt. Leo Smith astutely noted that Vogt was very much a Canadian who valued "material or concrete evidence of success and the winning of victories, of triumphs," which the taking over of the Academy certainly was. Smith also considered it thoroughly Canadian that Dr. Vogt should, in Conservatory matters, incline towards the advantages of bigness. He pictured a great national conservatory that would "occupy a place in the public mind similar to that occupied by the University."[132]

The agreement of sale included the Academy's buildings on 12 and 14 Spadina Road and its annex at 17 Walmer Road. The Academy's list of chattels was formidable: several grand pianos, furniture, bookcases, and even kitchen supplies. There were more than forty studios in the two main buildings and annex in addition to a recital hall and offices, all of which the Conservatory planned on using. Now the coast was clear; the TCM was indisputably Canada's leading music school, and it had a near monopoly on standardized examinations.

Unfortunately, the April 2 meeting that preceded the sale was clouded by the death of Sir Edmund Walker. An "In Memoriam," published in the May 1924 *Review*, described him as "a forceful and unique character in which, added to his natural and sedulously applied business faculties, were welded the more unusual graces of intellectual and artistic accomplishments." Losing his guiding hand, however, didn't impede the negotiations. The University governors approved a draft agreement between the TCM and the Academy on June 12. They also informed the delighted TCM trustees that Colonel

Sir Albert Gooderham.

Albert Gooderham, a university governor and president of the defunct Academy, had been nominated president of the enlarged TCM. Walker, himself, could not have found a better successor. In addition to his experience at the Academy, Gooderham clearly looked the part: he had an impressive bearing and even a waxed moustache.

The Academy's faculty would now be working for the TCM, including Frank Welsman and an already distinguished thirty-one-year-old organist and conductor, Ernest MacMillan. Welsman's student Percy Faith, an arranger and composer who would have an outstanding career in radio on the CBC in the thirties and then in the U.S. from 1940 until his death in 1975, wrote in 1971 about his teacher: "The discipline at the keyboard, the encouragement Mr. Welsman gave me, and the hinting at the sound and excitement of the large orchestra were all things that later became obsessions for me." Faith had burned his hands at age eighteen, which seriously affected his piano playing. Welsman "insisted that I take up harmony and composition.... A fortunate bit of advice for me."[133]

A revealing sidelight in this period of power brokering and empire building involved Vogt's piano study books, which were listed in the examination syllabi. Such listings guaranteed — and still do — substantial royalties for the composer. Between 1919 and 1923, Vogt had amassed $14,489 in royalties — a considerable sum — from the Frederick Harris Music Company, which published TCM piano examination material. Acknowledging that his favoured position might have given him an advantage over other composers of pedagogical material, Vogt turned over half of these royalties to the

Conservatory. In 1923 he proposed a new arrangement: the TCM board would give him a fixed royalty of $2,500 annually for the next ten years, the Conservatory keeping the balance. It seemed like a fair proposal, since Vogt was at work on new material that Harris would probably sell in great numbers to examinees. Vogt uninhibitedly wrote to Sir Edmund Walker, reminding him that his past publications "have exercised a great influence on the development of the Conservatory's local examinations, much of the rather remarkable increase in this part of the Conservatory's work being due to the existence of its clearly outlined and comparatively inexpensive examination material. It is probable that the same ratio of increase will continue for years to come." As they say, modesty gets you nowhere! The board promptly approved the proposal, although its implementation was delayed by one year.[134]

Vogt, although only in his early sixties, suffered from ill health. He took a leave of absence in the winter of 1924–25 and then, when he took a more extended leave in July 1925, suggested that Ernest MacMillan take charge during his absence. Ever alert to threats from other examination bodies, Vogt pointed out in his annual report on October 7, 1925, that the TCM's old nemesis and principal competitor, the Associated Board, was now giving full scholarships for study in England to the three highest ranking students taking its Canadian examinations. "This significant step," Vogt warned, "will doubtless compel the Conservatory to take similar action in the interests of our institution's prestige." However, there is no record of equally generous scholarships awarded to top TCM examinees.

Prompted by Vogt's failing health, the school held a banquet in his honour on October 25, 1925, at the splendid Great Hall of Hart House, the all-male student's union on the University campus that was completed in 1919, thanks to the Massey family. As described by Leo Smith, the hall had "flaring candles, old portraits, lofty roof and glittering tables … the Banquet itself was a splendid sight, the colour needed by the dim grey architecture being supplied by the dresses of the ladies, and the rose-paper caps of the men." It was a joyful occasion, with speeches, skits, and a special menu with teachers' names, musical terms, and other nonsense cheerfully injected: "Grape Fruit Squirtzando, Champion Celery, Knott Almonds, Geen Olives, Tough Spoiled Spring Bullock, Pamphylon Sauce, Shepherd's Pie, Virgina Prest Ham, Potatoes Guerrero, Tattersall of Fried Linoleum, Boneless Gravy, White Potatoes Browned, Frickered Cauliflower, Robb Rolls, Creighton Custard, Farmer's Delight, Fancy Cakes Hayunga, Demi-tasse Leo, and Punch McNally." There were toasts by University Chancellor Sir William Mulock, followed by "A Quiet Morning in the Principal's Studio, A burlesque translated impressively for this occasion from the French of Wat-Afoo-Liam by Non Da Capo." Thus was honoured the man who had in his twelve years as principal made the TCM into one of the largest — and richest — North American music schools.[135]

Vogt died on September 17, 1926, less than a year later. The obituaries praised his work as leader of the Mendelssohn Choir, which he had left eleven years before, and of the Conservatory. The critic Hector Charlesworth wrote with admiration in *Saturday Night* that Vogt was "the first native-born Canadian to do constructive work for music in his own country ... the child of a small Ontario rural community, a self-made man who fought his way upward in the face of adverse conditions as would any captain of finance and industry." Charlesworth said he was a lover of good talk and generous to a fault. Vogt watched over every aspect of the school, and "detested complacency in a teacher, a pupil or the community at large."[136] The memorial service was at St. Paul's on October 24. The Mendelssohn Choir sang, Sir Robert Falconer gave the benediction, and Canon Cody, who would succeed Falconer as president of the University in 1931, gave the address.

Although he didn't have much affection for Vogt, Ernest MacMillan wrote "An Appreciation" in the October 1926 *University Monthly*, which addressed his achievements on the podium:

> The wonderful feeling for musical colour which never failed to appear in Vogt's performances was compounded of an exceptional sense of rhythm and an almost uncanny sensitiveness to vocal tone. Many who sang under his baton have described to me his methods at rehearsal — his meticulous attention to such matters as intonation, his illuminating orchestral analogies, his clear mental conception of the effects he wished to obtain, and his rigorous discipline — but when all is said and done, any artistic whole is greater than the sum of its parts, and there was a quality in the man himself which counted for more than anything he did.

MacMillan also wrote about Vogt's personal virtues, noting that he was a genial host, frequently entertained visiting musicians, and had wide interests. "He was remarkably familiar with the movements of the Stock Exchange and had a passion for military and economic history. He had close personal friends in many walks of life, and was in every sense a man of the world."

Chapter Three

THE DEPRESSION YEARS

Augustus Vogt had wanted to be Conservatory music director when Edward Fisher died. Not so Ernest MacMillan. He was full of doubts when the board offered him the post of principal in October 1926. Should he head a school that he knew was essentially selling lessons to whoever could pay for them and directing an examination system that many thought was more devoted to making money than being a vehicle for learning? MacMillan was also concerned about the principal's administrative chores and about attending to the school's day-to-day affairs. And, finally, he feared that the post would limit his other musical activities.[137] Unlike Vogt, the thirty-three-year-old MacMillan did not intend to give up his performing career.

MacMillan was a brilliant musician. Of average height, he had a stocky build that made him seem shorter than he actually was. He always moved quickly and energetically. In his five years (1920–25) as organist and choirmaster at the Timothy Eaton Memorial Church, he had given several recitals annually of the organ music of J.S. Bach and had performed over those years — always from memory — Bach's entire vast output for the instrument. A great organist, he was surpassed in Canada only by Lynwood Farnham, who died prematurely in 1930 at age forty-five. In 1923, MacMillan had conducted the Eaton Memorial and St. Andrew's choirs in the first — for Toronto — complete version of Bach's *St. Matthew Passion*, with Luigi von Kunits as concertmaster. This became an annual and always superb event in Toronto's musical life over the next thirty years. MacMillan was also a fine chamber music pianist and accompanist, a talented composer with several important works to his credit, and an expert teacher.

After almost four years of internment in Germany during the Great War he had returned to Toronto, taken the Eaton post, and joined the faculty of the Academy. He resigned from the Eaton position in June 1925, fed up with complaints by the church's parishioners that he was doing too much German music and was dictatorial with the choir. In the same year, Vogt removed MacMillan's guarantee when the Academy joined the TCM because he had too few students, this despite his reputation and the outstanding pupils who literally revered him — Muriel Gidley, Frederick Silvester, and Charles Peaker, to name a few. To make ends meet he took a job at Upper Canada College, a Toronto boys' school, where he tried to start an orchestra, only to give up at the end of the season. He also took on the post of music director at Hart House Theatre; the position was terminated in the spring of 1926 due to lack of funds. How was he to support his wife and two sons on his limited TCM income?

And so, with his back to the wall, MacMillan accepted the principalship, a position he would hold until 1942. Several months later, as part of the package, he was, like Vogt, appointed dean of the Faculty of Music. The University had deliberately delayed the dean appointment to keep the two positions distinct from one another. His salary would be $6,000 per annum as principal, with no salary as dean. There was talk that Healey Willan should have been offered the dean's post, seeing that he was vice-principal, but those close to him knew he was not an effective administrator.

MacMillan first insisted, with good reason, that he must have a competent business manager (secretary/treasurer) to deal with non-musical matters. Next, to improve the Conservatory's teaching policies, he visited several leading music schools in the United States and Britain to see how they operated and what he could learn from them. He kept a diary for the two-month trip. His first stop was the privately endowed New England Conservatory, where composer George Chadwick had been director for thirty years. The school had several hundred full-time post-secondary students working towards degrees and diplomas. MacMillan was quite overwhelmed when he heard its symphony orchestra of eighty students do works with the school choir, a Brahms symphony, a near professional performance of the Lalo Cello Concerto, and the beginning of Act 3 of *Die Meistersinger*. How envious he was when he compared this orchestra to the TCM's.

Solfège was compulsory for all New England students (no sol-fa), which pleased MacMillan, since he believed in the importance of ear training, no matter what system was used. Students were examined by their own teachers and the director, and those seeking teaching diplomas had to first complete two years of actual teaching under supervision. MacMillan also noted the library's six thousand volumes, including the complete Bach *Gesellschaft*. It made his mouth water. The school also had a publicity office that kept the press informed of its concerts, operas, and other events.

Then MacMillan went to Harvard. Its program interested him particularly because Harvard actually held regularly scheduled classes, unlike in Toronto, where they were almost non-existent. According to MacMillan, Professor Archibald Davison had students on the edge of their seats in his medieval and renaissance music history classes, a subject usually difficult to get across. What he liked, too, were Davison's glee club and his mixed choir. The college also taught music to students in the teachers' course given by the Department of Education. MacMillan thought that this could be done in Toronto as well.

Moving on to New York, he visited the Institute of Musical Art, the undergraduate section of the Juilliard School of Music. It was a short and superficial review, with the school about to close for Christmas. Then he sailed to Liverpool. After seeing several musicians and trying several pipe organs, he went on to the Royal Manchester College of Music. There he admired the school's orchestra, the course material, and the rigorous auditions and written examinations given to all incoming students. The school was well endowed, and most teachers were on salary. Other music schools in England and Scotland taught him little. However, his stop in Edinburgh was rewarding for personal reasons; he had spent several years there in his early teens, and again, briefly, at the end of the war. Sick with influenza, he returned home determined to make the TCM a school that would measure up to the better schools he had visited. MacMillan also wanted it to be a *Canadian* school, with qualities that could be defined as Canadian, and not a carbon copy of American or British schools.

It would be a mighty task. Many of the changes MacMillan wanted were costly. Would the trustees pay for them? Vogt had used money to expand the physical plant and equipment, while MacMillan wanted money to develop instruction and musical groups, an altogether different matter that a layman board might not take to easily. Since the Conservatory Symphony was already making progress under von Kunits, MacMillan decided to form a school choir to complement the orchestra's work. On August 8, 1927, the school posted a notice at College Street announcing the formation of a Conservatory chorus to meet weekly, beginning September 13.[138]

It worked out as planned. On February 29, 1928, MacMillan and von Kunits conducted the TCM Choir (it had dropped the name chorus) and Orchestra at the University's Convocation Hall. Von Kunits led the purely orchestral works — A Suite for Strings by Henry Purcell and *The Lark Ascending for Violin and Orchestra* by Vaughan Williams, with Lillian Sparling as soloist. She later joined the TSO. Then came the Mozart Requiem with MacMillan on the podium and Healey Willan at the organ. Hector Charlesworth of *Saturday Night* wrote, "Few more distinguished programmes have been heard here.... Dr. MacMillan performed a feat remarkable in connection with a work so rarely performed, by conducting throughout without a score, and moreover with a complete grasp of every nuance." He went on to praise the choir and the professional soloists, notably the soprano, Dorothy Allan Park, and the tenor,

Reginald Heal.[139] Park, who was thirty-one, joined the TCM faculty three years later. She taught for the next four decades and numbered among her students Garnet Brooks, a prominent tenor, Catherine Robbin, an outstanding mezzo-soprano from the seventies until the turn of the century, Lillian Smith Weichel, and Margo MacKinnon.[140]

Lawrence Mason of *The Globe* said what MacMillan must have been thinking: "This is just the kind of work that a great Conservatory of Music should do, and yesterday's performance was a credit to the institution, to the community, and indeed to the Dominion." He praised the soloists and, not afraid to use superlatives, went on: "It must be about the best choir of its size in the Province." (It had about one hundred voices.) Mason, who travelled widely, concluded, "If the same absolutely first-class standard is maintained, the Royal Academy of Music and the Royal College of Music in London will be in no position to assert any superiority over the Toronto Conservatory in these fields."[141]

A performance the next year was equally arresting. The orchestra under von Kunits played the Beethoven Symphony no. 4 and Peter Warlock's Serenade for Strings, and the choir under MacMillan sang the Fauré Requiem. MacMillan again drew accolades from Lawrence Mason: "This performance surpassed all reasonable expectation. It was a really startling achievement to which the audience paid hushed and spellbound homage.... One felt that one could never have enough of such a heavenly experience." Organist Healey Willan was also lauded for his sensitive work in the Fauré. As for the orchestra, Mason and other press noted the steady improvement of the strings. Von Kunits's work, as always, was outstanding. "Principal MacMillan could well hold up his head with some pride as to the direction the school was going."[142]

Generally, the thirties saw fine performances by the choir. When Toronto celebrated its centennial in April 1933 with a week of concerts, it sang in the Beethoven Ninth Symphony with the TSO at Massey Hall. The next year it did performances of the *St. Matthew Passion* and, memorably, Gabriel Pierné's *Children's Crusade*, again with the TSO. The choir also sang in the Brahms Requiem at a memorial concert for Sir Albert Gooderham in December 1935; he had died earlier that year. In 1938 it did the *Children's Crusade* again, this time with the visiting Philadelphia Orchestra with MacMillan as guest conductor. MacMillan did other works with the choir and the TSO during his years as principal, including three by British composers: Parry's *Pied Piper of Hamelin*, Dyson's *Canterbury Pilgrims*, and Constant Lambert's *Rio Grande*.

Frequent vocal soloists with MacMillan were Jeanne Pengelly, Eileen Law, and George Lambert. Pengelly and Lambert were already members of the TCM faculty in 1933, when they sang in the

Beethoven Ninth. Law, an outstanding contralto and Conservatory graduate, joined the faculty in 1938. Lambert, a Yorkshireman who had studied in London and Italy, had a rich baritone voice and was one of the Conservatory's most outstanding vocal teachers. A partial list of Lambert's pupils is dazzling: Victor Braun, Donald Garrard, Robert Goulet, Gwenlynn Little, Ermanno Mauro, Bernard Turgeon, Jon Vickers, and Alan Woodrow. All have had or are still having illustrious international careers. Pengelly appeared briefly at the Metropolitan Opera and the Chicago Opera, and Law, for twenty-five years the contralto soloist in MacMillan's *St. Matthew Passion*, did the solo part in the Canadian premiere of Mahler's *Das Lied von der Erde* with the TSO in 1946.

To enrich the TCM's offerings, MacMillan introduced several free advantages in 1927–28: elementary ear training and sight-singing classes, score study lectures, and choir training. He also brought in Dalcroze Eurythmics, a teaching procedure in which young music students respond bodily to music to help them develop muscular control, rhythmic sense, musical feeling, and self-expression. The instructor was the Swiss musician Madeleine Boss Lasserre, a pupil of Jacques Dalcroze. For many years she gave her classes on the floor over the principal's office, which caused friction between her and the incumbent principal "when light fixtures started to shake and floors bounced during the movement exercises."[143] The Conservatory gave Dalcroze classes until the end of the century. Donald Himes (pianist and composer for television's "Mr. Dressup" for thirty years) joined Lasserre in the late fifties, followed by Elizabeth Morton, and then Wendy Taxis.

Another methodology used to introduce young children to music during MacMillan's tenure was the Kelly Kirby Kindergarten.[144] The Kindergarten was devised by May Kirby, assisted by her husband, who drew attractive pictures to help capture a child's interest. It caught on sufficiently for MacMillan to encourage Frederick Harris to publish a series of method workbooks in 1936. A number of Kirby disciples kept the system alive for the next fifty years.

In 1929, MacMillan launched the Conservatory String Quartet, led by one of his new violin teachers, Elie Spivak. Born in the Ukraine, Spivak had studied with Adolf Brodsky in Manchester and had played there and in New York before coming to Toronto. Still in his twenties, Spivak was a sensitive player and a gentle and likeable teacher; he led the Quartet until 1942 and was also concertmaster of the TSO from 1931 until 1948. Among his students were Walter Prystawski, David Zafer, and Campbell Trowsdale. One Spivak anecdote that had wide currency among faculty and students told of his stopping his car for a red light on College Street and noticing an elderly woman having trouble mounting the steps of a streetcar, which had stopped next to him. The kind and gallant Spivak quickly got out of his car to help her. Then, quite absentmindedly, he followed her onto the streetcar, paid his fare, and sat down. As the streetcar started to move along College Street, his driverless car was left to a barrage of horns and irate drivers, and caused a minor traffic jam.

Harold Sumberg, another TCM teacher, was the Quartet's second violin as well as the leader of the second violins in the TSO. Donald Heins, assistant conductor of the TSO, was the violist, and Leo Smith, the cellist. Although there were inevitable changes in the group's personnel, the Quartet managed to survive until 1946. The Conservatory board contributed $400 towards its first six-concert series, and the next year, 1930–31, granted the Quartet $1,000. Sad to say, it gradually reduced the grant during the Depression years.[145]

At the Quartet's first concert, MacMillan was the pianist in a quintet by the English composer and conductor Eugene Goossens. Other assisting artists during the season were TCM pianists Norah Drewett (the English wife of violinist Géza de Kresz), Viggo Kihl, and Alberto Guerrero. Over the years, the Quartet played an important role in Toronto's musical life and in other Ontario centres. It performed music by Canadian composers Patricia Blomfield Holt, who later taught at the Conservatory, John Weinzweig, who would become one of Canada's leading composers, Walter MacNutt, and others. Nor did it hesitate to have gifted students play with it. The eleven-year-old cellist Bobby Spergel, a pupil of Leo Smith, joined it in the Schubert C Major Quintet on February 14, 1935.[146]

The Quartet had access to the Hart House chest of viols, instruments of considerable value that Hart House guarded carefully. Leo Smith loved the collection's viola da gamba and played it frequently. According to Pearl McCarthy, his biographer, Smith would sometimes take it home at night and keep it in a bedroom of its own, "with curtains drawn to prevent drafts and a very light eiderdown plus a Shetland shawl ready for changes of temperature and humidity."[147]

One event clouded MacMillan's first year at the TCM. Paul Wells, one of the school's leading piano teachers, made advances to one of his senior students, Scott Malcolm, while they were travelling abroad. Malcolm, in shock, reported the incident to MacMillan. Macmillan evidently convinced Wells to leave the country, since, at the time (1927), Wells's action was unlawful. Whether MacMillan showed appropriate sympathy for Wells's predicament remains conjectural, since, undeniably, there was more than a bit of the puritan in MacMillan.[148] Wells wrote two imploring letters to MacMillan on May 3 and May 6 from the United States (he was born in Missouri) asking for a letter of recommendation to help him find another position, and also asking if the "scandal" had become known publicly. Wells was a popular teacher and informed MacMillan that he had already

Paul Wells.

received letters of support from ten of his students. Nevertheless, the situation seemed hopeless to poor Wells, and he committed suicide in Jacksonville, Florida, on May 25. MacMillan sent condolences to his family, which were gratefully acknowledged by Wells's mother.

MacMillan enthusiastically addressed opera in his first year at the Conservatory. Opera had always fascinated him, and now he had the opportunity to develop the first operatic training program in Canada. The school had already worked indirectly in opera, with Goltré-Fillion's 1923 productions, and members of the faculty and students had been involved in performances of the Gay-Pepusch *The Beggars Opera* at the Princess Theatre in 1925, with Healey Willan conducting, Alfred Heather, a tenor and voice teacher at the TCM, directing, and J. Campbell McInnes, a popular baritone, playing McHeath. Lawrence Mason of *The Globe* praised the "technical stage management" and felt the production was "carefully thought out."[149] Augustus Bridle of *The Star* wrote that Willan's "exquisite orchestration" was better than the Frederick Austin version he had seen at the Lyric Theatre in Hammersmith, London.[150]

Accordingly, the 1926–27 calendar offered opera ensemble study, to be directed by the retired singer Countess Laura de Turczynowicz. Born in St. Catharines, Ontario, Laura Blackwell had sung at the Hoftheatre in Munich and at Bayreuth before marrying Count de Turczynowicz, a Latin professor at Cracow University. After her marriage, she left the stage and turned to directing. De Turczynowicz and MacMillan worked well together and soon went beyond the ensemble classes to form the Conservatory Opera Company. Its first effort was a week of performances at the Regent Theatre in April 1928, with Humperdinck's *Hansel and Gretel* alternating with Gilbert and Sullivan's *The Sorcerer*. MacMillan conducted and de Turczynowicz directed. The *Hansel* performances were preceded by a short pantomime,

Bluebeard, for which MacMillan had written an orchestral arrangement of Beethoven's Piano Sonata op. 27, no. 2 (the "Moonlight"). The performers were either Conservatory students or graduates. The press praised the *Hansel* production but were lukewarm about *The Sorcerer*.[151]

On alternating nights in April of the following year a more experienced company did a week of Purcell's *Dido and Aeneas* and Franz von Suppé's *Boccaccio* at Hart House Theatre, a much smaller house than the Regent. Bach's *Peasant Cantata* was the curtain raiser for both operas. MacMillan conducted *Dido* and the cantata, the latter in his own English version, and Thomas J. Crawford, who had joined the faculty in 1923, conducted *Boccaccio*. Violinist Harold Sumberg led the Conservatory Orchestra, and the two *répétiteurs* were Weldon Kilburn and Reginald Godden. *Dido*, justifiably, got most of the press attention. Dorothy Allan Park sang Dido; Betty Priestman, Belinda; and Reginald Heal, Aeneas. *Saturday Night* lauded the singers and added that the presentation "owed much to the splendid verve and finesse of Dr. MacMillan as conductor."[152]

De Turczynowicz left the Conservatory in the fall of 1929 and thus missed the company's greatest triumph, the North American premiere of Vaughan Williams's ballad opera, *Hugh the Drover*, a work that splendidly expresses English rural life. It was performed at the new Royal York Hotel, the tallest, largest, and most costly hotel in the British Empire and the flagship of the Canadian Pacific Railway chain of hotels. *Hugh* was, in fact, part of a five-day festival of English music sponsored by the CPR.[153] MacMillan and Alfred Heather, de Turczynowicz's successor, teamed up for the memorable performance, with an assist from Canadian artist Arthur Lismer, who designed the sets. Allan Jones, an American tenor who would later appear in Hollywood films, was Hugh; the rest of the cast were local professionals and advanced students.

Hugh the Drover's central event is a boxing match between Hugh and John the butcher, and in Heather's production the fight was done so realistically that it made the sports pages of at least one Toronto daily. The audience was apparently carried away by the exertions of the two protagonists as they sang and fought in great style. One line in sportswriter Lou Marsh's account is worthy of special note: "John, the battling baritone, hit the ropes so hard that he finished out the piece as a soprano."[154]

Hugh was such a hit that it was booked for a week's run the following year at the Royal Alexandra Theatre. It alternated with *Hansel and Gretel*, which had the same cast that had played at the Regent two years earlier. The larger and more professionally equipped theatre helped improve both productions. Harold Tovell, chairman of the National Council of Education, was impressed with what he saw and heard but complained, as others would over the next seventy years, that Toronto needed a suitable opera house. "It is to be hoped that the Conservatory will erect a proper building for future productions. Given such a building with the musicians already at hand ... an opera centre can be formed by the utilization of the staff of the Conservatory in all of its departments. Canadian composers would then be given an opportunity of having their works produced."[155] These were the last Toronto Conservatory opera productions for sixteen years. The Depression hit the TCM hard, and opera was one of its first casualties.

An ailing Luigi von Kunits died on October 8, 1931, two weeks before the opening of the Toronto Symphony Orchestra's season. Colonel Gooderham, the president of both the TSO and the Conservatory, turned to MacMillan. He was von Kunits's logical successor, and, with none of the doubts he had had when the TCM position was offered him, he eagerly accepted the appointment.[156] However, there were problems. MacMillan had broken his right arm in an auto accident during the summer; until it healed he would have to conduct with restraint. In addition, he had practically no experience conducting a large symphony orchestra and knew little of the repertoire. To compound his difficulties, even before he led his first concert he indiscreetly announced to the orchestra his plans for its future, including personnel changes. This left the weaker players worried indeed. Next he wanted evening concerts only — the TSO mainly gave twilight concerts to enable its members to work in theatres. Luckily, this turned out to be a non-issue. With the onset of sound movies and the decline of vaudeville, traditional theatre work for musicians was rapidly disappearing. Von Kunits had been a popular conductor. MacMillan's high-handed manner troubled the orchestra.

Fortunately, hard feelings evaporated following the enthusiastic reception audience and press gave him after his first concert. The program included the funeral march from Beethoven's Third Symphony in memory of von Kunits, the Beethoven Eighth Symphony, and the Chopin Piano Concerto no. 1, with Ernest Seitz as soloist. Although MacMillan's conducting skill had already been shown demonstrably in his annual performances of the *St. Matthew Passion* and in his work with the Conservatory Choir, his ability as a symphonic conductor was yet to be proven. And it must be said that, good as von Kunits may have been with the TSO, MacMillan brought the orchestra to a higher level almost immediately.

The TCM board wondered if MacMillan could handle both his commitments satisfactorily, since the principal's job was supposedly full-time. (The dean's job at the Faculty of Music was limited to reviewing degree examinations.) However they soon realized that the TCM could only benefit from his association with the TSO. Gooderham, for one, was unconcerned, as was the teaching staff, but the issue would continue to fester.[157] With his three — for now — positions, MacMillan became, indisputably, the dominant figure in Canada's musical life.

Sadly, Principal MacMillan's aspirations to develop the Conservatory's instructional programs over the next decade came to practically nothing. The Depression caused a drop in student enrolments and in examination registrations. Profits declined sharply, inevitably followed by deficits. *Economize* was the watchword. Salaries were cut, including the principal's, but not teachers' commissions; yet lesson fees remained low. Examinations were zealously promoted but with only modest results, despite important and beneficial changes in the syllabi. Although the choir and symphony orchestra moved along, there was a shortage of wind, brass, and lower string players. The Conservatory String Quartet worked diligently, giving substantial programs but with little compensation. Free classes and other student advantages were limited. There was no advanced program per se, although students continued to take examinations for the ATCM and licentiate diploma.

Returning to 1927, MacMillan's first full year, the school opened a cafeteria, which became a successful meeting place for students and faculty. Then came a record library, a women teachers' clubroom, and a renovated women's residence. Failing to find a top-ranking piano teacher from abroad to join the faculty in 1928, MacMillan settled for Boris Berlin, a young Russian who had studied with Mark Hambourg and Leonid Kreutzer. An active and always-on-the-move man, Berlin was one of MacMillan's best appointments; he would teach at the Conservatory until his death in 2000. He composed many piano pieces and studies for beginners and intermediate students. In 1930 he co-authored *The Modern Piano Student* with MacMillan. This progressive book included photos and diagrams of hand positions, ear training and finger exercises, rhythms for clapping, guidelines for writing notation, interval work, and a good collection of beginning pieces. It innovatively encouraged children to perform action songs by rote before moving on to learning music *through* the piano. Nine years later, Berlin and MacMillan collaborated on writing an ear training manual. One of Canada's finest teachers of the young, Berlin also taught outstanding mature piano students, including Esther Hoffman, Adrienne Shannon, Christina Petrowska, Gwen Beamish, Bernadene Blaha, Dorothy Sandler, Andrew Markow, Peter Simon, and Rudy Toth.

Donald Heins, the Conservatory Quartet violist, succeeded von Kunits as conductor of the Conservatory Symphony. He was followed by Ettore Mazzoleni, an immigrant from England who had studied at Oxford and the Royal College of Music and had been a protegé of Vaughan Williams. He was slim, short, and handsome, spoke with an Oxford accent, and had an air of quiet efficiency. His criticism of others and their work was mostly well deserved, although it could be biting. Mazzoleni did well with the orchestra, but his abrasive personality on the podium did little to endear him to players. A fine pianist and an excellent all-around musician, he had commendable conducting technique, and in later years would teach conducting at the Conservatory. In 1932 Mazzoleni married Winifred MacMillan, an accomplished pianist and sister of Ernest MacMillan.

MacMillan, concerned about the future of the Conservatory, wrote a "manifesto" to the board of governors of the University in 1935 describing TCM conditions.[158] He pointed out that teachers with low fees were charged exorbitant commissions to cover costs and that the school's branches, where many of them taught, would be closing in ever-increasing numbers unless financial relief was forthcoming. "The TCM can never take its proper place ... so long as its operations are tied down to those of a self-supporting and even profit-making business institution." He lamented that the province spent enormous sums on education but nothing on music instruction. "The TCM wants to help children of all ages," he wrote, but "it has been fulfilling a public function without public support." The University ignored MacMillan's pleas.

Nevertheless, the Conservatory moved on and made lasting improvements in its graded examinations. In August 1935 Healey Willan announced that theory examinations would be graded in future by numbers I to V, thereby replacing grades formerly listed as elementary, primary, junior, and intermediate.[159] Grade I and Grade II would correspond to elementary and primary theory. Grade III (junior) would consist of two papers — harmony and history. Harmony would require adding three parts to a figured bass and a four-part harmonization of a simple melody. History would deal with music of the seventeenth and eighteenth centuries, for which — conveniently — Leo Smith had written a text. Grade IV, a new grade, would consist of three papers: advanced harmony, two-point counterpoint, and history from 1750 until the death of Haydn. Grade V, formerly intermediate, would consist of four papers: advanced harmony, counterpoint, history from 1800 to the present, and form in composition. Willan promised that more musical examples would be used, and that ear training and sight-singing would be stressed. After

1934–35, students who completed a graded practical examination would have only one year to complete the required theory paper. For example, Grade VI piano would require completion of the Grade I theory paper, and Grade VIII would require completion of the Grade II theory paper, and so on.

There were equally significant revisions in piano examinations beginning in 1935–36. Grades, which have remained essentially the same to the present, would also be identified by numbers rather than by introductory, elementary, primary, junior, intermediate, and senior. Junior grades would be I to VIII, and advanced grades, IX and X. The number of works required in the higher grades would be reduced. No works could be done at examinations unless listed in the syllabus.

In the 1935–36 syllabus Grade VIII material was listed in four categories, A through D, baroque, classical, romantic, and contemporary, respectively. A candidate was required to play one work from each category. The lists were comprehensive, with even a few minor works by Canadian composers included. Grade IX had five categories. For it, Category A was devoted solely to Bach, while Category B included Scarlatti, along with Mozart and Beethoven. Chopin and Schumann made up Category C, and romantic and contemporary music were assigned to Categories D and E. The associateship examination had six categories. Piano requirements in the higher grades were demanding and showed taste and discernment, and the levels of difficulty were as accurate as such an inexact process can be. This new graded system was sounder academically and encouraged students to take more examinations.

The Conservatory made a giant step forward in 1934 when it persuaded the Ontario Department of Education to accept some of its examinations as valid secondary school subjects. It meant, for example, that Grade VIII Piano and Grade II Theory certificates could be substituted for Ancient History, and Grade IX Piano and Grade III Harmony could count as one course for university entrance. This meant a great deal to students studying music seriously. G. Roy Fenwick, the forward-looking provincial supervisor of music from 1935 to 1959, was behind these changes.

In 1935 MacMillan was knighted by King George V. Colonel Gooderham was also knighted that year, as were eight others, including two in the arts, painter Wylie Grier and writer Charles G.D. Roberts.[160] Impressive as it might have been for a Canadian musician to be so honoured, many fellow Canadians objected to royal titles in principle. The *Toronto Star*, the only left-of-centre daily in Toronto, gave the news about one-tenth the space that the royalist *Mail and Empire* gave it. The *Star* editorialized: "The whole business of a titled class as opposed to a non-titled class is an unwelcome return of a custom which Canada thought it had rid itself some years ago."[161] Titles had been revived in 1934 by Conservative anglophile Prime Minister R.B. Bennett. They would end forever in 1936 when the Liberals returned to power.

Yet the title, controversial as it was, gave Sir Ernest more clout in his own country. He wrote elegantly to the prime minister:

> As a merely personal distinction, however gratifying, I should be most reluctant to accept knighthood. As a recognition of the importance of music and the musical profession in the Dominion, however, I accept it with gratitude. If the status of my profession is enhanced in the public mind — and I think it will be — I shall rejoice as I should have rejoiced had the lot fallen on another musician. I believe that those who have worked hard and faithfully on behalf of the institutions with which I am connected will be glad of my acceptance.[162]

Gooderham died in 1935, and Colonel Fred Deacon, another well-known philanthropist, succeeded him as president of the TCM. He quickly appointed Floyd Chalmers as vice-president. Chalmers, a self-made man, was, at the time, editor of the *Financial Post*, a leading Canadian journal. He was a tall cigar-smoking executive who got to the point in any discussion in record-breaking time. He described Deacon as a "cheerful, handsome giant of a man with white wavy locks; he had dominated Toronto business and the stock exchange for many years" and said, whimsically, that he had no choice when Deacon "commanded" him to accept the appointment.[163]

Much respected in the business community, Chalmers thought that the school's administration needed overhauling. He forthwith formed and chaired a TCM finance committee to address its income and expenses. First he asked board members to give up their fees for attending meetings, and they said they would. Then he went after the Ontario government to grant the Conservatory $15,000. Unsuccessful at first, he did finally wrest it from them in 1938. The payment was made through the University, which suggested to the TCM that it was merely a loan. Then, after an outcry from the TCM board, the University admitted that the government's original intention was that it be an outright grant.[164] Such provincial largesse was a first for the TCM. The University then came through with grants of $10,000 in each of the next two years, $11,500 in 1941–42, $10,500 in 1942–43, and $11,000 in 1943–44. The Conservatory repeatedly had trouble extracting these grants from its all-powerful ruler.

The finance committee straightforwardly recommended to the board on January 20, 1936, that Marion Ferguson, who was entering her fiftieth year of service at the school, be "released from her onerous responsibilities under an arrangement which would insure her of freedom from worry during the rest of her life." Miss Ferguson had become a living legend at the school. The committee also recommended that she retain the title of honorary registrar and be granted an annual honorarium of $1,000. Although a few Conservatory people questioned whether she was ready to retire, it was generally accepted by most of the teachers and staff. Alice Roger Collins had done a profile — "pen portrait" — of Ferguson in 1932, a fitting tribute to a very lovely lady.[165] Later, the Conservatory established the Marion Ferguson Foundation to grant scholarships to worthy students.

The committee's next recommendation, to abolish the vice-principal position, was met with more opposition. Obviously it would leave Healey Willan without a job. The committee had its reasons. Chalmers said years later that Willan "refused to deal with trivial problems by locking himself in his studio and refusing to answer knocks on the door or rings of his telephone. His secretary was instructed to bring him no mail or problems. He spent his time, profitably for posterity, on composing."[166] Godfrey Ridout, a Willan student, remembered Willan's office as "absolute chaos."[167] President Fred Deacon, in a letter to the faculty and graduates of the TCM on October 14, wrote: "It is unfortunate that it is not possible for the Conservatory to provide places on its salaried staff for outstanding musicians whose genius may not run to administrative or business routine. The Governors regret that the Conservatory finances do not permit it yet to indulge in salaried posts of this character." In truth, Willan was no help to MacMillan, who had many commitments outside of the school and needed a second-in-command to assist him in his daily tasks and take over during his absences.

There was an outcry when the news leaked prior to Deacon's letter. Some felt that internal politics was behind the move, not just money and administrative efficiency, and that MacMillan had not taken a strong enough stand with the board to retain Willan. On October 6, 1936, the *Evening Telegram*, having got wind that something interesting was going on at the Conservatory, addressed Willan's "retirement." It announced that the TCM Residence Alumnae Association (women who had stayed at the residence as students) would hold a meeting on October 8 to protest what it considered "a compulsory dismissal." Deacon, annoyed, then wrote to Mrs. Geoffrey Waddington, president of the association, asking her to get the facts from him, Chalmers, or MacMillan, since the *Telegram* article was inaccurate.[168] (Mrs. Waddington, a concert pianist, was the former Mildred Baker. Married women rarely used their own given names seventy years ago.) Deacon then discovered that Waddington also objected to the *Telegram* article. He subsequently explained to her that MacMillan had indeed tried his best to keep Willan on staff, even suggesting a cut in his own salary to make it possible.[169] Whatever,

MacMillan deplored the way the news was handled and gave notice that he would resign in three months.[170] Fortunately, he eventually saw reason and withdrew his resignation, satisfied that Deacon's letter had clarified matters and that a "better spirit" prevailed at the school.[171]

The Willan imbroglio didn't end there. The TCM had given him a full year's salary as severance pay that it could ill afford, plus the use of his office and secretary for the year.[172] After much debate, Willan was asked to continue teaching at the Conservatory. He refused, leaving matters at an impasse. He finally accepted an appointment to the Faculty of Music in May 1938 at $2,000 annually and agreed to do Conservatory classes and examinations in order to earn an additional TCM stipend of $2,000 annually.[173] These assignments were in addition to serving as University organist, a post he had accepted in 1932 and held until 1964. When Willan retired from the Faculty of Music in 1950 at seventy, the mandatory age of retirement, he presumed that he was also retiring from the organist post. University President Sidney Smith would have none of it. "Now look here, you are Organist to the University of Toronto, and that has nothing to do with the Faculty of Music; that's my affair, and as long as you can dodder over to the organ, you can be the organist." Over his thirty-two years as University organist Willan played at 250 convocations.[174]

In the same year as the Willan dispute, the TCM Residence Alumnae Association established the Vogt Society, its purpose to promote the performance and publication of contemporary Canadian music. At its first meeting on February 11, 1937, Elie Spivak and Leo Barkin played works by Willan and Leo Smith.[175] Was it a protest over the Conservatory's decision?[176] Much good came from this new group, which gave concerts of new works and sponsored composer competitions. It changed its name to the Society for Contemporary Music in 1941 and disbanded in 1945.

Prior to Willan's dismissal, Norman Wilks, an excellent pianist and teacher, had been named executive assistant to the principal. Wilks, who had joined the Conservatory a few years before, included Weldon Kilburn and Margaret Parsons among his students. (Wilks had also twice run for a Liberal seat in the provincial parliament only to be defeated both times.) After Willan left, he became the TCM's executive officer.[177] It was a wise choice. Wilks had won a Military Cross in the Great War, but despite his military demeanour he was always friendly and approachable. He took on his new job with enthusiasm and dedication and was an efficient and perceptive administrator for whom no task was too small. He made MacMillan's crowded life — an understatement — more tolerable.

MacMillan's activities while at the TCM included delivering countless public lectures, writing essays and articles, visiting teachers in their studios, assisting examiners at examinations, examining grade students, and adjudicating at music festivals across the country. Out of necessity he kept a high profile in the West, where a rival examining board was cutting into the school's profits. He had admirers everywhere. In Vancouver, Marjorie Agnew, a high school teacher, formed a "Sir Ernest MacMillan Fine Arts Club," which enabled students to gather together and "experience the arts" in a variety of ways. Over the next three decades these clubs spread to other parts of British Columbia, Alberta, the Yukon, and east to New Brunswick.[178] All the while, MacMillan was conducting the Toronto Symphony, Canada's leading orchestra.

From left to right: Frederick Silvester, Sir Ernest MacMillan, and Norman Wilks, c. 1937.

Following Wilks's appointment, the finance committee reviewed the non-Conservatory activities of MacMillan, Registrar Frederick Silvester, and, perhaps to make it look fair, Norman Wilks.[179] Chalmers believed that all salaried staff who did outside work "for gain" should "first obtain permission from the Board of Governors." MacMillan found this edict offensive and thought it petty to be asked to defend his TSO salary of $3,500, abysmally small for a conductor of a major orchestra.[180] Nevertheless, with good grace he offered to have his TCM salary cut from $6,000 to $4,000 so that Wilks's could be raised! The board complied by cutting his salary by $1,000. At one meeting, the board asked MacMillan and Wilks to leave the room so that it could consider in camera whether or not it would permit MacMillan to conduct the TSO and Wilks to adjudicate at a music festival.[181] MacMillan was humiliated, but he held his temper and actually kept the board informed of his outside work for the remainder of his term as principal. He even asked its permission on occasion and was never refused.

The Conservatory celebrated its fiftieth anniversary with a concert at Massey Hall on April 27, 1936. The choir and orchestra, with Mazzoleni conducting, did MacMillan's *Te Deum Laudamus* and a major a cappella work of Willan's, *An Apostrophe to the Heavenly Hosts*. Three student soloists performed: Esther Hoffman in the Shostakovich First Piano Concerto, Stanley Solomon in the Tchaikovsky Violin Concerto (he would later be the TSO's principal violist), and mezzo-soprano Jean McLachlan in shorter pieces (she went on to have an operatic career in England). The *Toronto Star*'s eccentric and unpredictable Bridle described the concert as "startling." This happy event notwithstanding, the TCM was still the same limited school it had been when MacMillan took office a decade earlier. In fact it had changed little since its founding a half-century back. Change was needed. When would the Conservatory become more than a collective? When would it have an advanced school like other self-respecting music schools south of the border?

To impress the teaching staff, the University, and the provincial government, MacMillan and the board proposed bringing in an outside authority who would, as they say, tell it as it is. The Carnegie Foundation agreed to pay for it. Juilliard President Ernest Hutcheson, a distinguished Australian pianist and teacher, was chosen. Hutcheson, who was booked to appear with the TSO on October 26, 1937, agreed to tack a few days onto his visit to report on the Conservatory's work and future.[182]

The Hutcheson recommendations, brief and to the point, were a compendium of the school's needs: it should be funded by the province much as any other public educational institution; an endowment fund should be established; student fees should be raised; the faculty should be smaller, salaried, better paid, and have no weak members; a professional division distinct from the preparatory division should be formed; professional students should be assigned to teachers by the school; a summer school should be established; there should be more scholarships; the school should set up an employment office to help students find concert engagements and other work; there should be music classes for the community; the school should work closely with the Department of Education; and more woodwind teachers should be appointed.[183]

MacMillan had made similar recommendations at various times in the past, but an outsider's words are usually listened to more carefully and given more weight. The report, additionally, helped MacMillan to see more clearly that the roles and functions of the two schools under his command needed more precise definition to avoid unnecessary duplication and even conflict. Unfortunately, Hutcheson's deliberations were shelved for almost a decade because of the Conservatory's lack of funds, the University's indifference to musical education, the continuing Depression, and the Second World War.

The Conservatory had, however, already acted on one of Hutcheson's recommendations even before his report — that a summer school be established. Faculty members Boris Berlin and Myrtle Rose had given a three-week summer training course in 1937. Berlin's courses dealt with music for very young children and "the art and science of pianoforte teaching." Rose's course dealt with group piano instruction. Rose (later Mrs. Alberto Guerrero) had trained with Guerrero, Alfred Cortot, and Wanda Landowska. All three courses were well attended. The next year the Summer School — now its official title — gave a number of standard courses in instruments, voice, and theory. It also included two that were quite innovative, "Folk Dancing of Many Nations" and "Musical Instrument Making." The school made a small profit. Summer School 1939 was more adventurous, with the outstanding Polish pianist Moriz Rosenthal giving master classes and European conductor Heinrich Jalowetz, an opera class. Although Rosenthal's classes were well attended, the tuitions collected fell well below his fee. As for Jalowetz's class, there was literally no interest. In sum, the school lost $678.

From 1940 to 1945 the prudent Summer School gave courses only to help teachers prepare their students for examinations. One course that stood out in 1945 covered Grades IX through ATCM piano requirements and was given by Lubka Kolessa. She was a Polish pianist of international stature who had studied with Liszt's pupil Emil Sauer and had played with leading European orchestras and conductors before coming to Canada in 1940. Later on, she performed in New York and other major North American centres.[184] Extremely attractive and flamboyant, she had joined the Conservatory faculty in 1942 and remained there until 1949, when she moved on to the faculty of the Conservatoire de Musique du Québec à Montréal. Among her Toronto pupils were Mario Bernardi, a gifted pianist who became one of Canàda's leading conductors; Howard Brown, who headed several university music departments in the Atlantic provinces; Carol Wright Pack, a fine accompanist and chamber player; and Gordon Kushner, who would hold senior administrative positions at the Conservatory in the seventies and eighties.

In 1937, in order to remain solvent, the TCM sold its imposing Academy of Music building on Spadina Road and its annex at 17 Walmer Road to the Toronto Bible College.[185] Since their acquisition in 1925, both buildings had been used primarily as branches, but had gradually become too costly to maintain. The sale price of $45,000 was a far cry from the $115,000 the TCM had paid for the buildings thirteen years before. Next, the TCM executed some money-making deals with the Hambourg and Hamilton conservatories: each would get 25 percent of gross TCM examination fees for examinations held at their schools. This, the TCM hoped, might encourage the two conservatories to have more of their students take TCM examinations.[186] Then, to help guard its

Sir Ernest MacMillan with Lubka Kolessa, 1942.

best examiners, MacMillan, of all people, suggested to the finance committee on November 24, 1938, that all TCM examiners get his permission before examining for other examining boards. The Conservatory's net revenue went up for the 1938–39 term, but lessons took a nose-dive the next year because of the onset of war. With the residence only about one-third occupied, Wilks asked the University to urge its women students to reside there; he also asked the same of TCM "lady teachers."[187] It worked: by September 1940 the residence was full again, with thirty music students and eighteen university students, but no "lady teachers." Registrations picked up, and the war years did not look as ominous for the school as anticipated.

Despite the death of von Kunits in 1931 the quality of violin instruction at the TCM improved during the thirties, thanks to Elie Spivak, Harold Sumberg, and Alexander Chuhaldin, a Russian violinist and conductor who had come to Toronto in 1927. Chuhaldin led a string orchestra — The Melodic Strings — in weekly broadcasts on the CBC beginning in 1933, and by the end of the decade it was estimated that the orchestra had done some three hundred programs. Many of its violinists and violists were Chuhaldin's students. A young Benjamin Britten heard the orchestra in 1939 and was so impressed that he accepted a CBC commission to write a work for it with piano solo. Britten called it *Young Apollo*, and he himself was the soloist for the August 27 broadcast.[188] He gave it an opus number, which he later withdrew.[189]

The violin had, for some time, been gaining in popularity, and by 1939 the TSO's violin section was outstanding, even though some Toronto violinists had migrated to New York and Hollywood. Like his brother Harry, violinist Murray Adaskin was constantly trying to improve his playing. He had heard that the great Canadian violinist Kathleen Parlow was living and teaching in New York. After taking three weeks of lessons from her, he returned to Toronto and excitedly told MacMillan how impressed he was with her playing and teaching.[190] As a result, Parlow was invited to give several lecture/recitals at the Conservatory in 1939–40 with MacMillan at the piano. In 1941 she was appointed to the TCM faculty.

Born in Calgary in 1890, Kathleen Parlow was a child prodigy who gave her first recital at age six.[191] She studied with Henry Holmes, a Spohr pupil, in San Francisco until she was fourteen. After concerts in London she worked with Leopold Auer at the St. Petersburg Conservatory; she was the school's first foreign student. Auer, one of Europe's leading teachers, numbered Mischa Elman, Jascha Heifetz, Efrem Zimbalist, and Tosha Seidel among his students. Parlow went on to give recitals and appeared with orchestras in Russia and later throughout Europe and North America. Before moving to Toronto, she taught at Mills College in California and then in New York, where she formed the South Mountain Quartet.

Parlow had a rather forbidding presence and few social graces. She was tall and gangly, and her wardrobe was dated and unattractive. She never married but had a close relationship with her mother, who accompanied her everywhere. Parlow had a wonderful tone and all-around musicianship that few violinists anywhere could emulate. MacMillan valued her so much that he convinced the

Canadian Trio, 1941: Zara Nelsova, Sir Ernest MacMillan, and Kathleen Parlow.

finance committee to give her a starting annual guarantee of $2,500.[192] At first she played duos with MacMillan, and then they formed the Canadian Trio with cellist Zara Nelsova. Although almost thirty years younger than Parlow, Nelsova had already had a considerable solo and chamber music career before being lured to Toronto to be the principal cellist of the TSO.[193] She was with the orchestra from 1940 to 1943 and also taught at the TCM for those years, returning to the Conservatory sporadically over the next fifty years to give master classes.

The Oxford University Press sponsored the Trio's first concert at Eaton Auditorium on November 28, 1941. The program included three of the most popular trios in the repertoire: Schubert's B flat Major, Haydn's A Major, and Tchaikovsky's A Minor. Hector Charlesworth said that since piano trios were more or less "unfamiliar" in Toronto the program had "the zest of novelty."[194] Such was the state of Toronto and its music criticism.

To return to Parlow, her outstanding pupils in the next decade and a half were violinists Andrew Benac, Charles Dobias, Victor Feldbrill, Morry Kernerman, Sydney Humphreys, and Joseph Pach, and violist James Pataki. She formed the Parlow Quartet in 1943, which performed in Canada and on the CBC for the next fifteen years. The group's membership fluctuated, for Parlow's ideas on playing chamber music were not always in accord with those of her colleagues. Not surprisingly, she was a demanding teacher.

The war may have been raging in Europe, but registrations began increasing at the main building as early as 1940. Fifty-seven "war guests" — children sent from England to escape the war's hardships — had enrolled at the school, all receiving either full scholarships or a 25 percent discount in lesson fees.[195] Then, in 1942, four young Germans enrolled in the school. These were young men who had fled from Nazi Germany and Austria to Britain in the thirties. When war broke out they were interned as enemy aliens, albeit friendly ones, and then sent on to Canada, where they were identified as alien internees. The Canadian government wisely agreed to set them free if sponsored by reliable Canadian residents. The happy outcome was that many of them made noteworthy contributions to Canadian life in the next half-century. Among those who enrolled at the TCM and the Faculty of Music were Helmut Blume, a brilliant pianist and later dean of music at McGill University, and Helmut Kallmann, pianist, historian, the first head of the music division at the National Library of Canada, and one of the editors of the *Encyclopedia of Music in Canada*.[196]

In the summer of 1941, conductor Reginald Stewart, whose Toronto career had been constantly overshadowed by MacMillan's, announced that he was leaving the city to be director of the Peabody Conservatory in Baltimore and, in the following year, to be conductor of the Baltimore Symphony.[197]

Stewart, also a fine pianist, had directed the popular summer Promenade Symphony concerts at Varsity Arena since 1935. The Peabody, one of the oldest independent conservatories in the United States, was at least as prestigious as the TCM, and the Baltimore Symphony was certainly comparable to the TSO.[198]

Stewart had not been overly active as a member of the TCM piano faculty. Yet the TCM board acknowledged his departure with a full-page resolution at their meeting of September 10, 1941. It summed up his accomplishments and contributions to the city's musical life, stated how much the board regretted his leaving, and wished him well in his new work. Floyd Chalmers, who had favoured Stewart over MacMillan, prepared the resolution.

At this same meeting MacMillan announced that the Mendelssohn Choir had asked him to become its conductor. Herbert Fricker, the conductor since 1916 — he had succeeded Vogt — was retiring. The Mendelssohn had long been Toronto's leading choir and, like the TSO, commanded much public esteem. In fact, the two organizations frequently did major choral/orchestral works together. Obviously, MacMillan's Mendelssohn appointment would be time-consuming, on top of his TSO position. MacMillan, who clearly wanted the post, explained to the TCM board that if he accepted the offer he would give up the Conservatory Choir and suggested merging it with the Mendelssohn. The board, especially Chalmers, was not ecstatic about this turn of events and approved the Mendelssohn merger in principle only. Chalmers insisted that the scheme fully protect "the interests of the TCM." Accordingly, a three-man committee was appointed to confer with the Mendelssohn. It all worked out — MacMillan's appointment was announced on October 1, 1941, Fricker conducted Bach's B Minor Mass at his farewell concert on February 23, 1942, and MacMillan conducted his first Mendelssohn concert, the TCM Choir included, on December 29, 1942, performing Handel's *Messiah*. The Mendelssohn rented the Conservatory's recital hall for its weekly rehearsals at $100 dollars a year, and the Conservatory generously donated its choral music to the Mendelssohn.[199]

Even before the *Messiah* performance, MacMillan resigned as principal of the Conservatory (April 27, 1942), although he would continue as dean of the Faculty of Music. Many of his admirers felt he should have left the post sooner, since his hopes for the school had not been realized and school obligations had inhibited his conducting career. The irritations and frustrations he had suffered, especially since 1935, had taken their toll. The board was relieved; it had already proposed unsatisfactory salary terms to MacMillan for 1942–43 that would have hastened his resignation.[200] It did, however, give him a generous separation allowance: $2,500 for the first year, $1,500 for the second year, and $500 for the third year. As dean, MacMillan would (for the first time) receive $500 per annum from the University, would retain his office, would stay on the TCM board, and would indeed still have a considerable presence on College Street. Furthermore, the TCM would pay $500 annually towards his secretary's salary.[201]

On October 7, 1942, the retiring principal gave his last annual report. It was longer than usual because, in addition to commenting on the school's current affairs, he reflected on his achievements and his failures in his sixteen years as principal. Then he moved on to the present. He stressed the need to send only the most qualified examiners to the West, where competing examining systems were taking root. He exhorted the school to maintain its standards, "for it is by earning the respect of the genuine musicians that we shall continue to play a leading part in Canada's musical life." MacMillan also urged competitive music festivals to use Canadians as adjudicators instead of the prevailing practice of using British musicians. He attributed the persistent lack of scholarship funds to prosperity in the pre-Depression years, when the Conservatory was a victim of its own success and saw no need for them. Later, when scholarships were needed, there were few donors. He suggested that without TCM scholarships talented music students have "many enticements from highly endowed institutions in the United States."

Still on money, MacMillan thanked the University for the recent annual grants that enabled the school to meet its yearly losses. He coupled his satisfaction in the establishment of the cafeteria and the "Women's Club Room" with his failure to continue opera, "the most notable lacuna in the Conservatory's activities." Then, resuming his "self-congratulatory retrospect," he praised the orchestra, the choir, the Conservatory String Quartet, and his colleagues. MacMillan went on to admonish those teachers who forbade their students to participate in chamber music classes directed by other teachers for fear that they might be lured away.

MacMillan closed his report movingly, reminding his audience of the troubled world of 1942 and the role music played in it. Thinking of his two sons in the armed forces, he said:

> It is strange that one should be able to write at such length of a great public institution and not mention what is always uppermost in all our minds — the War. Yet war-consciousness must be inherent in all our retrospects and all our plans are contingent on the outcome of the struggle. Many of our male teachers and more of our male students have joined the forces and are doing work of pressing importance — as are also many women on our faculty…. Yet we can justifiably think of our regular musical work as

also filling a war-need, for in preserving an institution that builds music leaders we are preserving one of those great civilising forces for which the Allied Forces are fighting. When we read of children still going to underground schools in Stalingrad, twelve students who wrote musical examinations last Spring in Malta, China establishing since 1937 three symphony orchestras, and when the Warden of the Royal Academy of Music in London writes me that during the Blitz of 1940, "every rehearsal, every lecture and every concert took place as scheduled" — we are preserving something that privation and peril need not induce us to relinquish.

The Conservatory staff and faculty honoured Sir Ernest, as it had Vogt seventeen years before, with a farewell dinner at Hart House, although it came a year after his resignation. Teachers humorously and affectionately acted out highlights of his life. Clara Baker read a poem, "Life Begins at Fifty," written by Donald Heins. A portrait of MacMillan in academic dress by the noted painter Kenneth Forbes was unveiled. MacMillan thought it conventional yet well done. He said with a smile that it would probably be on view long after he was forgotten and envisaged it hanging in a twenty-second-century salon entitled "Portrait of a Man in Academic Costume, Early 20th Century."[202] It now hangs prominently in the Faculty of Music's Edward Johnson Building.

Chapter Four

EXCITING TIMES

As expected, Norman Wilks was appointed the Conservatory's fourth principal in late 1942. He had been coping with the school's problems for five years, but now, without MacMillan's support and advice, he was on his own. He had to deal with a building that badly needed repairs, a difficult residence superintendent, and a president, Colonel Deacon, who had been inactive for several years because of ill health. He also had to negotiate with the Frederick Harris Company, the principal publisher of the Conservatory's examination material, about issues affecting the school.

First, Wilks dealt with a costly wartime measure requiring that the College Street building be converted from oil to coal.[203] Next, he took a trip to alleviate the West's ill feelings towards the TCM. The trip convinced Wilks that it would help the school's image to abandon "Toronto" on its masthead and adopt a more national name.[204] (The request to the Crown to call it "Royal" had been deferred by Westminster until after the war.) Yet the school's enrolment grew in spite of the war, and with many fine — mainly female — students. One was Gisèle LaFlèche, a violinist from Winnipeg. Still in her teens, she joined Kathleen Parlow's class and soon distinguished herself in recitals and chamber music classes. Yet, after several years of study, she abandoned a potential career as a concert violinist to turn to pop singing. The talented Gisèle was attractive, had a lovely voice, and could even accompany herself at the piano.[205] She changed her surname to MacKenzie — a family name — when she moved to the United States in 1950. Her first engagement was as soloist with the radio orchestra of another transplanted Canadian, Percy Faith. In all, she had an outstanding career on radio, television, and stage, and brought the Conservatory much reflected glory.

Then there were two young composers who studied and subsequently taught at the TCM, Godfrey Ridout and John Weinzweig. Both had works played at a special concert of Canadian music in New York on January 11, 1942. Ridout's music showed Healey Willan's influence, but not so Weinzweig's. He was an untraditional composer and proud of it.

Showing considerable originality, on September 19, 1943, the TCM began a series of weekly thirty-minute radio broadcasts devoted to graded examination material performed by Conservatory teachers. Sponsored by National Cellulose of Canada, these programs were demonstrably school showpieces and promoted examinations. The broadcasts continued for the next seven years.

In October 1943 the Conservatory Orchestra, with Mazzoleni conducting, did Willan's opera, *Transit Through Fire*, in a concert performance at Convocation Hall. The CBC had initially commissioned the work as its first radio opera and had aired it on March 8, 1942, with MacMillan conducting. John Coulter wrote the libretto, which was described as "a stinging denunciation of the plight of jobless young people of the 1930s."[206] What was not commonly known was that the composer/arranger Lucio Agostini orchestrated the work on short notice. It was so warmly received that the CBC commissioned another opera from Willan and Coulter, *Deirdre of the Sorrows*. A three-hour work, compared to the one-hour *Transit Through Fire*, it took almost three years to complete and was finally premiered on April 20, 1946. The Conservatory, which Willan had long forgiven, had its opera school mount the first staged production in 1965. Significantly, Willan considered *Deirdre* his finest work.[207]

Wilks made some new and important appointments to the TCM faculty in 1943: two cellists, Isaac Mamott and Joyce Sands, and pianist/harpsichordist Greta Kraus. Kraus would later distinguish herself as a teacher of lieder. Her teaching was always supportive, and she constantly probed for ways to bring out the best in a student. Her personality and intense devotion to her art left lasting impressions with two generations of Conservatory students.

Greta Kraus and Arnold Walter at harpsichords, c. 1942.

Not surprisingly, many TCM students were in the armed forces, and, sadly, several were killed in action. Voice student Glenn Gardiner, a pilot officer in the RCAF who won a Distinguished Flying Cross for participating in the long-range attacks on the German naval base at Trondheim, Norway, fortunately survived. The war notwithstanding, Fred MacKelcan reported to the board on October 21, 1943, that the architect A.S. Mathers was drawing up plans for a new Conservatory building. Wilks, echoing MacKelcan, urged the board to sell the College Street site, since it could command an enormous price. This was a topic for discussion, and nothing more, for several years. Chalmers, for one, envisaged a new Conservatory building as part of a performing arts complex on Bloor Street and Bedford Road, close to Varsity Stadium. He wasn't too far from the mark.

Wilks, a man of action, boldly urged the board to discard teachers' commissions and persuade leading citizens to form a new foundation to raise money for scholarships.[208] These were familiar cries, but they reassured his listeners that he was the man to take the school in hand, even if he had to wait until after the war. Charles Peaker, a prominent Toronto concert organist and church musician who had been on the TCM teaching staff since 1930, was appointed Wilks's assistant in November 1943.[209] One of Peaker's first tasks was to edit a new, brisk, and informative four-page *Monthly Bulletin*, the Conservatory's news organ for the next twenty years. A small man with an ever-present twinkle in his eye, Peaker was organist and choirmaster at St. Paul's Anglican Church from 1944 to 1975, where he organized concerts and made it one of Toronto's prime musical venues. Many who performed with him may remember how, after rehearsals and performances, Peaker would remove a book from his office bookcase and uncover a concealed bottle of whiskey, which he invited his thirsty visitors to share with him![210] His organ students included Fred Graham, John Hodgins, David Low, Stanley Osborne, and composer Charles Wilson.

Tragically, Norman Wilks died suddenly on November 20, 1944, at age fifty-nine. His death cast a cloud over the school. Wilks had worked hard — some said too hard — which might have hastened his early demise. He had journeyed west and east for the school in vast wartime Canada by rail, well before airplanes facilitated such travel. Yet Wilks had found time to write a study book with Boris Berlin, was active in the Ontario Registered Music Teachers Association, and was its president from 1940–42. Thomas J. Crawford, a long-time member of the faculty, wrote a poem about Wilks in the December 1944 *Monthly Bulletin*, that began:

Friend — why have you gone — so soon,
Brother — why leave us thus — your noon had scarcely passed —
and now — night.

Student string quartet: Gisèlle LaFlèche (MacKenzie), Joseph Pach, Rowland Pack, and Hillel Diamond, 1947.

Chalmers presented a resolution honouring Wilks at the December 6, 1944, board meeting. At the same meeting, TCM Chairman H.H. Bishop reported that the University would present the Conservatory's building plans along with its own to the provincial government. A formal letter, unsigned but probably from Bishop, went to President Cody on December 20 outlining the plans.[211] More pressing, however, was the need to find a replacement for Wilks. Peaker took over temporarily as overall director. Mazzoleni was subsequently appointed principal of the Conservatory, and Arnold Walter, vice-principal — later director — in charge of the soon-to-be-formed Senior School.[212] The board debated giving Walter the title of principal also but settled on the lesser title.[213] Walter, a German-speaking Moravian, had studied piano and musicology in Berlin and held a law doctorate from Prague University. He had fled Nazi Germany shortly after Hitler came to power and had had sojourns in Majorca and then London, where he worked on folk music at the Cecil Sharp House. Walter immigrated to Canada in 1937 to teach music at Upper Canada College. He was a good if conventional composer and an admirable pianist. Most of all, he had a profound interest in musical education.

There were two financial bonanzas in 1944. The first was a permanent bequest from the Frederick Harris Music Co., Limited. Harris had formed the company in London at the turn of the century. A few years later, in 1910, he established a Canadian company. It had extraordinary success with a number of songs, one of which, Carrie Jacobs-Bond's "A Perfect Day," was reputed to have sold 11 million copies. Harris also made large profits by holding the copyrights for a number of other music companies. Nevertheless, by 1940 the company's principal earnings were from sales of Conservatory examination publications. Four years later, just before he died, Frederick Harris turned over all of his 162 shares to the school, stipulating that after his death all profits and dividends be used for scholarships and musical education of talented students. If the annual sum available exceeded $15,000, then the TCM could at its discretion give up to $5,000 for the relief of indigent music teachers or their widows. (Evidently not widowers!) Thus both the Canadian and the London companies became TCM property.[214] There were several tiresome litigations over the next five years before the Conservatory assumed full control, but, when it did, it was indeed the fortunate beneficiary, and has continued to be so to the present day.

The second bonanza was due to the work of MacMillan's éminence grise, Floyd Chalmers. Wilks and Chalmers had prepared a survey of the TCM in 1944 shortly before Wilks's death. It was really an abbreviated history of the school and its continuing financial problems.[215] The survey was in great part motivated by the founding of the Conservatoire de Musique du Québec à Montréal in 1942, the first completely subsidized conservatory in North America. A second one in Quebec City opened its doors in

1944.[216] (Five more conservatories in other Quebec cities were founded within the next thirty years.) These conservatories gave free instruction to talented students and, if necessary, even provided them with instruments. The provincial grant for the two Quebec schools for 1944–45 amounted to $79,100. Chalmers and Wilks underscored Quebec's generous support of musical education in their survey.

Conducting class: Brock McElhran, George Hurst, Principal Ettore Mazzoleni, Victor Feldbrill, c. 1946.

Simply put, Chalmers and Wilks recommended that the provincial government replace the inadequate College Street building with a new building and establish and pay for a long overdue senior school. They further recommended that the University fund its affiliated Conservatory with much larger annual grants. To strengthen their case, they noted that the school had operated with a deficit almost every year since 1931–32, with possibly a small profit showing in 1943–44 (these figures were still incomplete), and that the TCM had an indebtedness of $200,000 in bonds that burdened it with crippling annual interest of $7,000. The survey cleverly hoped to arouse local and provincial pride by suggesting that the TCM's musical leadership in Canada might soon be eclipsed by the provincially supported Quebec conservatories. It pointed out that two of Quebec's most prominent and prestigious musicians, Wilfrid Pelletier of the Metropolitan Opera and composer Claude Champagne, were much involved in developing them. Accordingly, Bishop wrote to the newly installed president of the University of Toronto, Sidney Smith, asking for $50,000 to match Quebec's example. Smith did nothing.

Still, there were some sympathetic TCM supporters at Toronto's Queen's Park, where the legislature met. The Province had found itself with an embarrassing surplus of about $450,000 in the 1944 fiscal year, when initially it had predicted a deficit. Chalmers knew Chester Walters, the deputy provincial treasurer, and, with Walters paving the way, Chalmers brashly asked the treasurer, Leslie Frost, if he would grant the Conservatory $200,000 to pay off its bonds.[217] Lo and behold, the grant was confirmed several months later. The University, furious with the Conservatory for soliciting — and obtaining — the grant without University approval, was determined to get its revenge.

The Province first sent the money to the University, as the parent body of the TCM. Then, Colonel Eric Phillips, chairman of the Argus Corporation and the newly elected chairman of the University's board of governors, told his board on May 10, 1945, that he had received a cheque for $200,000 from the provincial treasurer, which he had turned over to the bursar to be deposited temporarily into a separate bank account. Phillips, who relished authority and power, and President Smith, a skilled diplomat and suave behind-the-scenes operator, proposed changing the terms of the governance of the TCM as retribution for the TCM having taken independent action. The governors drafted a plan to divest the TCM of all of its assets and take away its charter. It also proposed dissolving the Conservatory's board of governors and appointing an executive music committee of up to seven members selected by the University, with its chairman a member of the University's board of governors. Clearly, the University intended to keep the TCM on a shorter rein in the future.

Chalmers hit the roof.[218] He found the proposal high-handed, offensive, and a threat to the Conservatory's national identity. Things drifted for a short while. Then came a bright spot. The University asked Edward Johnson, general manager of the Metropolitan Opera Company in New York, to be the TCM's new chairman. Johnson, a native of Guelph, Ontario, accepted and promised to do all he could to enhance the Conservatory's profile, growth, and development. Not only had Johnson been a world-famous tenor before taking the Met job, but Ontario Premier George Drew was also his son-in-law, a state of affairs that might help the Conservatory's relations with the Province and, by extension, the University.

The University stipulated on December 13, 1945, that the Conservatory's board of governors be responsible to the University governors and that, "in the solicitation of donations, any approach to the Government for funds be made through the Board of Governors and not by individual members of the staff." It also included a reminder that all Conservatory property belonged to the University and that the Conservatory's board must always include ex officio the chairman of the University's board of governors, the chancellor, and the president. And so, almost a year after the University received the TCM's provincial grant, it deposited the money into the Conservatory's bank account. Yet it had the effrontery to say in a news release on December 5, 1945, a few days before it imposed its revised terms of governance, that it intended "to pay off the bonded indebtedness of the Conservatory and to insure the Conservatory of adequate financial support for carrying out its programme."[219] Whose money was it? No matter, the school was now, finally, out of debt. On September 12, 1946, the University's board of governors formally cancelled the Conservatory's debentures and recommended that they "be destroyed by burning."

With the war over, the school prospered as it never had in the past. It was flooded with demobilized veterans who wanted a musical education and had the funds to pursue it, thanks to a grateful government. With the triumvirate of Peaker, Mazzoleni, and Walter in place, the TCM announced, in its *Bulletin* of June 1945, the formation of the Senior School. H.H. Bishop had written to Sidney Smith informing him that Senior School funds were available, and Smith gave him the go-ahead.[220] Bishop also wrote about the new School positively in the *Bulletin*:

> … tuition fees would be such as to insure that no talented young Canadian
> would be denied a musical education because of limited financial

resources. We plan to provide opportunities that have in the past not been generally available in Canada. We wish to do our part in arresting the flight of native talent. Up to now, too many of our most promising students have had to go to the United States to complete their musical studies ... only a limited number to return.

It was becoming increasingly evident that Canada's young musicians were a valued resource needed to develop the country's musical culture. This was also true in the other arts in post-war Canada. Cultural nationalism flowered as never before.

Dorothy Johnson, an advanced piano student and branch teacher at the time, remembers how the entire ambiance of the school changed. Formerly, students attended the TCM once or twice a week for a lesson or class and then departed. Now a legion of full-time post-secondary students studied and practised at the school five or six days weekly.[221] They enrolled in traditional TCM classes and lessons or attended the Senior School and its offspring the Opera School, both long-overdue realizations of the Hutcheson report. Others attended the Faculty of Music's new school music course, which commenced in September 1946. Its objective was to train music teachers for Ontario's secondary schools. Students in this course also took their classes — three or four daily, sixteen to eighteen hours a week — at College Street.

What an exciting time it was! The Conservatory was bursting at the seams, even with the addition of two houses to its west purchased by the University in 1946 at a cost of $37,500.[222] No one complained, even though timetabling classes required enormous juggling acts in what were clearly inadequate quarters. John Beckwith, winner of a piano scholarship, had trouble even getting a practice studio because pianists from the women's residence had rented all of them. And everyone met in the meeting place, the school cafeteria. Victor Feldbrill praised it many years later: "It was a marvelous place for cross pollination.... A violinist would sit down with two singers, we exchanged ideas."[223]

Some forty new teachers were appointed to the school in 1945 to meet the demand, including voice teachers Ernesto Vinci and Leslie Holmes, cellist Cornelius Ysselstyn, bassoonist Elver Wahlberg, and percussionist Thomas Burry.[224] Vinci, a fine baritone, was a Berlin-trained medical doctor. While in Milan in the thirties he had sung in recital and opera before going to Halifax in 1938 to teach at the Maritime Conservatory. Vinci taught at the TCM for the next thirty years, and his pupils were a who's who of Canadian singers for the next two generations: sopranos Marguerite Gignac, Elizabeth Benson Guy, Mary Morrison, Maria Pellegrini, Sheila Piercey, Louise Roy, and Roxolana Roslak; mezzo-sopranos Joan Hall, Joan Maxwell, and Portia White; tenors John Arab and Glyn Evans; and baritones Maurice Brown, Alexander Gray, Robert Goulet (who also studied with Lambert), Avo Kittask, Andrew MacMillan, and Bernard Turgeon. Leslie Holmes, also an impressive baritone, had come from Lesser Slave Lake, Alberta, to study in Toronto with Albert Ham at the Canadian Academy, and then had a considerable career as a recitalist and oratorio singer in both Canada and Britain. He taught at the Conservatory for only two short periods and had in his class three excellent baritones, James Milligan, Harry Mossfield, and Jan Simons.

Emmy Heim joined the faculty the next year, 1946. Already sixty years old, she had been a prominent singer in her younger years. Born in Vienna, she had sung principally in Central Europe before moving to England in 1930. She met Ernest MacMillan in 1934 and made some unforgettable music with him on her annual visits to Canada prior to the outbreak of the Second World War.[225] Heim claimed that she had never worked with a better or more instinctive pianist than MacMillan. As for MacMillan, he was completely enchanted with her. A singularly fine interpreter of lieder, she devotedly shared her insights with her students: Frances James, Eileen Law, Lois Marshall, James Milligan, and innumerable others in the Senior and Opera schools.

Other returnees from the war who went back to teaching included pianist Clifford Poole and composers Samuel Dolin and John Weinzweig. Dolin, like Weinzweig, had the fresh outlook towards composition that was taking hold in Canada. It aimed to free itself from the British connection; it was atonal, twelve tone, radical, and implicitly Canadian, whatever "Canadian" might mean.

TCM profits doubled from 1945 to 1946, the residence was full, the orchestra was improving, and the library's holdings were being recatalogued. Sad to say, piano teacher Viggo Kihl died in 1945; he had taught at the school since 1913. Then Ernest Seitz, another one of the school's leading piano teachers, gave up his studio to manage his family's auto dealership in Toronto. His declining skill as a pianist may have contributed to this extraordinary decision, since he was only in his early fifties.[226]

Arnold Walter, the new Senior School's director, intended to have only a very limited number of teachers on the School's faculty. TCM teachers were, to say the least, concerned. Furthermore, Walter wanted complete authority not only to choose his teachers but also to assign students to them, an established practice in any reputable professional music school.[227] This was contrary to the prevailing TCM practice, where students chose the teacher they wanted from the several hundred available, with little or no guidance from the administration. Many top teachers now feared that, if Walter passed them up, they would lose income and prestige. Some even threatened to resign from the TCM.[228] They didn't know Walter well and didn't overly trust this confident, self-centred, and rather high-handed musician with a German accent — they called him "the Prussian" — who thought he knew more about musical education than anyone else. Walter, not one to back off, engaged only a few teachers for the Senior School, some of them relative newcomers like Kolessa and Vinci. He made no apologies, for he believed that the Senior School teachers he had selected were the best available and, therefore, there was nothing to argue about. To muddy the waters, however, nearly all of those he chose continued to teach students who were not in the Senior School, which put them in competition with those very teachers Walter had passed over. In 1948 some RCM teachers were even considering legal action and had engaged H.C. Walker, the son of Sir Edmund Walker, to pursue the matter.[229] No action was taken.

Yes, Walter didn't have an easy time. He even had to fight to enrol the best students into the Senior School. Teachers who were not among Walter's chosen few carefully guarded their students and discouraged them from attending the new school, despite its impressive offerings and large scholarships. Walter, frustrated, lacked the power to do anything about it. Even Senior School teachers like George Lambert resented and condemned the school and would have been happier if it had never happened. He and others did not agree that music students need a broader musical education. To them the ATCM and the more senior one-year resident licentiate was as valuable as the Senior School's artist diploma.

With opposition rampant among the TCM faculty, the Senior School had no recourse but to start slowly. There were approximately twenty students in the unofficial first year, 1945–46, and the next year's enrolment wasn't much larger. The calendar for 1946–47 spelled out a two-year course leading to the artist diploma, much like three-year courses at Juilliard and other leading American schools. There would be majors in piano, violin, singing, and composition; majors in organ and church music were also planned for but never happened. A year later, the program was extended to three years.[230] The extra year would outflank the Conservatory's licentiate diploma. The LTCM, as it was known, had increased its resident requirement to two years, in order to compete with the Senior School's two-year artist diploma course. Its program was roughly similar to that of the artist diploma, although it was more costly. Essentially, the LTCM was designed for a student wishing to continue with a teacher not in the Senior School.[231] But why have it at all if the TCM administration believed that the Senior School was the place where advanced post-secondary students should study?

The University only partially funded the Senior School, so Walter had to plead with the board for additional money and do so through Mazzoleni, since he was not allowed to attend board meetings. With reason, he complained about being responsible to Mazzoleni, who was ambivalent about the Senior School.[232] Walter did, after much protesting, obtain his coveted independence, but only for two years. In early 1948 President Smith abolished his entertainment allowance and — more important — ordered him, henceforth, to clear all Senior School and Opera School matters with Mazzoleni.[233] It was a bitter pill: Walter had tried to be free of the Conservatory and Mazzoleni and had lost on both counts.

The University sorted out a few other financial matters with the Conservatory in November 1948.[234] It decided to keep all fees from students at the Faculty of Music. (The TCM had been keeping fees of Faculty of Music students.) In return, the TCM would no longer pay any part of Willan's and Leo Smith's salaries. Further, the University would pay the TCM rent for the use of its facilities by the Faculty of Music and the Senior School, and the TCM would no longer be asked to supply capital items (e.g., furniture and equipment).

The Opera School, loosely part of the Senior School, took off almost immediately. Edward Johnson gave it his enthusiastic support, and students flocked to it from all parts of Canada. Walter engaged staff, selected students, and spent money, mostly without consulting Mazzoleni. Mazzoleni, more conservative and bureaucratic, went along with Walter, giving his approvals when asked, usually *ex post facto*. Walter needed a music director and a stage director. The engagement of Nicholas Goldschmidt as music director, as related by Goldschmidt to me many years ago, was serendipity at its best. Goldschmidt was in New York's *Musical Courier* office visiting the magazine's assistant editor Henry Levinger when the phone rang. It was Arnold Walter. He asked Levinger, who was an old friend and well informed about the New York musical scene, if he had suggestions for a musical director. Levinger promptly replied that he had just the man for the job sitting across the desk from him. Yes, it was Goldschmidt, the right man in the right place at the right time. It was a brilliant appointment.[235]

Goldschmidt, born in Moravia in 1908, studied in Vienna (Herbert von Karajan had been a fellow student), worked in opera houses in Czechoslovakia as a coach and assistant conductor, and came to the United States in 1937.[236] He taught at the San Francisco Conservatory, Stanford, and Columbia, and in Lenox, Massachusetts, and New Orleans. And he was looking for a job! Goldschmidt promptly moved to Toronto, took over the school's opera classes, and met his future wife, Shelagh Fraser. Tall, thin, and energetic, he enthusiastically and unfailingly conveyed his love of music to his students, nearly all of whom were devoted to him. Goldschmidt was a good if occasionally inaccurate pianist and a workmanlike conductor, even though he could become so infatuated with the music that he would forget to conduct! All in all, he gave the school a remarkable start.

Walter next engaged Felix Brentano, a Broadway director and student of Max Reinhardt, as stage director. The school held its classes in the recital hall, a euphemism for a catch-all large room used for classes, rehearsals, and junior recitals. There was, of course, no theatre, no place to store scenery and props, no office for the staff. Yet the school made do. The opera students were eager to learn opera, to sing, to act, to hope for a career.

On December 16, 1946, at the five-hundred-seat Hart House Theatre, after but eight weeks of classes, Goldschmidt and Brentano presented a program of operatic excerpts from *La Bohème*, *Otello*, *Faust*, *La Traviata*, *Fidelio*, and *Der Rosenkavalier* with a two-piano accompaniment. John Yocom of *Saturday Night* lauded the performance, calling it "a significant climax to the year in Canada — time may prove it significant for all Canada."[237] He praised the selections for their training value: "Here were no rich settings, no great spectacles, no ballets to relieve plot entanglements. But with the barest of settings and mostly in modern dress, with Dr. Walter introducing the scene, the excerpts were completely credible, even in foreign languages."

What an evening it was! Walter commented on it years later:

> Our singers had never been on stage before and acted accordingly. What was it that aroused so much enthusiasm among those who saw the show? … A mine of talent had just been discovered and a way of putting it to use — the lyric stage — had just been reinvented. The realization of that was so strong, the enthusiasm engendered so potent, that one forgot the gloomy cave of Hart House Theatre and the imperfections of the production and experienced the incredible: a credible Prisoners' Chorus from *Fidelio*; a credible finale from *Rosenkavalier*, as if it had been the most natural thing in the world to present Beethoven and Richard Strauss — and to do it so well.[238]

A few who sang that evening would go on to operatic careers, notably sopranos Mary Morrison and Elizabeth Benson Guy, tenor Pierre Boutet, and baritones Andrew MacMillan and Gilles Lamontagne.[239]

As for Hart House Theatre, it *was* a "gloomy cave." It had come about almost by accident while Hart House was still under construction. According to Ian Montagnes, Vincent Massey and his wife Alice "were touring the building one day … and had reached a large vaulted basement which lay beneath the central triangle. Two great supports for a terrace rose at the eastern end; with their connecting beam they formed a rough proscenium arch." Together they saw the possibility for a theatre almost immediately. Construction began, complicated in part because women — they were excluded from Hart House proper at the time — would have to be admitted as performers and audience, and thus access to the theatre had to be physically separated from the rest of the House. "A green room, dressing room and property and costume rooms were added to the plans, the finest equipment available was purchased, seats were installed. The result of the chance subterranean excursion was Toronto's first little theatre."[240] It would be the site for many of the Conservatory's small-scale operas for the next fifteen years.

The Opera School gave its first full-length opera, Smetana's *The Bartered Bride*, at Eaton Auditorium on April 28 and 29, 1947. It was sung in English with orchestra and chorus. Goldschmidt conducted, and the Boris Volkoff Ballet Company provided nine dancers. These performances led off the Diamond Jubilee Festival marking the TCM's sixtieth anniversary. Five other events followed. Two were talks, the first given by Mazzoleni at a faculty luncheon in the school's recital hall, and the second by John Erskine, author, English professor, and former president and chairman of the Juilliard School of Music, at an open luncheon of the Empire Club at the Royal York Hotel. Erskine's topic was appropriate for the occasion: "Ideals of Music Education in the New World Today." A fifteen-year-old Toronto pianist, Glenn Gould, ATCM, was scheduled to play at the Erskine luncheon, but there is no mention of him in the post-lecture reports.

Sir Ernest MacMillan conducted Pierné's *Children's Crusade* on the third night. He used impressive forces: the TSO, the Mendelssohn Choir, the Opera School chorus, and a three-hundred-voice children's choir. On the fourth night a "Senior School Quartet" — Gisèle La Flèche and Joseph Pach, violins; Hillel Diamond, viola; and Rowland Pack, cello — played the challenging Debussy String Quartet. A Handel Trio Sonata was on the same program along with the Schubert Octet. For the final night Mazzoleni conducted an all-Brahms program — the first movement of the Double Concerto, with Joseph Pach and Rowland Pack; the First Piano Concerto, with Yvonne Guiguet; and the First Symphony. Yes, with such a week of programs the Conservatory was beginning to look and sound like a major school of music. Certainly it was the richest and most significant series of programs that the school had given since its founding.

Even before the programs got underway Colin Sabiston of the *Globe and Mail* was heralding the Conservatory's jubilee efforts as not just a "culmination" of its past work but "rather a starting point toward new achievements."[241] He would not be disappointed. Sabiston considered the school's *Bartered Bride* "the finest amateur performance in local theatrical annals" and praised the singers and the fine ensembles, so well prepared by Goldschmidt and Brentano.[242] Although the singers had to sing over the orchestra on the floor in front of the stage — the auditorium had no orchestra pit — Sabiston believed that it did not seriously affect their efforts.

Sabiston praised Mazzoleni's conducting for the Brahms evening and noted that Yvonne Guiguet, a student of Lubka Kolessa, played "with remarkable poise and ease" in the D Minor Concerto. She built "tonal structures ... even in rapid running passages." He thought that Pach and Pack "acquitted themselves with great credit ... but their capacity for producing soaring volume in full ensemble passages is yet to be developed."[243]

At intermission on the festival's final night, Mazzoleni informed the audience that "His Majesty the King has agreed to allow the Conservatory to use the prefix 'Royal'." It was a happy conclusion to the Conservatory's 1939 petition for this right.[244] The official notice came on August 1, and a statute was passed by the Ontario legislature on December 12 enabling the school to change the Conservatory's diplomas from Toronto Conservatory of Music to Royal Conservatory of Music of Toronto. Having the designation "Royal" added much to the school's prestige across Canada and bolstered its claim that it was a national as well as a Toronto school. And whatever anti-royalists might say, "Royal" helped, and continues to help, its international image, especially in Britain and the United States.

As for the young artists, Guiguet, unfortunately, did not quite realize her performing talent in later life. She married Richard Johnston, a composer and professor in the Faculty of Music, and retired from solo work. Joseph Pach, who had been a child prodigy, made his TSO debut in the Tchaikovsky Concerto that same year and went on to appear as soloist with nearly every Canadian orchestra. Later Pach formed a duo with his wife, the pianist Arlene Nimmons, and still later created the resident string quartet at the University of New Brunswick. Rowland Pack, a pupil of Isaac Mamott's, was one of Canada's most gifted all-around musicians — as cellist, as keyboard player, as conductor. He became the principal cellist of the TSO and led several outstanding early music groups and choral organizations.

Opera meeting, 1947. From left to right: Nicholas Goldschmidt, Geoffrey Waddington (CBC), Arnold Walter, and Terence Gibbs (CBC).

He and his wife, Carol Wright — Arnold Walter once told me that she could sight-read anything — gave joint recitals for a number of years. Pack died prematurely at age thirty-seven in 1964.

Much of Toronto's recognition of the Conservatory's activities in the last half of the forties was due to the Women's Opera and Concert Committee chaired by Mrs. Floyd Chalmers.[245] Some of its members had been active in the Toronto Opera Guild in the thirties.[246] Arnold Walter had initially put the committee together to encourage Torontonians to attend the TCM's Five O'clock concerts and then to sell tickets to *The Bartered Bride* at the jubilee celebrations. The committee did all of its work admirably, underlining the importance of voluntary organizations in promoting the arts.

The CBC, eager to do its part in the development of Canadian opera, began a series of weekly opera broadcasts in May 1947. Participants included soloists from the school, a chorus, and an orchestra, with Goldschmidt directing. On June 11, 1948, Harry Boyle, CBC Trans-Canada program director and a skilled writer and producer, wrote to Walter proposing that the CBC cooperate with the school and give four operas on its Wednesday night programs. Boyle suggested having an advisory committee of Walter, Goldschmidt, and George Crum, a promising young conductor and coach who was working at the Opera School. Charles Jennings, Geoffrey Waddington, and Terence Gibbs would represent the CBC. Herman Geiger-Torel was added to the group after he settled in Toronto.

The outcome was the creation of the CBC Opera Company, which made its debut in the fall of 1948 with Puccini's *La Bohème*.[247] Britten's *Peter Grimes*, Bizet's *Carmen*, and

Smetana's *The Bartered Bride*, 1947, with Andrew MacMillan (Kecal) and Victor White (Vasek).

99

Gounod's *Faust* followed over the next three years. It was the Canadian premiere of *Grimes*, and when Britten heard a recording of the broadcast he was mightily impressed. A few weeks later he and tenor Peter Pears gave a recital in the RCM concert hall to a capacity audience. The highlight of that evening was Britten's *Seven Sonnets of Michelangelo*, "sung with superb taste by Mr. Pears."[248] Those were heady days for music in Toronto, and particularly for the CBC. Its leaders had both the will and the way to give Canada a national broadcasting system of quality that provided an alternative to American broadcasting and helped unify the country.

The Opera School gave a workshop in the summer of 1947 conducted by Ernesto Barbini, a coach and assistant conductor at the Metropolitan Opera Company. He collaborated with Andrew MacMillan, who was showing directorial talent in addition to his singing skills. Together they produced excerpts from *The Barber of Seville*, *La Traviata*, and *La Bohème*. Barbini, born in Venice and a graduate of that city's Benedetto Marcello Conservatory, had conducted in Italy before coming to the United States in 1938. He worked at the Chicago and Cincinnati opera companies immediately after the war before joining the Met in 1946. He would play an important role in the Opera School in the near future.

Just before Christmas 1947, the Opera School did two performances of Humperdinck's *Hansel and Gretel* in English at Eaton Auditorium. Bridle singled out the "trumpet-like clarity" of Jean Patterson's singing of Gretel and the "efficient" orchestra of thirty-two players conducted by Goldschmidt.[249] Gluck's *Orpheus and Euridice*, given in February at Eaton Auditorium, "reached a new peak of excellence," according to Colin Sabiston.[250] The stage chorus of twelve wore exciting masks (designed by Brentano) and costumes (designed by Stewart Bagnani). The three principals, Louise Roy, Mary Morrison, and Beth Corrigan, performed with skill and artistry. Sabiston poured on still more superlatives. "The production in both visual and musical beauty compares favourably with the best musical entertainment ever offered here." Assisting in the production was a newcomer to Toronto, Herman Geiger-Torel, a German stage director who was working in South America.

On April 9, 1948, at the Toronto Art Gallery, Geiger-Torel and Goldschmidt did a lean and sprightly version of Pergolesi's *La Serva Padrona* in English with a string quintet and harpsichord. Later that month the indefatigable Goldschmidt conducted the Opera School chorus and a chamber group in Mozart's Mass in C Minor on the CBC; it was advertised as the work's first performance in Canada. Then, to top off the busy spring, the school ambitiously tackled Strauss's *Die Fledermaus* in an English adaptation titled *Rosalinda*. Brentano had produced it on Broadway, where it had played for two years. He booked a two-week run at the Royal Alexandra Theatre and engaged Jeanne Merrill, who had created the title role in New York, to sing in the Toronto production. The rest of the cast was Canadian, with most of the singers from the Opera School. Goldschmidt conducted, with music arranged by Erich Wolfgang Korngold, a gifted Viennese composer who had immigrated to the United States. This

Glenn Gould with Alberto Guerrero, c. 1945.

was the school's first venture into commercial theatre, and it came off well, helped in part by the theatre's professional accoutrements. Although dusty and a bit down at heel — it had been built in 1907 — the "Alec" had a good stage and an orchestra pit sufficiently large at least for this show. Most important, the show's net costs came to just over $1,300, an astonishingly small sum.[251]

Brentano, who had been commuting between New York and Toronto since his appointment in 1946 and who really had little knowledge of opera, left Toronto for good after *Rosalinda*. He was succeeded by Geiger-Torel, who would devote the rest of his life to the Opera School and the opera company that evolved from it. Goldschmidt had recommended him to Walter, since they had worked together in Czechoslovakia in the thirties, where they had won one another's mutual respect and affection. Born Hermann Geiger in Frankfurt-am-Main in 1907 to a cultured German/Jewish family, he studied piano and violin and hoped to be a conductor, but finally turned to stage directing. Lothar Wallerstein, the chief stage director at the Frankfurt Opera, accepted him as an apprentice and took him to Salzburg in 1930, where Wallerstein was preparing the legendary performances of *Der Rosenkavalier*, with Lotte Lehmann as the Feldmarschallin and Richard Mayr as Baron Ochs.

Geiger fled Germany in 1933 and, after a brief and dangerous visit to his family in 1937, went on to Paris, where he dropped the final "n" in Hermann and changed his last name to Geiger-Torel. The French, he said, had trouble pronouncing the "g" in Geiger and were also getting tired of refugee Germans. Torel was, he thought, international in sound and would please everyone. Certainly it did in South American opera houses — Buenos Aires, Montevideo and Rio de Janeiro — where he worked after his departure from Europe. There he collaborated with leading conductors — Kleiber and Serafin, for example — and directed many of the world's great singers — Muzio, Pons, Schipa, Risë Stevens, Del Monaco, Sayao, Gigli, Milanov, and others.[252]

Torel was a dedicated teacher who treated students as young professionals. On occasion he would shout at them, but they soon became accustomed to his outbursts and suspected — rightly — that he usually staged them to get his point across. A practical director, he would only do works that he felt the students could handle. He had an encyclopedic knowledge of the standard repertoire that enabled him to deal confidently with minute details without referring to the score. Most important, Torel could see opera from all the vantage points — conductor, director, singer, and designer — thanks to his catholic training and experience.

Torel and Goldschmidt turned out to be a remarkable team. They did two operas in the next two years at Eaton Auditorium: Mozart's *The Marriage of Figaro* (the Dent English translation) in December

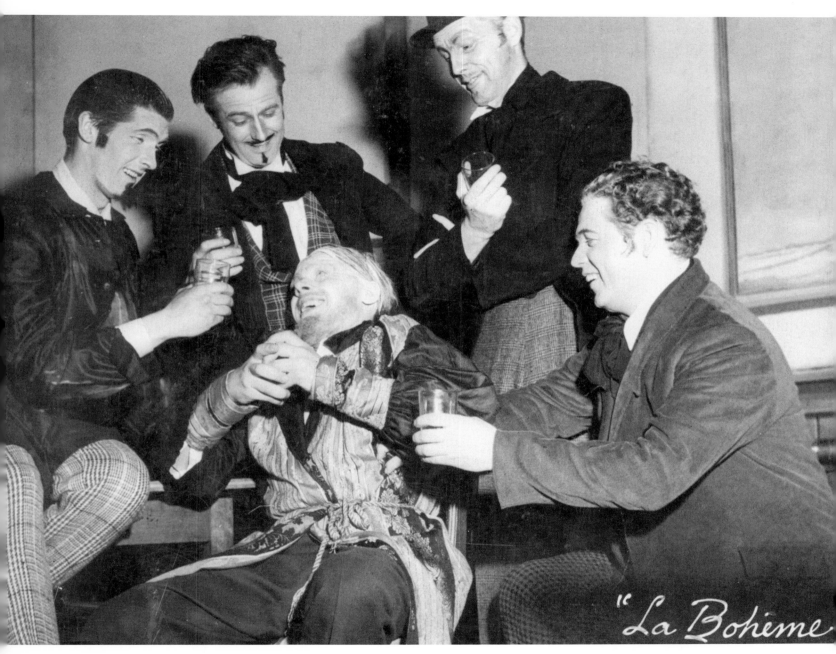

"*La Bohème*

Puccini's *La Bohème*, 1949. From left to right: Edmund Hockridge (Marcello), Andrew MacMillan (Schaunard), Glenn Gardiner (Benoit), Jan Rubes (Colline), and James Shields (Rodolfo).

1948 and *La Bohème* (in Italian) in May 1949. Marguerite Gignac, for one, was a charming Susanna in *Figaro*. Pearl McCarthy of the *Globe and Mail* hailed the Mozart as "another milestone in the history of the arts in Canada."[253] The School went on to present both *Hansel* and *Figaro* with piano accompaniment in several Southern Ontario cities.

None of these successes between 1946 and 1949 came easily. The University knew little about opera and operatic training and still less about the financial backing needed to produce opera at a professional level. It baffled Sidney Smith that an opera school must put on productions as part of its training. Arnold Walter impatiently wondered how Smith, educated and intelligent as he was, could know so little about opera and be so reticent generally about helping the School. This lack of support for opera, coupled with the constant need for money for the Senior School, left Walter debilitated psychologically and, on occasion, almost apoplectic. English Canada had a mindset that musical instruction should pay for itself. The combined deficit of the Senior School and the Opera School went from $17,000 in 1946–47 to a seemingly horrendous $35,000 in 1949–50. How small this was compared to expenditures in other university subject areas! Did the University authorities realize the key role the School was playing in establishing opera in Canada?

Another outcome of the Hutcheson report was the Conservatory's Concert and Placement Bureau, under the direction of Anna McDonagh (later McCoy). In its first full season (1946–47) she arranged fifty-two concert, banquet, and other miscellaneous engagements for students and the occasional faculty member, as well as church soloist and church organ positions. By 1949–50 the number of engagements she booked had grown to eighty-six, and in the following year to ninety-eight.[254] McDonagh, who had a gentle exterior, was hard-headed and resourceful in convincing sponsors to pay students professional fees. She was so successful that the board, in 1949, decided to charge students and faculty a 10 percent commission on fees earned through the bureau.[255] A charitable explanation for this tariff was that commissions were *de rigeur* in the profession, and so young professionals should get used to this fact of life. It was left unsaid that they also helped pay for McDonagh's salary. However, commissions were not charged for appearances on the CBC and on the university campus.

Perhaps the most distinguished of the many singers the Senior School trained between 1947 and 1950 was the soprano Lois Marshall. A student of Weldon Kilburn and Emmy Heim, she possessed an amazing, unique voice, with superb artistry to go with it. Unfortunately polio had crippled her when she was two, which ruled out an operatic career, although she did sing several roles on radio with the CBC Opera Company. Marshall first performed as soprano soloist in 1947, in the *St. Matthew Passion* under Sir Ernest MacMillan; it marked the beginning of a long career. Later that same year she was soloist in Alessandro Scarlatti's *Christmas Cantata*, with Mazzoleni conducting. Colin Sabiston wrote an eloquent passage in recognition of her gifts:

Lois Marshall in recital in the RCM Concert Hall, with Weldon Kilburn, pianist, 1952.

All the ordinary words descriptive of vocal excellence seem inadequate to describe the other-worldliness of Miss Marshall's singing. One became so transported that even the outer edges of consciousness were lost to the world, its affairs, and even its memories. It was the completeness of this spell, the totality of absorption in a single event, that brought a sensation almost like fear. Had one been transferred to a place where nothing existed but an extreme intensity of beauty?[256]

Lois Marshall won the Senior School's annual Eaton Graduation Award, as well as the first prize in the CBC's Singing Stars of Tomorrow competition in 1950. (Doreen Hulme, also an RCM student, won the CBC's second prize. She would become a leading musical comedy singer in England.) Two years later Marshall won the coveted Naumburg Competition in New York, which included a debut recital in the city's town hall on December 2, 1952. Torontonians relished what Peggy Glanville-Hicks of the *New York Herald-Tribune* wrote about this concert: "She is one of the most superb singers this reviewer has ever heard.... She has everything.... There is nothing this singer cannot do with ease, with insight and with the eloquence of the great artist."[257] This triumph was followed by an appearance with Arturo Toscanini in Beethoven's *Missa Solemnis*.

Another young Canadian, violinist Betty-Jean Hagen, had won this same Naumburg Award two years earlier. She was tall, rather imperious, and always "cool." Carol Wright, who accompanied her at the competition in New York, said that Hagen practised the minimum prior to the competition while she, Wright, slaved away on her parts for hours.[258] Hagen, a student of Géza de Kresz who had returned to Canada in 1947 after being in Hungary since 1935, went on to win several other prestigious awards over the next few years: the Paris Pathé-Marconi Prize, which entitled her to recitals in four Western European countries (1951); the Harriet Cohen Commonwealth Medal as the outstanding woman musician in the British Commonwealth (1952); the Carl Flesch Medal of the Guildhall School of Music in London (1953); and the New York Leventritt Foundation Award (1955).

Arnold Walter's Five O'clock concerts thrived in the post-war years.[259] Some high points were the Parlow Quartet playing the Schubert A Minor Quartet and the Beethoven op. 59, no.3 on November 20, 1946, Lubka Kolessa in recital on December 4, 1946, Goldschmidt leading the Conservatory Chamber Choir — an *ad hoc* group of Opera School singers — on March 10, 1948, and Ernesto Vinci performing

Schubert's *Die Schöne Müllerin* with Sir Ernest MacMillan at the piano on March 9, 1949. They also did *Die Winterreise* at a later concert.[260]

Music schools can be the scene of intriguing happenings outside of music. In 1948, a Toronto tabloid revealed that Lubka Kolessa and Arnold Walter were involved in an intimate affair and that Kolessa was behaving bizarrely, to put it mildly. Evidently she suspected Walter of having liaisons with other women and engaged private detectives to keep tabs on him. Unfortunately, there were leaks that ultimately led to Kolessa's abrupt resignation (she would otherwise have been dismissed) on November 18, 1948. President Smith was so incensed that he told Mazzoleni to get her off the University's premises within forty-eight hours.[261] Toronto's loss was Montreal's gain. Kolessa taught there for the next thirty years, although she continued to keep her Toronto residence. Mario Bernardi, a gifted piano student, gave up the Senior School to study privately with her, so much did he value her teaching.[262] Carol Wright, another Kolessa pupil, described her first lesson at Kolessa's residence/studio in staid Rosedale with its three grand pianos: "Madame, herself, dressed in black from head to toe, was very beautiful. She had dyed red hair, made-up eyes, high heels, and smoked cigarettes in a cigarette holder. She spoke in a heavy European accent. A large portrait of a nude man hung on the wall of her studio, where there was a general air of disorder." Wright thought her a superb pianist, with "style, character and brilliance rarely heard today."[263]

Kolessa's departure left a big hole at the RCM. During her time there her guarantee had been a considerable $7,000, higher than any other teacher. Fortunately, Mazzoleni and Walter had been negotiating for some months with a Hungarian pianist, Béla Böszörmenyi-Nagy, and he partially filled the gap. Bernardi later studied with Nagy, as did Wright, but they both found him ordinary compared to Kolessa. Nagy was a handsome man with a continental appearance — he usually wore a flashy over-the-shoulder cloak instead of an overcoat. He stayed in Toronto for only a few years before moving on to Boston.

The other Kolessa successor was the Swiss/Russian pianist Boris Roubakine. Trained in Switzerland and France, he was quiet, modest, and self-effacing. Roubakine had been violinist Bronislaw Huberman's accompanist for seven years before moving to the United States and, subsequently, Canada. He remained at the RCM sporadically until 1957, during which time he taught Arlene Nimmons, Arthur Ozolins, and several other promising young pianists. Roubakine accompanied Betty-Jean Hagen on her concert tours in the fifties and was a much sought after chamber player.

The school's neighbourhood branches were reviewed in 1950. David Ouchterlony, a Toronto organist who had been appointed the first supervisor of branches in 1947, reported to the board that it was pedagogically undesirable, impractical, and costly to maintain a large number of small rented premises. He believed that the best way for the school to serve the city was to buy suitable large buildings in developing residential areas.[264] The Conservatory owned only three buildings: 460 Avenue Road, purchased for $11,000 in 1946; 2 Alexandra Boulevard in North Toronto, purchased for $18,000 in 1947; and 366 Spadina Road, purchased for $19,000 in early 1950. The other thirteen branches were rented. Seven was considered the optimum number. Ouchterlony's cautious report wisely suggested that the school note carefully the Toronto Planning Board's deliberations before closing branches or establishing new ones. Some of the rentals continued, but several of the smaller ones were closed.

Two difficult matters persisted at mid-century. The first concerned the Senior School. A report by Arnold Walter to the board at its meeting of September 22, 1949, proposed a new school of music composed of the Faculty of Music's degree-granting department, the Senior School, and the Conservatory's licentiate diploma course. The new school would be responsible for all advanced instruction. Other conservatory instruction would be considered preparatory. Walter predicted that there would be no conflict between courses, a single budget would be set, and there would be a fully salaried faculty. The school would then be much like its U.S. counterparts, such as Eastman, Juilliard, and New England, even though — as Walter carefully avoided saying — these same schools employed performance teachers by the hour.

President Smith was wary of the aggressive Walter, whom he thoroughly disliked. In 1948 he had written to Johnson warning him that Walter's behaviour could cause a crisis at the Conservatory.[265] Smith wrote of Walter's "overwhelming ambition, Teutonic mentality, and an individualism to the extent of failing to work with others.... To my mind Mr. Mazzoleni has shown the patience of Job in his endeavors to work with Dr. Walter." Nevertheless, Smith set up a committee chaired by Edward Johnson to study reorganizing music at the Conservatory and the University.[266] No deadline was set for its report. Perhaps he hoped that the entire subject would go away.

The second matter, opera, was in some ways easier and in other ways harder to address than the Conservatory's academic reorganization. Walter wrote a brief in November 1949 on "The Present Stage of Opera in Canada" to the Royal Commission on National Development in the Arts, Letters, and Sciences, the conclusions of which were later known as the Massey Report.[267] His vision of the Opera

School was to set the stage for a permanent professional opera company that would continue to work closely with the school, as did the CBC. Walter stated that the school was limited in both the number and the scope of its productions since the parsimonious University had dictated that private funds must support them. He concluded his brief: "Canadian opera is on the verge of emerging as a major factor in Canada's musical life.... It will depend on grants from governments and municipalities, for opera has never been self-supporting, and probably never will be."

The flourishing Opera School was now ready to do an eight-day "festival" of three operas at the Royal Alexandra Theatre to prove its worth as a professional company. Walter, Goldschmidt, and Torel took their plans to the Conservatory board and asked for authorization and financial backing if things went wrong.[268] As expected, the board thought the plans risky and told Walter to clear them with Edward Johnson. Mazzoleni, who opposed the festival, went with Walter to New York to meet with Johnson. Johnson was of course enthusiastic; he had long felt that Canadians were too often sticks in the mud and rarely gambled on anything, especially in the performing arts.[269] He pointed out to the board that the *Rosalinda* run had been successful, that the private money already raised would release the Conservatory from any obligation, and that "such performances are not only an outlet for the students themselves but also a positive indication and affirmation of the accomplishments in the work of the Conservatory. Since Mr. Mazzoleni and Dr. Walter seem to be now in accord ... there could be nothing hazardous either in the way of financial responsibility, or to the prestige of the institution."[270]

Reluctantly, Smith gave his approval. Walter promised that the festival would break even, despite Chalmers's warning to expect a deficit of around $4,000. The school would do three operas: *Rigoletto*, *La Bohème*, and *Don Giovanni*, and the singers would be both students and professionals.[271] Undeniably, it *was* risky. Playing at the Royal Alec, as Walter knew from past experience, was more costly than playing at Eaton Auditorium and Hart House Theatre — the rent and the union pay scales for singers, orchestra, and stage hands were higher — but it was the closest thing Toronto had to an opera house. Its principal drawback was its orchestra pit, which could hold thirty players at best, and only after removing three rows of orchestra seats.

No matter, the intrepid Walter moved ahead, depending on his friends and the women's committee to raise the necessary funds. He told all doubting Thomases that he had a separate fund for costumes and that there would be no overtime, a frequent and costly drain on Opera School ventures in the past.[272] And he promised to stick to his budget. Operatic history in Canada was in the making.

Chapter Five

THE TRAVAILS OF REORGANIZATION

The year 1950 was a banner year for the sixty-four-year-old Conservatory. The Conservatory's opera festival was an enormous success, as Arnold Walter had predicted. It ran from February 3 to 11 with four performances of *La Bohème* and three each of *Rigoletto* and *Don Giovanni*. All three were operatic warhorses and bound to please. Many of the leading singers had already sung their roles in CBC productions, thus cutting coaching and rehearsal time and costs. The press loved what it saw and heard and even praised the marginally satisfactory orchestra. An astonished Toronto had never before seen or heard anything by local operatic forces to equal it. These were not haphazard performances with nondescript staging so typical of touring groups like the San Carlo, but thoroughly rehearsed operas with all of the trappings.

Rigoletto played first. The *Globe and Mail*, "recognizing the Festival as an event of importance in Toronto's musical history" brought in *Montreal Gazette* critic Thomas Archer, who reviewed it with boundless praise.[273] To identify Canadian expression in the arts, Archer dwelt on the company's all-Canadian cast, with leads from six different provinces. It was, he noted, "a striking example of what can be achieved by concentrating on ensemble work." Herbert Whittaker, the *Globe*'s drama critic, also wrote, rather backhandedly, of his relief that he "did not have to excuse everything but the singing. Here is opera which recognizes its heritage of theatre as well as music."[274]

The reviews of *Don Giovanni* were equally good. It was sung in English in the Dent translation the next night. Rose MacDonald of the *Toronto Telegram*, like Archer, was taken with "the establishment of a young company of Canadians. The performance was of such merit as made it stand firmly on its own ground; not to be praised especially because it is a Canadian product but with pride in the fact

111

that these accomplished singers are within the Canadian pattern."[275] More cultural nationalism! *La Bohème*, with Mary Morrison and James Shields in the leads, also received well-deserved laurels.

Still to come were the significant comments of Eric McLean of the *Montreal Star*.[276] The success of the festival, he wrote, "was the result of almost three years of painstaking work in which opposition was foreseen and forestalled, and support was detected and exploited." He praised the production for showing that Canada was capable of more than "hooked rugs and the Group of Seven." And, "Such an achievement was possible only through the Royal Conservatory Opera School." How germane were his comments! McLean must have known how Walter had to fight every inch of the way to bring the school to such a level.

Returning to money, as always a paramount concern, Walter gleefully reported that the festival had a small surplus of $3,405.[277] Plans for a 1951 festival were soon underway and Walter's budget got board approval on March 22. But by the fall he was having second thoughts. Costs had gone up and he could foresee a deficit of $10,000.[278] Rather than jeopardize his reputation for fiscal prudence with the board, he cancelled the festival. Goldschmidt and Torel, however, were unwilling to accept this decision. They saw all too clearly that dependence on the University's grudging support was a dead end. They wanted an independent company, but one working closely with the Opera School, which would continue to pay their salaries and supply singers, coaches, scenery, rehearsal space, and other services in the early stages. The company would be responsible for deficits, if any.

Soon, the two men got financial pledges from two prominent Torontonians who really loved opera, J.D. Woods and Conservatory board Vice-Chairman James Duncan. Less than two weeks after Walter's cancellation of the festival, Torel presented the Conservatory board with a plan for School/company collaboration.[279] The board, along with Walter and Mazzoleni, thought the plan too vague and were rightfully concerned that the company might exploit the School and its students in order to achieve commercial success. When Torel addressed the meeting, he gave assurances that he and Goldschmidt and the rest of the School's faculty would continue to have enough time to carry out their School obligations.

Much arguing back and forth ensued, with Edward Johnson and Sidney Smith insisting that the company must respect the School's prerogatives, and Torel promising that they had nothing to fear. Finally, the University pronounced that Goldschmidt and Torel must have a properly incorporated opera company in place before negotiating further. This was done in short order. Three meetings were held, on November 7, 11, and 13, between company and Conservatory representatives.

The incipient corporation had within a dramatic few days paved the way to obtaining its charter.[280] Its guarantors, including such luminaries as Vincent Massey, Floyd Chalmers, and Sir Ellsworth Flavelle, helped the company get all the University and Conservatory cooperation needed to clear the way. The new corporation and the Conservatory drew up an agreement that Edward Johnson brought before the University's board of governors on November 23. The many details, so typical of such agreements, were those that Goldschmidt and Torel had proposed less formally. They were to be in effect until June 1951. The governors, happy that the University was off the hook and out of show business, quickly approved the agreement. The Opera Festival Association, a rather unusual name for an opera company, was born.

Walter's pride in the accomplishments of the Opera School got a boost when the National Film Board of Canada produced a forty-five-minute docudrama, "Opera School," to coincide with the second opera festival. Directed by Gudrun Parker and produced by Guy Glover with a script by Lister Sinclair, it is an engaging and durable account of a young soprano who studies at the School for three years and ends up singing Susanna in *The Marriage of Figaro*. Marguerite Gignac, who had sung Susanna in the 1949 *Figaro* and Zerlina in *Don Giovanni*, played the lead. The film, well produced and a critical success, boosted the School's reputation and credibility.

Another offshoot of the Opera School was launched late in 1950 when six experienced graduates took part in a clever *divertissement* they called Opera Backstage. Created by Torel, with George Crum as pianist and coach, it was an operatic caricature/burlesque. As its brochure pointed out, it "poked fun at all the exaggerated stage mannerisms, wooden acting, and unlikely turns that make opera look ridiculous beside modern theatre." It capitalized on typical operatic themes, such as love, death, murder, curses, and vengeance, illustrating them with excerpts from the standard repertoire. Before each excerpt Torel would wittily point out to the audience how well or badly the opera dealt with the theme in question. In effect, he was doing what he did in actual rehearsals. The audience loved it. Opera Backstage was the first Canadian opera group to tour Canada from coast to coast.

Over the next few years the Opera Festival Association gradually weaned itself from the Opera School. Its productions were of a high standard, considering the budgetary restrictions and the limited possibilities of the Royal Alexandra Theatre. Its acoustics were more suited to spoken drama than to opera, and the orchestra pit was almost hopeless. Operatic warhorses were the order of the day: *Figaro*, *Faust*, and *Madama Butterfly* in 1951; *The Magic Flute*, *Manon*, and *The Bartered Bride* in 1952; *Così fan tutte* and *Butterfly* (again) in 1953; *Rigoletto* in 1954; and so on. The only twentieth-century operas

were Menotti's *The Consul*, which was such a success in 1953 that it was repeated the next year, and Wolf-Ferrari's *I quattro rusteghi* ("School for Fathers"), also in 1954. Talented School singers were given roles in the company, while others performed in the chorus. It was valuable training, especially for those heading for major careers.

School graduates distinguished themselves: Marguerite Gignac (Manon), Mary Morrison (Marguerite), Pierre Boutet (Faust), and Jan Rubes (Méphistophélès). Lois Marshall (her only appearance in staged opera) and Patricia Snell outdid one another alternating as the Queen of the Night in *The Magic Flute*. *The Bartered Bride* featured Elizabeth Benson Guy as Marie and Jan Rubes as Kezal — a role that seemed to have been created for him. Irene Salemka was an unforgettable Cio-Cio-San in *Butterfly*, and Theresa Gray was an equally unforgettable Magda Sorel in *The Consul*. Two RCM singers with great promise sang in the 1954 festival: tenor Jon Vickers as the Duke in *Rigoletto* and

Mozart's *Così fan tutte*, 1953, with Jon Vickers (Ferrando), Jacqueline Smith (Despina), and Donald Garrard (Guglielmo).

Filipeto in *I quatro rusteghi*, and baritone James Milligan as Marcello in *La Bohème*. Another young baritone, Robert Goulet, took minor roles in two operas that season.

A surprise of the 1953 season was Mozart's *Così fan tutte*. Following its Toronto run, the RCM Concert and Placement Bureau toured it in Ontario with a two-piano accompaniment. In Peterborough, where it played two nights in a row, a delighted Robertson Davies, then editor of the *Peterborough Examiner*, said all of the things the Toronto critics had, in good part, failed to notice — how technically difficult the work is, how the voices must match, how the singers "must have a musicianly regard for one another; balance and ensemble are everything in *Così*." The opera toured again in April 1956.

With the Opera Festival Association in high gear, the Opera School returned to producing its own small-scale operas annually at Hart House Theatre, with piano accompaniment. The first one, in March 1952, was Menotti's *The Old Maid and the Thief*. The next year there was a double bill: Kurt Weill's *Down in the Valley* and the Canadian premiere of a little-known Jacques Ibert opera, *Angélique*. Donald Garrard as the Preacher and Jon Vickers as Brock Weaver in the Weill opera were singled out by John Kraglund of the *Globe and Mail*, who wrote that Garrard was the "vocal highlight" and that Vickers, who was just getting his teeth into opera — he had until then been principally an oratorio soloist — "gave a superb performance vocally and dramatically."[281] George Lambert, Vickers's teacher, had heard him first in Winnipeg on an examination tour in 1950 and promptly offered him a scholarship to study at the RCM.[282] From the outset of his Toronto years there was no more serious student than Vickers. His career as one of the finest tenors in the world from the mid-fifties until the eighties speaks for itself. As for *Angélique*, its slapstick humour kept the audience in stitches. Lavone Skaven had the title role, a heartless woman who relentlessly persecutes her husband, Boniface. Two young baritones, Bernard Turgeon (Boniface) and Alexander Gray (Charlot), were excellent; they would both be leading singers in Canadian opera in the years to come.

The success of these two operas encouraged the school to do another double bill with double casts on April 12 and 13, 1954: Puccini's *Sister Angelica*, one of the operas in his *Trittico*, and a rarely performed work, Bohuslav Martinu's *Comedy on the Bridge*. In the Puccini opera Andrée Thériault shared the title role with Milla Andrew, who would come to prominence in Britain a decade later. Both were outstanding dramatically as Angelica. Patricia Rideout and Phyllis Mailing, two fine mezzo-sopranos, shared the role of the Princess. *Comedy on the Bridge*, in contrast to the tragic Puccini opera, was a slapstick comedy. Robert Goulet, as John the fisherman, drew plaudits. Hugh Thomson of the *Toronto Daily Star* was "taken with his stage presence and voice" and John Kraglund wrote of the "wonderfully confused and truculent interpreta-

Menotti's *The Old Maid and the Thief*, 1952, with Joan Hall (Miss Pinkerton) and Joanne Ivey (Miss Todd).

tion of the devoted but irate lover."[283] Mario Bernardi made his first appearance as conductor for the Martinu work, while Goldschmidt conducted the others. These productions, especially the less well known ones, were treats for opera buffs and provided invaluable experience for the school's students.

Theory, composition, and related subjects such as orchestration were not popular among students at the Conservatory or, for that matter, at the Faculty of Music, even though the latter's doctorate could be earned only by composing a satisfactory major work. A partial reason for this alienation was that budding young composers thought the teachers — Healey Willan, Leo Smith, and Ernest MacMillan — were too conventional in their outlook. Change was overdue. The end of the war brought a host of demobilized veterans, some of them gift-

Sir Ernest MacMillan and John Weinzweig, c. 1950.

ed composers. They literally landed on the Conservatory's doorstep and wanted instruction. The teacher most of them sought out was John Weinzweig.

Weinzweig, a Conservatory product of the thirties, had gone on to Eastman, where he had studied with first-class teachers who helped him to develop an individual and progressive approach to composing and the teaching of composition. Back in Canada, he wrote mainly incidental music for radio dramas and films for several years, only to have his work interrupted by military service. Blunt and outspoken, he made his views clear. In an article in the Conservatory's *Monthly Bulletin* of November 1949, he criticized the teaching of composition in the traditional B.Mus. course given by Willan and Smith. He accused them of "failing to give the creative musician a useful technical background." He went on to say that conservatory theory instruction does not help students in applied music. "Composition, as it is taught today, actually suppresses the student's natural capacity for creative thought. It has lagged far behind the teaching of instrumental techniques."

He maintained that theory teaching and its instructional materials had not changed since Fux's time, two hundred years before. He pointed out that "to confine teaching methods in theory to any one musical style, living or dead, is to confuse the student by shutting him off from the musical world in which he lives and in which he is going to work. Our theory students are taught their exercises as manoeuvres with notes, voice-leading patterns written for their own sake, and with no functional purpose." Returning to composition, he viewed teaching creative music "a matter of stimulating a natural creative instinct in music, for when people stop making their own music the art comes to a standstill. Is it not time we teachers ceased perpetuating a false tradition and started encouraging living music?"

Undoubtedly, Weinzweig's varied career had broadened his point of view. He had abandoned functional music after the war to devote his efforts to composing serious music expressive of the times. However, he would never leave his music in one mould for long. His pupils in the post-war years included composers Samuel Dolin, Harry Freedman, Harry Somers, John Beckwith, Phil Nimmons, and Murray Adaskin, all of whom were leaders in Canadian composition over the next fifty years. Freedman, for one, credits Weinzweig for helping him to establish his own identity as a composer.[284] Interestingly, some of Weinzweig's ideas were already in place at Juilliard, where traditional theory and harmony teaching had been abandoned after the war in favour of a course titled "Materials of Music." Whatever, Weinzweig was not the only new composition teacher at the Conservatory. Arnold Walter, an active composer until 1952, taught several students, notably Clermont Pépin and Paul McIntyre, in conventional middle-European ways.

Burning with curiosity, the Conservatory's composition students sought out the annual composition symposia organized by the American International Federation of Music Students. The first one had been at Juilliard in 1947. Student compositions from five major American schools — Juilliard, the Curtis Institute of Music, Eastman, the New England Conservatory, and the Yale School of Music — were performed. Discussion of the works followed. The next year the symposium was held at Eastman. Toronto students were admitted as visitors and played two works, Harry Somers's First String Quartet and John Beckwith's Five Lyric Pieces.[285] Soprano Freda Antrobus (later Ridout) sang the Beckwith pieces, with Beckwith at the piano.

The 1949 symposium at the New England Conservatory was extremely well organized. By then, the undergraduate association of Toronto's Faculty of Music had joined the federation and — with RCM students — was fully represented at the symposium. Each of the six member schools presented a chamber concert of works by its composers. Toronto's offerings were by Nimmons, Pépin, Somers, Beckwith, and Freedman, and their program was given a dry run in Toronto.[286] The symposium's orchestral concert included Clermont Pépin's *Symphonic Variations*. The *Boston Globe* said that Pépin's work was "the most polished, [its] style lush post-romantic whose last great — and non-Hollywood — master was Rachmaninoff. You can learn this style from text books and other scores, but the sustained motion (the only piece of the evening to exhibit it), the grasp of the structure and innate expressivity are instinctive. Pépin is evidently very gifted."

The *Christian Science Monitor*, in commenting on the orchestral program, thought that all the works, other than Pépin's, "were mainly in the neo-classic idiom, reflecting influences of such composers as Hindemith, Harris, Schönberg, or Copland. It was obvious that the students are striving to hew a new idiom of musical expression. Mr. Pépin's work, however, looks to the past and is quite Franckian in feeling." Symposium students roundly criticized Pépin's conservatism. They asked him when he planned to say something new. He answered that he sought "a thorough grounding in the classics first of all and would then use this basis for a more original expression." The *Boston Post* commented on the Toronto composers' conservatism generally but in no way disparaged their quality. Another Canadian composer, Violet Archer of Montreal, who was studying at Yale, also had an orchestral piece done; it got a mixed reception.

This symposium was summed up by John Beckwith in the April 1949 Conservatory *Monthly Bulletin*.

The general tone of the meeting was one of friendly interchange of ideas, a spirit which overflowed from the provocative, amusing, and often heated critiques into the smaller conversational groups. The New England Conservatory students were excellent hosts, and were anxious to ensure that the student delegations did not remain as separate "camps." Their attitude did much to break down the sense of competition and so increased the educational and social value of the symposium.

The Boston symposium's success gave Toronto much to think about when it hosted the next symposium, in March 1950. Were their composers *that* conservative, and, conversely, were U.S. composers trying to be radical just for the sake of being radical? Did serious music have to be in such ferment? If Walter and the old guard, Willan and Smith, were for tradition, certainly Weinzweig wasn't. Anyway, wasn't craft and inspiration what composition was all about? The Toronto symposium followed the same format as the previous ones. New works from the same six schools were performed. Freedman's Symphonic Suite, conducted by Mazzoleni at Convocation Hall, was one of eight works done at the orchestra concert, and it was well received. At Toronto's chamber concert, Beckwith's *Great Lakes Suite* was singled out for its originality. Lois Marshall and Glenn Gardiner were the singers, with Leslie Mann, clarinet, Rowland Pack, cello, and Beckwith, piano.

As in Boston, there was considerable press coverage. Thomas Archer of the *Montreal Gazette* gave Freedman's *Five Pieces for String Quartet* the most praise. He reported that some composers attacked Andrew Twa's String Quartet for using twelve-tone techniques, which they considered "foreign," and thought that the work had "no beginning no middle and no end."[287] But it was Leslie Bell, a prominent Toronto musician and music education professor at the University, who admirably summed up the symposium by writing that there was "ample evidence of those characteristics of 20th century music which are its strength and its weakness — on the one hand that insatiable curiosity for experimenting which has resulted in all sorts of new and wonderful things in music, on the other that unwarranted contempt for the 19th century and that mania for being original and '20th century' at all costs. There never was an age so concerned with the world about it as today." Bell thought that "restlessness, pessimism, and almost hysteria were evident more than once" in symposium works and that they reflect our society and civilization. Certainly a world of nuclear weapons and a war imminent in Korea concerned most thinking people. He added, however, that the music of some composers "could have been even better if the composers had spent more time learning to know themselves." Bell observed that the American students were "amazed" by the Canadian composers' "independence and ability to stand on their own feet without indicating that they must imitate others and belong to a particular school."[288]

And so Canadian music made a giant leap forward after the 1950 symposium, with RCM students in the lead. The CBC broadcast symposium works by Nimmons and Freedman on June 21, 1950, and eventually aired five other contemporary compositions. The stodgy image of Canadian composition was disappearing. Symposiums continued for several years afterwards in various U.S. locations. Conservatory students participated and were generally lauded for their work.

The Conservatory Orchestra, too, made progress. Although it still had to call in professionals from the TSO to bolster its weaker sections, the orchestra's programming and soloists merited attention from Toronto press and public. On April 18, 1951, Mazzoleni courageously did Bruckner's Ninth Symphony at the first of the two RCM annual closing concerts at Massey Hall. A Conservatory choir and soloists Lois Marshall, Margaret Stilwell, Jon Vickers, and James Milligan sang in the Te Deum (1883), which Bruckner had not assigned to the work but is usually done in lieu of a finale. (Bruckner died in 1896 before completing the symphony.) Leo Smith, writing in the *Globe and Mail*, claimed that Bruckner wanted the choral piece inserted. Smith, taking a populist point of view, also questioned "the appeal of this music [the entire symphony] to the average concert audience." The *Telegram* said, crankily, "one half of it was deliberately monotonous, meandering music."[289] The press responded more enthusiastically to the following week's concert: Graham George's *Dorian Fugue* (a short conservative piece), Bach's Three-Piano Concerto, Brahms's Second Symphony, and the Liszt Piano Concerto in E-flat with Ruth Watson (later Henderson) as soloist. Watson, also a composer, was praised by Smith: "This was the virtuoso astonishing us with her skill."[290]

Not to be forgotten in the early fifties were the growing opportunities for performers of all kinds. The principal provider was, of course, the CBC, which unwaveringly presented Canadian musicians and actors in order to fulfil its mandate as a Canadian network. The Concert and Placement Bureau continued to pursue concert engagements for Conservatory artists in Toronto, Ontario, and other parts of Canada. From 1949 until the late sixties, Toronto students and graduates gave about twenty-four weekly Sunday recitals annually in the Art Gallery's Walker Court. The Canadian National Exhibition (CNE), beginning in 1949, sponsored daily recitals by Conservatory musicians during its two weeks each summer. Glenn Gould and Lois Marshall were both on the 1950 series. Sunday evening concerts in the Great

Hall at Hart House were well attended, even if women were admitted only when escorted by a male. The gallery, the CNE, and Hart House all paid artist fees, albeit small ones.

Nor was drama neglected. After many years of limited instruction in elocution, the Conservatory engaged Robert Gill, the artistic director of Hart House Theatre, to give a thirty-week course in drama, beginning in October 1950. The outcome was that two plays were produced, *Craig's Wife* and *The Young and Fair*, each for two nights the following April.

The wishes of the Conservatory and the Faculty of Music to reorganize went as far back as the 1937 Hutcheson Survey. The key person in the events that followed the formation of Sidney Smith's reorganization committee in 1949 was Edward Johnson. His retirement from the Met in 1950 allowed him to spend more time in Guelph and Toronto. Johnson was impressive. He had handsome features, snow-white hair, and an erect carriage that made him look taller than his five feet, seven inches; he spoke well and had irresistible charm. Johnson had kept the Met afloat without compromising its artistic standards during the difficult years of the Great Depression and the Second World War. Now in his seventies, he was determined to develop Canadian music and generate opportunities for gifted musicians in Canada, opportunities he had missed when he was young.

The reorganization committee first wanted to survey leading music schools in the U.S. to see what might be applicable to the Conservatory. Accordingly, the committee assigned Ettore Mazzoleni and Secretary-Treasurer Roy Loken to visit Eastman, New England, Yale, Princeton, Juilliard, Manhattan, and Peabody in early 1950.[291] Mazzoleni already knew Eastman well: he had received an honorary doctorate of music from the school in 1949, which had elevated his prestige considerably. (Some wry observers said that he changed the sign on his office door to include "Dr." as soon as he returned from the ceremony and that he insisted everyone, henceforth, address him as "doctor.") Howard Hanson, who had presented the degree, described him in his citation as an "able administrator, gifted conductor, friend of American as well as Canadian culture, pioneer in the arts of the new world."[292]

In any event, the reorganization committee moved ahead slowly. An exasperated Johnson wrote Smith on June 25, 1951, that he was losing his enthusiasm and patience, as no real progress had been made. Thereupon Smith took matters in hand and put the committee to work. In October

Edward Johnson (right) with impresario Sol Hurok (left) and tenor Jan Peerce (centre), c. 1935.

1951, it tentatively decided on a single new college of music with two divisions — the Royal Conservatory of Music and the Faculty of Music. The Senior School and the licentiate diploma program — which would be a teachers' diploma — would become part of the Faculty of Music, thus assuring provincial funding for its students and University control of its standards. The Opera School would remain with the Conservatory because its flexible admission policies did not require attendance in the Senior School. Besides, Walter felt that the complexities of operatic training did not suit the Faculty of Music, at least for the time being. The Conservatory would continue to manage its examination system and award its associateship (ARCT). And there would be more flexibility in selecting teachers for the artist and licentiate courses.

The Conservatory and the Faculty of Music would each be headed by an assistant dean reporting to a full-time rector in charge of both. Walter was the obvious choice to head the enlarged Faculty of Music, especially since MacMillan had agreed to give up his post as dean once the reorganization was completed. Some insiders wondered if the position of rector was proposed to prevent Walter from becoming the top dog.

After the New Year, rumours about the deanship — the title of rector had been dropped — flew thick and fast, the most persistent one being that Mazzoleni, MacMillan's choice, would *not* get the job. Smith and Johnson, aware of MacMillan's partisanship, steered clear of him during the winter of 1951–52. Mazzoleni was, as we know, MacMillan's brother-in-law, and both men were deeply concerned about Mazzoleni's pianist wife, Winifred, who was dying of cancer. Neither Smith nor Johnson wanted Mazzoleni *or* Walter as dean, since either choice would invite conflict; it was common knowledge that there was no love lost between them. There were also doubts about Mazzoleni's administrative ability and his interest in musical education. Then, too, Johnson was wary of the MacMillan/Mazzoleni alliance and its effect on his power as chairman. Johnson, who had a sizeable ego, was jealous of MacMillan's importance in Canadian musical life. In fact, some said that he was still smarting over not having been knighted with or instead of MacMillan in 1935.

Reorganization plans now moved ahead. On January 30, 1952, the Conservatory board formally approved a college of music divided into two parts. There was some discussion about naming the college, and whether the designation "Royal" was "too good" to be relegated to a division of the college. The outcome? The college was newly named the Royal Conservatory of Music, with two divisions, the Faculty of Music and the School of Music.[293]

The RCM board then wrote full details of the reorganization to the board of governors for its meeting the very next day, February 28. The minutes state, "Johnson spoke very impressively of the future of music at the University and the Conservatory, and expressed the need and desirability of the proposed reorganization which would result in tremendous development." There would be one board to supervise all musical activities at the University, one budget, an academic council with representatives from both divisions, and one dean to oversee the policies of the two divisions. Also suggested was the appointment of a supervisor of graduate studies in music. The Opera School would be attached to the School of Music but would be financed from a different budget. The examination department would be attached to the School of Music but would issue certificates in the name of the Royal Conservatory of Music *and* the University of Toronto. The governors closed their meeting by accepting the plan in principle. They left it to the president and the Conservatory chairman to work out the details, and ruled that the new structure would take effect on July 1, 1952. It was all very tidy, but was it necessary? And would it work?

Still to be decided was who would head each division and who would be head of both. Walter seemed destined to head the Faculty of Music, but what of the other two positions? Then rumours spread, with reason, that the new dean would be none other than Edward Johnson. MacMillan, hearing this, promptly wrote to Smith on March 6 expressing his concern over the way things were going. He said that he was "in the dark as to what solution is contemplated." He also implied that he would not necessarily step down as dean if dissatisfied with his successor. Smith headed him off at the pass by writing him the very next day saying that "questions relating to personnel have not been settled" and pointedly reminded MacMillan, the conductor of the TSO and the Mendelssohn Choir, that "the success of the reorganization will be better assured by men who can give their full time to teaching and administration." Smith, master mediator that he was, continued, "I have been hoping that we could find for you in the Graduate School a position that would not take too much of your time but, on the other hand, would enable us to promote and develop our graduate work in the field of music, for which you would have direct responsibility." Smith promised to meet with him "once the personnel situation becomes clear."

MacMillan, unconvinced, then wrote Smith, "I hope that I may assume that no irrevocable decisions will be taken without my knowledge."[294] Sir Ernest MacMillan, so used to being at the centre if not in command of musical happenings at the University and elsewhere, may have suspected that Johnson had outmanoeuvred him and that his power was slipping away. MacMillan concluded by turning down Smith's offer to head graduate studies and then petulantly warned him not to depend on him in further reorganization plans.

Mazzoleni also wrote Smith the same day, saying that he could not sign teachers' contracts for next year until he was given "a full and clear explanation of the reorganization plan," which he would then relate to the entire faculty. It was his way of pressing Smith, who was wavering about appointing the seventy-three-year-old Johnson as dean. MacMillan, feeling certain that Johnson was the candidate, protested, and offered to stay another year until an appropriate appointment was made.[295] Needless to say, neither Smith nor Johnson wanted this.

Smith, Johnson, and MacMillan finally met on March 29. Johnson declined the dean's position, but, when MacMillan proposed postponing the reorganization for a year and appointing Mazzoleni as acting dean in the interim, Johnson and Smith turned him down.[296] Smith wrote Mazzoleni with finality on April 3, telling him that he would be principal of the new School of Music, effective July 1, and at no change in salary.

125

Winifred MacMillan Mazzoleni died on April 7. She was only forty-nine. Two evenings later, following the funeral, MacMillan led the TSO and the Mendelssohn Choir in his annual *St. Matthew Passion*. Three days later, MacMillan, in a dark mood, told Smith that he would not voluntarily resign "without being made aware of the full details of the proposed setup.... I hope that I am not going to be put into the somewhat embarrassing position of being asked to resign, but matters seem to be drifting in that direction."[297] Smith, looking to placate MacMillan, repeated his offer that MacMillan be head of graduate studies and added that he be dean emeritus of music as of July 1, 1952.[298]

A few days later, in an open letter to the Faculty of Music, MacMillan announced that he would be leaving on June 30 and went on to describe the reorganization and the forthcoming appointments of Mazzoleni and Walter.[299] Smith, after reading it, sent a more temperate and encouraging statement to the Faculty about the proposed reorganization, but failed to mention who would be the new dean. In fact it carelessly suggested that there would not be a dean — at least for a while — and that Mazzoleni and Walter would each head a division. This could mean that the two might do battle with one another without an umpire.

Mazzoleni, feeling more confident, wrote Johnson, declining to accept his new appointment as it stood, and then dispatched a letter to the Conservatory staff informing them of the reorganization and that he and Walter had each been asked to lead a department. He made no mention of a dean appointment.[300] Assuming that there would be no dean was presumptuous, if not downright silly, but Mazzoleni decided to ride with it and incited the Conservatory teachers sufficiently that they called a meeting of protest on Sunday, April 27. A substantial number attended, not so much out of affection for Mazzoleni, although he had many supporters, but more because they feared "the Prussian." Then the fracas hit the press, and MacMillan issued a lengthy statement explaining his position and why he supported Mazzoleni. One front-page story carried the headline, "MacMillan Retires, Mazzoleni Resigns, Discord Rocks Royal Conservatory."[301] The next night, a standing ovation and the dazzle of flash cameras greeted Mazzoleni at Massey Hall when he came on stage to conduct the Conservatory Orchestra and chorus in Godfrey Ridout's new oratorio *Esther*.

University Board of Governors Chairman Colonel Phillips brushed off a reporter's query about the controversy by snapping, "A tempest in a teapot."[302] He was right. On May 1, the Conservatory board called a teachers' meeting and officially announced the reorganization plans and the appointment of Chairman Johnson as unpaid coordinator until a dean was chosen.[303] John Weinzweig, vice-chairman of the Conservatory Faculty Association, the closest thing there was to a teachers' protective group, was in the chair, and, thanks to him, the Conservatory teachers took the news calmly.[304] Weinzweig was appointed to the Faculty of Music later that spring. Many teachers were apprehensive about offending the administration, and when they spoke to the press they requested anonymity. It didn't occur to teachers that they might have been consulted during the reorganization deliberations. This lack of respect and concern for teachers' views underlined the anomalous relationship between Conservatory teachers and their leaders. Legally, however, one could say that since they were only on one-year contracts they were not employees and, therefore, should not have a say in determining the school's policies or future.

Mazzoleni, concerned about his two motherless daughters, since he had no financial resources and no other job to go to, caved in and withdrew his resignation on May 6. The next morning MacMillan opened his *Globe and Mail* to read this news and to learn that Mazzoleni fully supported the reorganization and Johnson's role as interim coordinator. MacMillan, expecting Mazzoleni to hold to his resignation, was shocked. Their relationship cooled forever, although they kept up appearances in public and at family gatherings.[305]

Unquestionably, the Faculty of Music was strengthened by the addition of the Senior School. But the School of Music saw no change: it continued as a collective, and its commission system prevailed, as did its haphazard instruction program. There was still no properly structured course of study for talented young pre-university students. Thus the two divisions went their own ways, even more so than before. Faculty professors spoke of their school as the Faculty of Music, not the Royal Conservatory. Performance teachers waltzed between the Faculty and the School, eager to collect fees from both sources. Walter eventually dealt with the University directly on budgetary matters.

Problems persisted in the years following the reorganization. As for the beleaguered MacMillan in that unhappy spring of 1952, he lost his control of the Faculty of Music and, by extension, the Conservatory. To make matters worse, he had to cope with the "Symphony Six" problem — six of his TSO players were denied entry to the United States. The TSO fired them rather than cancel its short tour of Michigan. MacMillan's judgment was clouded in this issue, as it had been during the reorganization negotiations.[306]

Chapter Six

A DECADE OF WIDENING HORIZONS

I joined the Conservatory staff in September 1952 as director of the Concert and Placement Bureau and of the publicity department. The two had been merged, since their functions overlapped. Edward Johnson, Roy Loken, and Arnold Walter engaged me after a brief interview. I met Mazzoleni later the same day; he had probably been informed of the interview. I will never know whether he supported my appointment, for, although we got along well over the years, he was usually a bit aloof with me. On the other hand, Walter took to me from the outset, confided in me on many issues, and did much for my career.

I was overwhelmed to meet Johnson. As a native New Yorker, I had grown up with "Edward Johnson of the Metropolitan Opera," and had admired how he made the Met a truly American opera house, with American singers in leading roles. Now, here I was sitting in the same office with him! It was almost like a dream. We hit it off from the moment we met. It was the first time I had been close to a larger than life personality, and I relished it, especially since Johnson treated me with respect and some affection until his death. He would do much for the Conservatory in the next few years by presenting special programs of all kinds, usually with his own money, and he confidently entrusted me to administer them.

My new position was quite a change. I had been a professor and conductor for four years at two American universities, the University of Massachusetts in Amherst and Western Reserve University in Cleveland, and, although I had done some organizational work at both schools, administration, concert promotion, and publicity were new to me. Within days a number of students and faculty visited me about finding engagements. There was, first, tenor Jon Vickers. He was of average height, burly, barrel-chest-ed, muscular, and slightly bow-legged, and had a clamorous presence. Another visitor was James Milligan, a towering six-foot-four baritone with an imposing physique to go with his voice. I was most thrilled to meet Lois Marshall, especially since I had heard her sing on previous trips to Toronto and cherished her unique voice. For pianists there was Ray Dudley, modest and friendly and basking in the glory of having just won the Geneva International Competition on October 5. And, finally, there was Glenn Gould, who came shuffling into my office, unannounced, to size me up and see what I knew. He had heard about me, since I was playing clarinet at the CBC, and invited me to play in the Anton Webern Op. 22 Quartet sponsored by New Music Associates, a group he ran with his friend Robert Fulford. Naturally, I said yes, for I had already heard about Glenn Gould and his extraordinary musicianship. The performance went well. We had lots of laughs together — he had trouble doing triplets — and later, very informally, we read through the two Brahms sonatas for clarinet and piano. He played the rapid movements too slowly and the slow movements too rapidly for my taste. His idiosyncrasies, musical and otherwise, never bothered me. A friendship began that lasted until 1961 and resumed in 1980.

Johnson had engaged three senior people that autumn to teach at the school: Ernesto Barbini, Irene Jessner, and Gina Cigna.[307] Barbini, who had directed an opera workshop at the Conservatory's 1947 Summer School and had been a coach and assistant conductor at the Met for some years, was tiring of New York and wanted to continue to work for Johnson. (I always enjoyed hearing them converse in Italian, in which Johnson was fluent.) Barbini was now in his mid-forties and, although he had been in North America since 1938, still spoke fractured English with a heavy Italian accent. He was short and dark and volatile; he was once instructed by the musicians' union to apologize to a clarinetist in the opera orchestra for cursing him out, albeit in Italian. Barbini was a great asset to the Opera School and soon was conducting opera festival and school productions. He also formed a "Collegium Musicum," a string orchestra of advanced students and professionals that played engagements from time to time in Toronto and other nearby locations.

Irene Jessner, born, raised, and trained in Vienna, had been a leading soprano at the Met since 1936. Although she was much respected and sang major roles with the company, Jessner was apparently too nervous on stage to rank with the great sopranos of her time, like Milanov, Steber, Albanese, and Sayão. Johnson wanted her to give an introductory recital for the Toronto public to attract students. It was an agonizing exercise: she hadn't done a full recital program for many years, and her voice was already in decline even though she was only in her early fifties. However, she pulled it off moderately well on February 25, 1953, with Barbini at the piano. Jessner knew little about teaching voice but got better and better at it through the years until she retired in 1986. Among her women pupils were Teresa Stratas, Lilian Sukis, Jean MacPhail, Lois McDonall, Heather Thomson, and Jeannette Zarou. Her male pupils included Maurice Brown, Leonard Bilodeau, and Mark Dubois.

Just as the Conservatory was getting used to two new high-profile teachers, Johnson unveiled still another addition to the voice faculty, the great French/Italian soprano Gina Cigna. In November, complete with flowers, I met her and her husband Mario Ferrari at Union Station, made reservations for them at the Royal York hotel, and entertained them on Johnson's orders for several days until she found a residence. A prima donna of the old school, Cigna, now in her mid-fifties, was both gracious and unassuming. She'd had a distinguished career in Europe, having sung some seventy operatic roles, the most successful ones being Norma, Gioconda, and Turandot. And she was also a *premier prix* graduate of the Paris Conservatory in piano. Cigna did an introductory recital, and she managed to pull it off, too, after much travail. Cigna was relatively unknown in Toronto — she had been with the Met for only two years in the thirties — and, despite intense publicity, failed to attract students. She spoke little English and remained at the Conservatory for just three years before returning to Italy. Two new soprano voice teachers, both of whom received substantial guarantees, may have been too many to introduce in one year. It was a credit to established voice teachers like Lambert and Vinci that so many of their students stayed with them.

I met Boris Berlin in my first days at the Conservatory. We were kindred spirits who loved to get things done, so it was not long before he proposed that I help him revive the Conservatory Summer School. It had been lacklustre for several years and had been cancelled in 1952 because of the reorganization and the turmoil that went with it. Mazzoleni gave Berlin the green light, as did Johnson, and Berlin outlined a program with teachers' refresher courses and master classes in instruments and voice that included pianist Boris Roubakine, concertmaster of the NBC Symphony Mischa Mischakoff, Paris Conservatory cello professor André Lévy, and Cigna. Barbini would do an opera workshop with orchestra, Charles Peaker would preside over classes in church and organ music and choir training, and the distinguished Austrian composer Ernst Krenek would give a composers' workshop. In addition, classes in examination preparation, private lessons, lectures, and concerts were planned. The Canadian Federation of Music Teachers' Associations was meeting in Toronto two days before the opening of Summer School, and Berlin hoped that delegates would stay on to study at the school.

It was hectic. We prepared a glossy promotional booklet, but the binding was faulty and the booklets fell apart. Berlin's negotiations with some of the teachers were erratic, he worried about everything almost to distraction, and he fought to keep his well-known temper in check. No matter, the school was a success and even made a profit. Krenek made a lasting impression. Few could recall when Toronto had had an internationally known composer who was not of English background teaching at the school, and many young composers flocked to his classes.

Johnson, meanwhile, decided to father what he called a "special events series," principally lectures and chamber concerts by outstanding people in the arts. He felt that the Conservatory needed stimulation, and what better way than to bring stars from elsewhere to Toronto. For 1952–53 he invited Martha Graham, the founder of modern dance, and Virgil Thomson, the American composer and critic, to give lectures, and Alexander Tcherepnin, the Russian pianist/composer, for a lecture/recital. The Toronto dance fraternity turned out in force to hear Graham. She was bone thin, severely dressed, and strikingly beautiful. I couldn't take my eyes off her. I remember hearing chuckles and some derisive sounds from some of the classical dance mavens during Graham's talk, as she illuminated so well what modern dance was all about. It took Toronto some years to catch up with her, if it ever has.

Thomson was a revelation. He was drawing to the end of his term as critic with the *New York Herald-Tribune*, where over the years he had attacked icons such as Toscanini and Koussevitsky and deprecated twentieth-century composers he considered banal or old hat. Thomson told the audience the basics, that "a music reviewer should primarily report the musical life of his community, analyze the music and its execution, and describe it in words, since he is a man of letters. He is expected to know something about his subject since it will give penetration to his judgement and will prevent him from making irresponsible statements." He then addressed the more difficult task of describing the principles behind criticizing new music.[308] It was a fascinating evening.

There were other interesting events in 1952–53. The famed Canadian photographer Yousuf Karsh appeared at the Conservatory in January 1953 with two assistants and a camera to take pictures of the Opera School in action. He also photographed several Conservatory composers at work. Three RCM students won first prizes in CBC competitions that spring: bass-baritone Donald Garrard, "Singing Stars of Tomorrow"; soprano Roma Butler, "Opportunity Knocks"; and violinist Carolyn Gundy, "Nos Futures Etoiles." I published some impressive statistics about the school in the February 1953 *Monthly Bulletin* revealing its growth on all fronts: it was the largest music school in the British Commonwealth, with 7,000 students registered; there were more than 30,000 students taking its annual examinations; 181 pianos were in use; there were twelve branches and branch annexes; approximately $30,000 in scholarship and bursary aid was distributed to students annually; there were 200 teachers and 47 administrative personnel on its staff; that year there were 142 evening events in the concert hall and ninety in the recital hall.

But there still wasn't a dean to head the reorganized Conservatory. Edward Johnson was determined to get someone from England — there were few if any Canadians who seemed likely candidates. He felt that an English dean would create a proper Canadian balance, whatever that might mean, since the Conservatory was now developing along American lines. There is no evidence that he consulted Walter or Mazzoleni. On his shortlist were Boyd Neel, Sir Steuart Wilson, and Robert Irving. Neel, a medical doctor, had made his musical reputation as founder and conductor of the Boyd Neel Orchestra and seemed attracted to Toronto. Wilson, a senior administrator at Covent Garden, was considered too old (he was sixty-three), and Irving, conductor of the Sadler's Wells Ballet Orchestra, didn't appear interested. So Johnson zeroed in on the tall and handsome Neel and invited him to Toronto in April 1953 for interviews. (He had met Neel briefly earlier in the year and had seen him a second time in London.) That was when I met Neel, who seemed pleasant enough. I admired his orchestra, which dated back to the mid-thirties, but found it disconcerting that he had no experience with music schools — as student, teacher, or administrator. Neel asked me what the dean's main job would be. I replied that it would be to keep peace between the two heads and lead a drive to get a new conservatory building.[309]

Although Johnson was only mildly enthusiastic — he hadn't looked long and hard enough and should have had a committee to help him — he nonetheless offered Neel the position, which Neel promptly accepted. Then Johnson changed his mind. He had heard some things about Neel that worried him, mainly to do with his sexual orientation. He felt that a school should have a heterosexual person leading it. Neel didn't back down, and a two-year appointment was confirmed, with four months off each year to allow him to fill other commitments. The University board of governors gave its approval on June 18.

All in all it was a bad start. Neel, not quick to learn how the school functioned, openly admitted that he was at the Conservatory as a mediator, as a figurehead, if you wish, and wasn't interested in interfering with anything Walter or Mazzoleni did in the Faculty or the School, respectively. He met with them weekly to discuss matters of concern, and, according to Neel, these meetings went on amicably for many years.[310] Walter and Mazzoleni accepted Neel, since he was civil and generally let them be. His lack of involvement in the school facilitated his pursuing other interests, such as forming a Canadian version of the Boyd Neel Orchestra. Certainly orchestral musicians and the CBC welcomed him, since there were few Toronto conductors of stature. They hoped that Neel would be an important addition to Toronto's orchestral life. Whatever, the RCM provided him with a sinecure for the next fifteen years.

When he arrived in Toronto to begin work, he was not given an office! Bizarre as this may seem, Johnson had taken over MacMillan's office and obstinately refused to surrender it. Instead, Neel shared space with his — and Johnson's — secretary in Johnson's outer office. After several weeks Neel, rightfully, complained to President Smith, who intervened. This did little to improve relations between Johnson and Neel. The outcome was that Johnson now had to share space with the secretary! Smith also told Johnson to stay out of Neel's way and not interfere with school operations. From then on, Johnson and Neel saw each other as little as possible. In retrospect, Johnson could well have functioned as acting dean for a number of years. In fact, it may have been what he really wanted. As it turned out, he lost much of his interest in the school after Neel's appointment.

One of Neel's first utterances on arriving was to recommend that the school have five hundred students instead of its current eighty-five hundred, without realizing that at least 95 percent of the eighty-five hundred were part-timers taking perhaps one lesson a week, and that twenty-five hundred of these part-timers were studying at the branches. Further, there were two hundred RCM teachers who depended on these students for their livelihood, and few earned anything comparable to Faculty of Music professors, Neel's frame of reference. The School of Music Faculty Association demanded an explanation, which it never got. Neel simply didn't understand that the Conservatory was an amalgam of two departments, each needing his attention and support in different ways. He showed little or no sympathy for RCM teachers who taught by the hour and had only yearly contracts. His comments seemed to condemn them for teaching at a school that hadn't changed for the past sixty-five years. Whose fault was that? Nor was he aware of the importance of the Conservatory in the community.

In the midst of Neel's difficulties the Conservatory had a financial upset. Roy Loken, the affable secretary-treasurer and recently appointed president of the Harris Company, appeared to have gone off the deep end and wildly overspent school funds. Loken, eager and ambitious, wanted to increase the Harris Company's income, and imprudently took several financial shortcuts with RCM funds to implement his plans, including unauthorized travel to conferences and other expenditures. Neel, Walter, Mazzoleni, and especially the University's financial staff had simply failed to supervise him sufficiently.

Alex Rankin, the University comptroller, exposed Loken's mismanagement of funds in a letter to Colonel Phillips, chairman of the University board of governors, on December 9, 1953. Loken's records were in a shambles, there were unexplained bank overdrafts, and there had been no audits or financial reports at the RCM for two years. Loken was way off budget and had used trust money for operational purposes. Fortunately, the damage at the Harris Company was minimal, thanks to general manager Fred Collier, who kept a tight grip on its chequing account. Loken's salary was supposed to be drawn from both Harris and the RCM, and this was badly muddled. The well-intentioned Loken had even hired an assistant manager to help Collier, but he hadn't bothered to ask Collier if he needed or wanted one.

This, however, was only the beginning. Loken had bought fifty-six new Mason and Risch pianos from the T. Eaton Company, trading in forty used ones as part of the deal. The cost was $27,600, and the RCM didn't have the funds. He had also promised the Heintzman Company a purchase of eighty pianos ($58,400) and had ordered two electric organs. Here, however, the alert Conservatory Registrar Frederick Silvester had been able to cancel the organ order just prior to delivery. Rankin's list went on, detailing offences such as the purchase of expensive office equipment and hiring executive staff without clearance from the board.

The infuriated University governors arranged for special grants to get the Conservatory out of what they claimed to be a $70,000 hole, and, at the same time, they resolved to cancel the RCM's arm's-length relationship with the University and take it over completely.[311] They got the provincial legislature to pass the Act of April 6, 1954, which read: "All property, real and personal, and the undertaking, assets, rights, powers, privileges and immunities vested in, owned, held, possessed or enjoyed by the Royal Conservatory of Music of Toronto, are hereby vested in the Governors of the University of Toronto." All Conservatory gifts, trusts, deeds, and the like were now the University's. "The Conservatory shall for all purposes whatsoever be dissolved and its letters patent of incorporation … surrendered." The Conservatory would suffer dearly from this move in the coming decades. The initial cause of it all, Roy Loken, had already left the school and the Harris Company to be director of administration of the Stratford Festival. Rankin was appointed Harris president in his stead. Ironically, the review of financial statements by the auditing firm of Clarkson, Gordon in June 1955 was not as damning as Rankin had claimed. The University and the RCM covered the losses in due course.

The new Act had little immediate impact on College Street. The dean welcomed it, since, after all, it was the University who had engaged him, and *it* had secure finances. Johnson, upset, didn't comment, nor did Walter or Mazzoleni. A new secretary-treasurer, J.F. Brook, was appointed. A functionary, he did whatever the University told him to do, reporting the most minor infractions to his financial superiors at Simcoe Hall. The governors appointed a new Conservatory committee (not a board) with Johnson as chairman; it would have power to recommend to the governors, but not to enact decisions.[312]

Dr. Johnson's Special Events Series in 1953–54 brought two unusual attractions to the school in addition to more standard fare: lute, virginal, and recorder player Suzanne Bloch and the Indian Temple Dancer Shivaram. Bloch's appearance was as interesting and exotic as Martha Graham's of the year before, and Shivaram's was, in a word, extraordinary, especially for Toronto, which knew little in 1953 about Indian dance.

Warm-hearted and skilled Swiss pianist Pierre Souvairan joined the faculty in October 1953, replacing Böszörmènyi-Nagy. Souvairan had studied with Teichmüller in Leipzig, had performed with a number of leading European orchestras, and had taught at the Berne Conservatory. He would be an invaluable member of the school's piano faculty for the next forty-eight years, his recitals and recordings always demonstrating musicianship of a high order. Among his students were Mary-Nan Dutka, Mari-Elizabeth Morgen, Ralph Elsaesser, Ann Southam, Mary Kenedi, Helena Bowkun, and Philip Thomson.

The new RCM committee made its first report to the University governors on May 12, 1954. It assigned Neel to extract $5,000 from the Opera Festival — by now it had had four seasons — as "payment in part of the cost of the services rendered by the Opera School to the Association." Believing that a new face might be more effective in dealing with the festival, the committee further empowered Neel to deal with it in the future. The following January, Rankin wrote President Smith that the festival had still not given its "grant."[313] Neel, to his credit and showing rare statesmanship, then explained to Smith that the festival was still strapped for funds. "The continuance of this Festival is vitally essential for the future of our Opera School, so that I am afraid we shall have to exercise our clemency for some time yet to come. I see no solution at the moment of this extremely delicate situation."

The committee, urged on by Rankin, had been mean-spirited in the first instance to ask the festival for money. An equally thoughtless recommendation made at this same May meeting was to cut Mazzoleni's salary from $12,000 to $9,000 to match Walter's salary. Neel objected, but to no avail. One wonders why Johnson supported these recommendations. The committee's ambivalent and enigmatic behaviour seemed to be the order of the day.

There were more cheerful events in 1954. Conservatory students made an almost clean sweep of CBC competitions: James Milligan, "Singing Stars of Tomorrow"; coloratura soprano Lesia Zubrack, "Opportunity Knocks"; and contralto Joan Maxwell and bass-baritone Donald Garrard, "Nos Futures Etoiles." The Summer School looked at least as promising as the previous year's, with a faculty that included violinist Alexander Schneider, retired tenor from the Metropolitan Opera Frederick Jagel, composer Alan Rawsthorne, and clarinetist David Weber. Schneider, especially, was a great success. The students loved his playing, his teaching, and his uninhibited personality. Asked back for the 1955 Summer School, he combined his teaching with performing in Stravinsky's *L'Histoire du Soldat* at the Stratford Festival's third season. The 1955 Summer School also had an opera workshop and several visiting faculty members: Danish tenor Aksel Schiotz, cellist Zara Nelsova, saxophonist/clarinetist Alfred Gallodoro, and the distinguished American composer Roy Harris. Harris, like Ernst Krenek two years before, made a strong impression. The school also ran a well-attended master class at Stratford for the first time, featuring the great German soprano Elizabeth Schwarzkopf. The celebrated Schwarzkopf was sympathetic, knowledgeable, and personally enchanting.

Boris Berlin failed to make his teaching guarantee for 1954–55. He claimed that he was so busy running the Summer School that he had to turn down pupils wanting to study with him. The committee seized the opportunity to make Mazzoleni work harder — Johnson, particularly, felt that he didn't have enough to do — and assigned him to direct the 1956 Summer School.[314] I would continue as assistant to handle details when Mazzoleni was examining in June in Western Canada. Berlin would only teach. Visiting teachers were Gordon Jacob (he had practically no students), English baritone and teacher Roy Henderson, Gallodoro (again), and popular trumpeter Rafael Mendez. Classes at Stratford included a success and a failure. The success was the Chilean pianist Claudio Arrau, whose ten-day master class attracted twenty-seven students; the failure was the fine Swedish soprano Inge Borkh, who attracted only one. Arrau agreed to a smaller fee than usual because he was also a soloist with Neel's Hart House Orchestra at Stratford. Teachers' courses and private lessons were also given, as usual, in the non-air-conditioned College Street building. Toronto summers seemed to be getting hotter.

Mazzoleni summed up the dilemma of the Summer School to Neel in November 1956.[315] Enrolment was declining in teachers' courses, and master classes were a mixed bag. Any good summer school with master classes can only be a deficit operation, and Mazzoleni knew full well that the University, which held the purse strings, would never agree to this. He suggested as an alternative that the Summer School be held in a resort or festival location. Finally, he asked for an "acting director," since he, the principal, was too busy to give the Summer School the attention it deserved. Neel brought these concerns before the committee on December 14, 1956.

The committee, irritated that Mazzoleni — and Neel — had done nothing to plan the 1957 Summer School, instructed Neel to tell Mazzoleni to get on with 1957 and start planning the 1958 Summer School. Neel did take one of Mazzoleni's suggestions to heart and investigated possible loca-

Elizabeth Schwarzkopf, Stratford Summer School, 1955.

tions outside of Toronto: Kingsmere, MacKenzie King's old residence near Ottawa; St. Andrew's College, Aurora; and Glenhyrst, Brantford. None of them, according to Neel, was suitable. What was needed was a real commitment and know-how to develop a summer operation like some in the U.S., and neither Mazzoleni nor Neel had such a commitment, for whatever reasons.

Neel, however, had committed himself to something much closer to his heart: the creation of a new Hart House Orchestra. Towards the end of his first year at the school, he organized an eighteen-piece string orchestra made up of some of the best players in the city. The Concert and Placement Bureau helped by booking it for concerts in Ontario centres, on the CBC, and at the Stratford Festival for its 1955 season, where a number of top soloists performed with it: Schwarzkopf, Lois Marshall, Glenn Gould, Isaac Stern, and Zara Nelsova. Louis Applebaum, who

Pierre Souvairan, Summer School class for teachers, 1959.

was head of music at Stratford and composed music for the Shakespeare plays, had hopes that Neel and his orchestra would become a resident group from which a summer music festival could take root. Sadly, Neel was a disappointment. Although he had a fine sense of tempi and an ear for balance, he could not take the orchestra beyond clean but routine performances. If five hours of rehearsal were allotted he would finish in three or four, not understanding that rehearsing means more than getting the right notes. And Neel had a limited repertoire, although, admittedly, he did learn scores quickly. All in all, he was a talented amateur.

Nor was Neel the local conductor of stature the CBC, the TSO, and the Opera Festival were looking for. He did occasional guest appearances with these groups, but they were few and far between. His orchestra members liked him, for he was always friendly and reasonable and didn't push them too hard.

From time to time, he would spell Mazzoleni and conduct the Conservatory Orchestra. However, Mazzoleni left more of a mark on the group than did Neel.

The Concert and Placement Bureau was of special interest to Neel, since it managed his Hart House Orchestra. In February 1955 he proposed that the Conservatory committee fund an expanded bureau ($16,800), including the addition of a travelling representative to the staff. He didn't tell the committee that he had earmarked the post for his English secretary/manager.[316] The committee turned down his expansion plans but did allot $2,100 towards the travelling representative's fee, which would, in total, come to $4,000. Neel hoped that this appointment would lead to more engagements for the orchestra, but the representative stayed only a few months before he moved on to a concert management post in New York. However, the orchestra remained tied to the bureau until 1960. It represented Canada on Canada Day at the 1958 Brussels World's Fair, along with the Montreal Bach Choir conducted by George Little. The orchestra's soloists were Glenn Gould, who had done his remarkable tour of the Soviet Union the year before, and soprano Marguerite Lavergne. Neel shared the conducting with the young Canadian conductor and orchestra member Victor Feldbrill. In the autumn of 1958, Feldbrill took over the conductorship of the Winnipeg Symphony, a post he held for the next eleven seasons.

The 1954–55 season at the RCM began with a special lecture by Ralph Vaughan Williams at Convocation Hall on October 8. Recitals by new faculty members violinist Henri Temianka and baritone Leslie Holmes followed later in the month. Temianka was the first violinist of the internationally renowned Paganini String Quartet. A student of Carl Flesch at Curtis, he had appeared as soloist with major orchestras and had played sonatas with George Szell, Lili Kraus, and Rudolf Firkusny. Short, nervous, and energetic, Temianka was a great raconteur and wrote for leading American journals, not all of them musical. He promised to divide his time between the Quartet and the Conservatory. However, the latter made few demands on his time, since the number of serious student violinists at the School and the Faculty had inexplicably declined in the fifties. It was also true that a number of young violinists were already committed to studying with Alexander Schneider, thanks to his Summer School visits, and they did not hesitate to travel to New York for lessons.

To help consolidate his position, Temianka arranged for a bright young American pianist, Leonard Pennario, to join him in giving all of Beethoven's piano and violin sonatas in the concert hall over three nights at the end of April 1955. Pennario's playing was actually more impressive than Temianka's, who had persistent pitch problems. The pair also seemed under-rehearsed at times —

Temianka never liked to rehearse. The cycle was probably a "first" for Toronto. Pennario coupled his visit with a week of moderately successful master classes.

Neel had engaged Temianka completely on his own, much as Johnson had done with Jessner and Cigna three years before. It was clearly not a propitious time for such an appointment. With or without consultation — I'm not sure — Neel next appointed the Polish pianist Alexander Uninsky in September 1955. Uninsky had won the very prestigious Chopin Prize in his youth, but his career had never really taken off. His Toronto stay was no more successful than Temianka's, and they both left within two years. Leslie Holmes stayed on. He had taught at the school years before, and this was a sort of homecoming.

Sadly, the much-loved Emmy Heim died on October 13, 1955, so Holmes's appointment filled the gap she left in the voice department. Heim's teaching, coaching, and lieder classes are still lauded

Emmy Heim gives a lieder class, 1953.

by those who studied with her. Sir Ernest MacMillan wrote eloquently in the *Monthly Bulletin*, shortly after her death: "She loved to teach, she loved to talk with her friends, and she loved to live." He marvelled at how "she conscientiously made every note in a song 'a matter of special study' and every little phrase 'a miracle', and how she covered such a wide range of moods."[317]

A major event of 1955 was the Vegh Quartet's week-long series of performances of all of the Beethoven string quartets — it was called a Beethoven cycle. String quartet enthusiasts said it was the first time this cycle had ever been done in Toronto. The Vegh, a rough and ready Hungarian group, lacked finesse but made up for it in energy and style. Beethoven's quartets came vividly to life in their hands, and all six nights were sold out. This set a pattern, over the next few years, for other international quartets to play at the Conservatory for several consecutive nights to devoted and capacity audiences. The Vegh's appearances also gave local quartets the proverbial shot in the arm; groups like the Parlow moved ahead more determinedly than in the past. There was an amusing incident at one of the Vegh concerts. Midway through one of the movements, two bats flew high over the heads of the rapt audience, which gave a collective shudder but did not utter a sound. The musicians were totally unaware of the "bats in the belfry."

The 1955 Opera School production at Hart House Theatre of Menotti's *Amahl and the Night Visitors* was, to nearly everyone's surprise, a great hit. It ran as a Christmas event and was co-sponsored by the Junior League of Toronto. The young women happily collaborated with the Conservatory to help fill the houses. *Amahl*'s melodies and verses charmed the young — and the young at heart — as did its excellent costumes and sets. Earlier in the year the school had given two other Menotti operas, *The Telephone* and *The Medium*. Lesia Zubrack and Robert Goulet played the two roles in *The Telephone*, Goulet revealing an attractive voice and a natural flair for the stage. Some opera watchers criticized the school for performing too much Menotti. (His *Consul* had played at the 1953 Opera Festival and was repeated the next year.) They complained that his music lacked substance, even if it worked well with the dramatic action.

Conservatory staff and graduates gave a program of Bartók's music on December 1, 1955, on the tenth anniversary of his death. Géza de Kresz and Pierre Souvairan did Bartók's First Sonata for Violin and Piano. De Kresz, who had not played well, said to John Beckwith after the concert, "You do the best you can because you can no longer do it well."[318] It was Géza de Kresz's last public appearance; he suffered a stroke shortly afterwards. He had first come to Canada with his pianist wife, Norah Drewett, at Boris Hambourg's urging in 1923. De Kresz joined the newly formed Hart House Quartet the next year and remained with the group until 1935, when he moved back to Hungary to teach and

Menotti's *Amahl and the Night Visitors*, 1955.

ultimately be appointed director of the National Conservatory in Budapest. De Kresz was a pupil of Jenö Hubay in Budapest, then Otokar Sevcik in Prague, and, finally, Ysaÿe, and he diligently passed on what he learned from these masters to his Canadian students.

Mozart reigned supreme in 1956, as musical establishments, ensembles, and soloists everywhere marked the two-hundredth anniversary of his birth. The Conservatory was no exception. It sponsored the Paganini Quartet in all-Mozart programs in January and February, with local wind players assisting, and the Albeneri Trio, a leading North American group, also in February. And there were other ensemble programs of Mozart's music given over the rest of the year. Sir Thomas Beecham, one of the great Mozart conductors, received an honorary doctorate from the University on March 29. He chose to speak about Mozart and, as expected, was witty, scintillating, and opinionated. The Mendelssohn Choir, Sir Ernest conducting, did Mozart's Mass in C Minor at Massey Hall, with Lois Marshall and Mary Morrison

Boris Hambourg, cello, Géza de Kresz, violin, and Norah Drewett de Kresz, piano, c. 1950.

among the soloists. Arnold Walter wrote a short article "In Praise of Mozart" for the 1956 January/February *Monthly Bulletin*. Typically succinct, he provided the reader with insight into the composer's genius: "Mozart's music is the image of a world of cosmic order, beauty and peace. The generative power of his music has not yet spent itself; it is still alive and fills our hearts with gratitude and gladness." How right he was! The Mozart year brought about a minor renaissance of Mozart's music that continues into the twenty-first century.

The Opera School repeated *Amahl* during the 1956 Christmas season and then did a double bill at Hart House Theatre in April 1957: Act II of Monteverdi's *Coronation of Poppea* and a short opera, *Gianni Schicci*, from Puccini's *Triticco*. John Kraglund of the *Globe and Mail* said that, although it had been more than three hundred years since *Poppea* was written, "there is a contemporary quality in the psychological insight of this forerunner of Italian opera and German music drama." Two singers who were praised by Kraglund would have great operatic careers: soprano Teresa Stratas as Drusilla — she "reached passionate heights" — and bass-baritone Victor Braun — "his voice was rich, round and well controlled."[319] Baritone Bernard

Turgeon played Gianni Schicchi and drew many a laugh from the audience. Sung in English, the double bill was well received, especially the Puccini.

Unquestionably, the Opera School's triumph of the decade was in April 1958, when it gave a triple bill of one-act operas at Hart House Theatre. The triumph was not in the first of the three operas, *Marriage by Lantern* of Jacques Offenbach, a lusty comedy that came off well despite its thin dramatic material. Nor was it in Paul Hindemith's *There and Back*, an ingenious comedy in which the action reaches a midway point where husband and wife both die — he murders her, then jumps out of the window — only to go into reverse and work back to the beginning. Amusing but disquieting, it is typical of Hindemith's compositions in 1920s Germany.

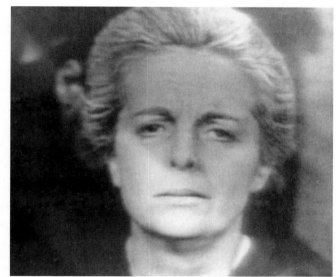

Yes, these two operas were extremely well done, but the greatest moments were yet to come with Vaughan Williams's *Riders to the Sea*, based on the Synge play of the same name. William Krehm of the CBC, an astute and articulate critic, said on his radio program "CJBC Views the Shows": "It is music so completely wedded to the dramatic situation and the words, that it rakes your innards.... The production was nothing short of a masterpiece." Patricia Rideout was an unforgettable Maurya, "as drab, drained, and battered as any driftwood cast up by the sea. Her walk, her stance, her keening tones curdled the blood in your veins." (I can remember her performance as if it was yesterday.) Krehm went on:

Patricia Rideout, contralto, as Maurya in *Riders to the Sea* (Vaughan Williams), 1958.

Teresa Stratas as the daughter Nora exuded wild forebodings by her very silences. The set was effectively dim and austere, a hut with the sea all but pounding on the door, and the white boards of the coffin portentously to the fore. Ettore Mazzoleni as conductor kept the tension unflagging. It was a stupendous performance. Let no one again be fooled by the modest shingle of the opera school. When you hear of their short productions, drop whatever you happen to be knitting, and queue up at their door.[320]

It should be remembered that these same students were also playing minor roles or singing in the chorus at the annual opera festivals. Few opera schools in the world offered training and experience to match Toronto's. Even though the School had to perform in the dreary Hart House Theatre it fearlessly staged new and significant works. Although Nicholas Goldschmidt left the school in 1957, Torel, Barbini, Mazzoleni, Andrew MacMillan, Mario Bernardi, and an experienced staging crew made going to the Opera School's productions a treat year after year.

Teresa Stratas, soprano, in the 1970s.

The School of Music had been languishing since the 1952 reorganization. In the spring of 1957, mainly due to the urging of teachers and staff, Dean Neel announced that the School would launch special organized courses of study for talented students, which would be a feeding ground for the Faculty of Music. The courses would be given at three levels: junior (Grades II to IV), intermediate (Grades V to VIII), and senior (Grades IX to ARCT). Course students would pay considerably less than if they took lessons and classes separately, and there would be substantial scholarships for those with excellent examination records, unmistakable promise, and high scholastic achievement. Since the School couldn't support the program in full, the newly created Musical Talent Foundation, led by James Duncan of the RCM committee, set out to raise scholarship funds from private, civic, and provincial sources. The Harris Company would also play a major role in funding course students.

The program was a singular achievement. Dr. Mazzoleni, with considerable pleasure, commented in March 1958 on the results of the program's first year. There were fifty-two places, for which two hundred auditioned. The senior course had thirty-nine students — twenty piano, twelve voice, five strings, and two composition. The intermediate course had nine students, and the junior, four. Mazzoleni recommended expanding the program if more scholarship support could be found. This was done. These special preparatory courses continued in various guises and with varying degrees of efficiency for years to come.

The Orff Method for introducing young children to music was launched at the School by Arnold Walter in 1956. Doreen Hall, an RCM graduate in violin, studied it in Salzburg in 1954–55 and then returned home to teach it. Walter had been instrumental in obtaining the funds for Hall to go to Austria, and he worked with her in preparing an English text, *Music for Children*, for Orff Method students. The composer Carl Orff, with Gunild Keetman, had created the Orff Schulwerk before the war. Music teachers soon flocked to the RCM to study Orff, much to the credit of Hall and her colleagues. Lois Birkenshaw-Fleming has succinctly described the Schulwerk:

> The Orff approach is based on the world of the child — a world of movement, songs, games, rhythms, chants, dances, and stories. These are often accompanied by sound gestures such as hand clapping, finger snapping, and stamping, and also by playing small instruments especially designed for the Orff approach. These instruments, which are extremely well made, sound beautiful and include hand drums, triangles, rhythm sticks, xylophones, glockenspiels, and metallophones.[321]

The Conservatory further honoured Orff by giving the Canadian premiere of his secular cantata *Carmina Burana* on February 9, 1958, at Convocation Hall. Mazzoleni conducted the orchestra and chorus admirably, and, as George Kidd of the *Telegram* said, it was "undoubtedly the most exciting and interesting thing [Mazzoleni] has done … and full credit for the evening's success must be given to him."[322] Kraglund of the *Globe and Mail* admitted grudgingly that "we were in for a very pleasant surprise, for this was a very good performance."[323] The lusty text and Orff's unsentimental and rhythmic score rather shocked the staid Toronto audience, but the exuberant applause at its conclusion spoke to its success. The three student soloists, soprano Barbara Strathdee, tenor Brian Beaton, and baritone Donald Young, handled their difficult parts well. The RCM, be it opera or symphony or chorus, was becoming something of a centre for new and little heard music. The next year Mazzoleni did Michael Tippett's oratorio, *A Child of our Time*, but with less success. The work is only mildly convincing, despite its moving theme — a young German-Jewish refugee, in despair on hearing reports of the Nazi's treatment of his mother, kills a German diplomat (the provocation for the infamous Kristallnacht).

There were other bright spots. The RCM Concert and Placement Bureau thrived throughout the fifties, arranging concerts and tours from British Columbia to Newfoundland for its student groups, the Opera School, staff chamber organizations (Neel's Hart House Orchestra and Ernest Barbini's group), and individuals such as Jon Vickers, James Milligan, Ray Dudley, Malcolm Troup, and Betty Jean Hagen. It had a clear mission: to find Canadian concert outlets for Canadian artists as an alternative to their going abroad. The bureau produced a weekly half-hour radio program on CFRB beginning in 1958 and continued its regular art gallery and CNE concerts. It assisted the CBC, the TSO, the Stratford Festival, and orchestras and choirs across the country by recommending qualified students and graduates to perform with them. No job was too small for the bureau — it also arranged soloists for club meetings, banquets, conferences, and churches.

The bureau had a major rival, Community Concerts, a group run by Columbia Concerts Management in New York City. This competitor had developed a scheme whereby music clubs presenting yearly concert series would first raise money annually by selling subscriptions, and only then would Community Concerts help them choose the artists whose costs would match the money raised. Of course, only Columbia artists were engaged. It was a difficult system to beat: Columbia had many well-known soloists and groups on its roster, nearly all American or U.S.–based, and booking them was uncomplicated. They would usually play at several community concert clubs in the same area, thereby keeping their fees lower. With the door to many communities closed, the bureau, using cultural nationalism as its weapon, developed, with some success, contacts with less affluent but independent music clubs interested in presenting Canadian artists. The creation of the Canada Council in 1957 helped bring the needs of Canadian artists to the forefront. Developing performing opportunities for RCM musicians led to more concerts. By extension, this enhanced the RCM's reputation as a breeding ground for the artists of the future.

A number of other string quartets — including Parlow, Budapest, Quartetto Italiano, Amadeus, and Hollywood — played on the annual special events series until 1960. There were soloists such as lutenist Julian Bream, in his first appearance in North America; tenor Peter Pears; and oboist Leon Goossens, who replaced horn player Dennis Brain after Brain was killed in an auto accident in November 1957. Also appearing were the Philadelphia Woodwind Quintet, pianist Denis Matthews, harpsichordist Ralph Kirkpatrick, French baritone Gérard Souzay, flutist Jean-Pierre Rampal and harpsichordist Robert Veyron-Lacroix in a joint recital, the great Hungarian violinist Joseph Szigeti, the French soprano Suzanne Danco, and prominent speakers from Canada and abroad.

There were several appointments at the Conservatory in 1958. Aksel Schiotz, who had taught at Summer School, joined the staff, as did Elemer Nagy, an operatic stage director. Schiotz's very promising career as a tenor had been cut short just after the war because of a brain tumour, but he continued to sing as a high baritone, with mixed results. Saxophone was finally given its due when Paul Brodie, a concert saxophonist, joined the woodwind teaching staff. Brodie, who had studied with two fine saxophonists, Larry Teal in Michigan and Marcel Mule in Paris, would do excellent work at the RCM for the next decade. Another instrument that had been given short shrift at the Conservatory was the classical guitar. Adding the Viennese-born Eli Kassner to the staff changed all of that, for within a few years he had a class comparable to those of other leading schools on the continent, both in numbers and quality.

The Conservatory mourned the passing of four of its prominent people in 1959–60. Edward Johnson died on April 20. He was eighty-one. People came from all parts of North America to attend his funeral in Guelph. Arnold Walter wrote in the September/October *Monthly Bulletin*:

> He was buried with great honours. The Prime Minister led the procession. A distinguished throng of high officials, artists, educators, and men of affairs paid him their last respects. He always reminded me of men like Benedetto Marcello or Agostino Steffani, famous musicians in their day but also diplomats and courtiers and adventurers. Next to life itself he loved singing. I remember him saying a few years ago, that he would cheerfully sell his soul to the Devil if he could once more sing as he sang in his youth — a most un-Christian remark, but very human and revealing; the operatic stage meant more to him than all the riches of this earth.

To honour Johnson the Conservatory Symphony played Elgar's *Nimrod* from the *Enigma Variations* at their concert on April 26.

Just six months later Géza de Kresz died. Ettore Mazzoleni wrote:

> On the morning of October 2, just a few hours after the conductor and members of the Philharmonia Hungarica had paid a moving tribute in Massey Hall to their illustrious compatriot ... came word of his passing. It was a heartfelt tribute, warm with the esteem in which he was held throughout the

musical world. What an insatiable enthusiasm he had for music and music making.... He was of vital temperament, full of zest for life, and completely selfless where music and those he admired were concerned.[324]

Then, on November 7, Alberto Guerrero died. Boyd Neel, the third member of the Conservatory's ruling triumvirate, wrote of his playing and teaching skills: "He was a splendid raconteur.... His reading was extensive and he was a real connoisseur of pictures, good food, and wine. An evening at Guerrero's home took one back into the atmosphere of the Proustian salons of the turn of the century."[325] Guerrero had a prodigious memory, spoke several languages, and encouraged his students to do things away from the piano. Several of them turned to composition, including Beckwith, Schafer, Watson Henderson, Gould, Laufer, Mather, and Morawetz.[326] Alas, the Conservatory suffered still another grievous loss on July 23, 1960, when Elie Spivak died. He had been on the RCM faculty for thirty years, first violinist of the Conservatory String Quartet from 1929 to 1942, and concertmaster of the TSO from 1931 until 1948.

Elie Spivak coaching Josephine Chuchman and Walter Prystawski, 1953.

Chapter Seven

BUILDINGS OLD AND NEW

The University of Toronto had begun planning new buildings well before the end of the Second World War. As already noted, the University had A.S. Mathers of the Mathers & Haldenby architectural firm prepare a submission for a new building, which the TCM board reviewed on October 21, 1943. A year later the TCM board prepared a short unsigned brief for President Cody stating why a new building was needed: the present one was too small, the building itself was obsolete, maintenance and repair costs were getting out of hand, the building was unsafe to the point of putting the public at risk, and anticipated expansion would be impossible in the existing premises.[327]

Twelve years went by. Then, in 1956, James Duncan of the Conservatory committee visited Juilliard at President Smith's request and reviewed its budget. He reported that Juilliard's top salaries were far higher than the RCM's and that the RCM was not overstaffed administratively. However, he pointedly supported Dr. Johnson, who had stated that the RCM dean and principal "devote but a portion of their time to the job. Our existing executive staff is not working hard enough."[328] More important, Duncan suggested to Smith that the provincial government should allot money "to build a new Conservatory of Music on its present valuable site. Do not delay," wrote Duncan, undoubtedly influenced by his Juilliard visit. Juilliard had a fine building, with ample studios and practice rooms, a theatre, and a recital hall. (It is now the home of the Manhattan School of Music.)

An advisory planning committee had been set up by the University to recommend what buildings were needed and to set priorities. Boyd Neel took the cue and wrote a brief to the committee, stating the case for music.[329] He quoted the five points in the 1944 brief and also cited Smith's two most recent annual reports, both of which gave a *raison d'être* for a new music building. Calling it a "disgrace" that "reconstruction has still to be undertaken," Neel pointed out that Conservatory enrolment had grown to ninety-five hundred (an exaggerated figure), the Opera School didn't have a theatre, and the orchestra had no concert hall. Conservatory expansion without enlarged facilities would thus be impossible, he said. This could be on the present College Street site or, if the land were sold, another option could be a move to Spadina Crescent, the site of the Connaught Laboratories.

The idea percolated. A Conservatory building committee was formed in June 1957 to determine space requirements. Its work became more urgent when it found that Ontario Hydro, through its chairman the same James Duncan, had offered $1,750,000 for the College Street site.[330] After some toing and froing the final price was set at $2,500,000, an amount roughly estimated to be 35 to 40 percent lower than its actual value.[331] Then Neel raised a pertinent question: who and what would be housed in the new Conservatory? He thought the new building should be the home of "the higher diploma courses of the School of Music," along with, naturally, the Faculty of Music and the Opera School. As for the casual students — this time he cited six thousand, down thirty-five hundred from his earlier figure — he said brashly that they could be sent off to the branches.[332]

Luckily, Neel's views were not publicized. In May 1958 the University's advisory planning committee recommended that the new building be on Queen's Park south of the Royal Ontario Museum and that the Law Faculty, which was also looking for new quarters, be sent to Spadina Crescent.[333] However, Colonel Phillips thought the Conservatory's plans too extravagant and did a *volte-face*. The governors, accordingly, decreed — the best word for this action — "that the discussions with the architect regarding plans for a new building on the Queen's Park site be discontinued" and that the Conservatory building committee examine the Connaught Laboratories "to see whether the present Conservatory facilities might be housed therein." Unbelievable? Yes, but such was the disrespect Colonel Phillips and his fellow governors had for the Conservatory and for music study.

But now there was new blood in the top echelons of the University. Claude Bissell, the president of Carleton University and before that Sidney Smith's assistant, was appointed president of the University of Toronto. He took the reins on July 1, 1958, and was formally installed in October. Now the University had a president who was a distinguished scholar, understood and loved music, and even had a brother, Keith, who was a prominent school music teacher and a nationally known composer. He was also an academic elitist who used the great American Ivy League universities as models for Toronto's programs — including music programs. During his years as president he would bring the University's libraries and its graduate school to a top position among North American universities.

Boyd Neel and Claude Bissell, 1959.

On December 18 Bissell wrote Neel a detailed memorandum about the Conservatory that would ultimately determine its future for the next thirty years. He explained that the problems of the RCM were "deeply imbedded" in its history. "The present organization grew out of an institution that even by 1919, when it was handed over to the University, was outmoded." It was a "commercial enterprise" that nonetheless "established itself as a central and important institution on the Canadian scene. There is a mystique about the Conservatory which is powerful and will be difficult to dissipate … a national symbol, in the same category with the mounted police." Bissell went on to say that without minimizing the accomplishments of the Conservatory — it had raised the level of music education in Canada through its examination system — the Faculty of Music was imposed on it, and although the reorganization of 1952 was "bold" it did not go far enough. It was a "forced relationship of two activities that are not bound together necessarily either by administrative practice or by theoretical need."

Bissell noted that the Conservatory made money; the Faculty of Music did not. Then Bissell said, deprecatingly, that it was manned entirely by part-time instructional staff who depended on individual lesson fees for a livelihood. (Bissell's "part-time" was not entirely accurate. He meant that nearly all conservatory teachers taught an undetermined number of hours weekly without a guaranteed salary.) Their economic existence was subject to many hazards. Consequently, "They have a very strong sense of group solidarity and would fight vigorously against any suggestion of encroachment." In another area, Bissell contended that mixing younger part-time Conservatory students with older full-time Faculty students had created problems. In theory the Conservatory fed its best students to the Faculty, but in practice, he noted perspicaciously, Conservatory teachers who didn't teach at the Faculty tried to hold on to their best students.

To summarize, Bissell said, "There is good reason for trying to bring about a greater degree of functional separation, which may also involve physical separation, and certainly a greater degree of financial and administrative distinction." The University would "have to accept additional financial responsibility for the Faculty and appoint more full-time staff, particularly on the performance side." The School of Music, which was essentially the old Conservatory, could then be left as an independent financial unit.

Bissell underscored the need for a physical separation, suggesting that the Faculty change its name to "School" and the present School revert back to "Royal Conservatory." "In the previous reorganization the word 'Conservatory' was retained because of its great emotional impact…. That impact is of a mixed nature, and as long as we retain it, as the over-all name for our work in music, we shall be doomed to misunderstandings and to confusion." How right he was!

Bissell's views were reflected in Neel's report on the reorganization of the RCM in relation to a new building, which he gave to the Conservatory committee a month later.[334] It clearly stated that the new building should house only the Faculty of Music and the Opera School and used the argument that there were insufficient funds for a new building large enough to house the present School of Music as well. However, wherever it may ultimately be located, he went on, the School must remain under the University's control, since its special courses were in part funded by the University and were student feeders to the Faculty.

Neel, after writing about the need for a high school of music (he had recently learned about New York City's twenty-year-old High School of Music and Art), informed the committee that he and Vice-President Murray Ross had visited the Economics Building (the former McMaster Hall) on Bloor Street and, after a "cursory examination," saw it as a "distinct possibility for the School." He described its concert hall and pointed out that the "cafés" on Bloor Street would make a school cafeteria unnecessary. Its parking lot, he said, could be used for Faculty events at its new building, which he hoped would be situated south of the museum. The new building's limited parking space would be a definite drawback, he said. (It still is!) His closing words showed that either he didn't know or he chose to ignore the history of the College Street buildings and site. "The School of Music might, over the years, pay back the outlay required for this particular conversion and, therefore, there might be a modified financial problem" — the cost of converting the Bloor Street building. Wasn't it enough that the University had pulled the rug out from under the Conservatory by almost giving away its building on one of the finest corners in Toronto? To expect the Conservatory to also pay the University for renovations for the Bloor Street Building was simply adding salt to the wounds.

The Canada Council granted close to $1 million to the University for a new music building — this in addition to the monies realized from the College Street sale. Did the School get its fair share of the proceeds? Who had bought College Street and maintained it with scant University help for six decades? For this, as we shall see, the School of Music got a building that was condemned in 1944, reconditioned a few years later, and now again in deplorable condition. It had but two assets: its location on Bloor Street between Bedford Road and Avenue Road and the facade and basic structure of its main building. Years later, when Toronto became more conscious of its history and its buildings, McMaster Hall (the main building only) was identified as an historic site and a pride of the city.

The continuing saga of music's two proposed buildings, one new and one old, was assessed by Luther Noss, dean of the Yale University School of Music, in February 1959.[335] It seems as if Neel and

McMaster University, Toronto.

Turn-of-the-century photo of McMaster Hall (Economics Building).

Bissell might have got to him first, because Noss's report certainly supported their views, albeit the language was altered. Noss wrote that the Faculty of Music should be the central authority for music at the University, that it should work more closely with, and be funded by, the University, and, bluntly, that the School of Music had no place in the University, whatever its contributions to musical education, which, he admitted, were considerable. He did recommend that students in the special courses be under the joint supervision of the Faculty and the School, with Faculty teachers instructing them, and that their classes be held in the Faculty of Music building. This did not happen.

In February 1959 Neel prepared another extensive report on the two buildings for James Duncan, who had succeeded Johnson as chairman of the Conservatory.[336] Duncan, pleased, gave a copy to Bissell a few days later and then called the committee together on March 5 to allocate space for both buildings, even though the sites hadn't been confirmed. The committee decided to cut the total area of the proposed new building by some ten thousand square feet. Then Duncan, with the best of intentions, told the RCM committee on April 7, 1959, that "the new organizational relationship recommended by the President has made it possible to accommodate the Faculty of Music and a multi-purpose auditorium in a considerably smaller new building." Neel did nothing to contradict this as he deserted the sinking ship — the School of Music. The committee thought that a renovated Economics Building would be adequate space-wise for the School unless there was a shortfall in funds. Neel told the entire Conservatory staff on June 16 that the new building would, in fact, be south of the museum, and that the east wing of the Economics Building would be renovated to make it the home of the School of Music. (The east wing had been constructed at the turn of the century and had little architecturally to commend it.) He suggested, cheerfully, that everyone could look forward to many happy years in the Royal Conservatory's new quarters.

A University press release on December 30, 1959, gave more details. The Faculty of Music building, costing $3 million, would have an opera theatre seating eight hundred, a recital hall seating five hundred, two rehearsal halls, an electronic music department, offices, a music library, and teaching and practice studios. The eastern half of the Economics Building would provide quarters for the University's School of Music. The two divisions would be only a few hundred yards apart. Total space for both the Faculty and the School would be more than double the space on College Street, and there would be "a sharper distinction between the work of the Faculty and School." The news release continued with details about the new building, pointing out that Falconer Hall and the president's residence, both of which still blocked its visibility from University Avenue and Queen's Park Crescent, would "eventually be taken down to make way for a garden and a semi-circular driveway." However, this was wishful thinking. The president's house did come down, but Falconer Hall still stands forty years later. The music building is tucked away behind it and shares a narrow driveway with the museum loading dock and a small parking lot with the Faculty of Law.

With the new building underway, the University now turned its attention to the Economics Building. A good part of its main building was committed to University classes, which limited RCM studio space. The concert hall would have about one hundred fewer seats than the College Street concert hall, but there would be more office space in the new quarters. A sub-basement area was designated for a cafeteria. There would be no common room. (The cafeteria, as at College Street, could be the meeting place.) The washrooms were poor and needed modernization. The superintendent of buildings, F.J. Hastie, proposed a freight elevator for moving pianos; he also planned to provide storage areas.[337]

To show how in flux matters were, President Bissell, after receiving warnings about costs from the University comptroller, begged off funding the special courses — let the School support them! — and

The completed Edward Johnson Building, 1962.

expressed doubts about having salaried performance teachers, since they would be more expensive than part-time teachers.[338] Two months later Neel supported Bissell.[339] Walter, not one to give up easily, showed, through a series of tables, that the cost was not as much as Bissell feared.[340] It was to no avail. Only new — and eminent — teachers would be salaried. Generally, performance teachers would be paid as in the past, some with guarantees fixed yearly, depending on the number of students taught the previous year.

The new building was named without sufficient thought. On September 8, 1960, Bissell wrote to Henry Borden, the new chairman of the board of governors, suggesting that the building be named after Edward Johnson.[341] The cornerstone was laid on April 21, 1961, by Fiorenza Drew, Johnson's charming daughter, who came from England for the event. Her husband, George Drew, who was Canadian high commissioner in London, was also present. Bissell, who had been appointed

Edward Johnson's daughter, Fiorenza Drew, laying the cornerstone of the Edward Johnson Building, with her husband, George Drew, looking on.

chairman of the Canada Council the year before, told the assembly about the council grant of $1 million towards its construction. "It will not only serve the University," he went on, but "will become a possession of the nation.... It will take a new place of centrality in the studies of this University." He thought it auspicious that its neighbours were the Faculty of Law to the south and Theology to the east, "for therein we have recalled to our minds the basic curriculum of the early universities."

What was wrong with the building's name? On January 26, 1962, fifteen months after the cornerstone was laid, Bissell asked MacMillan if he would give his approval to naming the opera theatre after him.[342] MacMillan said yes. Then it became all too obvious that the naming should have been reversed — the opera theatre in honour of an internationally famous Canadian tenor and opera administrator, and the building after a distinguished principal, dean, and conductor. But it was too late. MacMillan, always the gentleman, appeared pleased, no matter. The Canadian Authors, Publishers, Association of Canada (CAPAC) then sponsored the annual "MacMillan Lectures" in his honour — lectures that were given from 1964 until 1977 at the MacMillan Theatre during summer school.[343]

The Edward Johnson Building, not unexpectedly, was over budget some $267,000 as of October 1961.[344] A few items — the orchestra shell, the electronic studio, the furnishings — were deferred to keep costs down. The financial estimate for the Economics Building renovations was raised to $650,000. An October 25 memorandum about provision of space for the School of Music — unsigned, but probably written by Superintendent Hastie — stressed that the School be given satisfactory facilities. Interestingly, this brought up the question of a new building for the School instead of a renovated building. A totally new building would cost approximately $1,610,000. A new add-on to the Economics Building would cost $1,240,000. Both were ruled out. The memorandum also suggested sites for a new building and recommended the area between Varsity Stadium and Philosopher's Walk. Hastie, like Chalmers fifteen years before, must have had a crystal ball, considering what is now underway forty years later! A.S. Mathers, who had been in charge of the 1946 improvements to the Economics Building as a member of the University's architectural advisory committee, thought at the time that it would "still be good structurally for another twenty-five or thirty years."

At a Conservatory committee meeting held shortly after the laying of the cornerstone, Mazzoleni and Mrs. W.H. Clarke, a member of the committee, expressed concern that the public might think that if the School was physically separated from the Faculty it would no longer be an integral part of the University's undertaking in music. In reply, Bissell reassured them that the two divisions would "continue to bear the same relationship to each other. The Faculty is concerned with full-time students working toward a degree and the School with part-time students working toward a certificate." The committee quickly endorsed the president's statement, and Mazzoleni and Clarke, for the moment, accepted it.[345]

Yet this may have led to another "Memorandum on the Proposed Use of the Economics Building by the School of Music" addressed to Bissell by the "Building Committee" on December 5. Was this the building committee that had helped plan the Johnson Building, or was it a School of Music group? There were no signatures. It stated — among other things — that the Economics Building was "neither satisfactory nor really suitable. Does this mean a definite down-grading of the School, which, in the public mind, is still the Conservatory?" It reminded the president that the Conservatory was recognized as the main centre of musical training in Canada, that it had many fine students who were bringing prestige to the country, and that the University had assured the School that it would do everything possible to meet its needs. It gave a detailed summary of the building's shortcomings and concluded with dismay that the allocated sum for renovations would be only $624,000, a substantial cut from the million dollars promised.

Bissell took umbrage on reading the memorandum and replied (I am not sure to whom) on December 6. He detected "a querulous strain of dissatisfaction over the present arrangements, with the suggestion that there is a deliberate attempt to downgrade the School of Music.... It stands to gain substantially by the new proposals." He noted that the School will use parts of the Johnson Building for its Opera School, and that the new theatre cost well over $1 million, one-third of the cost of the entire building. So, he concluded — without tongue in cheek — "the School got $1.7 million for the conversion of the Economics Building and the opera theatre, leaving the Faculty with $800,000." What he didn't say was that the Opera School remained with the School of Music because it was the School that supported it financially, not the parsimonious University. Bissell added that the Canada Council money could only be directed to University buildings and not to the School, "which is essentially, in administrative terms, a form of extension education." He went on to say that the University had generously spent $4 million in total on the entire Royal Conservatory "and it is insufferable that such petulant criticism should be offered at this time."

Neel and Mazzoleni had tried to cancel the 1961 Summer School because of the uncertainty of the old building being available, but the RCM committee insisted on having one. The more cynical committee members suspected that the two administrators were looking for time off. In any case, although it was a routine program, with the usual lessons and classes, it produced income of $5,494, which led to an overall profit of $1,340.[346] However, the 1962 Summer School, held at the Edward Johnson Building, was far from routine. Richard Johnston, a theory professor in the Faculty of Music, was appointed director and took a firm grip on the proceedings: an international conference on the Orff Method, university classes, a training session of the National Youth Orchestra (NYO), and conservatory lessons and classes. (The NYO had had its first training session at College Street in December 1960.) The spanking new facilities, and especially the air conditioning, left most people happy. Faculty classes and lessons began there in the fall, although the formal opening of the building was delayed until 1964. Incidentally, the Summer School ended up with a slightly larger profit than the preceding year's: $1,486.[347]

The University's sale of College Street to Ontario Hydro was concluded in February 1962.[348] As the time approached to vacate the premises, questions arose once again about the outrageously small purchase price for such valuable real estate. Was it a deal cooked up by the University and its provider, the provincial government? One early casualty of the sale was the women's residence; it had been dark since 1961. A new residence was opened, temporarily, on St. George Street. The main RCM move to Bloor Street, however, was not until early March 1963. It marked the beginning of the end of the 1952 Conservatory reorganization. Perhaps it *was* the end. Pedagogically the Conservatory was back to where it had been in 1940. If it hadn't had the Opera School in the Johnson Building, it would have been total retrogression. All that was left to complete the picture was changing the name of the School of Music back to the Royal Conservatory of Music, but this would have to wait another seven years.

At Bloor Street the RCM staff found that the Economics Building was old and decrepit, but nonetheless impressive. Soon it would revert back to its favoured original name, McMaster Hall.[349] William McMaster, from County Tyrone, Ireland, had come to Toronto in 1833 at age twenty-two and had, eventually, become a millionaire dry goods merchant. He then founded and was, for twenty years, president of the Canadian Bank of Commerce. A devout Baptist, he gave $100,000 to the University of Toronto for the land on Bloor Street. He then engaged the architectural firm of Langley, Langley & Burke to erect a building on the site for $90,000, to be the home of the Toronto Baptist College. It opened in 1881 and, for a while, was not only the city's largest and generally most magnificent building but also, it was said, the tallest, thanks to a decorative tower that was later taken down.[350] McMaster left the bulk of his estate to the college, which was renamed McMaster University after his death. When McMaster University moved to Hamilton in 1930, the building and its east wing became the property of the University of Toronto, and the name McMaster Hall was dropped.

Looking at it objectively, the building was better than expected, although still a far cry from what it should have been, despite Bissell's rationalizations. David Ouchterlony, the supervisor of branches, wrote a positive piece about it on March 2, 1963.[351] Using the metaphor of a four-movement symphony, he thought the studios spacious, with up-to-date acoustical treatment, and the office space vastly improved over College Street (*Introduction — Allegro*). The soundproofing (sound isolation) was generally good, and there was "a splendid lecture hall for instruction in theoretical subjects, and, for the nervous artist, a room designed for his refuge and comfort" prior to recitals. Happily, there were two new practice organs "in studios of splendid height," with a third one on the way (*Andante-Sostenuto*).

Ouchterlony drew attention to the eurhythmics room, now completely separated from other rooms, which the long-suffering Lasserre and her colleagues could use with impunity. He also joshed that the freight elevator was large enough to use as a studio (*Con Moto*). In addition to a recital hall, with seating for 120, there was an excellent concert hall with a well-lit stage and a new three-manual Casavant organ on the way. "One was witnessing old meeting new in rather wonderful ways," concluded the sanguine Ouchterlony (*Finale*). The organ would have thirty-three stops and twenty-two hundred pipes, and cost $32,250. (It would be some years before the Johnson Building purchased its first organ.)[352] What Ouchterlony did not anticipate was the attention McMaster Hall would get from passers-by on Philosopher's Walk, as they stopped in their tracks upon hearing music from the wide-open windows.

Theory teacher Fred J. Horwood wrote "The Exodus" for the 1963 January/February issue of *The Bulletin* to remind Conservatory teachers what they were leaving behind. "While this is the exodus we shall generate the spirit of happiness as soon as we have unpacked our bags in the new Conservatory on Bloor Street." Horwood was a long-time teacher and had written an earlier piece about the school for its fiftieth anniversary in 1936. In "The Exodus" he reminisced about when the College Street parking site was a vegetable and flower garden, the cafeteria sold three-course meals for thirty-five cents with no extra charge for second helpings, and lessons could be had for fifty cents. "Not much happened to interfere with our happiness, apart from a leaky radiator or a piece of ceiling which always fell down in the night," wrote Horwood.

Dorothy Howarth of *The Telegram* also wrote a sympathetic piece about College Street, although she said mistakenly that the RCM had been there for seventy-five years instead of the actual sixty-six.[353] She quoted several leading RCM figures. Charles Peaker said the building was "cramped, shabby, not to say squalid, and wholly lovable"; the ten-year-old Glenn Gould was "as fluent as all get-out even at that time, with Bach fairly bubbling out of him"; and the late pianist Viggo Kihl had "a thick Danish accent, always wore a Prince Albert tail coat, heavy watch chain and gold pince-nez — the better to see pretty girls. But beauty never dimmed Kihl's judgment. 'You may look like a peach, honey,' Kihl told a student, 'but you sing like sour apples.'" Lois Marshall recalled how the building had terrific atmosphere: "all that screaming, clashing, and bawling. I have the greatest affection for it." Teresa Stratas credited the Conservatory gossip mill, the cafeteria, with her opera debut. "Massey Hall auditions were not posted, but the kids told me at lunch. So I got mad and tackled Herman Geiger-Torel for not giving a girl a break in her home town. He got mad, too, and said if I thought I were ready, I'd better try. I did." Mazzoleni told Howarth that he was delighted to move, "but there is music in these old walls, and it will take a long time for it to seep into the new sterile building."

Ontario Hydro moved into College Street on March 31, yet it permitted organists to practise there for two more months. It also gave the Conservatory until May 1964 to find a buyer for its concert hall organ. (It was eventually sold for $750 to a Hydro employee.)[354] Hydro promised that if the building were torn down, the four stained glass portraits of great composers would be saved and turned over to the Conservatory. (Two are presently stored in the McMaster Hall attic.) The building had memories galore, which inspired the staff to put on a series of skits on a "nostalgia night" a few days before moving. This helped soften the psychological shock teachers endured, especially the older ones, in moving after so many years at College Street.

Yet, for those teachers who remembered the Conservatory in the twenties and thirties, McMaster Hall had a similarly quiet orderly feeling, interrupted from time to time by young children carousing about while waiting for lessons. There were few full-time students and few over eighteen. It was once again a collective, with an efficient registration desk and an examination centre. The Conservatory Symphony, which met in the Johnson Building, improved as the performance program at the Faculty improved, especially when bachelor's degrees in performance were initiated in 1964. Few School of Music students could qualify for it. "Ringers" — TSO members — were now rarely called in. However, it should be noted, a good many of the top teachers who taught for both divisions preferred the McMaster studios, since the Johnson studios were generally smaller and, in some cases, had poorer pianos.

To report events chronologically, the Edward Johnson Building held its formal opening on Monday, March 2, 1964, at three o'clock, at the MacMillan Theatre. Charles Peaker provided music on a temporary electronic organ, and I led a student brass choir in fanfares written by Keith Bissell and Sir Ernest MacMillan. (I had joined the Faculty in 1960.) There was an academic procession, speeches, and a presentation of the key to the building to Sir Ernest by the dean. In the evening, Sir Ernest conducted his *England*, for orchestra and chorus. He had written the work while interned in a civilian prison camp in Germany during the Great War. That performance was followed by Mazzoleni conducting Ridout's *Esther*. Geoffrey Payzant, who reviewed the concert for the CBC, was annoyed that the dignitaries arrived late to the concert because they were attending a celebratory dinner. Whatever, the concert went off well.

There followed an entire week of special events, all in the MacMillan Theatre. On Tuesday, Greta Kraus arranged a student chamber concert of works by Bach, Buxtehude, and Bach's son Johann Christian. Performances of Britten's *Albert Herring*, with Mazzoleni conducting, played on Wednesday and Friday. This was what opera buffs had been waiting for. The MacMillan was Toronto's first real opera house, and they were eager to see how good it was. Certainly its dimensions were impressive. The stage was 134 feet wide, 50 feet deep, and 85 feet high, almost as large as the stage at the O'Keefe Centre. The orchestra pit could seat 80, and the hall 815. *Herring* was hardly an ideal choice to show off the new hall, but Neel and Mazzoleni were taking no chances: it was a relatively easy opera to mount and needed only a chamber orchestra of the Faculty's best student players along with a couple of professionals. Garnet Brooks was a fine Herring, and there were several top sopranos in the two casts — Roxolana Roslak, Lilian Sukis, and Jeannette Zarou. The audience reserved judgment about the theatre's acoustics, since hearing the words was a problem. Later, when operas given at MacMillan used full orchestra, the technical staff employed some subtle amplification to help the singers. The theatre had a commendable thirty-foot rake, but the rather plain walls made it look a bit like a school auditorium. For sure, it was not the opera house Toronto was waiting for, although it was an admirable training theatre and, as Bissell had promised, an important addition to the city's musical life.

On Thursday night, Neel conducted the Conservatory Symphony, although the first work on the program, Brahms' *Academic Festival Overture*, was conducted by one of his students, Wilson Swift. Other works on the program included Richard Johnston's First Symphony, which was politely received, and works by Bartók, Debussy, and Elgar. On Saturday night Sir Ernest and Boyd Neel conducted the CBC Symphony in a concert of Canadian music, including works by Morawetz, Beckwith, Somers, Gellman, and Walter. As an orchestra hall the theatre still needed some fine tuning. The University's concert band, conducted by Robert Rosevear, wound up the week on Sunday afternoon. All in all, the celebration was well planned and engendered much excitement about the Johnson Building's future.

Chapter Eight

COOPERATION ENDS

Putting buildings aside for the moment, there were other happenings at the Conservatory in the first years of the sixties. The ninth and final Special Events Series in the College Street concert hall was given in the 1960–61 season. To open the series, Maureen Forrester from Montreal sang an all-English program. Her wonderful voice had already put her in the top rank of contraltos in the concert world. Violinist Fred Grinke (he was from Winnipeg but had made his career in Britain) and pianist Kathleen Long did a sonata recital, followed by the Vienna Philharmonic Wind Ensemble with the versatile and remarkable pianist Friedrich Gulda. The supreme harpist Marcel Grandjany was next. Then came the Fine Arts Quartet of Chicago in a cycle of three concerts — its broadcasts had for many years attracted much attention. And the extraordinary counter-tenor Russell Oberlin closed the season.

There were two piano appointments in 1960, mainly replacements for Guerrero: another Chilean, Rafael de Silva, who had been teaching in New York since 1942, and American Jacques Abram, a pupil of Josef Hofmann and Ernest Hutcheson. Abram had been soloist with many of the leading orchestras of the United States and Europe. Yet he had limited success in Toronto, as did de Silva. It was, in some respects, the same old problem: teachers of long standing clung to their good students like glue, and the Faculty, which was paying the newcomers' salaries, could do little about it. Both de Silva and Abram stayed but a few years. The same was true of Aksel Schiotz, who taught only one year before accepting an appointment at the University of Colorado. With Lambert, Vinci, and Jessner all teaching large classes, Schiotz simply couldn't make any headway.

The 1961 appointment of the newly formed Canadian String Quartet as the University's quartet-in-residence caused a great stir inside and outside the Conservatory. It was assigned to give an annual series of concerts, teach students privately in both the Faculty and the School, coach student string ensembles, and broadcast on the CBC. The Quartet was a project of violinist Albert Pratz and CBC music director Geoffrey Waddington, its objective to be a quartet of international stature. The Conservatory favoured the scheme, hoping it would stimulate string study, which was still only creeping along despite a $5,000 annual grant from the McLean Foundation to provide full scholarships to twenty string students. The new quartet had its first meeting in July 1961 and, after extensive rehearsing, performed for the first time after the New Year.

The group's members had outstanding credentials. Albert Pratz, the first violin, was certainly one of Canada's finest violinists. He had been teaching at the Conservatory since returning to Canada in 1953 after a nine-year stint with the NBC Symphony that concluded when Toscanini left the orchestra. Pratz had also been soloist with almost every major Canadian orchestra, played chamber music with Glenn Gould and others, and was highly regarded by both musicians and public. Bernard Robbins, the second violin, had been a member of the New York Philharmonic and, like Pratz, of the NBC Symphony. David Mankovitz, viola, the most experienced chamber player in the Quartet, had been a member of the Kroll, New York, and Stradivari string quartets. The cellist, George Ricci, like his violinist brother, Ruggiero, had been a child prodigy, a soloist with many American orchestras, and principal cellist with the ABC New York orchestra.

The Quartet's name caused a problem; many considered it a misnomer with three of its members Americans. Since it was supported by University, Canada Council, and CBC money, couldn't Pratz find at least one other Canadian to be in the group? One could ask why Waddington and Neel, who had jointly made the appointment, didn't take a stand in this regard. Having said this, the Quartet was undoubtedly needed at the RCM, with de Kresz and Spivak gone and Kathleen Parlow ailing. The Quartet, it was hoped, would give violin, viola, and cello instruction a much-needed shot in the arm.

Controversy aside, the group, as promised, gave more than fifty CBC radio recitals and a good many public concerts before it disbanded in July 1963. It did some 150 works and played a fair amount of Canadian music, including four quartets that it or the CBC had commissioned — quartets by Weinzweig, Morel, Somers, and Murray Adaskin.[355] Murray Schafer wrote in the Spring 1962 *Canadian Music Journal* that he was "overwhelmed" with their performance of the Ravel Quartet, while their Beethoven op. 59, no. 2 was not convincing. "This is," he said, "a quartet of true stature in some, if not yet in all fields. Provided they are able to stay together long enough to adjust their individualities and have patience in developing their rich resources, we may expect rewarding results."[356] As teachers, the Canadian String Quartet members were unimpressive, partially due to the paucity of advanced students, but mainly because they were simply not interested in teaching.

Did Schafer have some foreboding about the Quartet's future? Laszlo Varga, an accomplished Hungarian/American cellist, replaced George Ricci in 1962. Sadly, the Quartet lasted only one more year. No matter, it had proved its worth as a performing organization and helped leave the door open for another resident group, the Orford String Quartet, which joined the University in 1968 and had a splendid history until its demise in 1991.

As the country's population grew and music instruction in elementary and high schools improved, gifted performers attended the Conservatory in ever-increasing numbers. The winners of the first CBC Trans-Canada Talent Festival in 1960 were Gordana Lazarevich, a piano student at the Faculty, and baritone Cornelis Opthof, a student at the Opera School. Lazarevich would ultimately become a professor of musicology at Victoria University, and Opthof would have a distinguished international operatic career and be a close colleague of Joan Sutherland; in fact, Opthof was still singing with the Canadian Opera Company in 2004. Then there was Teresa Stratas, who had won the grand prize in the 1959 Metropolitan Auditions of the Air and was now taking leading roles at the Met; Jon Vickers, who was rapidly becoming the world's leading *heldentenor*; Lois Marshall, who had just done a round-the-world tour; and James Milligan, who had joined the Basle Opera Company and sang the Wanderer in *Siegfried* at Bayreuth in the summer of 1961. Milligan was, as expected, a great success at the Wagner shrine, but tragically he died suddenly on November 27 in Basel at age thirty-one. It was a tremendous loss to the musical world, and his wife, teachers, and friends mourned his passing.

The Orff Schulwerk was now known throughout North America. To encourage the growing interest in it, Arnold Walter and Doreen Hall directed an international conference at the 1962 Summer School. They invited Orff, Gunild Keetman, Lotte Flach, Barbara Hasselbach, and Wilhelm Keller — all members of the Orff Institute in Salzburg — to teach and lecture. Walter served as simultaneous translator of Orff's lectures, since Orff spoke no English. Keith Bissell and Laughton Bird, both leading Canadian music educators, spoke in addition to Hall. Hugh Orr, a fine recorder player, also performed. The conference confirmed that Toronto was the continent's leading centre for Orff studies. Of interest is that some of the instruments brought by Hall from Germany more than fifty years ago are still in use. Alison Kenny-Gardhouse and Catherine West now direct the extensive Conservatory Orff program and teacher-training course.

The Conservatory and the University had been dodging the subject of pensions for Conservatory teachers for many years. They used the excuse — a good one — that RCM teachers were contract employees and therefore could not participate in the University pension plan. (The administrative and clerical staff were members of the University plan.) However, by 1962, the teachers were increasingly restive. The Conservatory bit the bullet and proposed a pension plan into which it would pay its share but would also require raising teachers' fees and commissions.[357] Although the plan appeared to be a mixed blessing, it was unveiled at a Conservatory committee meeting on April 20, 1966. Using a "career-earning basis" and integrated with the Canada Pension Plan, it would be available as an option to teachers between the ages of twenty-five and sixty-seven with an estimated annual income of not less than $1,200. Only 124 of the 182 teachers would thus be eligible. The cost to the RCM would be $47,000 annually, including its contribution to the Canada Pension Plan. To help meet these new costs, the School, as predicted, raised its instruction fees 15 percent and boosted teachers' commissions from 20 to 25 percent. The University gave nothing. The plan was duly put in place.

Repairs for the Bloor Street building were proving very costly. An additional $68,000 was needed to repair roofing and windows and for interior painting, as well as $20,000 for furniture.[358] Superintendent Hastie reminded the Conservatory committee and, by extension, the governors, that the original allocation for renovation was $900,000, but the University had cut it to $650,000. Hastie had consistently tried to give Bloor Street what it needed, but it wasn't easy.

Gordon Mudge, the secretary-treasurer of the School, died at the end of 1963 and was replaced by George Hoskins, whose title was changed to business administrator.[359] Hoskins, genial and easygoing to a fault, stayed with the Conservatory until the nineties. Mazzoleni proposed that the "of Toronto" in the title of Royal Conservatory of Music be dropped for advertising and publicity purposes, although it would, by statute, continue to be included on certificates and diplomas.[360] In the meantime, the Frederick Harris Company went from strength to strength, and its scholarship and bursary awards topped $34,000 for the 1965–66 session.[361]

Glenn Gould spoke at the Conservatory ARCT graduation at Convocation Hall on November 11, 1964. Gould was now a world-famous pianist who, to everyone's astonishment, had just renounced public concert giving. He told the young graduates at the beginning of his address not to take too much advice from others. Later, acknowledging that teaching was an "awesome responsibility" for which he lacked the courage, he stated that success in teaching "would very much depend upon the degree to which the singularity, the uniqueness of the confrontation between yourselves and each one of your students is permitted to determine your approach to them." To clarify his theme of independent thought and action, he said, "As performer or composer you will in all likelihood exist, or at any rate, should try to exist, more for yourself and of yourself than is possible for your colleagues in musical pedagogy." A bit heavy for a graduation speech for people mostly in their late teens, his message comes through more clearly on the printed page. The RCM's business was teaching, and anything that helped its present or prospective teachers to appraise and reappraise their profession was bound to be useful.

Maureen Forrester, a favourite in Toronto as elsewhere, took to teaching and gave a revealing master class in German lieder and art songs, as well as a recital, at the 1965 Summer School.[362] Since 1962 the School had recaptured some of the spirit of the exciting summers of the mid-fifties, thanks to director Richard Johnston, assisted by Gordon Kushner. Johnston was a large man with a brash manner who would be hard to miss in a crowd. Kushner was just the opposite. A fine pianist, he was small, soft-spoken, and always agreeable. Of lasting value was Johnston's work on the methodology of teaching music to children developed by the composer Zoltán Kodály and other Hungarian teachers working under Kodály's guidance. Johnston had first visited Hungary in 1964 to observe the method in action. He then arranged for Ann Osborne, who had studied in Hungary, to give a pilot course at the 1965 Summer School. Like the Orff Schulwerk, the Kodály method was taught at future summer schools and at other music schools in North America. The Kodály method, put simply, is based on folksinging and movable-doh solmization. Kodály was the MacMillan/CAPAC lecturer in 1966. Johnston continued as Summer School director until 1968, when he became dean of fine arts at the University of Calgary. Gordon Kushner then took over the Summer School.

In 1966 the RCM committee, in a spending mood, approved $14,000 for the establishment of two electronic music studios at McMaster Hall to rival the one at the Johnson Building.[363] Composition teacher Samuel Dolin was behind the plan. He had visited several electronic music centres in the United States and Europe to help him decide what he wanted. Once these studios were in full swing, Dolin happily reported that eighteen students had enrolled in the thirty-week electronic music course in its first year. Dolin, who had independent and rather opinionated views, built up a large following of composition students who preferred to work with him rather than with composers at the Faculty of Music. Brian Cherney, a professor at McGill for many years, said of Dolin, "His attitude is unique, I think, in that he's genuinely interested in what his students are doing.... He makes you feel that what you're doing is

Samuel Dolin with student composer Steven Gellman, c. 1970.

important." Ann Southam, another leading composer, added, "He allows a great deal of freedom, never intimidates you with rules. He guides people into situations where they just inevitably learn." And Allan Rae, who has composed in almost every genre, said enthusiastically that Dolin "instills in you the desire to write. I've done so much writing while I've been studying with him that it's hard to believe, and I'm sure it's because of him making me realize that perhaps I can write."[364]

COOPERATION ENDS

Composition had generally taken a leap forward with the 1965 revival of the student composers' symposium. A short "trial balloon" one-and-a-half-day session was held at the RCM on February 27 and 28. Works by composers from Eastman, Juilliard, and the RCM were performed at two concerts. There was a panel discussion with four older composers, George Rochberg and Morton Feldman from the United States and John Weinzweig and François Morel from Canada, with Louis Applebaum as moderator, as well as lively meetings of students from eleven different schools. Works by three Conservatory composers — Nick Slater's Symphony Movements, Steven Gellman's Andante for String Orchestra, and Ann Southam's Sonatina for Orchestra — were given at the orchestral concert. Performed at the chamber concert were David E. Williams's Woodwind Quintet and John Felice's Five Songs for Soprano and Clarinet. BMI, CAPAC, and the University helped to fund the event.

The next year a three-day symposium was held at the University of Buffalo. More than one hundred people attended. Eastman was the host in 1967, and Bennington College in 1968. Student composers from Toronto whose works were heard at the 1966 symposium were Douglas Riley and Brian Cherney (each wrote a woodwind quintet), Ann Southam (a piano suite), and Stephen Pedersen (a movement for string quartet.) Given at the 1967 symposium were John Mills-Cockell's *Fragments for Two Pianos and Stereo Magnetic Tape* and Kathleen Solose's *Reflections for Piano*.[365] In 1968, the Conservatory chartered a bus to attend the Bennington symposium, where works by Solose, Pedersen, John Fodi, Richard Henninger, and John Rimmer were played. The School of Music and the Faculty of Music worked together to sponsor the three out-of-town symposia.[366] Symposia continued into the seventies, with the Conservatory an active participant, along with McGill and the Québec Conservatoire.

There was sad news too. Frederick Silvester, who had been in charge of TCM examinations from 1929 to 1946 and then School registrar, died on June 24, 1966. A friendly Lancastrian, he was a prominent Toronto organist and choirmaster at Bloor Street United Church for twenty-eight years and had conducted the Mendelssohn Choir from 1957 until 1960, succeeding Sir Ernest MacMillan. Silvester also had the distinction of opening the School of Music's new three-manual Casavant organ at McMaster Hall on October 17, 1964. Mazzoleni, MacMillan, and Peaker all praised the departed Silvester for his administrative ability, his musical gifts, his wit, and his loyalty to the School.[367] Warren Mould, who had been assistant registrar, was promoted to registrar. The examination department needed attention, and Mould, an excellent pianist and teacher, was well qualified to tackle its problems. He had already been supervising revision of the piano examination requirements, grade by grade, with a board of ten leading piano teachers. The revision was long overdue and produced excellent results over the next few years.[368]

Reginald Godden playing Bach on his knees.

RCM Board of Studies, 1966. From left to right: Clifford Poole, Elsie Bennett, Douglas Bodle, Margaret Brown, Boris Berlin, Warren Mould (Chairman), Earle Moss, Walter Buczynski, Madeline Bone, Gordon Hallett, and Patricia Holt.

Speaking of pianists, Reginald Godden returned to the RCM faculty in 1966 after five years as principal of the Hamilton Conservatory (1948–53) and another stretch of eight years in San Francisco, where he studied the music of Bach. Godden was a maverick who had taught at the RCM in the thirties and forties and had also been a member of a two-piano team with Scott Malcolm and a five-piano team with Malcolm, Seitz, Stewart, and Guerrero. To show his increased understanding of Bach, he did a CBC broadcast of the master's music on January 11, 1967, playing, literally, on his knees. Godden felt that this position would reduce the percussive sound of the piano. In his words: "The articulation is vertical but the source of energy is moving horizontally."[369] The next year he gave thirteen critically acclaimed public lectures on Bach's keyboard music.[370] Godden, who had taught a number of fine pianists, including his lifelong friend and avid supporter Harry Somers, liked to do complete cycles, and in the next eleven years did the twelve études of Debussy, which he recorded, and Beethoven's thirty-two sonatas. Then, on December 7, 1978, to climax his career at age seventy-three, the gifted and eccentric pianist performed Hindemith's extraordinarily difficult *Ludus Tonalis*.

Early in 1968, Healey Willan died. He was eighty-eight. Although he had done little teaching at the RCM since 1936, he had worked closely with the Opera School when it gave the first staged performance of his *Deirdre* in 1965. The Canadian Opera Company (COC) did it the following year at the O'Keefe Centre. Godfrey Ridout, one his finest pupils, wrote after his death, "Lessons were fun. He was never dogmatic, and he never imposed his style of writing on us … he insisted on technical mastery. He also helped break down our musical inhibitions. 'Never be ashamed of being vulgar, old man,' he said, 'be as vulgar as you like.' This was good advice, especially at a time when Toronto music was steeped in an atmosphere of pretty-pretty gentility."[371]

The Opera School forcefully moved ahead in the sixties. The introduction of a wide variety of mainly lesser known works to Toronto by Canadian and non-Canadian composers, living and dead, was the order of the day. In 1960, following the 1959 performances of Menotti's *Amelia Goes to the Ball* and Arthur Benjamin's *The Prima Donna*, the School repeated *Riders to the Sea*, with another remarkable performance by Patricia Rideout. To balance the evening the School did two short comic works, Rossini's *The Marriage Contract* and Douglas Moore's *Gallantry*. Leon Major, a promising young theatre director, directed the Moore work, which turned out to be a piece of fluff, but the one-act Rossini opera had the great composer's stamp.

In 1961, the School gave performances of *The Mother* by Stanley Hollingsworth and Respighi's *Marie Egiziaca*, using a small orchestra. Leon Major had more success with the Hollingsworth piece. Gwenlynn Little, a talented lyric soprano who would go on to sing with major opera companies in Canada and the United States, played Maria in the Respighi work. Maria Pellegrini, who had a warm and truly exciting soprano voice that would lead her to an international career, made her first appearance in a small role in the same opera. The next year *The World of the Moon*, a one-act work in three scenes by Giovanni Paisiello, shared the evening with Lennox Berkeley's *A Dinner Engagement*. Heather Thomson, a versatile soprano who would sing leading roles with the COC and other companies in the years to come, was in the Berkeley piece, as were Jean MacPhail and Mona Kelly, mezzo-sopranos, and Garnet Brooks, tenor, all of whom would have important performing and teaching careers.

In 1963, the young Canadian composer Raymond Pannell took the spotlight with his short opera *Aria Da Capo*, sung to a text by Edna St. Vincent Millay. It was the School's first Canadian operatic presentation. A bit like Hindemith's *There and Back*, with the beginning and the end the same, it is both farce and tragedy. Torel and Mazzoleni, after reviewing the manuscript, recorded their enthusiasm in the *Toronto Star*.[372] Torel stated that Pannell was a "powerful imaginative composer who has a tremendous talent and the potential to become a very important composer — and that is by international standards, too." Mazzoleni said it was "bloody marvelous." Apparently Pannell, an accomplished pianist, wrote the fifty-five minute work in five weeks while teaching twenty-five hours a week at the RCM and writing a score for a TV film! Unfortunately, *Aria Da Capo* didn't do well in the press. The *Globe and Mail* thought the work too eclectic, while the *Telegram* thought the libretto too complex.[373] Whatever, it was given short shrift and merits a rehearing. (Pannell's *The Luck of Ginger Coffey*, commissioned by the COC for the 1967 centennial year and given at the O'Keefe Centre, would suffer roughly similar criticism — an ineffective play with music that drew too heavily on Bernstein, Weill, and Menotti.)

Nino Rota's *Silent Night* shared the 1963 double bill with *Aria Da Capo*. It was equally unsuccessful, although Andrew MacMillan's staging helped make it more enjoyable. In all of these double bills, conducting tasks were divided between Barbini and Mazzoleni, and, later in the decade, Alfred Strombergs and guest conductors. With Torel increasingly busy at the Canadian Opera Company, Mazzoleni engaged other opera directors from time to time, including Leon Major, Andrew MacMillan, Joan Cross, Werner Graf, and Heinar Piller. Graf also served as administrator for three years. The Pannell and Rota operas were the last ones given at Hart House Theatre. All future productions would be staged at the MacMillan Theatre, with its large orchestra pit and stage, its state-of-the-art lighting board, and its spacious backstage facilities and storage areas.

Albert Herring was the first work given at the MacMillan. The following year the School did two contrasting works, the stark folk drama *Le pauvre matelot,* by Darius Milhaud, and *Angélique*, a light piece by Jacques Ibert that the School had done a decade earlier. Having the MacMillan Theatre allowed at least two opera performances each season. In 1964 Wallace Russell, the technical director of the theatre, took advantage of its facilities to initiate a course for incipient stage managers and electricians that continued sporadically for several years.

Christmas 1964 brought back *Amahl and the Night Visitors*, with much satisfaction for all concerned. The following Christmas the School presented Prokofiev's *Love for Three Oranges*. (The COC had done it in 1959 at the Royal Alexandra Theatre.) It has a fairy-tale plot, and so, according to one critic, the production "emphasized its fantastic elements." It was "staged lightly and sung with great musical and verbal clarity" to enhance its attractiveness for the young.[374] Ermanno Mauro, an outstanding

Italian/Canadian tenor whom Barbini had discovered in Edmonton, did the Prince, and his voice at times seemed almost too big for the theatre. Mauro would have a major career with leading opera companies in Europe and North America. *Hansel and Gretel* was done at Christmas 1966, and *Amahl*, again, in 1968. Less successful was *The Magic Flute* in 1967, which, of course, is hardly a children's opera. The Canadian Opera Junior Women's Committee sponsored these Christmas productions, and the houses were usually filled to overflowing.

Planning *Deirdre* (Willan). From left to right: Lawrence Schäfer, Ettore Mazzoleni, John Coulter, Healey Willan, and Herman Geiger-Torel, 1965.

Deirdre, staged by the Opera School in 1965 for three nights, was quite moving despite its fundamental shortcomings. Jeannette Zarou, truly sympathetic in the title role, possessed a mellow lyric soprano voice that led to a distinguished career in Germany over the next thirty years. Lilian Sukis, equally gifted, did one performance. The next year, when the COC did *Deirdre* at O'Keefe's with Zarou as Deirdre, Kenneth Winters described its music as "semi-resplendent Elgarian/Wagnerian ... retailored with fine sense, respectable craft, a clear-eyed decent sincerity, and other qualities short of genius. Broadly speaking, it is still relentlessly rhapsodic in the treble, rather square in the bass, and pitilessly chromatic in the middle, without quite enough relief anywhere."[375] In short, Willan lacked the instinct and feel for music *and* drama, the two vital elements of successful opera.

The highlight the next year was Orff's *Die Kluge* (*The King and the Wise Woman*), a one-act opera in eleven scenes. Orff wrote the libretto as well as the music. Innovatively, designer Lawrence Schäfer used slides and films as backdrops to highlight the opera's moods and characterizations. His circular multi-level stage also helped. The MacMillan Theatre was offering stage designers and lighting experts opportunities heretofore unknown in Toronto except at the O'Keefe Centre. Harry Somers's *Riel*, done by the COC at O'Keefe the next year, took its cue from *Die Kluge*'s visual effects, using slides, films, and imaginative lighting.

Yes, thanks to the MacMillan Theatre, Opera School productions were becoming more demanding musically, more lavish scenically, and more costly. Although run by the School of Music, the Opera School's location made it very much a part of the Edward Johnson Building, with students from the Faculty of Music playing roles and singing in the chorus. Mazzoleni, in addition to conducting many of the School's operas and orchestral concerts, still had to run the School of Music, for which student registrations continued to increase at the main building and branches. He was left with insufficient time and inclination to address the Opera School's problems.

With Torel thoroughly occupied at the COC, it was clear that the Opera School needed a new and experienced full-time director. Thus Peter Ebert, an internationally known stage director, was appointed to the post in January 1967. In his first spring season he produced two operas: Britten's *The Rape of Lucretia* (February 17 and 19) and Francis Poulenc's *Dialogues des Carmélites* (March 31 and April 1 and 3). The productions made great demands on the singers and staging staff. Wisely, *Lucretia*'s chamber orchestra was composed of top Toronto professionals while the Poulenc used the increasingly proficient school orchestra. Ebert wanted the Opera School to use the theatre more than it had in the past, much like a professional company.

Orff's *Die Kluge*, 1966.

After three months in Toronto, Ebert told the RCM committee that changes were needed in the School's structure and finances. In short, he wished to make the Opera School a separate entity, with appropriate funding and more reasonable student fees. (They paid far more for instruction than Faculty of Music students.) He made no mention of the orchestra players, all of whom were Faculty students, and without whom, manifestly, opera could not be done. Ebert's concerns soon led to the formal sepa-

Stravinsky's *Oedipus Rex*, 1967.

ration of the Opera School and the School of Music. Within two years (by June 1969) the Opera School became part of the Faculty of Music's performance department.

The end result of this change was that the University would fund the Opera School through the province's new "formula funding," a per-student amount known as the basic income unit (BIU). Enrolment would be limited to twenty-four students (twenty-four BIUs), who would pay the lower

181

Debussy's *Pelléas et Mélisande*, 1968, with Danielle Pilon (Mélisande) and Paul Trepanier (Pelléas).

University fees and be granted an opera diploma upon successful completion of the required work. The course took two or three years, depending on the student's level of advancement. Such changes were long overdue; in addition to lowering student fees, the Opera School could now raise funds independently.

The adventurous Ebert produced Stravinsky's *Oedipus Rex* for four nights in November 1967 and then did his final production, Debussy's *Pelléas et Mélisande*, the following March. *Pelléas* was, in a word, superb. John Kraglund wrote that the production was "sensational.... Not only was it the greatest ever presented by the Opera School but it would vie for a place among the greatest operatic productions ever offered in this city."[376] Barbini conducted, Brian Jackson did the sets and costumes, and the student orchestra outdid itself. Danielle Pilon was a beautifully sensitive, vulnerable, and ambiguous Mélisande. In the spring of 1968 she followed Ebert to Augsburg, Germany, his next port of call, to sing with that city's opera company. The English director Anthony Besch succeeded Ebert.

The Opera School was now in its final year as part of the Conservatory. Besch did Rossini's *Turk in Italy* before the New Year, and, in February 1969, Humphrey Searle's *Hamlet*; the latter had had its first performance in German in Hamburg in March 1968. The School's production was its world premiere in English — Covent Garden would do it in April. In the spring, Besch did Strauss's *Ariadne auf Naxos* and then wound up his one-year tenure as the School's director. Mary-Lou Fallis, an undergraduate student in the Faculty of Music, was an amazing Zerbinetta, a challenging role even for the most experienced high lyric sopranos. Fallis would later become a delightful singing comedienne. Besch also helped in designing the new opera diploma course. The two-and-a-half years of Ebert and Besch was an unforgettable high point for student opera study and achievement.

Tragedy struck the Conservatory when, in the early hours of June 1, 1968, Dr. Mazzoleni was hit by an auto while walking on Yonge Street in Richmond Hill. He was sixty-two. The Fall 1968 *Conservatory Bulletin* devoted most of its issue to tributes to him by friends and colleagues. Sir Ernest MacMillan wrote about his first contacts with "Mazz" when he did *Hugh the Drover* in 1929. When it played at the Royal Alec the next year, "Mazz conducted a few of the performances, proving his ability as an opera conductor." Sir Ernest also spoke of his achievements as Conservatory Symphony conductor. Torel highlighted Mazzoleni's three conducting triumphs, the radio premiere of Arthur Benjamin's *The Tale of Two Cities*, the television premiere of Britten's *Peter Grimes*, and the stage premiere of *Deirdre*. George

Lambert recalled his performance of Ridout's *Esther* and, along with York Wilson and Herman Voaden, spoke movingly of Mazzoleni's personal qualities. Boyd Neel, at the memorial service on June 4, muddled a few facts, but otherwise expressed his affection for Mazzoleni as a good colleague. David Ouchterlony was at the organ, and F.J. Horwood gave the prayers.

Mazzoleni's daughter Clare Piller recalled that, following her father's election as an Honorary Fellow of the Royal College of Music, a reporter from the *Toronto Star* asked him to name his principal frustrations. He replied: "That so many talented children have to have parents. That I have tried for years without success to get season's tickets to hockey games. Organ recitals, although some of my best friends are organists. When I am required to conduct the night of a hockey game. That I never have time for a haircut and I'm always mistaken for a musician."[377]

The University of Toronto *Bulletin* reported a singular event in its December 2, 1971, issue: Joanne Ivey Mazzoleni, Mazzoleni's second wife and former student of the Conservatory and its Opera School, had donated to the Conservatory an outstanding collection of contemporary Canadian paintings, which would be hung in McMaster's concert hall. Assisted by Cleeve Horne and York Wilson, Mrs. Mazzoleni had chosen works by Paul-Emile Borduas, Bertram Brooker, Jack Bush, Charles Comfort, Peter Haworth, Jean McEwen, Toni Onley, Jean-Paul Riopelle, Francois Thépot, Harold Town, and York Wilson. Mazzoleni, she said, had always wished that "each of the arts should be aware of the other. In making our selections consideration was given to the fact that audiences would spend a considerable amount of time with these paintings, and for that reason we felt that they should act more as an accompaniment rather than make too strong a statement of their own." Unfortunately, the Haworth painting, *Swordfish Boats*, was stolen early on and was never recovered. The collection remained in the hall for more than two decades.[378]

David Ouchterlony, branch supervisor since 1947, stepped in as acting principal after Mazzoleni's death. In his "Message from the Acting Principal" in the Christmas 1968 *Conservatory Bulletin*, Ouchterlony, carried away with emotion, said that he would "get on with the job" (a favourite Mazzoleni phrase) and that he found the work "challenging, demanding, exhilarating, exhausting, and enormously exciting." With fatuous modesty he concluded: "I am humbled by the realization of my own deficiencies compared to so many who have created the glorious eighty-three year history of this institution, but I promise to give everything I have to try, at least in part, to offset my limitations." Ouchterlony was appointed principal by the board of governors a year later.[379]

Known as "Mr. O," Ouchterlony represented a change of pace in Conservatory principals. He was very tall and always amiable. Organist at Timothy Eaton Church since 1946, he gave music appreciation programs on radio and television, mainly, although not exclusively, for children. He also directed a popular choir, The Songmen. And, as further evidence of his versatility, he invented a Multiple Student Keyboard (MSK). It has been described as "several individual electronic keyboards all of which fed into a central control board equipped with tiny lights representing hundreds of notes and a sound system which could be turned on or off. By means of lights the teacher could remain stationary and, even without hearing, detect student errors."[380] The MSK has since been in use by some teachers in piano and keyboard harmony classes.

Boyd Neel retired as Conservatory dean in 1969. In a news release of October 28, 1970, President Bissell announced changes in the Conservatory's administrative structure: John Beckwith, who had succeeded Neel the previous July, would now head the Faculty of Music, thus eliminating the position of director. (Walter had also retired.) The news release announcing the changes stated: "The School of Music has been replaced by the more popularly known and more historically accurate term Royal Conservatory of Music, which, it was felt, was no longer necessary as an omnibus or umbrella designation." A principal would lead the Conservatory and a dean the Faculty, as it had been prior to the 1952 reorganization.

"The two bodies are basically different," the news release went on. "The Faculty's academic programs are supported by the University directly through the use of provincial grants. The Royal Conservatory is a self-supporting affiliated institution, owned by the University and operated under the direction of a committee of its Board of Governors." The Conservatory would be "concerned with community teaching in the studio sense, with preparatory courses, and with the operation of a large extra-mural examination system."

There would be, the release continued, "a close interrelation of the two departments: the Faculty would rely on the Conservatory for part-time teachers, particularly in performance, while the Royal Conservatory sends gifted students to Faculty performance teachers." The two would share scholarships from the Musical Talent Foundation, and Conservatory students would have "full borrowing and listening privileges at the Edward Johnson Music Library." The Summer School would "continue to be held at the Johnson Building while the Faculty would benefit from the use of practice and hall space at Bloor Street at overcrowded hours." The principal would remain a member of the Faculty council, and the dean and two other Faculty delegates would be members of the principal's advisory council, made up of the principal, the registrar, and six elected members of the teaching staff. The principal would also be a member of the Board of Musical Studies of the University senate, "the body presently charged with ultimate legal approval of all academic policies over which the Dean presides as chairman."

Concluding, it said that the new "alignment of duties" will aim "to clarify the similarities and differences between the structures and programs of both the Faculty and the Conservatory and to create a practical day-to-day set-up for the direction of work in both divisions, with due regard to their natures, their points of interrelation, and the main lines of responsibility, both financial and academic."

The change in structure brought things back to pre-Second World War days, only now the Faculty of Music was a thriving post-secondary enterprise, the kind of school Hutcheson, Noss, and Walter envisaged. Would the Conservatory be content in its subordinate role? One thing was certain — the Faculty had irrevocably lost the name "Royal Conservatory." When people talked informally about music instruction in Toronto over the next twenty to thirty years, they were usually referring to the Conservatory. The Faculty would have to fight an uphill battle with the public to achieve comparable identity as a music school, even though it held all the cards. When the Faculty sought private and corporate donations it often had to explain its position vis-à-vis the Conservatory. As for the Conservatory, the University was intransigent — no fundraising because it would compete with the Faculty. The far-sighted saw that an independent Conservatory would have a far more promising future. But for now it would continue, as Bissell called it, an "extension department" of the University.

Chapter Nine
STRUGGLES FOR DIRECTION

Giving back the name Royal Conservatory of Music to the School of Music was at best a partial solution for the continuing differences between the University of Toronto and the RCM. It was nothing new that the University was determined to maintain control of the Conservatory, both because it served as a feeding ground for the Faculty of Music and to prevent the Conservatory from competing with the Faculty at the post-secondary level. These two points, especially the second one, remained paramount as events unfolded over the next fifteen years.

The University had little trouble ruling the RCM, since nearly all RCM teachers, as in the past, wanted the university affiliation to continue. A number of them gave lessons in instruments and voice to Faculty students, especially to those in the music education course. Teaching well at the Faculty led to more work and increased income and prestige. There were also theory and history teachers at the Conservatory who had classes of students preparing to qualify for entrance to the Faculty. Examinations, too, reinforced the RCM's ties to the University, since all examination certificates, as in the past, carried the University masthead. This made a difference, not only in Toronto, but in Moose Jaw and Victoria and St. John's; examinees and their families liked seeing the name of the Royal Conservatory on a certificate, but even more so the name of the University of Toronto. Conservatory teachers feared that without the University the school would go downhill and ultimately cease to exist.

There were, however, a small number of advanced and qualified RCM post-secondary students who scorned the Faculty because they thought that its performance program was too academic, that it did not provide enough time for practice, that it had unreasonable entrance standards, and that, generally, it had little sympathy for performers and their needs. These RCM students did not want to spend

187

four years preparing for a profession when, so they thought, one or two years of concentrated study on their instruments would be just as valuable. Attending the Conservatory meant that they could take the subjects they wanted — lessons, theory, ear training classes, and anything else they thought they needed — not what was laid out in the Faculty's formal and rigorous course of study. It was costly, more costly than the Faculty, but there were substantial scholarships.

RCM mezzo-soprano Catherine Robbin with teacher Dorothy Allan Park and pianist Mary Rezza.

On the whole, the RCM leaders did not sympathize with Arnold Walter's argument that a performing musician needs a thorough musical education beyond his or her instrument. In actual fact, the Faculty's performance course was much like ones given at major schools of music in American universities and conservatories. It was thriving, with swelling enrolments, a fine orchestra, two choirs, opera, and small ensembles. The Conservatory had none of these groups. It was hardly a serious competitor and looked like it never would be. Nor did the Faculty or its big brother the University ever consider *two* post-secondary music schools in mushrooming Toronto. (York University had started a music program, but it was not directed toward preparing performers.)

Canada's musical world had developed enormously since 1950. Professional musical organizations were springing up across the country with positions for qualified musicians. In 1950 there were three fully professional orchestras in Canada; by 1970 there were eleven. In 1950 there was one opera company, and now every major city had an opera season. The Canada Council and, to a lesser degree, provincial arts councils, seeded professional groups and provided study grants for talented young musicians. There was a National Arts Centre Orchestra and a National Youth Orchestra, both of which were the envy of the Western world. The fallout from the outstanding music programs at the 1967 exposition in Montreal had also had a favourable impact on the country's musical development.

A contributing factor in all this growth was the country's expanding population — from 14 million in 1951 to 21 million in 1971.[381] Metropolitan Toronto had more than doubled its population in these same twenty years, from 1,261,000 to 2,628,000. Canadian orchestras were hastily engaging Americans because, they claimed, there were not enough qualified Canadians. When Canadians were qualified, they had difficulty competing with Americans because they were outnumbered, often ten to one, at auditions. And yes, orchestral training at the best schools in the United States was better than at any school in Toronto — perhaps taken more seriously would be more accurate.

Could the RCM provide better training than the Faculty of Music? It appeared unlikely, so long as the RCM was prohibited from giving a post-secondary course of study. Nevertheless, the University, trying to be an honest broker, decided to wrestle with the Conservatory's future and its relationship with the Faculty. Three reports between 1973 and 1984 addressed these issues, as did one memorandum of understanding (1981). The only report that solved anything at all was the final one in 1984. Even then, it took another six years to implement. The Faculty may have dispatched the Conservatory to Bloor Street, but the latter wouldn't go away.

Dr. John Hamilton of the University of Toronto's Medical School assembled a committee of Conservatory and Faculty representatives in 1973 to address "the problem ... that the University of Toronto offers musical education through two separate and distinct institutions. The governance is different and no mechanisms have developed whereby an effective dialogue can continue towards clarification of roles, optimization of facilities, and avoidance of duplication of educational courses."[382]

The committee first recommended that the RCM stay in the University and that "the administrative structure and governance be similar to an academic division." It finessed the question of how the RCM could actually be an academic division with no salaried teachers and no post-secondary program. The second recommendation dealt with the establishment of a "Faculty Assembly ... to have the responsibility and powers normally held by Faculty Councils of academic divisions." It would report to the provost. Membership would consist of officials representing the University, the Faculty of Music, and the Conservatory, and RCM teachers and students. There would be committees for curricula, examinations, and syllabi, an awards and admission standards committee, an appointments committee, and a publications committee. The report urged that the assembly "define the goals and objectives of the RCM and its role in the education of music students."

The Hamilton committee underlined what everyone knew already: "The future of the Conservatory cannot be assured without gaining recognition from the Ministry of Education that it is an educational institution, and eligible for public support." It pointed out that the University now receives "statutory support for the University of Toronto Schools." Why not the RCM? It urged the Harris Company to work more closely with the RCM and appoint an advisory committee to "investigate" Canada Council subsidies for non-commercial music publications. It also asked Harris to issue an annual report. Presumably it had not been doing so. The assembly was duly formed and committees struck. More Conservatory teachers than in the past were now involved in school decision-making.

Three years later (in 1976) the University appointed another committee to review the Royal Conservatory of Music and the Faculty of Music.[383] It was chaired by Principal Archibald Hallett of University College. I was one of its five members. Hallett, like Hamilton, was struck by the RCM's anomalous position in the University. He solicited briefs from the chairs of the five assembly committees and Dean Beckwith of the Faculty. In addition, there were six unsolicited briefs from Faculty of Music professors, one of which was signed by the six members of the music history department who more or less denigrated performance studies at the university level and urged the committee to assign them all to the RCM. There were three unsolicited briefs from the Conservatory.

Hallett recognized that the Conservatory had no formal reporting procedure to the academic affairs committee of the University, which normally would approve or not approve of programs and other academic matters. And there were no procedures for staff evaluation or recruitment of new teachers. Hallett stated that "the unity and integrity of an academic institution devolves from the Programme it offers far more than from its individual components," and he highlighted the need for a program that would "prepare professional practicing musicians." This was tantamount to admitting that the RCM could and should have a professional department, which would, undoubtedly, irritate the Faculty of Music. What was needed to make Hallett's proposal come to life was an advanced three-year RCM program eligible for provincial funding. However, Dean John Beckwith, in a letter to Hallett of October 21, 1976, when the committee first began its deliberations, opposed any new professional programs for the RCM.

And so, after several months of meetings, a thoroughly frustrated Hallett prepared a final report that was eventually buried in the University's archives. It is of interest, in view of future events, that the report proposed that the RCM should settle for one of three courses of action: 1) separate from the University, 2) integrate the staffs of the Faculty and the Conservatory "in some way and in some degree," or 3) remain more or less as they were. Of course the third recommendation was the outcome, at least for the time being.

The low incomes of most RCM teachers rightfully disturbed Hallett. Only 4 teachers out of 197 earned over $20,000 per year. Nine earned between $15,000 and $20,000, thirty-five between $10,000 and $15,000, and eighty-nine between $5,000 and $10,000, and nearly all of these teachers were full-time. There were an astonishing sixty who earned less than $5,000. Granted that some teachers, especially in the lower income categories, may have had other sources of income, but, nonetheless, the figures were especially damning when compared to University teaching salaries. For 1976–77 (excluding the medical and dental faculties) full professors earned an average of $34,580, associate professors an average of $25,666, assistant professors an average of $19,700, and lecturers an average of $16,708.[384]

The sympathetic Hallett noted, too, that the normal terms of teachers' contracts at the RCM "permit them to teach only in the RCM, yet they draw incomes so very much less than their counterparts in the school system as any reader of the newspapers of 1976 will recognize instantly." The committee, Hallett said, deplores this situation and believes provincial government funding is an absolute must. The Ministry of Colleges and Universities (MCU) did seem to respond to the Conservatory's entreaties by coming through with one grant of $100,000 for 1977–78. However, the MCU had been led to understand that it would be used for specific projects and was upset to find that the Conservatory simply put it into its bank account. Right or wrong, the ministry did not renew its grant the following year.[385]

Routine if not downright somnolent best describes the RCM during the first eight years of the seventies. It had been emasculated and could do little to improve its profile. That is not to say, however, that good teaching didn't go on, for it did. Margaret Parsons and her husband, Clifford Poole, were among the most successful RCM piano teachers. In 1974, journalist Michael Schulman interviewed Boris Berlin, who was marking his forty-fifth year on the faculty.[386] Berlin explained that his aim was to create material that would be a "blend of pedagogical usefulness with musical interest, both at the level of the child," and boasted that sixteen to twenty thousand of his beginners' books were being sold annually. Berlin's children's pieces were being lauded from as far away as the Soviet Union. He was busy giving workshops all over Canada, showing teachers how to help pupils like and understand the music that they were playing. He believed that all children should be able to play by ear and to write music. From his early collaborations with Sir Ernest MacMillan, Berlin had now moved on to an eight-volume *Four Star Series* devoted to sight-reading and a *Basics of Ear Training* in collaboration with Registrar Warren Mould.

Registrations continued to increase, and the space allocated to the Conservatory at McMaster Hall was becoming glaringly inadequate. The University finally moved its academic classes to other campus locations.[387] By 1978 the RCM had taken over the entire building. In 1972 the MCU agreed that "in future full-time conservatory students are eligible for student loans and grants on the same basis as students who are enrolled in the Colleges of Arts and Technology."[388] This Ontario Students Assistance Plan (OSAP) was a financial godsend for the RCM. However, the Conservatory's entrance standards were not rigorous. It may not have been wise to encourage students to mortgage their futures with large student loans unless they clearly showed the talent and degree of advancement necessary for a professional musical career. As for the Musical Talent Foundation, it was of little use to the RCM, since nearly all of its scholarships were given to Faculty of Music students. Yet, when the RCM asked to have the scholarships' sizeable administrative chores transferred to the Faculty, its request was refused.[389]

David Ouchterlony retired in 1977 to become the director of the Kiwanis Music Festival. One of his favourite projects while principal was establishing a branch of the RCM in Sarnia, but after several years it closed because of excessive costs. Gordon Kushner, Ouchterlony's executive assistant since 1972 and director of the Summer School, became acting principal for six months prior to my appointment as principal in July 1978. I was given a leave of absence from the Faculty of Music to take on this assignment.

In some respects it was much like a homecoming, since a number of teachers I had known in the fifties were still there. However, the position presented more of a challenge than I anticipated, for developing post-secondary programs at the Conservatory held little promise. After acknowledging the University's constraints, I turned to implementing non-competing programs that would in part bring the school back to its position of thirty years before. Yes, the Opera School was now with the Faculty, but there could be ensemble programs and a revival of the special preparatory courses, whose enrolment had sadly declined.

Initially, I addressed orchestral and conductor training. Professional orchestral musicians were persistently critical of orchestral training at the Faculty of Music. For four years before going to the RCM

I had directed an annual conductors' workshop, with top musicians such as Andrew Davis instructing. The workshop, designed for four or five aspiring conductors, was administered through the Faculty. They met weekly to conduct assigned scores with piano and, once monthly, a small professional orchestra. A grant from the Ontario Arts Council (OAC) made this program possible. When I moved to the Conservatory I brought the program with me, and it continued for several more years. The most talented conductors in the program eventually found positions with orchestras, opera companies, and ballet companies, mainly in Canada.

The other new program about which the University could not quarrel was the Orchestral Training Program (OTP). In 1979, orchestras, opera companies, and ballet companies were booming. Altogether they employed approximately six hundred orchestral musicians. Additionally, there was a pool of symphonically trained musicians who were used by these groups as extra players. There had been many openings in these orchestras in the preceding ten years — a period of great orchestral growth in the country — and most of them, as has already been suggested, had been disproportionately filled by American musicians. (American and Canadian musicians belong to the same union, so there was — and still is — no problem employing Americans.) The Canada Council, the Association of Canadian Orchestras, and Canadian musicians' unions were all concerned and blamed the situation on the country's inadequate training institutions. Right or wrong, in 1978 Quebec addressed the issue by sponsoring a six-month course in orchestral training for young professional musicians administered through its provincial conservatory system.

In May 1979, I brought forward a roughly similar plan for the RCM. The TSO was supportive, and Canada's Ministry of Employment and Immigration decided to fund it substantially. From this emanated the OTP. Its first session began in January 1980 and ran until May. Outstanding conductors and top players for master classes were engaged for its faculty. OTP conductors also taught in the conductors' workshop, whose student conductors attended OTP rehearsals and, on occasion, conducted the orchestra. Thanks to federal and OAC backing, the RCM sponsored as close to an ideal program as one could find anywhere for advanced instrumentalists and conductors, nearly all of whom already had degrees and/or diplomas from universities and conservatories. From the beginning of the second term, the forty students in the program earned $70 weekly.

The program was first managed by Philip Morehead (now head of the music staff at the Chicago Lyric Opera), with the help of an advisory committee of leading local musicians. The OTP continued until 1991–92, although funding was reduced in its later years. The program met and gave its concerts in the nearby Church of the Redeemer at Bloor Street and Avenue Road because there was insufficient space at McMaster Hall. Occasional requests to use the MacMillan Theatre at the Johnson Building were rejected by the Faculty of Music.

The first OTP conductors included Andrew Davis (TSO), Mario Bernardi (National Arts Centre), Victor Yampolsky (Atlantic Symphony), Lucas Foss (Buffalo Symphony), Iona Brown (St. Martin in the Fields), Kazuyoshi Akiyama (Vancouver Symphony), Sidney Harth, Lawrence Leonard, Seymour Lipkin, Oscar Shumsky, Laszlo Varga, and James Yannatos. Master classes were given by Joseph Silverstein (concertmaster, Boston Symphony), Daniel Majeske (concertmaster, Cleveland Orchestra), Ronald Leonard (principal cellist, Los Angeles Philharmonic), Steven Staryk (concertmaster, TSO), John Mack (principal oboe, Cleveland Orchestra), other top-notch players from both Canadian and American orchestras, and soloists including violinist Alexander Schneider, flutist Jean-Pierre Rampal, and oboist Heinz Holliger.

In addition to orchestral reading sessions and rehearsals for concerts, there were seminars on preparing for auditions, a vexing and stressful procedure yet all-important for orchestral players. The musicians union insisted that players at auditions for orchestral positions play behind a screen to protect their anonymity so that the audition jury's selections would be fair. In effect, a nerve-wracking four-minute audition could change a musician's life. How fair was it? The OTP also had seminars in section playing, chamber music classes, and instrumental instruction from RCM teachers.

The OTP concerts were well-attended. The orchestra, for want of a name, was called the Royal Conservatory Orchestra. Even though it was a small orchestra and played in an unsuitable hall, its quality was without question. During the OTP's first term, Philip Morehead told a reporter that the "essential ingredient of the project has been the cooperation and involvement of the Toronto Symphony and its conductor Andrew Davis."[390] It was in some respects like the COC's involvement in the Conservatory Opera School in the fifties and sixties. Both were contemporary versions of the apprentice programs of one or two centuries earlier. (In fact, the COC's Lotfi Mansouri and his assistant John Leberg, after studying the OTP, successfully sought a similar grant to start the company's ensemble program for young professional singers. It continues to this day.) Morehead also noted that many of the TSO's principal players were on both the OTP and the RCM faculty. Michael Colgrass, a leading composer and percussionist, was interviewed for the same article and echoed what other musicians had been saying, that orchestral players need truly exacting training to succeed in a highly competitive field.

In its early years, the OTP kept careful records of its students. Thirty-seven of its graduates found jobs in Canadian orchestras from 1980 to 1985. Canadian conductors were used more frequently as the program continued. The OAC sponsored an annual conducting competition for the Heinz Unger Award — Unger had been a prominent Toronto conductor in the fifties and early sixties — and the OTP served as the competition orchestra for several years. Robert Sunter, of the CBC and former music officer at the OAC, spoke at an OTP press conference on April 13, 1984. He stated that the conductors' workshop evolved out of discussions seeking ways to train Canadian conductors. "It was 1968 and, although we didn't know it then, they were the halcyon days of the arts in Ontario. There was irresistible energy, vaunting ambition, and a bloody minded determination to make governments understand that a nation can only define itself through its artists." A maverick at heart, Sunter berated the arts councils and the CBC for not doing more for Canadian artists. Canadian orchestras should have a Canadian conductor or, at least, a Canadian assistant conductor, he said. Also, there were still too few Canadians at every level in the orchestral world, and there seemed to be less and less will to address the problem. Sunter deplored, too, the lack of militancy of arts organizations in pressing for more funds from governments.

The administration of the examinations department needed attention. Its head, Helen Bickell, had been with the Conservatory for fifty-one years and ran an efficient but not cost-effective operation. All the record-keeping was done manually, as it had been done since the days of Edward Fisher. Computers had become a fact of life, but introducing one to a long-standing and competent department wasn't easy. (I turned up studies going back to the sixties that recommended that the department's antiquated system needed computer assistance.) Mrs. Bickell retired in 1979, and shortly after, on April 1, 1980, the RCM announced that theory and practical examinations would now be processed by computer. The changeover didn't go smoothly, with the usual mix-ups and errors. However, by the mid-winter examination period (1980–81) most of the glitches were gone. Fears of negative effects on examination registrations in the transition period were groundless. On the contrary, there was a 10 percent increase in candidates from 1978 to 1981.

This computerization didn't happen without disputes with the University's computing service, which the RCM was using for the examination department. It was very costly. A report from an independent consultant stated that it was charging 25 percent more than similar services. When I voiced an objection to President James Ham, he was not pleased. He had little sympathy for the

University's poor self-supporting ward on Bloor Street. Unlike the rest of the University, the RCM bravely chose to discontinue the University's computing service and engaged an outside firm. I found out later that other faculties had also complained about the excessive cost of the University's computing service.

I broadened my view of examinations with a visit to the Associated Board of the Royal Schools of Music in London. I knew nothing at that time of the RCM's disputes with the Associated Board (AB) eighty years earlier.[391] The RCM and the AB were not far apart in believing in the importance of examinations. They both viewed an examination as a learning exercise and an evaluation tool for teacher and student, showing the candidate's strengths and weaknesses and motivating him or her to greater achievement in the future. The AB's grades went as high as VIII, and its theory requirements were less stringent than the RCM's. The Conservatory's theory requirements suggest that an RCM Grade X student — more or less equivalent to the AB's Grade VIII — had a wider knowledge of music and its anatomy, although the performing skills might be comparable. (As a point of interest, in 1980 the AB had three hundred thousand worldwide registrations annually, four to five times more than the RCM.)

On this same trip I visited the RCM branches in Lahr and Baden, Germany, to review the RCM's contract with the Royal Canadian Air Force (RCAF). The branches served those Canadian families at the RCAF installation who wanted Canadian teachers to prepare their children for RCM examinations. The two conservatory teachers, Patricia Lemoine and Majorie Lea, did extremely good work. A third Canadian teacher who had headed the branches initially and who had stayed on to teach in the area was Warren Mould, former Conservatory registrar. This was in the land of Beethoven and Brahms! The RCM closed the branch some years later when the RCAF left Germany.

The preparatory course registrations had dropped from over one hundred to thirty-three by 1978. With Vice-Principal Kushner in charge (the vice-principal position was reinstated in 1978), the Conservatory publicized it more widely and urged teachers to have their best students apply for it. By 1981 its numbers had grown to eighty, including a blossoming string enrolment. Two string orchestras, conducted by John Barnum, and two choirs, directed by Denise Narcisse-Mair, were organized. There was also a chamber music program for outstanding teenage students. Ofra Harnoy, who would become an outstanding cellist in the concert world, played in one of the string quartets. Others in the program included Stephen Sitarski, later concertmaster of the Kitchener-Waterloo Symphony, and Barry Shiffman, a charter member of the St. Lawrence String Quartet.

In 1978, a newly formed local film company, Rhombus, made a charming film about three twelve-year-old RCM pupils: pianist Yuval Fichman, who would win a number of international prizes in the future, violinist Barry Shiffman, and cellist Wendy Morton. The film showed them preparing sections of Beethoven's op. 1, no. 1, with Conservatory teacher Robert Spergel coaching. Titled *Opus 1, No. 1*, it helped the school's image and contributed towards Rhombus's growing reputation as a filmmaker of musical subjects. Five years later, Rhombus did a sequel, *Opus 2*, with the same group, this time with Spergel's sister, Mildred Kenton, coaching.

Two new programs were begun — one in early music and the other for Suzuki strings. These new programs contributed to growing enrolments — from 7,620 registrations in 1977 to 8,950 in 1981, an increase of about 17 percent. The teaching staff now numbered three hundred, with most of the

Opus 2 class. From left to right: Barry Shiffman, Mildred Kenton, Yuval Fichman, and Wendy Morton.

recent additions orchestral instrument teachers. Metro Toronto granted $10,000 annually to support the work of the branches, and a new RCM division opened in September 1981 in Mississauga, an expanding community west of Toronto. Teacher welfare was also addressed. In 1977–78, the RCM paid $122,000 towards health plans, pensions, and unemployment insurance. After introducing dental, group, and disability insurance in 1980–81, its contribution increased to $230,000. A thriving Summer School announced an enrolment increase of 40 percent from 1978 to 1980.

The 1982 Summer School was comprehensive, touching on many different areas, and the CAPAC lectures were revived, with playwright/actor Mavor Moore speaking on two nights. The American voice teacher Daniel Ferro returned for a second term, such was his success, as did the great American pianist Leon Fleisher; Fleisher would work at the RCM intermittently for the next two decades and more. Greta Kraus gave a German lieder class. Jeanne Baxtresser, principal flute of the TSO and soon to be the principal of the New York Philharmonic, presided over a master class along with her teacher, Julius Baker. Jazz flutist Moe Koffman, oboist Ray Still, cellist Tsuyoshi Tsutsumi, and clarinetist Joaquin Valdepeñas also gave master classes. A Baroque week, with Stanley Ritchie, Nigel Rogers, Mary Springfels, and Colin Tilney, all internationally known early music performers, was another high point. Margaret Hillis of the Chicago Symphony and Denise Narcisse-Mair gave choral conducting sessions. There were other classes too numerous to mention, even a reed-making session for oboists given by Patricia Morehead. Finally, there was a percussion week with Fred Hinger of the Metropolitan Opera Orchestra, members of the Toronto percussion ensemble Nexus, tympanist David Kent of the TSO, Columbian expert in Latin jazz Memo Aceved, and Indian classical drummer Trichi Sankaran.

The Conservatory was giving more concerts in its concert hall. Although access to the hall was, and continues to be, awkward, the excellent acoustics, much like the hall at College Street, made up for it. Off campus, the Yamaha Piano Company sponsored an RCM "Monster Concert" at Massey Hall on October 31, 1980. The hall was full, and twenty top RCM piano teachers performed a variety of two-hand and four-hand music on ten grand pianos supplied by Yamaha. The American pianist Eugene List, who had played for world leaders at the famous 1945 Potsdam Conference, was the soloist. Ten young pianists — average age twelve — joined the performers in the finale, each child seated between two adult pianists. It was lovely for both eyes and ears. And it netted approximately $25,000 for the RCM.

Without consulting the string department of either the Faculty or the RCM, the University sold a fine Bergonzi violin to an anonymous buyer, the sale money ($50,000) going to the RCM. Lady Eaton had initially loaned it to the National Youth Orchestra and appointed the University its custodian. The

RCM matched the money realized from the sale and then applied, successfully, for a provincial Wintario grant to match the new total.[392] With the grand total, the Conservatory bought twenty-five new 3CD Yamaha grands, two larger model L Steinway grands, a one-manual harpsichord built by Harvey Fink, and a two-manual harpsichord built by Wolfgang Kater. These purchases met the RCM's keyboard needs for the next five to ten years. Although the RCM profited enormously from the sale, it remains debatable whether the Bergonzi violin should have been sold in the first instance, since gifted RCM students could have used it in the years to come.

The Windsor Weinstein Stradivarius, donated to the RCM by philanthropist and amateur violinist Leon Weinstein, had a different story. The RCM helped restore it, thanks to a $15,000 grant from the Ontario Heritage Foundation. It eventually found its way to the Canada Council instrument bank, which loans valuable instruments to leading young musicians for two or three years at a time. Such instruments are national treasures.

Another windfall of Wintario grant money in September 1980 enabled the RCM to pay for a feasibility study of McMaster Hall, its east wing, and the surrounding land.[393] The brilliant architect Barton Myers and his team of associates — architects, engineers, and acousticians — produced a plan with a number of significant ideas: a new west wing with an auditorium and rehearsal halls, a new fifteen-storey east wing (the engineers deemed the present east wing bordering on the unsafe!) with teaching studios and practice rooms on the lower floors and a residential condominium above, a major renovation of McMaster Hall, and a new small building to the rear for a café and teaching studios. The study should have led to major construction, but the University wouldn't let the RCM raise money for the project. Besides, it didn't want a condominium next to Philosopher's Walk. Myers left Toronto in the eighties, but his younger colleagues, Kuwabara, Payne, McKenna, and Blumberg, did eventually lead the RCM into a major building program.

In 1980, the RCM sponsored a national meeting in Toronto of eleven English-speaking Canadian conservatories and community colleges with substantial music programs. Ontario's Ministry of Culture and Recreation and Ministry of Colleges and Universities also sent delegates, as did two local boards of education. The conference addressed two major concerns: 1) the need for music schools to share information about their instructional objectives and procedures and to show how these fitted into the educational scheme of the country; and 2) the positions music schools should take when approaching boards and ministries for funding. Those attending felt that communities take conservatories for granted too readily, and that few assist them financially. The meeting also addressed relationships conservatories have with universities, conservatory diploma standards compared to university degree standards, and relations with provincial music teachers groups. Out of this meeting came the formation of a new association, the Association of Conservatories and Colleges of Music (ACCM).

The ACCM was an alliance of schools formed to review curricula; share information; investigate sources of funding; and canvas non-profit conservatories, music schools, departments of music in colleges and CEGEPs (Quebec's pre-university colleges), and Quebec conservatories. The group met the next year in Banff, and then in Montreal in 1982, where conservatoire directors from different parts of Quebec explained how their schools operated and how they were subsidized. Conservatory directors from other parts of Canada, including the RCM's, were green with envy. However, when asked to join the ACCM, the Quebec directors declined because they were civil servants. The ACCM didn't meet again for five years.

Glenn Gould, the Conservatory's most famous alumnus, died on October 4, 1982. I missed the funeral at Mt. Pleasant Cemetery and the memorial service at St. Paul's Anglican Church because I was on an examination goodwill tour. However, I wrote in the November issue of *Con Notes*, the RCM's news journal, what thousands of other felt: "He was one of the great musicians of our time. For those of us who knew him there is a huge void, a gnawing sense of deep personal loss. He will not play again as no other has, talk to us with his rare insight on all things musical and non-musical; there will be no new writings of his, so rich in language and colour."

There was a happier event at the school a month and a half later. The RCM conferred an honorary associateship on Louis Applebaum, the first such honorary diploma in the school's history. Applebaum, who had studied piano with Boris Berlin, was one of Canada's finest composers and creative arts administrators. He was just winding up his report as co-chairman of the Federal Cultural Policy Review Committee, its goal to set policies that would assist the arts in Canada. There was a change in government after the committee embarked on its work — Conservative to Liberal — and the new government assigned Jacques Hébert to be its co-chair; the report thus became known as the Applebert Report.[394] It addressed an immense subject replete with political overtones, but had little effect on musical education.

It was not, as they say, all sweetness and light in my years as principal. Some teachers were earning disproportionately large fees in summer schools and, to a lesser extent, in winter terms, by teaching large theory and history classes at substantial individual student rates.[395] Bringing this to a halt — paying teachers by the class and moderating student rates — was reasonable by any standard, but the teachers affected were, understandably, not happy with this change, even though I gave one year's notice before implementing it. Several of those affected were on the Faculty Association executive and wielded considerable influence. Other executive members had been denied teaching opportunities at the Faculty of Music when I was head of its performance department and saw an opportunity to retaliate. Surprisingly oblivious to the executive's ill feelings, I was thus unprepared for disturbing events later in my term of office.

The administrative staff also resented one or two persons

Louis Applebaum (left) receives the first RCM honorary diploma from Principal Schabas, November 1982.

I engaged to assist me, as much for their personalities as for the way they carried out their tasks.[396] In retrospect, I should have been more careful to employ staff who would not irritate my colleagues. This was not the case, however, when two of my more ebullient assistants at the Faculty of Music, on their own volition, quit their posts there to join me at the RCM. It may have given me the false impression that I could do no wrong in staff selection and supervision.

On February 23, 1979, halfway through my first year at the RCM, I submitted a detailed plan for reorganizing the school to John Sword, executive assistant to the University's president, James Ham. I recommended an independent conservatory and a resident ARCT program. I also suggested that with independence and a formal program the RCM might then obtain provincial grants similar to those given to the Ontario College of Art and to community colleges. Then, in September 1979, I brought my views out into the open, first in the University's student newspaper, *The Varsity,* and then in two "Notes from the Principal" to the faculty and staff. I said that there were no substantial reasons for the RCM to remain part of the University of Toronto. I explained that the MCU grant of 1977–78 would not be an annual one and that all other RCM fundraising was either totally forbidden or, if allowed, had awkward and restrictive conditions. Hopes for an RCM post-secondary diploma course and a music high school would remain nothing more than dreams as long as the University's restrictions remained. True as this was, it was premature to raise the issue of separation with the faculty. I should have prepared the ground more carefully for such an important and controversial issue. Many RCM teachers, as in the past, looked to the University as a prestigious and income-enhancing connection and a protective umbrella.

In March 1981, the RCM concluded an agreement with the RCM's Faculty Association that gave the association powers and rights approaching that of any union in Ontario, even though its members were technically self-employed and contracted yearly. The University, as always eager for peace to reign at the school, approved the agreement. (The RCM paid the teachers, so why not?) The teaching staff, aware of this support, more than ever sought to remain with the University.

The trial balloon suggesting separation from the University had other unfortunate ramifications, since it also annoyed the University and the Faculty of Music. It resulted in a memorandum of understanding being drafted by University, Faculty, and RCM officials, dated February 13, 1981, which listed twenty-one points of reference, none especially new except that henceforth the Conservatory would be treated as an academic body, much like any other University faculty, and report to the office of the provost. It was just another way to keep a close watch on the Conservatory.

Robert Dodson was chosen by a search committee that I chaired to succeed the retiring Gordon Kushner as vice-principal. He was tall, handsome, and bearded (rather Lincolnesque in appearance), and extremely well-spoken and articulate. A cellist and member of the Vaghy Quartet-in-Residence at Queen's University until his appointment at the RCM, he did his work well and helped me a great deal as I tried out further innovations in the school's operations.

In the spring of 1982 I took a six-month leave of absence. Dodson took over for this period. In April he suggested that I appoint Andrew Shaw, a former Dodson cello student and manager of the Kitchener-Waterloo Symphony, as assistant principal in charge of all performing groups: the OTP, the small string orchestras, and the choirs, all of which, collectively, became the Professional Training Program. Shaw left the RCM at the end of the 1982–83 season, but the seeds for more professionalism in RCM programs had been planted.

The good news was that, during my first three years, the RCM's accumulated deficit had been reduced by 30 to 35 percent. Academic matters in the examination department were under control, but its administration needed tightening, so George Hoskins was appointed examination director. His position as business administrator had been voided by the University's appointment of Ian Ross as assistant principal (administration).

When I returned in September 1982, I found Vice-Provost Roger Wolff, to whom I reported, plainly antagonistic. He had been listening to the woes of the Faculty Association executive and anticipated difficulties between it and the principal. The University's custodianship of the Conservatory didn't include a principal who confronted issues, and thus Wolff didn't support me. Favourable representations by leading faculty members who supported me had no effect on the provost's office, nor did my accomplishments as principal, since the University saw most of them as competition for the Faculty of Music.[397] I announced in March that I would conclude my five-year term in June 1983. The Faculty Association executive were pleased, but I got the feeling that the rest of the teaching staff were surprised to hear that I was not staying on at least another two years, my option when I took the post. The University, unprepared, asked Gustav Ciamaga, dean of the Faculty of Music, to be acting principal. He accepted.

What was going on at the RCM? The kettle came to a boil when, a month before my departure on May 25, 1983, the University advertised in the *Globe and Mail* that there was a "Development Opportunity" on the RCM property. The University "plans to relocate the present occupants of the building, so that the building and land will be available for non-university, income producing use." This announcement came without warning, and the proverbial "something" hit the fan. The RCM faculty was thoroughly incensed. My hands were tied, thanks to the Faculty Association executive's help in discrediting me with the University. However, I did manage to get a promise from President Ham that "there must be satisfactory financial provision to replace McMaster Hall and provide a new facility." Furthermore, Ham said that the new facility must be in place before the Conservatory vacates McMaster Hall and it should be near the Faculty of Music to be accessible to Conservatory students.[398] Where in the world that could be only Ham might know. Fortunately, the University backed down and nothing more was said for a while about selling or disposing of McMaster Hall.

There was, however, an epilogue to these curious happenings. The so-called Wolff Committee, the third committee in ten years to address the relationship between the RCM and the Faculty of Music, was struck. Its members were Alexandra Johnston, principal of Victoria College; R.W. Missen, who had preceded Wolff as vice-provost for music; G.P. Payzant, professor in the philosophy department and an organist and writer on aesthetics and music; Walter Pitman, at the time executive director of the Ontario Arts Council; and D.W. Lang, a top university administrator. Members of the committee were shocked when they found that I was leaving the RCM because of an embittered Faculty Association executive and a non-supportive vice-provost.[399] And there was Wolff chairing their committee!

In December 1983 the committee published a "Summary for Discussion" report that received wide circulation. It recommended that the Faculty of Music take over all professional music training and set up a separate division for community music teaching operated by the University for a transitional period of ten years, after which time this separate division should be separated from the University.[400] The committee, fed up with the Conservatory's pretensions as a school, said the obvious, that it was a teachers' collective and as such had no place at the University and should eventually be set free to function as a community music school.

The Summary was yet another attempt to solve the problems (enigma?) of music at the University, while continuing at all costs — it hoped — to give the Faculty of Music what it needed. The RCM's Faculty Association executive, led by its president Joseph Macerollo, wrote a seventeen-page response to Wolff on February 17, 1984, attacking the committee for exceeding its terms of reference. Macerollo wrote that it had not had "proper consultation or input from those most intimately affected; and its recommendations are based on inadequate information and flawed reasoning."

The press, as expected, took up the cudgels for the nearly hundred-year-old Conservatory and how much it meant to Canada. It was almost like a replay of the press's treatment of the 1952 reorganization. Critics did not look beyond the superficial, failing to see that the RCM was neither healthy nor dynamic. To spin the story, the press claimed, without documentation, that the University had approved the sale of McMaster Hall to a private developer who hoped to create a hotel on the site. Indeed, the Conservatory's future appeared ominous. The Wolff Committee, after a stormy public hearing on its discussion paper, returned to its deliberations.

In June 1984, the committee submitted its final report to Provost Frank Iacobucci. (He had succeeded Provost Strangway, was later appointed to the Supreme Court of Canada, and in 2004 was appointed interim president of the University of Toronto.) It said the obvious, that the RCM should be an independent institution. Both the Conservatory and the Faculty had mixed feelings about the decision, but for different reasons. Joseph Macerollo, at a press conference, said, "integration of the two institutions was logical since they already share facilities and staff." He did admit, however, that "autonomy could make it easier for the Conservatory to raise money."[401] As if on cue, a group of Canadian musicians, including Lois Marshall, Steven Staryk, Liona Boyd, Oscar Peterson, and Gordon Lightfoot, promptly set up The Friends of the Conservatory Foundation of Canada to raise funds for the school and, according to Macerollo, to participate in the separation plans.[402]

On the other hand, the Faculty of Music was worried anything might happen with an independent Conservatory. Carl Morey, dean of the Faculty of Music, was no less troubled by Wolff than I had been. Wolff seemed antagonistic to the Faculty and any proposals it made.[403] In fact, nearly everyone was concerned about Wolff's attitude. The University's plans to sell McMaster Hall were put on hold — and eventually dropped — because the University was committed to finding the RCM new quarters if it did so.[404] Over sixty years of varying degrees of conflict with the University, which held the trump card at all times, was drawing to a close. Now the RCM had to face the rigours of legal separation.

Acting Principal Dodson, who succeeded Ciamaga in 1984, favoured the separation but had difficulty getting a "detailed collective response" to the report from the RCM assembly, so he prepared one independently and distributed it to all teachers and staff. He singled out several points that needed clarification and asked that the door be left open for other points he might address during the separation process. Dodson agreed with two of the report's four premises: that the University sever its connection when satisfied that the Conservatory is able to function independently, and that the Conservatory be governed by a strong independent board at the time of separation. The report had referred to the University as a "patron" of the Conservatory. Dodson, to his credit, felt this undeserved, given its sporadic financial support for the past fifty years. Dodson also declared that the RCM would initiate new programs even while separation was going on.

The wheels turned slowly: Provost Iacobucci and University President Connell were helpful in getting things underway, but the intricacies, the paperwork, and the endless meetings took many hours, days, weeks, and months. Gordon Kushner returned to the RCM as acting vice-principal from 1984 to 1986. Then Joseph Macerollo, at Wolff's suggestion, was appointed special assistant to the acting principal to help Dodson develop "proposals for systems of governance for the new Conservatory."[405] Macerollo's appointment upset the Faculty Association executive, who thought he was going over to management. Its concerns were short-lived. His appointment lasted only three months, ending when Macerollo resigned from the RCM because of a dispute with Dodson over music history examinations.

The University Governing Council had been heavily involved in RCM decisions, but now the stakes were much higher. Its membership was composed of sentimental partisans for the RCM, serious-minded supporters of the professional Faculty of Music, others determined not to give away University assets (they knew little of the RCM's history and *its* lost assets), and, thankfully, some who saw the big picture and believed that Toronto could and should have two schools of music. Toronto now had two universities (Toronto and York), with a third one (Ryerson) in the wings. Compare Toronto with Montreal, which had three music schools in 1985: the provincial conservatory, McGill University, and the Université de Montréal.

And so the first decision of the University governors on April 18, 1985, was that, in principle, the University would take action to create an independent Conservatory by July 1, 1986. The outcome would be a Royal Conservatory of Music corporation without share capital, with a board of trustees that would control all of its assets, including the Harris Company, the branches, and all funds and assets held in trust. The next decision would result in five years of disputatious wrangling between the RCM and the University: the University would provide the new corporation access to McMaster Hall or equivalent facilities, but nothing was said about *giving* it to the Conservatory. And, finally, it stated that an act of the Ontario legislature was needed to separate the RCM from the University and to establish the new corporation.

One wise governor warned that July 1, 1986, was a mere fourteen months away, and that it might be too soon to address the complex details involved in separation: the formation of a new corporate structure, settling the division of labour between the Conservatory and the Faculty, securing leadership for the Conservatory (Dodson was still acting principal), making arrangements to ensure RCM financial viability, providing accommodation, transferring ownership of the Frederick Harris Music Company, securing tax-exempt status, and the inauguration of fundraising efforts. Other unforeseen issues requiring resolution appeared as the negotiations proceeded.

Dodson spoke at a general meeting of the school over a year later, on May 15, 1986, to dispel rumours by bearers of gloom and doom that the school was in trouble. He said that separation was moving along, that a principal's advisory committee and an implementation committee had been meeting to address corporate structure and resources, and that a legal firm was exploring the Conservatory Act. A new RCM board of management was established by the University in early 1986, the first board with any real power in almost twenty years. Its chairman was Lac Minerals President Peter Allen. Robert Dodson, Gordon Kushner, and Steven Staryk represented the RCM. The other members were Vice-Chairman Ben Wilson, chairman of the Ontario Manpower Commission; two businessmen, Lawrence Heisey and J.C. Wilson; lawyer William A. MacDonald; and Patricia Wardrop, a researcher at the *Encyclopedia of Music in Canada* and as such well informed about Canadian musical life. The acting principal would report to the board, and the board would report through the president of the University to the Governing Council until separation was achieved.

The board met several times in the spring and summer of 1986. It had some daunting tasks: setting the terms to free McMaster Hall and the surrounding lands from the University; deciding on who — the RCM or the Faculty — owned equipment such as pianos, music, and books; distributing named scholarships between the RCM and Faculty (particularly those given to the RCM in the fifties and sixties when it was divided into two divisions); resolving the ongoing collective agreement negotiations with the RCM's Faculty Association and the University; establishing modes of payment for administrative and clerical staff, which had previously followed University guidelines for salaries, pensions, and other benefits; and working out pensions and benefits for teachers.

Dodson greeted the staff in his Principal's Letter of October 20, 1986, with news about the impending RCM centennial celebrations. There would be an open house on November 20, at which the plans for a gala would be unveiled. Dodson promised that Jon Vickers, the Mendelssohn Choir, the Orpheus Choir, Zara Nelsova, and other artists would perform. He noted enthusiastically that the RCM would soon have a new logo — combining the school's founding date with a lyrebird, to represent both instrumental and vocal music. The *RCM Bulletin* would replace *Con Notes*, and there would be a new audio-visual series featuring Conservatory faculty. The first a-v release would be an updated version of a film, *A Lesson with Steven Staryk.*

The same letter announced that a search committee was in place to select a principal, with the headhunting firm Woods Gordon assisting it. Darryl Irvine, a prominent piano teacher, would succeed Hoskins as director of examinations, and the assembly membership had been set at twenty-six: ten elected by the teachers, six appointed by the principal, one representing the Faculty of Music, one representing the Faculty Association, and eight ex officio — the president and vice-provost of the University, the dean of the Faculty of Music, and five RCM administrators, including, of course, the principal.

A number of fine musicians had joined the teaching staff in the late seventies. From Russia came Marina Geringas, an outstanding piano teacher of gifted children, and Boris Lysenko, former head of the piano department at the Leningrad Conservatory. Then there was Marietta Orlov, a Hungarian pianist who had come to Toronto with her cellist husband, Vladimir Orlov. Mrs. Orlov's teaching has gone from strength to strength with each passing year. Another especially outstanding pianist who joined the RCM in 1979 was Antonin Kubalek from Czechoslovakia. Kubalek was well known in Central Europe before coming to Canada. He is a powerful performer of the standard repertoire and, additionally, of contemporary mainstream Canadian music. Two young Canadian pianists, James Anagnason and Leslie Kinton, who were successful in the concert world as duo-pianists, were also developing large RCM classes, as was pianist Andrew Markow, who had studied at the Faculty of Music and in the Soviet Union. There were also Victor Danchenko and Leo Wigdorchik, Russian violinists, and Adelina Burashko, a Russian theory teacher.

New voice teachers included Patricia Kern of the English National Opera (formerly Sadler's Wells) and Jean MacPhail, an ARCT and Faculty of Music and Opera School graduate who had sung widely in Canada, Europe, and the United States. MacPhail was appointed singing coordinator in 1981. Another 1979 faculty entry was Sandra Cannon, who became speech and drama coordinator in 1981. This department had done excellent if unsung (!) work for many years, thanks to teachers Clara Baker and Florence Aymong, among others.

Orff teachers Angela Elster and Alison Kenny-Gardhouse succeeded Doreen Hall in 1978. They directed the growing program at the RCM and encouraged its expansion to other schools in Canada and the United States. The Suzuki method, imported from Japan, was initiated at the school in 1979 with

Erica Davidson teaching violin and cello to young children. A year later Spiro Kizas launched Suzuki piano classes. Suzuki enrolments increased steadily from its very first days at the RCM. Parents were expected to attend the Suzuki lessons and classes and to help their children study at home. The principle behind Suzuki, as described by Alfred Garson, is that children "look, listen, and imitate." Children can start studying as early as two and one-half years old. They are "introduced to music one step at a time.... No child proceeds to the next step until the previous one has been learned, no matter how long it takes. They learn to play the same way they learn to speak, by hearing a sound and then reproducing it."[406] Mechanical? Many think so. There were other approaches to early music education. In the eighties, Edith Lantos, a pupil of Zoltán Kodály, introduced the Kodály method for children, and Donna Wood started her classes for pre-kindergarten children. Both earned well-deserved followings.

Separation plans were more or less put on hold as the school geared up for its centennial gala on February 10, 1987, at Toronto's Roy Thomson Hall. Titled "Stars of the Royal Conservatory" and subtitled a "Benefit Gala," it would be fundraiser for a "Scholarship Endowment Fund." Dodson engaged Edwina Carson, an experienced manager, to plan and execute the celebration, and she did an outstanding job. As Dodson had promised, the Conservatory hosted a press conference and open house on November 20, 1986, the actual hundredth anniversary date of the school's incorporation. Prime Minister Mulroney sent the RCM his personal greetings. "For one hundred years, the Royal Conservatory of Music has been fostering the growth of many young talented people. Whether it be by voice, the hand, or the pen, music is perpetuated and enhanced through dedication and hard work."[407] Ontario Premier David Peterson also conveyed his congratulations to the school, proudly noting that he was a Grade IV graduate.[408]

A program committee under the leadership of Patricia Wardrop admirably assisted Carson and her two associates in coping with details. Every Conservatory artist of the past or present who was asked to perform *gratis* happily agreed. The Department of Communications of the federal government, through its minister Flora MacDonald, and the Ontario Ministry of Citizenship and Culture, through its minister Lily Munro, each gave $25,000 towards costs, and Metro Toronto and the Toronto Arts Council each granted $5,000. The CBC paid $25,000 to broadcast the gala. There was a two-tier ticket scheme: regular tickets cost $15 and $25, and benefit tickets cost $150, $115 of which would go to the Scholarship Endowment Fund. The end result was that donations and benefit receipts netted more than $56,000.

It was a great night. Young groups, including the Suzuki violin class, played in the hall's lobby as the public arrived. The concert itself was magnificent. Harry Freedman's *Fanfares for Century II* opened the program, and Louis Applebaum's *Play On, A Caper on a Well-known Tune* closed it. Joining Applebaum in his fun-song on "Happy Birthday" was Elmer Iseler, who conducted the Elmer Iseler Singers, the Mendelssohn Choir, the Orpheus Choir, the RCM orchestra, members of the TSO, and, of course, the audience. After the concert, a birthday cake was brought into the hall by ministers MacDonald and Munro, as complimentary champagne flowed in the hall's bars. The cake's sparklers, to everyone's amusement, set off the building's fire alarms.

As for the actual program, the first half was mainly instrumental, with three generations of soloists participating: for the younger generation, violinist Corey Cerovsek and pianist Katja Cerovsek played a Wienawski *Polonaise*, and violinist Martin Beaver, clarinetist Michael Rusinek, and pianist Marc Widner played a movement from Bartók's *Contrasts*; for the middle generation, pianist Arthur Ozolins played a Rachmaninoff Prelude, mezzo-soprano Catherine Robbin (with Greta Kraus) sang "If Music be the Food of Love," and flutist Robert Aitken played the Fauré *Fantaisie*; and for the older generation, cellist Zara Nelsova played a movement from the Dvorak Concerto and violinist Steven Staryk played a movement from the Tchaikovsky Concerto. Victor Feldbrill conducted the orchestra.

The second half began with the Mendelssohn and Orpheus choirs singing Harry Somers's *Gloria*. A quartet of fine voice graduates, Caralyn Tomlin, Sandra Graham, Glyn Evans, and Ingemar Korjus, with duo pianists Anagnason and Kinton, next did selections from Brahms's *Liebeslieder Waltzes*. Maria Pellegrini and Donald Garrard sang arias from Cilea's *Adriana Lecouvreur* and Verdi's *Simon Boccanegra*, respectively. A duo from Offenbach's *Tales of Hoffmann* was sung by Rosemarie Landry and Janet Stubbs, followed by the finale from *Le Nozze di Figaro*, with Derek Bate conducting. Jon Vickers then sang the gripping "Vois ma misere" from the last act of Saint Saëns's *Samson et Dalila*, Lois Marshall and Greta Kraus did Schubert's *An die Musik*, and "Play On" wound up the program. When Robert Dodson, who had just been appointed principal and who was enjoying every minute of the proceedings, asked all those in the capacity audience who had ever taken RCM lessons or examinations to raise their hands, he seemed to get a total response. In reviewing the concert, William Littler of the *Toronto Star* called it a "musical smorgasbord....Yes, but that is because the Royal Conservatory has produced many chefs in its time."[409]

Chapter Ten

FREE AT LAST

The RCM sped up the separation process after Robert Creech joined the staff as vice-principal in 1987. Ironically, he had been the first choice for the same post in 1981, but, because of his other commitments involving lengthy absences, he had turned down the offer. Creech had, however, been advising Dodson on a variety of matters since 1986. Of average height and modest bearing, he was reserved and taciturn with staff and faculty, but when it came to drafting plans, proposals, and documents and doing the necessary homework, he was brilliant. Creech had been principal horn of the Vancouver Symphony for many years, the founder of the Courtenay summer music camp in British Columbia, founder and chair of the music department at Vancouver Community College, and, most recently, professor in charge of applied music at the University of Western Ontario's Faculty of Music. He had a trenchant grasp of the legal implications of the RCM/University separation and a clear vision of the school's future. He also had considerable assistance from Peter Simon, director of academic studies. A pianist graduate of the Faculty of Music, Simon also studied at Juilliard and in London, England. He subsequently earned a doctorate in music at the University of Michigan with Leon Fleisher and went on to join the faculty of the University of Western Ontario.

Separation negotiations were tortuous and seemingly endless. There were more than twenty-five meetings between the University and the Conservatory from the fall of 1985 to November 1987. When one issue was resolved, another one was sure to emerge. James Keffer, Alexander Pathy, and Daniel Lang represented the University, and Peter Allen, John Wilson, and Robert Dodson represented the RCM. Although there were positive results, it was clear that the University would not easily give up anything it valued to the RCM.[410] In 1988, the University finally agreed to divide trust funds and scholarships between the Faculty of Music and the RCM. Architect Barton Myers, who had done the 1980 feasibility study, was consulted again about the state of McMaster Hall. He gave a poor prognosis, suggesting large sums be spent on repairs. He estimated that it would cost $36,412,000 to replace the building.[411] This interested neither the University nor the RCM.

As for other Conservatory matters, on June 22, 1986, Dodson reported that Andrew Shaw would become general manager of the Harris Company, beginning in 1987.[412] Shaw soon worked out the complex royalty payments between Harris and the RCM to the latter's satisfaction. On the academic front, Dodson happily reported that the Ontario Arts Council had granted the school $57,000 for its Senior Program pilot project. The OAC was interested in backing a concentrated RCM professional program as an alternative to university performance programs.

In the summer of 1988 questions arose among teachers, administrative staff, and the board of management about Robert Dodson's performance as principal. There were complaints that he had been too arbitrary with senior staff, appointed and dismissed teachers without consultation and due process, and denigrated efforts of other academic officers. The board's very involved and dedicated chairman,

Vice-Principal Robert Creech.

Peter Allen, attacked Dodson for departing from the school's financial plan, for budgetary overruns, for making binding agreements without informing the board, for inconsistencies in teacher management, for negotiating in bad faith with the Faculty Association, and for taking independent action with federal and provincial governments without board approval.[413] Dodson left the Conservatory in September 1988. It should be noted that not all board members supported Allen. Harlequin Books publisher W.L. Heisey, on hearing the news, resigned from the board in protest, saying he knew nothing about Dodson's "performance being less than satisfactory. My own impression was the contrary. No matter what the reality, I cannot accept being presented with a *fait accompli* on such a critical matter."[414]

In his letter of resignation to President George Connell, Dodson said, "Differences with the Board have led me reluctantly to conclude that it is best for me to step aside as Principal."[415] The University's relatively brief news release announcing the resignation said that Gordon Kushner would be acting principal.[416]

Dodson told the *Globe and Mail* that he was "disappointed to leave behind unfinished tasks, most notably the common goal of the University and the Conservatory to establish independent status for the Conservatory." Kushner said Dodson's resignation could have been due to the difficult conditions he worked under. "He tried to do an awful lot and may have ruffled some feathers."[417] According to William Littler, Vice-Provost Keffer said that the differences with Dodson had nothing to do with the Conservatory's separation from the University.[418] Keffer said later, "It's clear to me that the Conservatory now has strength. During the period Rob was administrator, the Conservatory has become a very vital institution."[419] Such contradictory statements and obfuscation went with the territory. Dodson is now provost of the New England Conservatory.

For the next two and a half years Kushner directed the RCM's everyday business, while Creech dealt with academic planning and, especially, the separation. Peter Simon left Toronto in 1989 to become president of the Manhattan School of Music in New York City, to be succeeded as director of academic studies by John Kruspe, an RCM and Faculty of Music theory teacher.

After a six-month lapse, separation negotiations resumed in February 1989. The University's business officers, led by Administrative Vice-President R.L. Criddle, wanted the University to keep McMaster Hall and its immediate surrounding grounds.[420] Criddle had no sense or feeling for the RCM's rights to it. Seeing it simply as valuable University property, Criddle set up as many roadblocks as he could to stymie the RCM from taking possession of it. One especially onerous condition he proposed was that the RCM must build on the land surrounding the Conservatory within ten years, or the land would revert back to the University. Yet, the Conservatory would need $10 million just to renovate the ailing McMaster Hall, which made addressing new buildings by 2000 patently unreasonable, if not impossible. Furthermore, the RCM's lawyers warned that if the school wanted to use the land as security for a loan to help it cope with repairs and other immediate needs, banks might balk at extending a loan with this reversion condition.

Another condition was that the University have the privilege of first refusal — the option to purchase if the Conservatory wished to dispose of the property. The terms of this option — they are too detailed to enumerate here — were absolute and impractical. Finally, the University refused to assist the Conservatory in any way to meet existing liabilities concerning building repairs and renovations. The question arose again and again — wasn't it unethical, if not downright immoral, for the University to have sold the College Street property, its functioning buildings and 106,722 square feet of land, and in return to have given the RCM a crumbling building and land totalling only 69,363 square feet? Thanks to the uncooperative University, RCM legal bills for separation were mounting, and negotiations were far from over.

To strengthen its case, the University said that the RCM was in poor financial shape and thus couldn't handle independence. To fend off this rearguard action, Creech prepared a "Business Plan 1989/90–1992/93" that proved, at least on paper, that the RCM's current fiscal position was sound. He pinpointed items to show how responsible the school was: that it paid for University services (heating McMaster Hall, etc.), that its earned income was growing, and that government grants — always uncertain and sporadic — represented less than 2 percent of the school's total revenue. Approximately 11,500 students attended the school, of whom 122 were in the preparatory and advanced programs, the only sections requiring direct subsidy. Tuition fees in 1988–89 brought in more than $6.1 million, 58 percent of the school's total expenditures. There were eighty-two thousand examination candidates that year, paying fees totalling in excess of $3 million. Creech then spelled out anticipated growth in the school's operations, including fundraising. The hard-nosed Criddle questioned the validity of the optimistic projections and remained unimpressed.

In June 1989 Creech made several additional proposals and concessions: that the RCM would use its property for school purposes only; that it would agree to a restrictive covenant to make the University's need to revert the property unnecessary, but, if the University insisted on reversion rights, they not be imposed until 2010; that for the first refusal right, if and when the RCM might sell its property, the University could have sixty days to accept or not accept the offer from the Conservatory; that any profits from such a sale would be divided 80 percent to the RCM and 20 percent to the University; and that the statute legalizing the RCM as an independent school should not require application to the City of Toronto for conveyance permission and other troublesome details connected with transferring McMaster Hall.[421]

Incredibly, the University's lawyer Gordon Dickson phoned the Conservatory's lawyer Jeremy Johnston on July 27 to report that there were still thirty-one points to be settled and, if not settled by that afternoon, the separation documents could not go to the Governing Council's business board for its meeting on July 31, four days away! Some points were being raised for the first time. One might ask what the council had been doing for the past three years? For example, it wanted two of its members on the RCM board; it wanted a five-year limitation on the RCM's use of the Faculty of Music Library; it wanted to prohibit the RCM from building any kind of overhang in the area leading to Varsity Arena to the south of McMaster Hall because it would inhibit fire and emergency access; and so on.[422] Creech, who had to clear all substantive matters with the RCM's board and Faculty Association, managed to do this with both groups in a detailed memorandum the same day.

Moving on, the business board met on October 23 and December 4. The board grudgingly went along with the RCM's proposals on everything except giving up McMaster Hall and the surrounding land, the reason being that the University might, in the future, want the site for academic or residence use or for a commercial/University project. However, the conscionable President Connell, using dollars and cents rather than ethics and morality, reminded the board that if the University retained McMaster Hall it was in for a $7.5-million repair bill to meet fire and safety standards. No matter, the business board dug in its heels. Creech spoke to the academic board of the Governing Council on December 7. Both the academic board and the planning board approved the separation. Nevertheless, the Governing Council postponed its final decision because of the business board.

The RCM Faculty Association denounced the business board's wish to retain McMaster Hall and its veiled threats to leave the RCM without a home.[423] Ironically, the association was by now almost rabid in its support of separation. What a difference ten years had made! It had approved its collective agreement with the RCM administration on October 22, 1989, with amendments added in the months following. The final agreement, however, could not become law until the Ontario legislature approved the legal independence of the RCM.

The all-important Governing Council meeting was scheduled for February 8, 1990. In the weeks prior to the meeting, the Toronto chapter of the RCM National Alumni, led by its national president and Conservatory administrator John Milligan, along with piano teacher Lynda Metelsky, took drastic action. Alumni members were stationed at McMaster Hall to give away buttons cleverly created by Publicity Director Andrew Stewart. The buttons said "Our Heritage Our Home" and included a tiny yet visible picture of McMaster Hall. The alumni urged all and sundry to save the RCM and asked for donations to help the cause. The January 8 *Varsity* reported Vice-President Criddle as saying that the RCM should move, and that, as a business deal, the RCM's proposals didn't make sense.

Michelle Landsberg's piece in the *Toronto Star* on February 6 was headlined, "Real estate madness hits university." Landsberg wrote, "The city does not exist solely for the benefit of real estate moguls. And public institutions that adopt the corporate mentality can expect to become the target of citizen fury and resistance." This didn't stop Paul Cadario, a member of the business board and an official at the World Bank in Washington, from telling the *Globe and Mail* prior to the February 8 meeting that "we're not satisfied that we have the truth on the value of the land. McMaster Hall might be worth an estimated $10 million to $20 million," he said. This statement was rather reckless for a banker — there is, after all, a considerable difference between those two figures![424] Cadario wanted the RCM to lease the land, not own it.

Another board member, Brian Hill, said the Conservatory didn't have enough money for renovations. He went on, "U.S. universities have endowments, we don't. Our endowment is our land…. It would be bad stewardship to give away this land."[425] Rob Behboodi, an undergraduate student representative on the Governing Council, said that council members were trustees for future generations of students, not "to supervise the dismemberment of the University."[426] Such was the tenor of the opposition.

The Governing Council voted after an hour's closed session in camera. The vote was close, twenty to seventeen in favour of the University granting the RCM its independence, its building, and its land. Conservatory officials were elated. Connell said what needed to be said: "The value of their land is not of fundamental importance. We have the obligation to set the Conservatory free with a prime piece of land in downtown Toronto."[427] That seventeen governors voted against ceding the property to the Conservatory is a sorry commentary on their values. Land, buildings, and money were more important to them than helping a hundred-year-old music school, its four hundred teachers (some of whom were among the finest musicians in Canada), its ninety-five hundred students (half of whom studied at McMaster Hall), and its eighty-five thousand examinees. In appreciation of George Connell's efforts — the clear-headed voice among the philistines — the RCM created a scholarship in his name in 1993.

Few at the Governing Council meeting considered how advantageous the Conservatory's proximity to the Faculty of Music was. Nor did anyone bother to recall President Ham's promise of an adequate RCM building close to the Johnson Building. In 1990, RCM teachers gave instrumental and vocal lessons to 161 Faculty students, taught 28 Faculty courses or sections, and coached 9 Faculty chamber ensembles.[428] In all, forty-nine RCM teachers worked for the Faculty, whose students, incidentally, used

RCM facilities for lessons, practice, and rehearsals during daytime hours when the Johnson Building was overcrowded and before the late afternoon rush of young RCM students. Also, the Conservatory's music store was useful for Faculty students. It takes about four minutes on Philosopher's Walk to go from one school to the other. Consider the inconvenience to both schools — students and teachers — if they were further apart.

The next fifteen months were devoted to preparing new employee and pension regulations for teachers and staff and a myriad of other agreements to do with the building and land, from which, ultimately, would come "An Act respecting The Royal Conservatory of Music."[429] Wording the Act was complicated, with the RCM's Faculty Association posing additional problems in its concern to guard the rights of its members.

Robin Fraser, now the RCM's lawyer, took the draft of the Act to the Attorney General's office at Queens Park for appropriate revisions. The final draft went to MPP Tony Silipo, who moved the Act's acceptance in the provincial legislature at its first reading on May 27, 1991. After some delay it was brought before the committee dealing with private acts and their regulation. The committee had only the weekend to review the Act because the legislature was breaking for the summer later the next week. There was at least one committee member who opposed such hasty approval. However, he backed off after being persuaded by the University's Vice-President for Development Gordon Cressy, who was observing the proceedings, that the University was in favour of the Act and would like to see it go forward. The committee passed it unanimously. There were second and third readings on June 26 and Royal Assent was given on June 27, 1991.

In short, the Act legalized the RCM's form of governance and set forth schedules for building and land transfers from the University to the Conservatory. It confirmed that the RCM would have absolute ownership of McMaster Hall, the areas around it, the Conservatory branches owned by the RCM, and the Harris Company. A board of up to fifteen members and an eleven-member academic council would govern the school. It would have an operating agreement with the University to carry out the intent of the statute to do with University services, the Faculty of Music Library, insurance, pensions, and the continuing exchange of RCM and Faculty teachers. And so the Conservatory was now its own boss after seventy-two years of domination — should one say subjugation? — by the University of Toronto.

Between 1984 and 1991 the Conservatory had done a great deal besides winning its independence. Professional training held centre stage. In a lengthy 1978 report on Canadian performance training commissioned by the Canada Council, Helmut Blume, dean of Music at McGill University, had considered establishing a National School of Music.[430] Although Blume's report was never implemented, it did give university music schools and conservatories cause for reflection. By the late seventies, as has already been mentioned, there was a disproportionately large number of American orchestral players in Canadian orchestras due to a shortage of qualified Canadians. True or not, some schools took heed. The RCM's Orchestral Training Program, begun in 1980, had stimulated and improved orchestral training and influenced all Canadian performance training for the better. But Canadian universities moved slowly. Their composition, musicology, and music education programs were well in hand, but not so performance. Perhaps universities weren't well suited to performance study.

Lorne Watson, the concerned head of music at Brandon University in Manitoba, convinced the Canadian Music Council to initiate a study of Canadian music schools. The Canada Council, provincial arts councils, provincial cultural ministries, and private foundations funded the study, with more than fifty schools participating. The task was assigned to Campbell Trowsdale, concertmaster of the CBC Vancouver Orchestra and a professor at the University of British Columbia. He completed his report in December 1988.[431] It was rich in information — an invaluable sourcebook about Canadian music schools from coast to coast.

Trowsdale's conclusions were limited to the obvious: little or no public money goes to English-speaking Canadian conservatories. The opposite is the case in Quebec, where music education is completely funded by the province. "Unlike the Americans, who retained their philanthropically funded conservatories as a major vehicle for providing professional musicians ... English Canadians have dismissed the Conservatory. Our financial eggs have been placed in the basket of the university."[432] Without public funding, Trowsdale concluded, Canadian university schools of music will continue to ape American university music schools, and professional performance training in conservatories will inevitably be limited in its breadth and scope.

The study stimulated a revival of the Association of Conservatories and Colleges of Music (ACCM), which met in Calgary in 1987 to discuss Trowsdale's work in progress. The group then assembled again at the RCM in June 1989.[433] Carefully prepared, this "Partners in Music" conference made a number of resolutions, including that the musically gifted should be given substantive musical education from childhood onwards, and that music schools should be encouraged to interact with public schools, independent private teachers, and universities. It also urged the federal government to fund the CBC more substantially and stressed that schools, festivals, and competitions must include works by Canadian composers for general study and performance. Bur the main thrust of the conference was that the scope and quality of performance study needed improvement. As expected, university music faculties and departments weren't listening.

The Trowsdale Report and the ACCM conferences reaffirmed that the RCM had been heading in the right direction since 1978 when it gave overt support to the ARCT resident program, however tentative its efforts were because of University restrictions. Then it started the OTP and, after 1984 when Conservatory independence seemed inevitable, it uninhibitedly structured its Professional Studies Program, which formally began in 1987. Robert Dodson, Robert Creech, Peter Simon, and John Kruspe all played key roles in its evolution. There were four levels of instruction in 1990–91 schedule of courses, the first two part-time. These were the Preparatory Performance Program, for gifted children ages eight to eleven leading to the Grade VIII certificate, and the Pre-college Performance Program, for ages twelve to eighteen and leading to the ARCT. Next came the full-time Performance Diploma Program (PDP), for ages eighteen and over, and, finally, the Artist Diploma Program (ADP) for those with the PDP or its equivalent. Enrolments in 1990–91 for the four levels were, respectively, thirteen, twenty-four, nineteen, and sixteen. There were also a resident four-year ARCT Honours Program and a three-year Artist/Teacher Program for those wishing to teach and/or take other important roles in the musical life of their communities. These two programs were begun in 1988. Their first enrolments were, respectively, forty-two and eight.

The faculty for the professional studies programs was impressive indeed. The instructors for the 1990–91 master classes included Leon Fleisher, Marek Jablonski, and John Perry, piano; Lise Elson, Jaime Laredo, and José Luis Garcia, violin; Jon Vickers, voice; and Norbert Kraft, classical guitar. Class instructors included critic William Littler, radio pundit and writer Lister Sinclair, theory teachers John Kruspe, Adelina Burashko, and Anthony Dawson, and pianists James Anagnason, Andrew Markow, Lynda Metelsky, and Boyanna Toyich. Applied performance teachers included pianists Carol Pack Birtch, Marc Durand, and Boris Zarankin, violinists and violists Lorand Fenyves, David Zafer, Mark Childs, and Victor Danchenko, and cellists Vladimir Orloff and David Hetherington. The sharing of teachers with the Faculty of Music continued.

The RCM could claim some prize-winning piano students in the eighties: Yuval Fichman, Francine Kay, Kevin Fitzgerald, Alan Hobbins, Peter Longworth, Andrew Burashko, and Henry Becker. The great Polish composer Krzysztof Penderecki conducted the Orchestral Training Program for a week in November 1987. It culminated in a concert of his music on November 13 with mature soloists Rosemarie Landry, soprano, and Rivka Golani, viola. RCM students who would make their mark in the performing world in the early nineties were Martin Beaver, violinist, Naida Cole, pianist and flutist, and the St. Lawrence String Quartet, which coached with Denis Brott and Lorand Fenyves at the school.

Edith Lantos directs a children's Kodály class, 1988.

One of the school's leading accompanists, John Coveart, died in January 1987. This sparked a benefit scholarship concert in his honour on September 25, 1987, with artists Victor Braun, baritone, and Catherine Robbin, mezzo-soprano, among the soloists. Coveart's career had included playing for the outrageously delightful Anna Russell on several of her national tours in the United States in the fifties. On a happier note, on November 28, 1988, the school conferred an honorary ARCT on Adelmo Melecci to celebrate his ninetieth birthday. Melecci, principal of the Willowdale branch and still maintaining a full piano teaching schedule, had been a member of the RCM's faculty since 1921. Ten years later the school celebrated his hundredth birthday. He was still teaching!

Fundraising for repairs to McMaster Hall and the branches had begun even before independence, with a "Heritage '89" benefit concert at Convocation Hall on April 21, 1989. José Luis Garcia was conductor and violinist with the OTP orchestra performing Vivaldi's *Four Seasons*, and Nicholas Goldschmidt conducted the school choir in Schubert's Mass in G Major. A year later, on April 6, 1990, the OTP did a "Heritage '90" concert. Garcia conducted again and also played in the Beethoven Triple Concerto along with cellist Denis Brott and pianist Angela Hewitt, one of the youngest ARCTs on record and winner of the Toronto International Bach Competition in 1985. John Barnum conducted. With oboist Senia Trubashnik, Garcia also played the Bach D Minor Concerto, and John Tuttle conducted Parry's *Blest Pair of Sirens* with the RCM choir. Net receipts of the concerts totalled $37,725 in 1989, and $19,335 in 1990, impressive for the time.

Two monster concerts were given in October 1990. The first was on October 29, the tenth anniversary of the first monster concert, and it was repeated the next day. Held at Massey Hall, both were benefit concerts, sponsored jointly by the House of Remenyi, a music store across the street from the RCM, and radio station CFMX. Remenyi, celebrating its hundredth anniversary (the firm had been founded in Budapest), provided the ten Steinways played by thirty-two members of the school's faculty. Unfortunately, the expenses outdistanced any profits for the RCM. Remenyi also generously renovated a large room on McMaster Hall's second floor, to be used for master classes and the like and known henceforth as the Remenyi Room. The company loaned an Ibach grand piano for the room for three years. The warm relations between Remenyi and the RCM led to Remenyi taking over the school's music store in early 1991. Remenyi agreed to manage it for the RCM for ten years. Long & McQuade now operates the RCM Music & Book Store.

The RCM continued its "General Studies Program," a new name for its traditional lessons and classes. Its objective, as in the past, was to serve students of all ages in the Greater Toronto Area wanting to study music. Fulfilling its community function remained paramount for the school, even though outside funding was almost non-existent. Branch expansion continued with the leasing of the Cawthra Adamson estate on the shores of Lake Ontario in Mississauga in 1989. The RCM already had six hundred students in its Mississauga branch, but having the historically interesting and beautifully located Adamson house was a welcome addition in this growing city to the west of Toronto. A year earlier, the school had opened a branch in Oakville, west of Mississauga, which would be short-lived.

Then the indefatigable Creech, not satisfied with the status quo, commissioned a long-overdue study of the RCM's examination system. In 1989 he engaged Campbell Trowsdale, Warren Mould

The Cawthra Adamson estate on Lake Ontario, Mississauga.

(former RCM registrar), and Norman Burgess (director of the Mount Royal College of Music and Speech Arts in Calgary and president of the ACCM) to be the commissioners. They reviewed RCM examinations and other examination systems across Canada, assessed examination systems in Britain and Australia, and turned in an in-depth report with much data about examinations and recommendations for their improvement.[434] However, the report brought little change.

The teaching and examining of theory and history also had a thorough review in 1989. John Kruspe's report was a revelation.[435] He was eminently qualified to speak his mind, having been a piano and theory teacher and member of the RCM's board of examiners since 1969 and a teacher of theory and composition at the Faculty of Music since 1973. It had been twenty years since the last review, and, since theory and history were so important in the examination system, Kruspe's study was long overdue. Brutally frank in his appraisal of the RCM theory program, he wrote in his preface that changes would not be easy to implement because of the "force of tradition." The school had "a mistrust of new ideas which tend to become more entrenched with age." There was no "efficient mechanism for consistent curriculum review or implementation of revisions," he wrote, and this made teachers all the more reluctant to retrain or to alter their teaching approaches. He also warned that change could also mean "increased costs to teachers, students and parents because of changing texts or additional examination fees."

Kruspe, nevertheless, soldiered on. He prepared the report in four sections: using present material for immediate implementation, using present material but with alterations in the next few years, general recommendations for the future, and a new and expanded theory/history curriculum when the current syllabus expires. Fundamental in his recommendations was that the ear be used more in theory *and* history examinations and that sight-singing and dictation should be included in theory examinations. Theory study should be started in the lower grades, as should two-part harmonizations. As for history, it should be taught chronologically with reference to actual music heard. The recommendations, which can only be appreciated by studying the report, are as relevant today as they were fifteen years ago.

Has there been any change since Kruspe's report? More than one would think in

The cover of *Celebration Series* showing the new RCM logo.

PIANO REPERTOIRE ALBUM

4

Celebration SERIES

Official Examination Repertoire of the
Royal Conservatory of Music - Grade 4

Répertoire officiel des examens du
Royal Conservatory of Music - Niveau 4

223

areas such as recognizing modes, using foreign terms, and the return to an RCM history text. Kruspe's problems with theory/history examinations go right to the heart of the examination problem generally — standardized examining in music requires more time at examinations, good study books, and more opportunities to examine and evaluate individual creation.

The Harris Company was in financial difficulties in 1987. Board Chairman John Whitten and General Manager Andrew Shaw astutely published all of the RCM graded piano books in one phase, along with study guides and recordings. Peter Simon, mainly assisted by Andrew Markow, Boris Berlin, and Dianne Werner, edited the series. The *Celebration Series,* as it was titled, showcased favourably at conferences

From left to right: Ontario Premier David Peterson, Principal Robert Dodson, Sam "the Record Man" Sniderman, and Maureen Forrester at the launching of *Celebration Series*, June 22, 1988.

and earned good reviews from professional journals such as *Clavier.* The resulting sales were a financial bonanza for the company and provided it with a sound base for the future. The 1990–91 Harris catalogue stated that two hundred thousand teachers and students used the series worldwide. Harris served nine hundred music dealers in Canada and others in the United States and abroad. The company happily reported that its recent three-volume choral series, *Reflections of Canada*, had won the National Choral Award from the Association of Canadian Choral Conductors for an outstanding choral publication.[436]

One major task remained — to find a principal for the new Conservatory. In the fall of 1990, Chairman Peter Allen assembled a large search committee and engaged a headhunting firm to seek out applicants. Robert Creech was seen by most as the obvious choice. He had written many studies and action plans in his four years at the RCM. He loved his work and had many staunch supporters, including Manhattan School of Music President Peter Simon. The committee moved along, and by March there seemed to be only two candidates on the shortlist, one of whom was Creech, the other a prominent musician from Western Canada. Allen, however, favoured someone who hadn't yet applied and urged him to do so. It was none other than Peter Simon. In his second year at Manhattan, Simon was tempted but was ambivalent about seeking the position, given his friendship with Creech. He was also concerned about the RCM's financial viability and its resistance to change. He anticipated the need for a comprehensive reorganization involving reductions and changes in staff and faculty. Yet, he missed Canada, wanted his children brought up in Toronto, and believed that the future of the RCM offered a unique opportunity to develop the kind of school he wanted. He had also been in Toronto several times during the year to engineer an exchange of performing groups between the RCM and Manhattan, so he knew about the school's important happenings.

In any event, Simon did apply in the closing days of the search. Now it was down to a choice between Creech and Simon. One was bound to be hurt. In the second of two closed ballots — Creech and Simon were tied in the first ballot — the committee chose Simon. Allen did not vote in either ballot. Sorely disappointed for professional as well as personal reasons, Creech left the RCM in the summer to become chief executive officer of the Liverpool Philharmonic Society. He now directs a music school in Ennis, Ireland, and a summer music festival in Limerick. As for Simon, his title was changed to president after the Act became law.

Chapter Eleven

AN INDEPENDENT SCHOOL

The Royal Conservatory of Music was now independent. It had its own board of directors and a new vision. But first came housekeeping. The RCM had to set personnel practices for the administrative and clerical staff, such as hiring, firing, benefits, and pensions — practices administered in the past by the University. The Community School also needed a fresh look. It had about 340 teachers, of whom roughly half taught in the branches. Some teachers taught fewer than five hours a week and yet had unlimited access to studios — a costly privilege, since the studios could have been rented to students when not used for lessons. To complicate matters, there were forty-five different fee structures for individual and/or group lessons — an administrative nightmare. This confused students and encouraged divisiveness among the faculty. The Conservatory extracted a commission of 25 percent from fees, approximately half of which went towards teachers' benefits, leaving little to operate the community program. In the past the RCM had covered teaching losses through examination and publishing profits. However, building and equipment needs were being ignored, a state of affairs that was no longer an option: life-safety systems had to comply with new building codes; heating, cooling, and electrical systems needed improving; and the leaking roof and brickwork had to be restored. The Community School, by hard-nosed accounting standards, was losing $1 million annually. And 50 percent of all students were not returning for a second year, suggesting that some RCM teachers were not teaching as well as they might. Yet teachers could not be released without the approval, or at least the acquiescence, of the RCM Faculty Association. Would the president of the new independent Conservatory live with these conditions? Should he?[437]

And so McMaster Hall continued to deteriorate, as did the RCM's branch buildings. There was a huge accumulated deficit. The examination department had leadership problems, and the retired George

Hoskins was brought back temporarily to keep things going.[438] There was no fundraising department, yet fundraising strategies had to be developed. Here, too, initial investment funds would be needed before a return was available. Program and teaching quality could not be fully verified, and this discouraged potential donors. Governments gave only small grants. Some cynical observers in 1991 said that it would have been easier if the new RCM had started all over again, instead of having to cope with too many self-important teachers, a leaderless examination department, worn-out buildings, no investment capital, and poor management resources.

President Simon began his work by engaging two senior assistants, Norman Burgess, the former Mount Royal Conservatory head, as dean of the school, and Mark Jamison as director of the examination department. Jamison, a graduate of the Faculty of Music, had started his music studies at the RCM with piano teacher George McElroy. He was a skilled double bass player and had played in several Canadian orchestras before moving into administration. The two men couldn't have been more different — Burgess was quietly introspective, gentle, and retiring, while Jamison was decisive, forthright, and outspoken.

Simon moved quickly to bolster the two areas of the RCM that had the greatest immediate potential to improve the fiscal situation — examinations and the Harris Company. Examinations, which had been a department of the RCM and in effect of the Community School, became a new division of the organization. This was the first of several steps taken to change the structure of the organization and establish five distinct units, each with a specific objective and leadership but sharing the overall mission and direction of the RCM. Simon also allocated funds for information systems development as a means to improve efficiency and to lower processing costs. The examination area was profitable, and with a small investment Simon anticipated large gains. It was a good start. The board was pleased, but money problems persisted.

Thanks to Jamison's work, there was a 5 percent increase in the number of examination candidates (the first increase in five years), and eighteen new examination centres had been established in Canada and the United States. During Jamison's first year, the examination department moved to an office building on the north side of Bloor Street facing the school, a more hospitable setting than its shabby McMaster Hall basement offices. Within two years the RCM examination department had increased its net contributions to the school by 22 percent.

The Frederick Harris Company moved to more commodious quarters in Mississauga in 1996, and in 1997 sold its Oakville building. RCM Examinations moved to the same site from its Bloor

The first ruling triumvirate in the independent RCM (from left to right): Peter Simon, Norman Burgess, and Mark Jamison.

location. Clarke MacIntosh succeeded Andrew Shaw as Harris president in 2002, and also manages the examination department.

To improve its long-term financial stability the school soon established a development department. Several fundraising initiatives followed. One was the Friends of the Royal Conservatory of Music. Almost seven hundred donors from this group gave up to $1,000 each, and another twenty gave more than $1,000. Another fundraising project, Open the Door to Music, also attracted donors, including a number from Mississauga, their special interest being the renovation of the Cawthra Adamson estate. The next year, the Ontario government gave the RCM $670,000 towards restoring the roof of McMaster Hall.[439] The Conservatory's name, place, and prestige boded well for future fundraising.

Simon commissioned John Milligan and Karen Castelane in December 1991 to prepare strategies for RCM expansion.[440] They proceeded to interview students, parents, teachers, and teaching associations. Their resulting report addressed the school's national presence, its revenue production, its standards of teaching, and its marketing. Also addressed was the musical public's commitment to RCM examinations. The report was useful to the community program, but, practically speaking, it simply covered old ground more clearly and succinctly than previous ones.

Legal costs continued to escalate, as did building repair costs, the latter due to the University's disclaiming its responsibility to pay for at least part of them. And there were other mainly unforeseen expenses, all of which weighed heavily on the RCM. By the fall of 1992, the school seemed to be heading for bankruptcy. The time had come for a hard look at the branches. Some were owned, some were rented, and several were clearly run down. One was located in a strip mall with the RCM logo displayed in neon next to a fish and chips shop. In 1981–82 total branch registrations had been 5,163, while in 1988–89 they were down to 4,519, this in spite of Toronto's burgeoning population. For better or for worse, branch principals had been renamed branch administrators during Robert Dodson's term as principal, which may have made some of them feel undervalued. Unfortunately Ian Ross, who left during Dodson's term, had ignored the decline in branch registrations. Things had changed, however, when John Milligan took over as branch consultant in 1989. His 1991 report showed a considerable improvement in registrations in just two years, thanks to aggressive marketing.[441] However, profits remained elusive and the future looked grim.

With several million dollars needed for urgent repairs at McMaster Hall, the Conservatory decided that selling the branches provided the light at the end of the tunnel. And so, in 1993, the Conservatory boldly sold the four branches it owned — Avenue Road, North Toronto, Forest Hill, and Etobicoke — and closed all its rented branches except the Adamson estate. Teaching would now be limited to McMaster Hall and Adamson. This was a blow not only to those who believed in the mission of the branches but also to the branch teachers, most of whom would be left without jobs. Some of them had been teaching at the RCM for four decades.

The terms were straightforward. All RCM teachers who taught fewer than fifteen hours weekly would be let go. It was anticipated that most of them would continue teaching their pupils at home and in the process retain their full earnings. More than half of them taught eight hours or fewer weekly, which suggested to President Simon that they might have other jobs or were not all that committed to or dependent on their teaching. He hoped that separation would not be too traumatic.[442] A February 5, 1993, letter to one long-standing branch teacher informed him that his services would terminate on June 30. He would receive a lump sum severance payment equal to twenty-three weeks of fees based on his

Boris Berlin's eighty-fifth birthday concert and celebration, 1991. Standing from left to right: Andrew Shaw, Margot Onodera, Andrew Markow, Marek Jablonski, Linda Ippolito, Leslie Kinton, Angelo Calcafuoco, Peter Simon, Louis Applebaum, and, at the piano, Laura Ippolito and Boris Berlin.

average weekly earnings for 1992–93. The pension plan surplus of about $2.5 million made this severance allotment possible.[443] However, teachers not on the pension plan left the RCM with only memories. A few teachers grieved their discharges, and some of them eventually won back their positions. Some selective judgment was applied — certain teachers, mainly of orchestral instruments, were retained.[444] In all, 125 teachers were let go.

Naturally, there were complaints, and the press was quick to pick them up.[445] Change never comes easily. One observer speculated to the *Globe and Mail* that the school's deficit was due to a mushrooming administrative staff — eight new well-paid managers had been hired since the school's independence. Simon refuted talk about a growing administrative staff by pointing out that in fact most of the appointments were replacements for existing positions and that he had cut staff numbers in other areas. He explained that the Community School had to reach a break-even position if it were to have a chance to expand and reach more people. The painful truth was that it had been losing money for many years, certainly since pensions and benefits were granted to the teaching staff. Nor did it, as we know, receive any grants to cover its costs, which grew each year. Returning to the branches, the real estate market had taken a plunge in 1992–93, and the branch buildings were sold for disappointingly small sums. Still, their sale helped to alleviate the RCM's financial woes and, as time would tell, helped its long-term growth.

To further soften the blow, the school initiated a Teacher Services Program for departing teachers, which included a number of teachers' development aids. The first was John Milligan's "Studio Management Guide." It laid out suggestions to help teachers operate independently, including tips on marketing, teaching venues, publicity, accounting, and even image development.[446] Subsequently, Nancy Bell and Geoffrey Sangwine developed the Affiliate Teachers Network — a master list of music teachers across Canada to which students could refer when looking for a teacher.[447] This grew into the Affiliate Teacher program, officially launched in May 1995. Qualified music teachers across the country could now formalize their relationship with the Conservatory for an annual fee of $125 (free to those RCM teachers who had been let go). Much like Community School teachers, they would have access to services designed to enhance their teaching, a toll-free telephone number to reach RCM resource people, workshops, RCM master classes, digital keyboard instruction, a *Guide to Music Education*, and two newsletters. Four-day workshops were held in July 1995, which helped to placate those who still felt that the Community School was dying. Affiliate membership also included a $2 million liability insurance coverage, optional group insurance benefits, and an annual luncheon at the RCM. The well-intentioned program had reached a membership level of 950 by 1997, when it closed because existing teachers' organizations were concerned about competition from the RCM.[448]

Still another initiative was launched in 1995: the Community School Task Force. Members of the Community School faculty participated with the RCM Faculty Association's full support. Aiming to renew the school's programs, the task force surveyed faculty viewpoints in a wide range of areas. Its final report three years later said that it hoped the Conservatory would be restored to "its traditional position of national leadership in musical pedagogy."[449] The report recommended that the RCM provide more innovative and creative programs unavailable in private music studios or small schools. RCM programs "do not have consistently high quality; evaluations are inadequate; there is little to distinguish it from other institutions; and McMaster Hall is not located in an area of market growth." The report supported President Simon's long-held views that the Community School needed a fresh look. Accordingly, new strategies were tried: developing programs offering extra value, improving quality through evaluation, developing community links, and capitalizing on areas of strength such as the ensemble matching program for students who voluntarily wished to play music together. The Community School also heeded the task force recommendations to offer a variety of adult classes of all kinds. In the 1998–99 RCM student handbook, for example, there were thirty adult classes listed, including Hand Drumming, Saxophone from Scratch, For the Love of Mozart, Bach — There Is No substitute, and Women Composers: The Lost Tradition Found.

Back to 1993. With more funds available, thanks to the sale of the branches, faculty reductions, and increased revenue from examinations, repairs and renovations at McMaster Hall gct underway. Simon made other moves that eliminated the operating deficit and made some headway in reducing the RCM's accumulated deficit. Altogether, a substantial $3 million was spent on facilities, instruments, computers, and programming from 1991 to 1994.[450]

Mark Jamison was appointed executive vice-president in 1993. He had multiple duties, including that of secretary-treasurer. Rennie Regehr, a leading Winnipeg violist, was brought in to head the Professional School in 1992. He was appointed dean a year later. Regehr, who had been manager of the Manitoba Chamber Orchestra for ten years, had literally no academic experience and was in for a long learning curve. He was a large man with a beard and bushy hair. He visualized a professional training program that would teach young musicians how to become community music leaders using communication techniques and technology.[451] This was Simon's vision, too. It got its inspiration from an independent program for professional musicians, Musical Performance and Communication, which had been sponsored by the federal government and the Ontario Arts Council from 1987 to 1990. In addition to new appointments, the school gave the thirty-five-year-old Preparatory Program a more positive identity by renaming it the Young Artists Performance Academy (YAPA) in 1992–93.

Eileen Keown was appointed dean of the Community School and held the post until 1997. Shaun Elder, a composer, violist, and experienced fundraiser, was engaged to direct the development department in 1995.[452] Elder and Simon focused their energies on finding funds for innovative ideas and working out long-term plans.[453] Norman Burgess, who had made the Regehr and Keown appointments, moved laterally to direct the new Pedagogy Institute, from which would evolve the Learning Through The Arts program. He left the RCM in 1996.[454] Jamison left the RCM in 1996 to be general manager of the Kitchener-Waterloo Symphony. Colin Graham replaced him as vice-president of finance and administration; he had just retired from the Ernst & Young accounting firm.

In the fall of 1993 President Simon believed that he could move ahead on his plans to bring the arts back to the public schools and, by extension, improve the quality of education itself. He described the concept behind what would be known as Learning Through The Arts (LTTA) to the Weston family. Impressed, the Weston Foundation granted the program a start-up fund of $500,000. Norman Burgess and Mitchell Korn of New York's ArtsVision did the preliminary work, and in October 1995 a fully integrated LTTA program, conceived and directed by Angela Elster, assisted by Nancy Bell, was launched in partnership with the North York Board of Education. Elster, an experienced educator, specialized in curriculum design and integrative education.[455]

LTTA addresses the developmental needs and varying learning styles of children from kindergarten to Grade 12. It is an inspiring success story. By 2004 it has reached students from kindergarten to Grade 12 in three hundred schools in more than twenty cities across Canada, with pilot projects and presentations in ten other countries, including Great Britain, Italy, the United States, Singapore, and Sweden.[456] Three hundred artists in the different arts work in Toronto's LTTA programs. LTTA essentially provides arts-based experiences that heighten a student's opportunity for academic success. Artists from all disciplines and class teachers work together in selecting a common theme and then find the art forms that best enhance the theme and the curricular outcomes.

An early example of LTTA is Elster's use of a Grade 1 theme: Community. It focuses on Orff procedures, drama, African percussion/storytelling, visual arts, and a string trio performance. A more recent example is Dance and Geometry. Dancers work with Grade 2 students, who are taught to understand geometric concepts such as perimeter and area. The students create communal dances that require them to stand or move inside or outside specific shapes such as circles, squares, triangles, and trapezoids. An interesting Music and Science example is used in Grade 5. The students learn about heat transference with music and movement. By following changing beats played on percussion instruments, students react as if they were water molecules being heated by a uranium bundle in a nuclear power plant. When water is heated, molecules move more quickly and further apart from one another. In another lesson, children shuffle along the floor, representing electrons moving along power lines. Then they pretend to be atoms joining together and then breaking apart.

The LTTA program is based in part on American educator Howard Gardner's theory of multiple intelligences, which states that each person has his or her own particular blend of intelligences, and therefore his or her own unique learning style, be it linguistic, logical/mathematical, musical, spatial, bodily/kinesthetic, interpersonal, or naturalist. The theory provides a conceptual framework for developing new approaches to meeting the needs of diverse learners. In fact, the RCM Professional School uses LTTA to improve its students' communication techniques with young audiences.

LTTA has, fortunately, been well funded.[457] In 1998 the Ontario government, with strong support from its minister of culture, Isabel Bassett, granted $3.7 million to expand LTTA's work in the province. The federal government next allocated another $1 million to LTTA. These government grants have encouraged substantial corporate donations, the most significant being $2.5 million from the TD Financial Group.

In 2002, Upitis and Smithrim of Queen's University concluded a three-year quantitative study of 6,700 LTTA students in five cities across Canada.[458] They were overwhelmingly positive. Certainly LTTA, with its creative thrust, is one of the most significant teaching areas at the RCM, and it has done much to enhance the school's reputation as a leader in pre-university musical instruction.

Simon believes that the arts have a significant impact on general education and Canadian society and musical life. In a talk given in Calgary in 1998, he argued that the arts are a natural partner of the sciences and that arts programs are essential if test scores in other areas are to increase. He questioned education's current preoccupation with mathematics and science at the expense of arts programs, saying this "relegates the exploration and utilization of the intuitive, creative side of people to a secondary position. Education in the arts provides the tools for thought. For example, analysis, synthesis, and evaluation of information are implicit and explicit in music instruction. The inherent mathematical underpinnings of music reinforce the analytic dimensions of higher cognitive skill." On another tack, he pointed out that the arts "are of course the very essence of communication." Concluding, he advocated arts activity because it "facilitates the kind of self-awareness or consciousness that results in fulfilled lives." According to Simon, the RCM was moving from being a conventional school to being an agent of social change.[459]

Children's classes flourished at McMaster Hall, thanks to excellent instructors and quarters. The 1989 publication "Children's Programs" told the musical world what the RCM was doing. Orff, Dalcroze (now called Eurhythmics), Kodály, Suzuki, and Keyboard Classes (formerly the Kelly Kirby Kindergarten) were all well attended. The pre-kindergarten classes of Donna Wood, titled the Preparatory Music Program, also attracted many children. Wood started teaching her classes at the RCM in 1972; her mentor was Madeleine Boss Lasserre, the school's first Dalcroze instructor. Wood used children's chants with a limited range and repetitive language, rhythmic patterns (beat, accent, and meter) derived from nursery rhymes, finger plays, and children's poetry, especially when combined with movement. She also used sound-play and percussion instruments to highlight basic elements of music. She believes that all children are musical and all can enjoy the pleasures of music through active play.[460]

Donna Wood was a magnificent instructor, not only for children, but also for adults. She gave summer courses for prospective early childhood teachers from 1973. Her achievements were formally recognized when she was awarded the fellowship *honoris causa* from the Royal Conservatory of Music of Toronto (FRCMT) at the school's graduation on January 27, 2002. When Wood retired in 1993, Mary Stouffer, who had trained in

Eurhythmics class.

Toronto, Calgary, and Hungary, took over her work. Stouffer initiated the Music With Your Baby program for children under three years old in 1990.[461] As of 2003 there are about sixty preparatory and baby classes given weekly at McMaster Hall.

Still another initiative was the use of digital pianos, begun in 1988 by Susan Hamlin. She started with three Roland digital pianos, giving weekly class lessons for children aged six to eight, each child also taking an individual weekly lesson on a traditional piano.[462] By 1992 there were sixteen digital pianos in operation. Then, in 1997, the RCM acquired a sixteen-piano Yamaha laboratory, and the Roland pianos were moved to the Hugh Mappin Children's Learning Centre, named after a generous donor to children's programs. By 2002 there were approximately 130 people taking digital piano classes at the RCM, including some adults.[463]

An important outgrowth of the RCM's work in children's classes was the Advanced Certificate in Early Childhood Music Education, begun in partnership with Ryerson University in 1991. For it the RCM gives courses in music education, early childhood educational theory and practice, music in early childhood, music and movement for young children, and other applied subjects. Ryerson gives courses in psychology and related subjects.[464] In 2000, the RCM Community School took over the program's administration. The graduation certificate is now issued by the RCM.

In 1995 the Conservatory established the Historic Register. Conceived by Shaun Elder, its aim was to reconnect alumni to the school through a central worldwide registry.[465] The school estimates that through instruction and examinations it has touched the lives of 3 million Canadians over the years and reaches approximately 250,000 annually. Lacking funds for database development, mailings, and promotion of the register, Elder enlisted prominent RCM alumni to volunteer for thirty-second television ads that were then played on major networks as free public service announcements. Graduates Robert Goulet, Lois Marshall, and David Foster volunteered to help the campaign, and the number of registrants swelled. There were thirty thousand calls for information about the register in its first six months, some from students who graduated as long ago as 1919, and one from remote Baffin Island.[466] Personal anecdotes were legion. Myrtle Leishman, a caller from Atikokan, Ontario, recalled that, as a child, "she would take the train every Monday to Thunder Bay for her piano lesson. The journey took five hours each way!" Myrtle was determined to become a piano teacher and, when she began instructing in her hometown, she formed an RCM examination centre to save her students from the same five-hour trip.[467]

Jumping ahead, the Historic Register was formally published in 2000. RCM staff member Debra Chandler then took the register, musical memorabilia, and the Yamaha Disklavier Grand Piano across the country, showing her display in such places as the refurbished immigrant hall in Halifax and the West Edmonton Mall. Many attendees played on the Disklavier and went home with their performance recorded on a CD. In Ottawa, Madame Aline Chrétien, wife of the prime minister and chair of the RCM National Advisory Board, signed the register, as did other luminaries who had taken RCM examinations or studied in Toronto. In all, more than fifty thousand names were collected. It was a public relations triumph.[468]

Pleasant surprises came in 1995 and 1996. First, the Toronto Historical Board gave a matching grant of $21,598 towards the restoration of McMaster Hall's foyer. Then, a year later, the Historic Sites and Monuments Board of Canada designated the RCM a school of national historic significance.[469] The board's decision was based on the RCM's "influence on the musical life of Canada over the last century … its graduates include some of the most prominent musicians and music teachers in Canada."

At the 1995 fall meeting of the board, President Simon summed up the accomplishments and innovations implemented in his first four years. He noted that the number of examination candidates were at an all-time high of 111,500, a growth of 26 percent since independence. Learning Through The Arts had just been launched as the RCM's response to the decline of arts education in public schools and the Historic Register had created a new source for fundraising. He praised the Harris Company for sponsoring 150 workshops attended by 10,000 teachers, for commissioning three Canadian composers to write pedagogically significant works, for registering a 20 percent increase in U.S. sales, and for its remarkably successful new piano series, which had been launched that year. And finally, he reported that the RCM had recorded its second consecutive operations surplus in the 1994-95 fiscal year, totalling $498,129.

Another crop of outstanding young musicians emerged in the nineties, including a number of pianists, some of whom won or placed in major international competitions, much like in the great days of the fifties: Lisa Yui, David Louie, Sonia Chan, Richard Raymond, Naida Cole, and Stewart Goodyear. Soprano Isabel Bayrakdarian, a science graduate of the University of Toronto and a pupil of Jean

MacPhail's, won the 1997 Metropolitan Opera Auditions of the Air first prize, to join several Canadian singers of the past who had been in the finals of this prestigious competition.[470] Bayrakdarian made her concert debut in New York in 1997 and by 2003–04 was singing major roles at the Met and the COC. Other voice students on the brink of international careers in 2004 are two young baritones, Robert Pomakov and Robert Gleadow.

The student orchestra began developing after the wind-up of the Orchestral Training Program in 1992. It showed initial promise on February 9, 1996, with Leon Fleisher conducting and Martin Beaver as soloist in the Haydn C Major Violin Concerto. The orchestra played Mozart's "Prague" Symphony and Boccherini's Symphony in C Minor on the same program. Master classes around this time included groups such as the Berlin Philharmonic Quartet, the Haydn Trio of Vienna, and the St. Lawrence Quartet (it had already achieved international standing), and top instrumentalists including cellists Aldo Parisot, Steven Isserlis, and Desmond Hoebig and pianists Angela Hewitt, André Laplante, and Marc Durand.[471] Laplante and Durand both teach regularly at the school.

In February 1996, the Conservatory announced that it would renovate and restore the concert hall to its turn-of-the-century elegance and rename it the Ettore Mazzoleni Concert Hall.[472] Mrs. Joanne Mazzoleni generously offered to help pay for the renovations. Much as she loved the paintings she had donated to the hall twenty-five years earlier, they were sold at auction to raise almost $400,000 toward the renovation. Then the family contributed an additional $100,000, and the Ivey Foundation did the same.[473] Other fundraising for the hall was done with imagination and flair. For example, after the seats were torn out on June 2, 1996, a gala black tie fundraising dinner/dance, with music by Peter Appleyard, was held in the hall. Over 150 attended. Conceived by Louise Yearwood of the development office and titled "A Royal Occasion," it netted some $17,000.[474] Too good an idea to let die, it became an annual event, always with some stellar attraction to head the evening. The next year it was given at the Royal York hotel and earned $50,000, the year after $70,000, and, when Oscar Peterson was the guest of honour, $130,000.

Money was also raised by the sale of individual seats in the restored hall at $1,000 each. Plaques with donors' names were then secured to the seats in perpetuity. In less than a year, virtually every one of the 243 seats was sold. The restoration campaign brought in about $1.6 million, part of which went to the hall's costs, and part to the creation of new classroom space below it.[475]

Isabel Bayrakdarian with her teacher Jean MacPhail at the opening of Mazzoleni Hall in October 1997.

Ettore Mazzoleni Hall opened with a gala concert on October 17, 1997. The hall's excellent acoustics delighted performers and audience. The program included words of Mazzoleni's made shortly before his sudden death in 1968: "The Conservatory is now over eighty years old; but let me serve notice upon you all — she may be over eighty, but she has no intention of retiring. She will be happy to accept at any time a large endowment to carry on — but not a pension."

For the gala, distinguished faculty members and top students from both the Professional School and YAPA performed short works, from Purcell to Pépin, from Mozart to Messiaen, from Bottesini to Britten. Students and parents were equally delighted with the new facilities on the floor below the hall — three children's classrooms, two toilets (a godsend), and a parents' lounge, all of which made up the Hugh Mappin Children's Learning Centre.

YAPA now has over 125 students aged nine to eighteen, and its students have won all kinds of competitions. It also has its own orchestra, which performed Shostakovich's First Symphony, Copland's *Appalachian Spring*, and the Tchaikovsky Violin Concerto with soloist Maria Krechkovsky in 2002. YAPA students gave fifty chamber and soloist performances that same year.[476]

In January 1997, the Professional School had been renamed the Glenn Gould Professional School (GGPS): Simon's announcement explains why:

> [Gould] personifies the highest standards of musicianship, creativity and performing ability. His emphasis upon performance excellence, broadly based communication skills, and use of technology to reach new audiences is reflected in our curriculum. The linking of Glenn Gould with the Royal Conservatory produces a very powerful and recognisable name that

The refurbished Ettore Mazzoleni Concert Hall.

will help to attract the finest students and bring international recognition to the institution.[477]

And so it did. The Professional School had been moving ahead slowly in the early nineties, its enrolment buoyed up by an influx of foreign students, mainly from Asia, some of whom were not all that qualified and others who had great language difficulties. Now, GGPS enrolment mushroomed. In 1995–96 there were 36 students in the school, with 11 from other countries.[478] By 1997–98 there were 73, with 19 from other countries, and five years later, there were 159 — perhaps the ideal enrolment — with 37 from other countries, mainly China (11) and the United States (10). Of the 122 Canadian students, 83 were from Ontario, 15 from British Columbia, 9 from Alberta, and 8 from Saskatchewan. Ten years earlier nearly all the students had been piano majors. Now there was far more diversity. In the two post-secondary programs, the Professional Development Program (PDP) and the Artist Diploma Program (ADP), one-third were pianists, another third were string players, one-fifth played other orchestral instruments, and the rest were singers.

Shortly after the naming of the GGPS the Conservatory arranged with the Open University in Vancouver to offer qualified GGPS students a bachelor's degree in music performance. The Open University's requirements for this degree are similar to those of other degree-granting professional university music schools and conservatories and include several non-music courses. This affiliation came about because Ontario's Ministry of Colleges and Universities prohibited the RCM from giving its own degrees, unlike professional music schools in the United States. Nor has Ontario funded the RCM, as it does the Ontario College of Art & Design and its community colleges. Simon and his staff had to scramble for funds. Then, fortunately, the Heritage Ministry of the federal government stepped in. Beginning in 1998, after several favourable assessments of the school's work, its National Training Institutions Program has granted $1 million or more annually to the GGPS, thus assuring the school of its continued existence.

Campbell Trowsdale did a penetrating assessment of the Glenn Gould School (GGS) for Heritage in 2003. (The "Professional" part of its name had by this time been dropped.) After talking with several students and making other observations, he concluded that the school's main strength rests in its practical courses, or, as he put it, theory in practice. He praised a new course, Materials 3, given by composer Omar Daniel. Its students perform music of different styles — practical examples of what they study in theory. Trowsdale also lauded the master classes given by internationally known artists (there

Honorary Fellows of the RCM.

Top left: 1995, Maureen Forrester, President Simon, David Mirvish, Oscar Peterson (seated).

Bottom left: 1999, Teresa Stratas, Tomson Highway, Jeanne Lamon.

Below: 2002, (front) Lois Birkenshaw-Fleming, Carol Pack Birtch; (rear) Ezra Schabas, Michael and Sonja Koerner, President Simon.

were sixty-seven in 2002–03) and courses in Art History by Francis Broun, Performing Arts Criticism by William Littler, and Aspects of Creativity by Lister Sinclair.

With due respect to master classes and their impact, it is, in the long run, the permanent faculty who sets achievement standards in performance at the GGS. Its piano faculty as of 2004 includes Leon Fleisher, Marc Durand, André Laplante, John Perry, James Anagnason, Andrew Markow, Boris Lysenko, Dianne Werner, Marina Geringas, Leslie Kinton, Antonin Kubalek, Monica Gaylord, and Marietta Orlov. The string staff includes: violinists Mark Fewer, Erika Raum, and Mayumi Seiler; violists Stephen Dann and Rennie Regehr; cellists Brian Epperson, David Hetherington, and John Kadz; and double bass Joel Quarrington. Voice teachers include Roxolana Roslak, who also directs the opera program, Jean MacPhail, Joel Katz, Donna Sherman, and Ering Schwing-Braun. Some of the best wind and brass performers in Toronto are on the staff, as are baroque specialists, including Jeanne Lamon, the leader of Tafelmusik.

The RCM orchestra continues to grow. On November 16, 2001, at Massey Hall, Leon Fleisher conducted the Beethoven Ninth Symphony and the Brahms Second Piano Concerto, with André Laplante as soloist. The concert was a revelation. Guest conductors in subsequent years have included Franz-Paul Decker, Simon Streatfeild, and Bramwell Tovey, all of whom work well with younger players. The orchestra's repertoire — Stravinsky's *Le Sacre du Printemps*, Strauss's *Don Juan*, Mahler's Third Symphony, Ravel's *La Valse*, and the standard classical and romantic works of Mozart, Beethoven, Schubert, and Brahms — demands a level of playing expected in the professional world. The orchestra is on its way!

GGS fees are substantial but not as high as those at most leading American music schools. The Ontario Students Assistance Plan continues to benefit Ontario residents, while revenues from the Harris Company and the RCM endowment fund — $628,000 in 2004 — provide scholarship assistance. Scheduling GGS classes and practice studios is difficult due to the Community Program's competing demands for space. Trowsdale thought the administrative staff, from Dean Regehr down, were competent and sympathetic in meeting student needs. Dr. Jack Behrens, former dean of the Faculty of Music of the University of Western Ontario, is in charge of academic programs, and David Visentin, a former symphony violinist, is associate dean.

Regehr is attentive to the thrust of professional music training.[479] He believes that the preparation of students for musical careers needs transforming, that students should grapple with what some fear is a declining interest in classical music and its relevance in today's world. Communication courses, also given at the GGS, help students to apply attention-getting techniques in introducing good music to schools and communities.

Artists of the Royal Conservatory (ARC) was organized in 2002 to serve as the school's flagship ensemble-in-residence. Its core members are pianists James Anagnason, Leslie Kinton, David Louie, and Dianne Werner, violinists Marie Berard and Erica Raum, violist Steven Dann, cellist Brian Epperson, double bass Joel Quarrington, and clarinetist Joaquin Valdepeñas. The group frequently collaborates with outstanding guests and students from the school. ARC focuses on performing traditional chamber music and "an eclectic repertoire of music typically ignored as a result of either political change or musical fashion."[480] In its first year the ensemble gave two concerts in Mazzoleni Hall and four concerts in New York as part of that city's bargemusic series. Directed by Simon Wynberg, the 2003–04 season included a weekend series of concerts and lectures devoted to Jewish composers in the Nazi period, and two programs of early twentieth century English music. ARC has also toured and recorded.

On the administrative side, the RCM's Faculty Association, led by John Graham, has enjoyed a collective bargaining agreement with the RCM. Pension terms were changed in January 1996 from a defined benefit plan to a defined contribution plan, which most of the teachers preferred. And the RCM board continues as an effective governance and support group for the school. Bob Rae, a former premier of Ontario, followed Alan Goddard as chair in 1999 and deserves much credit for the RCM's expansion in his five-year term. Florence Minz, a prominent business executive, succeeded Rae in 2004.

Chapter Twelve

A BUILDING FOR THE FUTURE

In 1990 the RCM had engaged the architectural firm Kuwabara Payne McKenna and Blumberg (KPMB) to create a master plan for developing the RCM site. Nothing was done over the next ten years since the school spent all of its available funds, some $8 million, to maintain its facilities.[481] By 2002, a new building would require a minimum of $50 million (later raised to $60 million). The Canada-Ontario Infrastructure Program, developed after the turn of the century, provided a welcome answer. After a year of intensive work by President Simon and his staff to frame their plans and to lobby, the fund awarded the school $20 million to create a new performance and learning centre. With this funding as a start, the Conservatory then launched a major fundraising campaign to raise the remaining $40 million.

Here is Peter Simon's vision of the centre:

> When completed, the new Performance and Learning Centre will stand among the greatest arts education facilities in the world. The new Centre will be a locus for the development and nurturing of culture and creativity in Canada. It will be a world Centre for the professional development of educators interested in integrative education; it will be a destination for the most gifted artists wishing to study and to intersect with the community; it will provide hundreds of performances annually at the highest level; and it will be a place for Canadians of all ages to weave the arts seamlessly into their lives. The new Performance and Learning Centre

will also help the RCM distribute the music and ideas of the twenty-first century to an eager public throughout Canada and to place Canada at the forefront of educational innovation. The new facility will provide the educational space, the technology, and the tools to make the most of the RCM's extraordinary potential.

Is this all too good to be true? Only time will tell.

Scheduled to open in 2007, the Centre for Performance and Learning has been designed by award-winning architect Marianne McKenna. It will include seventy practice and teaching studios, fully wired classrooms, a library, and a new media and broadcast centre. At its heart will be a 1,140-seat concert hall. Not only will it provide a venue for performances by internationally acclaimed artists but it will also be used for community school events, academic conferences, and a host of other activities. It will provide a unique venue for LTTA lectures, artist and teacher training, worldwide videoconferencing, not to mention works exploring the integration of music with other art forms.[482]

The centre plans to deliver concerts, lectures, and other educational programs through the Internet. Sean McShane, formerly a vice-president of Enterprise Technology at Sheridan College, is now vice-president of information technology at the RCM and will be a key person in this work. He studied double bass at the Conservatory in the late seventies and was an assistant to the RCM principal from 1986 to 1988.[483] According to President Simon, "The Conservatory is now posed to move assertively into the area of technology, multimedia, and broadband video-conferencing."[484] Indeed, this work has already begun. In 2003, the RCM, in partnership with Acadia University, Yamaha, and CANARIE (a Broadband Research Network), began a research project, Music Path, to test the use of two-way transmission and video-conferencing for music instruction.[485] On February 26, 2004, Music Path's first remote music lesson — truly a milestone — was enacted between twelve-year-old Lucas Porter, a piano student in Atlantic Canada, and RCM teacher Marc Durand. The *New York Times* described the event: "Mr. Durand sits 700 miles away … watches and listens to his young charge on a large video screen as he plays and talks to him through a headset, giving him tips and at times humming, even growling, along with the music…. Lucas listens dutifully, in turn watching his teacher on a monitor beside his sheet music. They interact as if they were two people alone in the same room."[486] MusicPath manager Karen Wilder described what happened in a nutshell: "You see his hands move here and you hear the sound in Toronto."[487]

A BUILDING FOR THE FUTURE

TELUS Corporation, a major leader in telecommunications, is the principal donor for what has now been named the TELUS Centre for Performance and Learning. TELUS CEO Darren Entwistle agreed to chair the fundraising campaign.[488] Sections of the TELUS Centre have been named in honour of other major donors: the Michael and Sonja Koerner Concert Hall, the Leslie and Anna Dan Galleria, the Wilmot and Judy Matthews Family Centre for Integrative Education, the R. Fraser Elliot Centre for Keyboard Studies, the Evelyn and Bert Lavis Promenade (in memory of donor Marilyn Thomson's parents), the Siemens Hall, the TD Centre for Orchestral Studies, and the Rupert Edwards Library.[489]

The RCM is not standing still. Its future is bright. Its importance is assured.

The TELUS Centre for Performance and Learning.

The Michael and Sonja Koerner Concert Hall.

Appendix A

CHRONOLOGY

1886	The Toronto Conservatory of Music (TCM) is founded by Edward Fisher, music director.
1897	The TCM moves from Wilton Avenue to College Street.
1910	The TCM becomes a non-profit private trust.
1913	Edward Fisher dies. A.S. Vogt is appointed music director.
1919	The University of Toronto assumes authority over the TCM through an Act of the Ontario legislature.
1924	The TCM purchases the Canadian Academy of Music.
1926	A.S. Vogt dies. Ernest MacMillan is appointed principal of the TCM.
1942	Norman Wilks succeeds MacMillan as principal. Dies in 1944.
1944	Frederick Harris gives The Frederick Harris Music Co., Limited to the TCM.
1945	Ettore Mazzoleni is appointed principal. The Senior School and the Opera School are formed, with Arnold Walter as director.

1947	The TCM becomes the Royal Conservatory of Music (RCM).
1952	The RCM is reorganized into two departments: the School of Music and the Faculty of Music. Boyd Neel is appointed dean of the RCM in 1953.
1954	RCM letters patent is revoked. All RCM property and assets are vested in the University of Toronto by an Act of the Ontario legislature.
1957	Special courses for gifted children begin.
1963	The School of Music moves to McMaster Hall. The Faculty of Music and the Opera School move to the Edward Johnson Building, which is formally opened in 1964.
1968	Ettore Mazzoleni dies. David Ouchterlony is appointed acting principal, to become principal in 1970.
1969	The Opera School is transferred to the Faculty of Music. The School of Music is now the RCM.
1977	David Ouchterlony resigns as principal.
1978	Ezra Schabas is appointed principal and serves until 1983.
1980	The Orchestral Training Program begins.
1984	Robert Dodson is appointed acting principal.
1987	Professional programs begin. The RCM celebrates its hundredth anniversary at Roy Thomson Hall. Dodson is appointed principal. He resigns in 1988.

APPENDIX A

1988   Gordon Kushner is appointed acting principal. Robert Creech is appointed vice-principal.

1990   The Governing Council of the University of Toronto grants the RCM independence. An Act of the Ontario legislature formalizes it in 1991.

1991   Peter Simon is appointed president of the RCM.

1995   The Examination Department is transferred to the management of the Frederick Harris Company.

1997   The professional school is renamed the Glenn Gould Professional School. The Ettore Mazzoleni Concert Hall is opened.

2003   Plans for a Performance and Learning Centre are announced.

Appendix B
LIST OF ABBREVIATIONS

AB	Associated Board
ACCM	Association of Conservatories and Colleges of Music
ADP	Artist Diploma Program
AGM	Annual General Meeting
ARC	Artists of the Royal Conservatory
ARCT	Associate of the Royal Conservatory of Music
ATCM	Associate of the Toronto Conservatory of Music
BMI	Broadcast Music Incorporated Canada Limited
CAPAC	Composers, Authors and Publishers Association of Canada Limited
CNE	Canadian National Exhibition
COC	Canadian Opera Company
CQR	*Conservatory Quarterly Review*
EMC	*Encyclopedia of Music in Canada*, 2nd edition
FTCM	Fellow of the Toronto Conservatory of Music
GGPS	Glenn Gould Professional School
GGS	Glenn Gould School
LTCM	Licentiate of the Toronto Conservatory of Music
LTTA	Learning Through the Arts
MCU	Ministry of Colleges and Universities
NAC	National Archives of Canada
NYO	National Youth Orchestra

OAC	Ontario Arts Council
OTP	Orchestral Training Program
PDP	Professional Diploma Program
RCM	Royal Conservatory of Music
TCM	Toronto Conservatory of Music
TSO	Toronto Symphony Orchestra
UofT	University of Toronto
UTA	University of Toronto Archives
YAPA	Young Artists Performance Academy

Appendix C
LIST OF INTERVIEWS

Allen, Peter	10 February 2004
Barrett, Joan	15 February 2004
Beckwith, John	10 November 2003
Behrens, Jack	2 March 2004
Bernardi, Mario	6 December 2003
Burgess, Norman	15 February 2004
Connell, George	21 February 2004
Creech, Robert	8,9 September 2003
Dodson, Robert	5 February 2004
Elder, Shaun	20 March 2004
Elster, Angela	8 February 2004
Freedman, Harry	18 November 2003
Graham, Colin	8 March 2004
Hoskins, George	26 January 2004
Jamison, Mark	7 February 2004
Johnson, Dorothy	3 June 2003
Kenton, Mildred	21 May 2003
Krehm, William	11 January 2004
Kruspe, John	17 February 2004
Kushner, Gordon	18 June 2003
Macerollo, Joseph	21 January 2004

Markow, Andrew	26 June 2003; 22 January 2004
Mazzoleni, Joanne	1 March 2004
Milligan, John	8 February 2004
Piller, Clare	1 March 2004
Regehr, Rennie	18 March 2004
Seitz, Burke	20 May 2003
Shaw, Andrew	15 March 2004
Simon, Peter	12 March 2004
Solomon, Stanley	7 May 2003
Spergel, Robert	21 May 2003
Trowsdale, G. Campbell	29 May 2004; 1 June 2004
Weinzweig, John	2 December 1992
Welsman, George	5 May 2003
Yearwood, Louise	26 February 2004

Endnotes

Prologue: The Setting

1   *Encyclopedia of Music in Canada (EMC)*, 2nd Edition (Toronto: University of Toronto Press, 1992), pp. 1292–6.

2   Ezra Schabas and Carl Morey, *Opera Viva: The Canadian Opera Company, The First Fifty Years* (Toronto: Dundurn Press, 2000), p. 8.

3   Joan Parkhill Baillie, *Look at the Record: An Album of Toronto's Lyric Theatres 1825–1984* (Oakville: Mosaic Press, 1985).

4   John Becker, "The Early History of the Toronto Conservatory of Music," MFA Thesis, York University 1983, pp. 60–73.

5   Ibid., p. 45.

6   Ibid., p. 47.

7   *EMC*, p. 1293.

Chapter 1: Toronto Has a Music School

8   Ibid., p. 467.

9   Gaynor G. Jones, "The Fisher Years: The Toronto Conservatory of Music," *CanMus Documents* 4 (Toronto: Institute for Canadian Music, 1989), p. 69. For more about Fisher see also Donald Jones, "Edward Fisher gave Toronto a truly 'noteworthy' institution," *Toronto Daily Star*, 2 April 1983. V.P. Hunt, one of the TCM's first teachers, wrote TCM Principal Mazzoleni on 12 May 1947 about his positive experiences with Fisher.

10   Coincidentally, Anna McCoy, who was on the administrative staff of the RCM from 1947 until 1952, resided until recently in the house with her husband, William McCoy. He gave me this information.

11   Harry Adaskin, *A Fiddler's World: Memoirs to 1938* (Vancouver: November House, 1977), p. 67.

12   Becker, pp. 31–8. Gaynor G. Jones, pp. 68–76. *EMC*, pp. 1153–4. F.J. Horwood, *The Toronto Conservatory of Music: A Retrospect (1886–1936)* (Toronto: 1936), pp. 3–7. There are a few minor inaccuracies in Horwood's piece. See also TCM Board Minutes.

13   TCM Board Minutes, 14 December 1886. The Conservatory's Board of Directors Minute Books are at the Royal Conservatory of Music. The University of Toronto Archives (UTA) has Conservatory material from its founding until 1975. Information on courses and other study material is from annual calendars and other Conservatory publications found in A75-0014 (118 boxes), and from Faculty of Music materials found in A75-0015 (36 boxes).

14   Ibid., 7 May 1887.

15   *EMC*, p. 346.

16   Ibid., p. 466.

17   Ibid., pp. 382–3.

18   TCM Board Minutes, 21 March 1887.

19   Ibid., 15 March 1889.

20   Mildred Kenton and Robert Spergel, interview with author, 21 May 2003.

21   TCM Board Minutes, 30 August 1887.

22   Horwood, p. 6.

23   Becker, p. 58.

24   *EMC*, pp. 1053–5. See also Wayne Kelly, *Downright Upright: A History of the Canadian Piano Industry* (Toronto: Natural Heritage/Natural History Inc., 1991).

25   Gaynor G. Jones, pp. 79–80.

26   TCM Board Minutes, 16 November 1887.

27   Ibid.

28   Ibid., 10 June 1887.

29   Ibid., 2 April 1889.

30   Louise McDowell, *Past and Present, A Canadian Musician's Reminiscences* (Kirkland Lake, ON, n.d.), pp. 27–8. McDowell graduated from the TCM in 1892.

31   *EMC*, p. 1314. Tripp's teaching appointment was approved at the TCM Board Meeting, 28 June 1888.

32   TCM Board Minutes, 29 September 1887.

33   Ibid., 9 May 1888.

34   Ibid., 10 October 1888.

35   *EMC*, pp. 586–7.

36   TCM Board Minutes, 7 May 1889.

37   Ibid., 28 June 1888.

38   *EMC*, pp. 1348–9.

39   TCM Board Minutes, 16 November 1888. See also Gaynor G. Jones, p. 88.

40   Ibid., 30 August 1888.
41   Ibid., 10 October 1888.
42   *EMC*, p. 275.
43   TCM Board Minutes, 26 March 1897.
44   *EMC*, p. 24.
45   William Kilbourn, *Intimate Grandeur: One Hundred Years at Massey Hall* (Toronto: Stoddart, 1994).
46   Gaynor G. Jones, pp. 104–7.
47   *EMC*, pp. 571–2.
48   H.H. Godfrey, *A Souvenir of Musical Toronto* (Toronto: Miln Bingham, 1898), pp. 14–5.
49   TCM Board Minutes, 20 July 1897.
50   *EMC*, p. 467.
51   Canadian Protesting Committee. "An Account of the Canadian Protest Against the Introduction into Canada of Musical Examinations by Outside Musical Examining Bodies" (Toronto: 1899).
52   Ibid.
53   Ibid.
54   TCM Board Minutes, 5 July 1899.
55   *EMC*, p. 53.
56   TCM Board Minutes, 14 December 1897.
57   *EMC*, p. 469. See also Lois Birkenshaw-Fleming, *A History of Childhood Music Education at the Royal Conservatory of Music* (Toronto: RCM, 2002), p. 2.
58   TCM AGM, 18 January 1899.
59   TCM Board Minutes, 1 February 2001. The whereabouts of the portrait is unknown.
60   *TCM Journal,* December 1901.
61   Unidentified clipping, 12 March 1910.
62   TCM Board Minutes, 13 December 1901, 9 January 1902. The letter to the University is attached to the Minutes.
63   *EMC*, pp. 1345–6.
64   TCM Board Meeting, 25 November 1904.
65   TCM AGM, 2 October 1907.
66   J.W.F. Harrison, "Conservatory in the North," *TCM Journal,* September 1909, p. 133.
67   The subject of Fisher vs. Torrington is admirably covered in Gaynor G. Jones, pp. 59–64.
68   *EMC*, pp. 1305–6.
69   Kilbourn, p. 21.
70   "Toronto Orchestral School, 1891 …," Toronto Reference Library, AR, PAM, 785.06271, T587.
71   TCM Board Minutes, 27 March 1906.
72   *The Welsman Memoranda* (Toronto: 1971), p. 8.
73   TCM Board Minutes, 24 April 1906.

74   *The Welsman Memoranda,* p. 9.

75   Ibid., p. 13.

76   TCM Board Minutes, 6 October 1908, 24 November 1908.

77   George Welsman (son of Frank Welsman), interview with the author, 5 May 2003.

78   John Beckwith, interview with the author, 11 November 2003.

79   Gordana Lazarevich, *The Musical World of Frances James and Murray Adaskin* (Toronto: University of Toronto Press, 1988), p. 60.

80   TCM Board Minutes, 11 June 1910.

81   Ibid., 28 September 1909, 11 July 1910.

82   Ibid., 25 October 1910, 7 June 1911.

83   *EMC,* p. 194.

84   Ibid., pp. 572–3. See also Eric Koch, *The Brothers Hambourg* (Toronto: Robin Brass, 1997).

85   TCM Board Minutes, 24 September 1912, 12 October 1912.

86   Becker, pp. 220–33. These figures about graduates are drawn from the 1914–15 TCM Yearbook. Other figures cited are from other TCM yearbooks and board minutes.

Chapter 2: Music Education and Money

87   TCM Board Minutes, 6 June 1913.

88   Ibid.

89   F.R.C. Clarke, *Healey Willan: Life and Music* (Toronto: University of Toronto Press, 1983), p. 14.

90   TCM Board Minutes, 26 June 1914.

91   John Beckwith, *Music at Toronto: A Personal Account* (Toronto: University of Toronto Press, 1995), p. 19.

92   F.R.C. Clarke, p. 17.

93   *EMC,* p. 697.

94   Kenton/Spergel, interview. Kenton later studied with Alberto Guerrero and B. Hayunga Carman, which gave her some basis for comparison.

95   Jonathan Krehm, conversation with author, 9 January 2004.

96   *EMC,* p. 1395.

97   Ibid., pp. 368–9. Also, see TCM calendars.

98   TCM Board Minutes, 24 February 1914.

99   Ibid., 31 March 1914.

100   TCM AGM, 7 October 1914.

101   Adaskin, p. 78.

102   Ibid., pp. 90, 98.

103 TCM Board Minutes, 26 February 1915.

104 TCM AGM, 6 October 1915.

105 Ibid., 6 October 1916.

106 Burke Seitz (son of Ernest Seitz), interview with author, 19 May 2003.

107 *Conservatory Quarterly Review (CQR),* Winter 1925–26, p. 53.

108 Jack Hutton, *The World Is Waiting for the Sunrise* (Bala, ON: Bala's Museum, 2000).

109 Ernest MacMillan, "August Stephen Vogt — An Appreciation," *University of Toronto Monthly,* October 1926, pp. 20–1.

110 "Memorandum for Senate's Committee, 19 February 1918," Falconer Papers, Box 50, UTA. See also Earl Davey, "The Faculty of Music of the University of Toronto, 1918–1945," 3 April 1975, in "Higher Education," 1801, UTA.

111 Falconer Papers, UTA.

112 Beckwith, p. 10.

113 TCM Board Minutes, 6 October 1920.

114 TCM AGM, 1918.

115 TCM Board Minutes, 12 November 1919.

116 Ibid., 15 June 1920.

117 Pearl McCarthy, *Leo Smith* (Toronto: University of Toronto Press, 1956), p. 21.

118 *CQR,* November 1918, p. 23.

119 Ibid., p. 24.

120 *CQR,* 1920–1921, p. 6.

121 TCM AGM, 30 September 1920.

122 *Toronto Daily Star,* 14 April 1923. Cited in Dorith Cooper, "Opera In Toronto and Montreal: a Study of Performance Traditions and Repertoire, 1783–1980," PhD Dissertation, University of Toronto 1983, v. 3, pp. 715–6.

123 *Saturday Night,* 4 November 1922.

124 TCM AGM, Financial statement, 3 October 1923.

125 Helmut Kallmann, "The Conservatory Remembered," *Performing Arts,* June 1987, pp. 9–11.

126 TCM Board Minutes, 7 December 1920.

127 Ibid., 10 May 1921.

128 See Kevin Bazzana, *Wondrous Strange: The Life and Art of Glenn Gould* (Toronto: McClelland & Stewart, 2003) for material about Guerrero.

129 See Eric Koch for a detailed account.

130 TCM Board Minutes, 11 June 1924.

131 Ibid., 23 May 1924.

132 *CQR,* Autumn 1926, pp. 2–5.

133 *The Welsman Memoranda,* p. 48.

134 A.S. Vogt, letter to Sir Edmund Walker, 8 December 1923.

135 *CQR,* Autumn 1925, pp. 6–8.

136 Reprinted in *CQR,* Autumn 1926, pp. 8–9.

Chapter 3: The Depression Years

137 Ezra Schabas, *Sir Ernest MacMillan: The Importance of Being Canadian* (Toronto: University of Toronto Press, 1994), pp. 60–83.

138 The author has the notice.

139 The quotations are from the concert reviews reprinted in part in *CQR,* Spring 1928, pp. 133–4.

140 *EMC,* p. 18.

141 *Toronto Globe,* 1 March 1928.

142 Ibid., 30 January 1930.

143 Birkenshaw-Fleming, pp. 3–4.

144 Ibid., p. 5; *EMC,* p. 679.

145 TCM AGM, 1 October 1930.

146 *EMC,* p. 313.

147 McCarthy, p. 27.

148 The author has copies of the letters.

149 *Toronto Globe,* 9 January 1925.

150 *Toronto Daily Star,* 13 January 1925. Lawrence Mason and Augustus Bridle are quoted in Cooper, pp. 722–3.

151 *Toronto Globe,* 17 April 1928. *Toronto Mail and Empire,* 21 April 1928. See Cooper, pp. 721–31.

152 *Saturday Night,* 6 April 1929. Cited in Cooper, p. 731.

153 See Cooper, pp. 732–9 and Schabas, pp. 80–3, for background of this performance.

154 *Toronto Daily Star,* 18 November 1929.

155 Harold Tovell, letter to Henry Button, March 1930. Cited in Cooper, pp. 738–9.

156 Schabas, p. 100.

157 Ibid., pp. 104–5.

158 TCM Board Minutes, 6 March 1935.

159 *CQR,* August 1935, pp. 80–1.

160 Schabas, pp. 130–3.

161 *Toronto Daily Star,* 3 June 1935.

162 Ernest MacMillan, letter to R.B. Bennett, 25 May 1935.

163 Floyd S. Chalmers. *Both Sides of the Street: One Man's Life in Business and the Arts in Canada* (Toronto: Macmillan, 1983), pp. 120–4.

164 Ibid. See also TCM Balance Sheet, 30 June 1939.

165 Alice Roger Collins, *Real People: Pen Portraits: Marion G. Ferguson* (Toronto: 1932).

166 Chalmers, p.122.

167 Schabas, pp. 124–5.

168 F.H. Deacon, letter to Mrs. Waddington, 8 October 1936.

169 Ernest MacMillan, letter to F.H. Deacon, 8 October 1936.

170 Ernest MacMillan, letter to F.H. Deacon, 9 October 1936. UTA, A73-0054104. It is uncertain whether MacMillan actually sent the letter.

171 Ernest MacMillan, letter to F.H. Deacon, 28 November 1936.

172 F.H. Deacon, "To Members of the Faculty and to Graduates of the Toronto Conservatory of Music," 14 October 1936.

173 TCM Board Minutes, 24 June 1938.

174 Clarke, pp. 44, 61.

175 *EMC,* p. 1379.

176 Clarke, p. 30.

177 TCM Board Minutes, 5 June 1936; TCM Finance Committee Minutes, 11 September 1936.

178 Schabas, pp. 142–3.

179 TCM Finance Committee Minutes, 2 April 1937.

180 Schabas, p. 147.

181 TCM Board Minutes, 1 June 1938.

182 Ibid., 6 October 1937.

183 Ernest Hutcheson, "Report: On a Short Survey of the Toronto Conservatory of Music," (n.d.).

184 *EMC,* p. 692.

185 TCM Board Minutes, 21 October 1937.

186 Ibid., 29 September 1939 (Hambourg), 24 January 1940 (Hamilton).

187 TCM Finance Committee Minutes, 20 October 1939, 15 May 1940.

188 Lazarevich, pp. 56–7.

189 Humphrey Carpenter, *Benjamin Britten: A Biography* (London: Faber and Faber, 1993), p. 139. Carpenter does not mention Chuhaldin. Lazarevich does not mention the CBC commission.

190 Lazarevich, pp. 61–2.

191 *EMC,* pp. 1018–9.

192 TCM Board Minutes, 30 January 1941.

193 *EMC,* pp. 938–9.

194 *The Globe and Mail,* 29 November 1941.

195　TCM Board Minutes, 30 January 1941.

196　See Eric Koch, *Deemed Suspect* (Toronto: Methuen, 1980). It includes a list of the internees and their activities after the war.

197　Schabas, p. 168. Reginald Stewart resigned as conductor of the Prom concerts a few weeks before leaving Toronto.

198　*EMC*, p. 1252. Reginald Stewart, personal talk with author, 1958.

199　TCM Board Minutes, 15 April 1942.

200　Ernest MacMillan, letter to Elsie MacMillan, 5 May 1942.

201　TCM Board Minutes, 3 June 1942.

202　Ernest MacMillan, quoted in *The Varsity*, 15 December 1943.

Chapter 4: Exciting Times

203　TCM Board Minutes, 24 February 1943.

204　Ibid.

205　Dorothy Johnson, interview with author, 3 June 2003.

206　Clarke, pp. 37–8.

207　*EMC*, p. 1406.

208　TCM Board Minutes, 21 October 1943.

209　*EMC*, p. 1027.

210　Author's reminiscences.

211　H.H. Bishop?, letter to President Cody, 20 December 1944. Norman Wilks might have written the letter before his death.

212　TCM Board Minutes, 18 May 1945.

213　Ibid., 21 June 1945.

214　Dana Porter, "Memorandum to RCM Board," n.d. but probably 1950. For a more detailed account of the company see Wayne Gilpin, *Sunset on the St. Lawrence* (Oakville, ON: Frederick Harris Music Co., 1984).

215　Norman Wilks and Floyd Chalmers, "Memorandum: The Toronto Conservatory of Music," 1 October 1944.

216　*EMC*, pp. 310–2.

217　Floyd Chalmers, letter to Leslie Frost, 22 December 1944.

218　Floyd Chalmers, memorandum to H.H. Bishop, 10 September 1945.

219　President's office, publicity release, 5 December 1945.

220　H.H. Bishop, letter to Sidney Smith, cited in Cooper, p. 750.

221　Dorothy Johnson, 3 June 2003.

222　TCM Board Minutes, 9 December 1946.

223 Jeannie Williams, *Jon Vickers: A Hero's Life* (Boston: Northeastern University Press, 1999), p. 34.

224 TCM Annual Report, 29 November 1945.

225 Schabas, pp. 139–40.

226 Burke Seitz, interview with author, 19 May 2003.

227 Arnold Walter, letter to Edward Johnson, n.d. but probably Spring 1946.

228 Albert Whitehead, letter to Ettore Mazzoleni, 29 July 1947.

229 H.C. Walker, letter to Hamilton Cassels, 19 May 1948. Cassels sent on the correspondence to Mazzoleni.

230 TCM Board Minutes, 14 April 1946; RCM Board Minutes, 25 September 1947.

231 Arnold Walter, "An informal history of the Senior School," 1949.

232 TCM Board Minutes, 13 September 1946.

233 University Board of Governors Minutes, 8 January 1948. Arnold Walter lost his independence at the TCM Board Meeting, 20 May 1948.

234 Ibid., 11 November 1948.

235 Schabas and Morey, p. 17.

236 See Gwenlynn Setterfield, *Niki Goldschmidt: A Life in Canadian Music* (Toronto: University of Toronto Press, 2003).

237 Cited in Cooper, pp. 755–7. Cooper, Schabas and Morey, and Kenneth Peglar, *Opera and the University of Toronto 1946–1971* (Toronto: Faculty of Music, 1971) are three informative sources on the history of the Conservatory Opera School.

238 Quoted in Peglar, p. 10.

239 See *EMC* for brief biographies of these singers.

240 Ian Montagnes, *An Uncommon Fellowship, The Story of Hart House* (Toronto: University of Toronto Press, 1969), p. 19.

241 *The Globe and Mail,* 26 April 1947.

242 Ibid., 29 April 1947.

243 Ibid., 3 May 1947.

244 Under Secretary of State E.H. Coleman, letter to Sidney Smith, 22 April 1940. The *Toronto Daily Star* reported the announcement on 3 May 1947.

245 Cooper, pp. 757–60.

246 Ibid., p. 759.

247 Ibid., p.760.

248 *Toronto Evening Telegram,* 2 November 1949.

249 *Toronto Daily Star,* 19 December 1947.

250 *The Globe and Mail,* 7 February 1948.

251 University Board of Governors Minutes, 24 June 1948.

252 Schabas and Morey, pp. 19–22.

253 *The Globe and Mail,* 10 December 1948. Cited in Cooper, p. 768.

254 Anna McCoy, "Summary of the Activities of the Concert and Placement Bureau, 1946–51," 5 June 1951.

255 RCM Board Minutes, 13 December 1949.

256 *The Globe and Mail,* 11 December 1947.

257 Cited in *RCM Monthly Bulletin,* January 1953.

258 Carol Elizabeth Wright, *My Stories, My Life* (n.d.), pp. 22–3.

259 See Cooper, who cites Joan Chalmers, p. 758.

260 John Beckwith, 11 November 2003.

261 RCM Board Minutes, 25 November 1948.

262 Mario Bernardi, interview with author, 6 December 2003.

263 Wright, pp. 20–1.

264 RCM Board Minutes, 9 March 1950.

265 Sidney Smith, letter to Edward Johnson, 18 February 1948.

266 RCM Board Minutes, 2 November 1949.

267 Cooper, pp. 776–7.

268 RCM Board Minutes, 24 March 1949.

269 Ibid., 27 April 1949. Edward Johnson wrote Vice-Chairman James S. Duncan giving his reasons for approval on 15 April 1949.

270 Ibid., 15 April 1949.

271 Schabas and Morey, pp. 25–9.

272 Arnold Walter, letter to Fred MacKelcan, 22 November 1949.

Chapter 5: The Travails of Reorganization

273 *The Globe and Mail,* 4 February 1950.

274 These citations are also noted in Cooper, pp. 780–1.

275 *Toronto Evening Telegram,* 6 February 1950.

276 *Montreal Daily Star,* 11 February 1950.

277 RCM Board Minutes, 9 March 1950.

278 Ibid., 13 October 1950.

279 Ibid., 25 October 1950.

280 Schabas and Morey, pp. 30–3.

281 *The Globe and Mail,* 2 May 1953.

282 Williams, p. 30.

283 *Toronto Daily Star,* 13 April 1954; *The Globe and Mail,* 13 April 1954.

284 Harry Freedman, interview with author, 18 November 2003.

285 John Beckwith, telephone conversation with author, 23 November 2003.

286 The full program is in the *RCM Monthly Bulletin,* March 1949.

287 *Montreal Gazette,* 18 March 1950.

288 *Toronto Daily Star,* 11 March 1950.

289 *The Globe and Mail*, 18 April 1951; *Toronto Evening Telegram,* 18 April 1951.

290 *The Globe and Mail*, 25 April 1951.

291 *RCM Monthly Bulletin,* March 1950.

292 Ibid., September 1949.

293 RCM Board Minutes, 27 February 1952.

294 Ernest MacMillan, letter to Sidney Smith, 18 March 1952.

295 See Schabas, pp. 214–9, for a more detailed account of this correspondence.

296 Ernest MacMillan, "Summary and Commentary on My Correspondence with the President of the University of Toronto," n.d.

297 Ernest MacMillan, letter to Sidney Smith, 10 April 1952.

298 Sidney Smith, letter to Ernest MacMillan, 14 April 1952.

299 Ernest MacMillan, letter to members of Faculty of Music, 21 April 1952.

300 Ettore Mazzoleni, letter to Edward Johnson, 22 April 1952. Mazzoleni, letter to RCM faculty, 23 April 1952.

301 *The Globe and Mail,* 28 April 1952.

302 *Toronto Daily Star,* 2 May 1952.

303 *The Globe and Mail,* 2 May 1952.

304 John Weinzweig, interview with author, 2 December 1992.

305 See Schabas, pp. 222–4, for MacMillan's response to Mazzoleni accepting his demotion.

306 See Schabas, pp. 225–36, for an account of the Symphony Six episode.

Chapter 6: A Decade of Widening Horizons

307 All information on these three artists is from my personal files.

308 See the *RCM Monthly Bulletin,* January 1953, for a synopsis of Thomson's lecture.

309 Boyd Neel, *My Orchestras and Other Adventures* (Toronto: University of Toronto Press, 1985). This volume, printed four years after his death, is a composite of his writings prepared by J. David Finch. Some of Neel's assertions while in Toronto are exaggerated, some would not stand up to documentation, and a few are simply wrong.

310   Ibid., p. 156.

311   University Board of Governors Minutes, 10 December 1953.

312   Ibid., 23 April 1954.

313   Alec Rankin, letter to Sidney Smith, 27 January 1955; Smith, letter to Boyd Neel, 27 January 1955; Neel, letter to Smith, 31 January 1955.

314   RCM Committee Minutes, 23 June 1955.

315   Ettore Mazzoleni, memorandum to Boyd Neel, 22 November 1956.

316   RCM Committee Minutes, 24 February 1955.

317   *RCM Monthly Bulletin,* November 1955.

318   Beckwith, 11 November 2003.

319   *The Globe and Mail,* 26 April 1957.

320   William Krehm, "CJBC Views the Shows," 27 April 1958.

321   Birkenshaw-Fleming, pp. 6–8.

322   *Toronto Evening Telegram,* 10 February 1958.

323   *The Globe and Mail,* 11 February 1958.

324   *RCM Monthly Bulletin,* November/December 1959.

325   Ibid., January/February 1960.

326   Bazzana, pp. 58–64.

Chapter 7: Buildings Old and New

327   TCM Board, Brief to President Cody, 20 December 1944.

328   James Duncan, letter to Sidney Smith, 9 April 1956.

329   Boyd Neel, "Report to the Advisory Planning Committee," December 1956.

330   Secretary E.B. Easson, Hydro-Electric Power Commission of Ontario, letter to Sidney Smith, 30 July 1957.

331   Various estimates have been made since the sale. In 1989 the College Street land was estimated to be worth $20,000,000.

332   RCM Building Committee Minutes, 7 October 1957.

333   University Advisory Planning Committee, "Report to the University Board of Governors," 8 May 1958.

334   This report was dated 13 January 1959.

335   Luther Noss, "A Report to the President of the University of Toronto Concerning proposed Plans for the Reorganization of the Royal Conservatory of Music," 24 February 1959.

336   Boyd Neel, report to Duncan, February 1959. Duncan wrote to Bissell on 23 February 1960.

337   "Notes on Use of Economics Building," 24 February 1960. (Unsigned)

338   G.L. Court, letter to Claude Bissell, 29 March 1960.

339   Boyd Neel, letter to Claude Bissell, 3 June 1960.

340   Arnold Walter, memorandum to the President, 3 June 1960.

341   The cornerstone correspondence and Claude Bissell's address are in the Presidential files at UTA.

342   Schabas, pp. 292–3.

343   Ibid.

344   F.R. Stone, letter to Claude Bissell, 2 October 1961.

345   RCM Committee Minutes, 26 April 1961.

346   Ibid., 12 December 1961.

347   Ibid., 8 November 1962.

348   University Board of Governors Minutes, 28 February 1962.

349   *Toronto Daily Star,* 24 August 1974. See also a provincial one-page description of "Senator William McMaster" (n.d.).

350   Ibid., 24 April 1974.

351   *Toronto Evening Telegram,* 2 March 1963. Reprinted in the *RCM Monthly Bulletin,* March/April 1963.

352   RCM Committee Minutes, 22 November 1962.

353   *Toronto Evening Telegram,* 25 February 1963.

354   "Stature Without Status: 103 Years of The Royal Conservatory of Music," (RCM Toronto n.d.) p. 12.

Chapter 8: Cooperation Ends

355   *EMC,* pp. 213–4.

356   "Canadian String Quartet," *Canadian Music Journal,* Spring 1962, pp. 29–30.

357   RCM Committee Minutes, 25 April 1962.

358   University Board of Governors Minutes, 15 April 1964. The memorandum on the furniture was written on 13 April.

359   Ibid., 16 December 1963.

360   RCM Committee Minutes, 29 April 1965.

361   University Board of Governors Minutes, 12 January 1966.

362   RCM Committee Minutes, 4 March 1965.

363   Ibid., 20 April 1966.

364   Allan Rae, "Success of Dolin's Students Evidence of His Teaching Skill" *Music Scene,* September/October 1972, pp. 4–5.

365   *RCM Bulletin,* Spring 1966, Spring 1967.

366   Ibid., Mid-Winter 1968.

367   Ibid., Winter 1967.

368   Ibid., Summer 1966.

369   *The Globe and Mail,* 5 December 1966.

370   *EMC,* p. 534.

371   *RCM Bulletin.* Mid-Winter 1968.

372   The clipping is undated.

373   *The Globe and Mail,* 6 April 1963; *Toronto Evening Telegram,* 6 April 1963.

374   *The Globe and Mail,* 14 December 1965.

375   *Toronto Evening Telegram,* 30 September 1966.

376   *The Globe and Mail,* 2 March 1968.

377   RCM, "Music in Our Lives," Summer 1996.

378   RCM Committee Minutes, 18 April 1972.

379   *RCM Bulletin,* Spring 1969.

380   *EMC,* p. 634.

Chapter 9: Struggles for Direction

381   *The Canadian World Almanac* (Toronto: Global Press, 1987), pp. 71–2.

382   "Committee to Study Relationships Between the Faculty of Music and the Royal Conservatory of Music," 1973.

383   Hallett Report, 1976. No official name was given to the committee.

384   These figures are from the records of the University of Toronto Faculty Association.

385   George Hoskins, conversation with author, 19 April 2004.

386   Michael Schulman, "Boris Berlin, Music for all our children," *The Canadian Composer,* February 1974, pp. 4, 6, 8, 46.

387   RCM Committee Minutes, 27 May 1971.

388   Ibid., 24 February 1972.

389   Ibid., 4 May 1972.

390   Pamela Cornell, "Playing For Real," *The University of Toronto Graduate,* January/February 1982, pp. 7–10.

391   See *ConNotes,* September 1980.

392   Reuben C. Baetz, Minister of Culture and Recreation, letter to Schabas, 19 February 1979.

393   Reuben C. Baetz, letter to Schabas, 11 September 1980.

394   See Walter Pitman, *Louis Applebaum, A Passion for Culture* (Toronto: Dundurn Press, 2002) for a detailed account.

395   Joseph Macerollo, interview with author, 21 January 2004.

396   George Hoskins, interview with author, 27 January 2004.

397   Andrew Markow, interview with author, 22 January 2004.

398   James Ham, letter to Ezra Schabas, 13 June 1983.

399   Walter Pitman, conversation with author, 24 January 2004.

400   "Report of the Committee on the Future of Music Studies offered by the University of Toronto," 19 December 1983, reproduced in the *University of Toronto Bulletin.*

401   *Toronto Daily Star,* 27 June 1984.

402   *The Globe and Mail,* 26 June 1984.

403   Carl Morey, conversation with author, 24 January 2004.

404   Ham, 13 June 1983.

405   "Principal's Letter," 18 February 1985; Robert Dodson, interview with author, 5 February 2004.

406   *EMC,* p. 1267.

407   The letter was received by the Board on 23 October 1986.

408   David Peterson, letter to RCM, 27 October 1986.

409   *Toronto Daily Star,* 11 February 1987.

Chapter 10: Free at Last

410   This group held six meetings between 25 June and 26 November 1986.

411   Robert Creech, memorandum to Peter Allen, 6 February 1990.

412   Andrew Shaw, interview with author, 15 March 2004.

413   Peter Allen, letter to Robert Dodson, 19 August 1988.

414   W.L. Heisey, letter to George Connell, copies to members of the board, n.d.

415   Robert Dodson, letter to George Connell, 31 August 1988.

416   University News Release, 2 September 1988.

417   *The Globe and Mail,* 5 September 1988.

418   William Littler, *Toronto Daily Star,* n.d.

419   *The Varsity,* 14 September 1988.

420   There was extensive correspondence between Robert Creech and R.L. Criddle, and between the lawyers on both sides. The letters are in the author's files. Only the most significant ones are singled out.

421   Robert Creech, letters to R.L. Criddle.

422   Jeremy Johnston, letter to Gordon Dickson, 27 July 1989.

423   *Toronto Daily Star,* 26 December 1989.

424   *The Globe and Mail,* 8 February 1990.

425   Ibid.

426   *University of Toronto Bulletin,* 12 February 1990.

427   *The Globe and Mail,* 9 February 1990.

428   Robert Creech, memorandum to Peter Allen, 6 February 1990.

429   Robin Fraser, conversation with author, 7 February 2004.

430   Helmut Blume, "A National School of Music" (Canada Council 1978).

431   G. Campbell Trowsdale, "Independent and Affiliated Non-Profit Conservatory-type Music Schools in Canada, A speculative Survey" (Canadian Music Council 1988).

432   Ibid., p. 236.

433   Robert Creech, "Partners in Music: A National Conference on The Role of Conservatory Training in Canada," June 3–6, 1989.

434   Norman Burgess, Warren Mould, and G. Campbell Trowsdale, "Report of the Royal Conservatory of Music Commission on the National Examination System," May 1991, 374 p. There is also a synopsis of the report, 29 p.

435   John Kruspe, "Report on Theory/History Curriculum Review at the Royal Conservatory of Music," October 1989.

436   *Music Magazine,* November/December 1990, pp. 26–9.

Chapter 11: An Independent School

437   Peter Simon, interview with author, 16 March 2004.

438   George Hoskins, conversation with author, 19 April 2004.

439   RCM Annual Report, 1992.

440   Karen Castelane and John Milligan, "Expansion Strategies Project 1992," 1992.

441   John Milligan, "A Report on the Royal Conservatory of Music's Branches and External Teaching Centres," 8 March 1991.

442   *Toronto Daily Star,* 8, 9, February 1993.

443   Colin Graham, interview with author, 10 February 2004.

444   Eileen Keown, conversation with author, 21 April 2204.

445   *The Globe and Mail,* 13 February 1993.

446   John Milligan, "Studio Management Guide," 1993.

447   Geoffrey Sangwine, conversation with author, 11 March 2004.

448   Louise Yearwood, interview with author, 26 February 2004.

449   "Task Force Final Report," May 1998.

450   Peter Simon, written communication to author, 11 September 2004.

451   Rennie Regehr, interview with author, 18 March 2004.

452   Simon, 11 September 2004.

453 Ibid.

454 Norman Burgess, interview with author, 15 February 2004.

455 Simon, 11 September 2004.

456 Angela Elster, interview with Dorith Cooper, 8 February 2004.

457 Simon, 11 September 2004.

458 Upitis and Smithrim, "Learning Through the Arts, A National Assessment, 1999-2002," Queens University, 2002.

459 Peter Simon, letter to author, May 2004.

460 *Music Magazine*, June/July 1990, pp. 26–8.

461 Birkenshaw-Fleming, p. 4.

462 Ibid., pp. 11–12.

463 Ibid., p. 8.

464 Ibid., pp. 4–5.

465 "Music In Our Lives," v. 1. no. 2. Louise Yearwood, 26 February 2004.

466 RCM AGM, 1994–95.

467 Ibid.

468 Debra Chandler, conversation with author, 20 September 2004.

469 *RCM Crescendo*, February 1996.

470 *EMC*, pp. 853–4.

471 RCM Annual Report, 1995–96.

472 See *RCM Life*, February 1996, Summer 1996.

473 Joanne Mazzoleni, interview with author, 1 March 2004.

474 Louise Yearwood, interview with author, 26 February 2004.

475 RCM Annual Report, 1995–96.

476 Ibid. 2003.

477 *RCM Crescendo*, January 1997.

478 Comparative registration figures provided to the author by the GGS, 8 March 2004.

479 Regehr, 18 March 2004.

480 Simon, 11 September 2004.

Chapter 12: A Building for the Future

481 Simon, 11 September 2004.

482 Ibid.

483 Ibid.

484 ibid.

485 Ibid.
486 *The New York Times*, 11 March 2004.
487 Ibid.
488 "Campaign Gifts," RCM, 8 June 2004.
489 "Campaign Gifts," RCM, 4 May 2004.

Photo Credits

PHOTO CREDITS

Chapter 6

Page 138	UTA
Page 139	UTA
Page 141	UTA
Page 143	Ken Bell
Page 144	UTA
Page 145	Patricia Rideout
Page 146	Beth Bergman
Page 150	UTA

Chapter 7

Page 153	UTA
Page 156	City of Toronto Archives, Fonds 1497, Item 33
Page 158	UTA
Page 159	UTA

Chapter 8

Page 172	RCM
Page 174	*The Globe and Mail*
Page 175	RCM
Page 178	Art Associates Photography
Page 180	U of T Opera Division
Page 181	U of T Opera Division
Page 182	U of T Opera Division

Chapter 9

Page 188	Catherine Robbin
Page 197	Rhombus Media
Page 201	RCM

Chapter 10

Page 212	Robert Creech
Page 220	RCM
Page 222	RCM
Page 223	RCM
Page 224	Photo-Canada Wide

Chapter 11

Page 229	RCM
Page 231	RCM
Page 236	RCM
Page 240	David Griffith
Page 241	Design Archive
Page 243	RCM

Chapter 12

Page 250	Kuwabara Payne McKenna Blumberg Architects
Page 251	Kuwabara Payne McKenna Blumberg Architects

Index

INDEX

INDEX